BY Ch. ....

COVER AND ILLUSTRATIONS BY CHRIS LOPARCO

Of His Might

Chris LoParco

www.astorytoldbook.com

Quotations in this book were taken from the New American Standard Bible (NASB)

ISBN-13: 979-8748322560

ISBN-10: 8748322560

Cover Design, Illustrations, and Page Layout by Chris LoParco

Characters created by LoParco, Olivera, Santarsiero

GOD BLESS !

Christopher James

Thanks be to the True and Ever Loving God,
without whom none of this would be possible.

And to all of those saints out there who have believed in and
continually help in this great journey
– Thank you.

*And the Word became flesh, and dwelt among us, and we saw His
glory, glory as of the only begotten from the Father, full of grace and
truth." John 1:14*

*Finally, be strong in the Lord and in the strength of His might.
Ephesians 6:10*

DAY I

CHAPTER I
DEATH KNOCKS ONCE

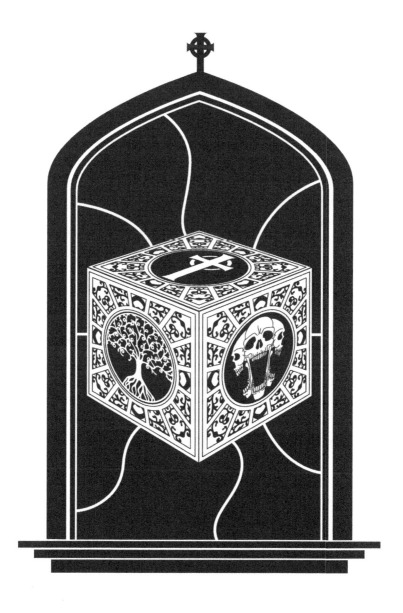

Time goes by and stands still, all at once. Life is the beginning of death, and death is the beginning of life. I, Death, sit and watch over the Earth from Limbo, from my thicket throne. The lives of mortals seem so futile from here, but they have a resolve unlike any other creation of God. I have watched countless civilizations rise and fall, men and women trying to become their own gods throughout the universe. But there is but one God, even I know that, and so does the Devil. God created the angels first. And from the beginning they fell. A third of them followed that wicked dragon, Satan, to Hell. Then, God created mortals. They also fell to the same evil that corrupted the angels before them. That is when Death came; that is when I was born. Adam and Eve fell to the wicked schemes of the Devil. The Darkness corrupted their hearts like it did his, and all humanity was born with a curse after this. Their seed was cast among the stars. Satan brought God's very creations to the nethermost regions of the universe, inhabiting thousands and thousands of worlds throughout the cosmos. All this happened overnight. Satan played god and reveled in the fact that he placed life on thousands of planets, while God only did so on one planet. But God created from nothing. All Satan had done was clone that which God created. These mortals on the distant worlds were only reproductions of what God made from the dust. They were created from the DNA of the first humans after the Fall. Because they were biologically created, God rightly gave them souls. Therefore, like all men and women, they would be allowed to take part in the salvation that God offered through His Son. The only problem was that Christ came to Earth and these mortals from other worlds knew Him not.

As in the days before the great flood on Earth, the men and women born on distant planets lived almost one thousand years. Any that died before the resurrection of Christ went to Sheol as all mortals did. Most of the worlds fell before Christ came, except for a few. For the worlds that fell afterward, God gave way for evangelism across the cosmos, just as He did on Earth. For there were survivors of the fallen worlds who knew Christ and brought his message to the other planets in hopes of bringing salvation and rescuing them from the Darkness. Some of these people were saved and others were taken into the Darkness to suffer. Now all the planets have fallen, except the Earth.

The planets that fell were betrayed by the very demon that put life on them. Satan, through his daughter, Pandora, brought the Darkness to each of these planets. The embodiment of all evil devoured each and every one of the souls that lived on those planets. It sucked every drop of life and energy that those planets had, leaving them desolate. The souls of those people who were taken are still trapped inside the Darkness to this day, being drained like human batteries. They are not dead, but still alive, body and soul inside the Darkness, which resides in the Abyss. But out there in the universe are those believers who survived. They are saints waiting to bring an end to the Darkness and bring light to the universe.

I was created the day that Adam and Eve fell. From one man's sin, Death was born. But the day I was born I was not yet awakened. I was in a trance-like state. I could see the world, and all that inhabited it. I could see the stars and the planets throughout the cosmos. I saw Satan put life on each of those distant worlds. I remember the first one. The planet known as Gaia, a name taken by the mortals of Earth in their own mythologies. Gaia was a beautiful planet and very similar to Earth. Satan handpicked it because it had everything he needed. God had made other planets inhabitable like the Earth, and even put water and plant life on them, and some microscopic beings. Gaia was one of them. The planet was serene, with blue skies, fresh air, thriving green plants, and clean water. It was pristine in every way. That is until Satan corrupted it. The father of lies, took the stolen DNA from our fallen first parents, and biologically engineered life on these planets. The first mortal that he planted was a girl, who he watched quickly grow into a woman. She lived alone on Gaia and her father visited her often, teaching her the knowledge that he himself had gained from the Darkness. He corrupted her mind, her heart, and her soul.

One day when she was still young, Satan gave her a puzzle box to play with. It was made from a strange dark metal and had symbols carved all over it. The girl played with the toy every day. She touched all the symbols, spun it on its point. It was her only toy, and the only gift her father had given her. She asked Satan, whom she called "father," what this box was for. This is when the Devil knew it was time. He took out a book, one that he had made in the flesh of demons from the very pits of Hell, and one that he wrote in his very own blood. Yes, he took out the *Necronomicon*, and read to her from that book. Her eyes were opened and she touched the symbol carvings again. The box flew into the air and glowed with a blue light. On that day, I awoke from my trance. I sprang forth from that box, the very place I was slumbering and I took it into my own hands. Then I appeared here in Limbo. That very day, the Angel of the Lord told me who I was and what my life's work would be – to collect the souls of all mortals who died.

Satan spread the seed of man around the cosmos. The worlds were inhabited and fell. Men and women died on Earth and all around. I collected their souls and brought them first to Sheol and later to Heaven to be judged by the Spirit. I do not know all of how I came to be, or about this box I hold, but this much I know now. The very day I came from that box, Cain slayed his brother Able and I collected my first soul. My eyes were opened to the wickedness of the world. Yes, from one man's sin Death was born. But there is hope because by one Man's death came eternal life. My job will end one day, and I still do not know what will come of me when that happens. But Christ died so men and women can live. Not live as they have been in this cursed universe, but live as they were created to, in the glory of God.

Pandora is out there still. She destroyed her own world first, then she went on to destroy the rest of the planets. Now she is coming for Earth. For many millennia, she has been trying to bring the Darkness to the very planet where God placed His creation. But she has been stopped by the power of the Spirit that covers the Earth's atmosphere, not allowing her to enter it. For her to enter, the world would need to reject God so completely that the Spirit would no longer be over its people. The world is in a state like that now, but God has remained faithful. Unfortunately, there is still a way the Earth could fall. If a true Temple of the Darkness was constructed on Earth, and the proper rituals conducted, then the Three Days of Darkness will begin. The world will be shrouded in thick Darkness, and on the third day Pandora will enter and complete the ritual to bring in the Darkness itself. Evil unlike any other would be unleashed onto the Earth, to devour it just as it has devoured every other planet. Pandora is on her way. She is just beyond the Earth, inside its very solar system, waiting. But the saints who are also out there in space are on their way as well, coming to stop her. They have fought her before, though until now they have failed. But God has a plan and each of these men and women hold the hope of Jesus Christ in their hearts. Through the power of the Holy Spirit they have lived well beyond the years they should, and will continue on until they are killed or until the final judgment. Because of the way they were cloned by Satan, even though they have souls and are saved, the men and women from the other worlds cannot take part in the rapture. For God decreed them to endure until the end of all time.

I, Death, am watching and waiting. I collect the souls of the dead. I am Death in every way. But my eyes see beyond all of that. I have no emotions, but I see hope, love, and life. That is what I yearn for – to know what it is like to truly live.

***

In the Shaanxi Province of China, the order of Magi known as the Keepers of the Light rebuilt a new home not far from their mountain abode that was destroyed by Legion. The order spanned throughout China, but their headquarters and their leader, called the Great Teacher, always resided in Shaanxi. That was where the priests taught by Daniel had settled to pass on their teachings and prepare the world for the coming of the true King, the Christ. This order had existed for over two thousand years, but it took a young girl to turn their hearts to the true God and Lord. Nathaniel Salvatore's niece, Bianca, who was only four years old at the time, showed these Magi that Jesus was in fact God made man, that He died for their sins, and rose to give them eternal life. She shared with them the message that if they believed in His name and believed that He died for their sins, then and only then could they be saved. Almost fourteen years had passed since this event occurred and on that day Chien, one of the Magi, was absent from her teaching. His heart had been hardened in those days. But he

9

fought alongside Lyles and other great heroes to defeat Legion and through this battle he had learned more about God and the Christ. After these years of studying Scripture and praying with his brothers over the body of Lyles Washington, his very dear friend, even Chien's heart turned to Jesus and he embraced Him now as his Lord and Savior.

Lyles had fallen almost fourteen years ago in his battle against the evil Nephilim, Legion. But Lyles was not dead, he was in a deep sleeplike state. Lyles' soul along with Legion's were trapped in the Skull of Miacha. Lyles' body and the skull lay in the center of the newly established Temple of Luminescence. The headquarters of the Keepers of Light, known as the Temple of Luminescence, was now underground, hidden alongside dark and ancient catacombs where many of their deceased brothers were buried. The place was built centuries ago and used during times of war as a shelter. With much hard work and great artistry, this order of Magi transformed these barracks into a beautiful underground paradise. There were picturesque reliefs of animals and plants carved into the stone walls. Pillars were erected with fanciful flutes on top and extravagant bases. In the center was a large circular room, with pillars all around. They used this room to worship the Lord every morning and evening, with a special service also on Sundays where they shared the Lord's Supper. In the center of this room was a stone altar, closed in on all sides, and on top of that altar was Lyle's body. The young African-American man, who was born and raised in Harlem, was placed there nearly fourteen years ago, yet he did not age a single day. His wife, Kimberly, was back home in Manhattan, and thirteen years ago she gave birth to his son, Bo, whom Lyles had never met. This man was a hero, a man of God, handsome, six foot tall, clean shaven, even the top of his head. The trance he was in was strange. Michael, the Archangel, had told Chien that Lyles' body would stay intact and it would be as if he were asleep. Through the years, his hair and nails never grew, and not one wrinkle appeared on his face. It truly was as if no time passed by at all.

Chien, who was now the Great Teacher of this order of Magi, was kneeling on the ground of the very room where Lyles' body lay. He wore his usual brown sackcloth robe, as did all those in this order. They were all men, brought into the order as young boys, when they were either found abandoned on the streets of China or given to the order by their families. All of their heads were shaved completely bald and they wore simple leather shoes with leather soles. This was how they have dressed since the order began. The Magi who followed Chien were all around him, and together they prayed to the true and living God. Beside each of them was a sword. They were Magi but also warriors, and you never knew when the agents of Darkness would show up to attack. Even in prayer they were ready for battle, and rightly so, for even now enemies stormed their gates. The candles that lit the room all blew out at once. Each Magus grabbed his sword and prepared to fight. None of them could see, but these men were trained to use all of their senses, not just their eyes. They could hear the sounds of faint footsteps, and feel a great dark energy all around. Something had invaded the Temple of Luminescence, but what? There was a powerful blessing over the place that guarded it from evil, much like their last abode had had. Legion had chanted a spell that took away that protection, but this time, that was not the case. Whatever broke into their home had found a way to simply materialize into the place, without entering from the outside. Some of the Magi ran and lighted the candles that had been extinguished in the room. They could see now, but no threat was visible. That was when Chien was struck from behind. His back was cut open. Several of the other Magi were struck also. Demonic shadows began to rise up from the ground all around the room, and took on solid forms. These shadow demons were large and hunched over with long sharp claws on their hands and feet. When they opened their mouths, the Magi could see that they also had sharp teeth like wild beasts. These monsters had no skin, but only appeared as silhouettes, like living shadows. What were these creatures, and why were they here?

All of the shadow demons began to crowd around the altar where Lyles lay. They knew the skull was there – the Skull of Miacha. They were after the skull and Legion's soul inside of it. Chien said a prayer in his heart, and then shouted out to his men that God was with them and to attack. Filled with the Spirit, the Magi attacked the army of shadow demons. They slashed at them with their blades, but the weapons only passed through them. Distracted from their goal of acquiring the Skull of Miacha, the demons turned on their attackers and fought back. They went right for the Magi. When the demons attacked, the Magi were able to block them with their swords but when they struck back at the shadow demons, their blades passed right through them. It was as if the demons had to take on physical properties to attack, but otherwise could make themselves to be truly as shadows and nontangible. Chien and the Magi fought hard, but their foes were fast and powerful. The creatures evaded the men's blades, and then struck the Magi one by one, cutting their flesh. Chien cried out to God for help. He could not let these creatures get the skull, he could not let them release Legion back into the world.

***

Thousands of miles away in the Arabian Desert, Puck sat on the desert sand, when one of his Djinn brothers appeared to him in a puff of smokeless fire. The Djinni were a race of desert demons created by Iblis, a former angel, who had been sent to Earth to live after he refused to bow to Adam when God created the first man. After realizing God's true intentions – for the angel to bow in reverence and worship of God's ability to create a living being – Iblis rejoined the side of light during the battle against Legion. Now he and his children, the Djinn, served the living God. Puck had already seen the truth, thanks to his close friends Nathaniel Salvatore, Lyles, and Ravenblade, and he had fought on the side of good even before his master repented of his sins. Iblis was uncertain what his final judgment would be at the end of time, for angels do not take part in the salvation of Christ as mortals do. Though, like Ravenblade, Iblis had never truly fallen. Both of them were sent to Earth to learn a lesson, and they were transformed into new creations known as immortals. Some believe that these beings are angels preserved by God in this form so that He can forgive them their sins once they have repented and turned back to Him. And they would rejoin Him in His kingdom one day. As for the Djinn, they have no souls and therefore their fate is to return to the smokeless fire from which they were created. That is, except for Puck. For on the day that he risked his own life to try and save the life of his friend Nathan,

Puck was granted a soul.

The Djinn all looked the same, like small goblins with large pointed ears, pig-like faces, two small tusks protruding from their lower lips, and vertically slanted eyes. They were covered in hair and had sharp claws on their hands and feet, and though their musculature was similar to a human male, they had no gender or reproductive organs. They were creatures like no other.

The two Djinni spoke and Puck was startled by the news that he was given. Instantly, Puck disappeared in his own puff of fire to find his friend Ravenblade. The immortal nomad was in a sand dune dueling with the very young man that he took under his apprenticeship a little over a year ago. Bo, the son of Lyles and Kimberly Washington, was born with an innate ability to tap into the raw power of the Holy Spirit. In order to use the power that God granted him, Bo still had to have faith in God and accept Christ as His Savior – which he did. God blessed Bo from conception with an anointing of the Holy Spirit. Even with only the faith of a mustard seed, Bo's body naturally harnessed the essence of the Spirit and turned it into solid energy, which could be used to fight evil. Ravenblade sensed this was the case even before the child was born, and once Bo began to display his gift, the immortal sent Puck to bring Bo to the desert so he could be trained to control his power and use it wisely. Ravenblade had told Kimberly that he would come for her son when he was thirteen, but the boy's powers were even stronger than the immortal had thought, and he could not risk Bo losing control of his power or even worse, falling into the scheme of the Devil. The child was excelling fast. He had just turned thirteen years old today in fact, and by Hebrew standards, he was a man. His mother had missed the milestone and even Bo did not realize that it was his birthday or even know what day it was. But Raven knew, for Bo's power had just fully awakened, and the immortal could feel it surging through the young man before him. If Bo did not learn to control it, it might even destroy him from the inside out. God had given this young man this gift for a purpose, and He also put Ravenblade in Bo's life to make sure the boy was properly trained to use it for good. Over the last almost eighteen years, Ravenblade's heart had softened and turned back to the

Lord. And the once feared and deadly killer was now a kind, yet stern, teacher.

The master and his pupil dueled back and forth with their blades. Ravenblade used the double-edged sword of the same name, while Bo used another Angel metal blade that Raven had collected from the desert many years before – a short sword with a knobbed hilt with ridges for the fingers and a short, rounded, cross guard. The immortal Ravenblade's skin was bronzed from the Desert sun, and he dressed in his usual weathered garb. His brown hooded cape draped over his shoulders and blew in the wind as he moved. His tanned leather boots dug into the sand, helping him to keep his footing. The knee pads and elbow pads, made of the same tanned leather, were the only armor he wore. The immortal's reddish brown hair was tied back. He stared with his dark brown eyes into his student's own. The child, who dressed very similar to his sensei, was not much of a boy anymore. Even though he was only thirteen years old, he was nearly six feet tall, and well-muscled from his training this past year. His skin was a mid-hazelnut brown, and helped him to not burn up in the hot desert climate. His hair had grown out a little bit, but Raven helped the boy cut it from time to time so it was still kept short.

Puck appeared before the teacher and his pupil and shouted for them to stop their practice. Ravenblade turned, but Bo took this opportunity to sweep his legs and push his sensei down.

"Well, that was a dirty trick," Ravenblade said and stood up. "You're learning."

Bo smiled, and the two stood in front of Puck. Ravenblade was just a little taller than Bo, and both of them dwarfed the much smaller Djinni, Puck, that stood before them. The kind desert demon looked troubled and Raven asked him what was wrong. Puck explained that one of his Djinn brothers told him that the new Temple of Luminescence had been invaded by shadow warriors. They were trying to steal the skull, and that Chien had been badly injured trying to protect it and Lyles' body. Puck feared that Chien would be killed and that Lyles' body may be destroyed and his soul lost, if the skull was taken by the shadow demons.

"Wait," Bo said. "Did you just say Lyles? I thought my dad was dead?"

"Death is relative," Ravenblade answered. "But no, he's not dead. Not yet. We have to go there now and make sure they don't get the skull. We can't afford Legion to be released again."

"Wait a minute!" Bo exclaimed. "My dad's not dead? Why didn't you tell me?"

"We don't have time for this," Ravenblade spoke. "We have to get to China."

"But how will we get to China fast enough?" Bo asked.

"You should know the answer by now. The same way we got you here," Ravenblade said. "Grab your sword and let's go. Puck, we're ready."

The teacher and his pupil placed their hands on the Djinni, and in a puff of smokeless fire they vanished.

***

Back in the Temple of Luminescence, Chien was lying on the ground. Blood poured from his side where one of the shadow demons had ripped into his flesh with its claws. Many of his brothers lay on the ground as well. The group of shadow demons crowded around the altar again, for they could sense the skull was present. One of the demons groped along the walls and then a blue light shone from its hand. The light grew in intensity, and all of a sudden a panel opened on the side of the altar, revealing the Skull of Miacha. The small crystal skull looked ominous and began to glow with the same blue light as the demon's hand. Triumphantly, the creature held up the skull and prepared to leave with its horde. But before it could, a blade cut through the air and also through the shadow demon's wrist. Its hand was severed and the skull fell to the ground. The blade that stuck the demon was no ordinary sword – it was the Ravenblade, a flawless double-bladed sword, sharp from end to end. The former angel, Ravenblade, had arrived with Bo and Puck. His Angel metal sword struck again at the demon whose hand it had chopped off. The blade moved swiftly, and was aimed at the demon's heart. Unfortunately for the immortal wielder of the blade, the demon did not perish but instead the sword passed right through it. Ravenblade was confused. The first strike cut through the wrist, but now the creature seemed to be ethereal. Then, he understood. These creatures were created by magic from the shadows, he could sense it. In order to hold the skull the shadow demon had to become solid, but otherwise it had no physical form.

Now was not time to worry about all the logic behind these shadow demons. No, it was time to fight and make sure they did not get the skull, and with it the soul of their friend and Bo's father, Lyles. Raven and Bo swung their swords at the advancing enemies before them. Their blades passed through these strange shadow demons each and every time. The Magi who had not been struck down earlier fought back as well. On the ground, the Skull of Miacha was kicked and rolled about, until one of the shadow demons finally got its hands on it. In a puff of smokeless fire, Puck appeared before the demon and grabbed the skull from its grasp. Then he disappeared again. He appeared before Ravenblade, but as soon as he did, the Djinni was slashed from behind by one of the creatures and the skull flew into the air. Bo jumped and grabbed it with his free hand, but fell right on top of his father's sleeping body.

The creatures grew more and more agitated, and all at once they let out a howling moan. The horrific sound pierced the ears of all around. It was like nails against a chalk board. They all went for Bo at once. Raven saw this. Puck and he went straight to help their comrade. Over the last year, Ravenblade had grown very close to his pupil. Lyles was like family to the immortal, who never really had one – except his angelic brothers when he was first created in Heaven. Ravenblade almost felt in some ways like a father figure to the boy. Bo had never known his own father, and though the immortal was tough and cold at times, Bo felt a warmth from him that he was missing. He knew Ravenblade cared for him deeply and was training him to not only fight, but also to live. It was like a father raising up his son to be a man. But now Bo was face to face with his real father – Lyles. He looked at his face and could see some of himself in the man before him, and Bo got lost in his thoughts. It was as if time stood still and everything around him disappeared. All he could see was the man who helped make him. The man who fought in the name of God and even sacrificed his very soul in doing so. The man who never had the chance to see his son born. But all around the demons came, and they were about to grab the boy and take the skull.

"When they go to grab him strike!" Ravenblade yelled. "They will have to make themselves physical when that happens. But go for the head! That is the only way to stop them."

The immortal was correct. The Magi and he all struck with their swords when the demons went to grab at Bo. Each sliced the head off one of the demons. And then they did it again and again. The shadow demons began to disappear one by one. Puck attacked as well, but only seemed to aggravate the demons that he struck. His claws were not long enough to take their heads like the swords of his allies.

While his sensei fought, Bo looked at his father. The Skull of Miacha was on Lyles' chest and Bo's hands were on top of it. Out of nowhere Bo began to glow with a bright, white light. The room began to shake, and then the skull began to glow as well. Instantly, light burst from the skull and sent a current of energy into Lyles' body, causing him to glow with the same white light. That was when one of the demons grabbed Bo's leg and threw him from his father's chest. The boy fell hard to the ground and so did the skull. The demons all ran for it. Raven and the Magi tried to stop them from getting their hands on it. They slashed violently at the shadow demons as one by one they scrambled to grab the object that they had come for. Finally, one of the evil creatures grabbed the skull. It no longer glowed with the blue light as before, but the demon was not wise enough to pay attention to this sign. All at once it disappeared, and the rest of the shadow demons vanished along with it.

The Magi looked around and so did Ravenblade. Puck went to Bo and did his best to help his friend to his feet. The immortal walked over to them.

"They got the skull," Raven said. "We are all in grave danger. If they bring that monster back, it can mean the end of the world!"

"What can we do?" Bo asked.

Before Raven could speak they heard a cough, and then Lyles sat up on the altar. The immortal and Puck were shocked, and so were the Magi that remained standing. On the other hand, the emotions that Bo felt were far different from them all. His whole life he thought his father was dead, and now that very same man was alive and in front of him. Bo ran to the altar where his father was sitting and threw his arms around him.

"Who are you?" Lyles said, his voice weak from his years in a trance. "And where am I? Raven, Puck is that you?"

Bo continued to squeeze his father in his arms as tightly as he could; everything else around him meant nothing.

"Can you let me breathe?" Lyles said and laughed.

He didn't know who the boy was, but he did not mind the hug. It was just so sudden and he still felt so weak.

"He is your son," a voice came from the ground. "I can see it from here. Am I right, Raven?"

It was Chien. He was still alive, but blood still poured from his wound. Puck teleported over to his dying friend and held his hand. Chien looked into the Djinni's eyes.

"Yes, God has shown me the next chosen hero, and now I can rest in peace," Chien spoke. "It will reassure you to know, Lyles and Raven, that I found my Savior after all these years. I gave my life to Christ and now I will go into His Glory until we meet again, my brothers. I am filled with joy today, for I saw you open your eyes, Lyles. I have sat and watched you, cared for you all these years. And now I get to see your son also. Praise God indeed."

With those final words, Chien closed his eyes and went home to the Lord. His Magi went over to his body and also saw their other fallen brothers on the ground. It was a sad day. But there was happiness, as well, for Lyles had woken after all this time – bittersweet.

"My son?" Lyles said surprised. "But how? You can't be?"

The man got up slowly. He tried to step forward but his body was still too weak. Bo caught him, and held him.

"Yes, he is your son," Raven stated. "You've been asleep for almost fourteen years."

"No!" Lyles exclaimed. "No! It can't be! Did we stop him? Did we beat Legion? What about Kimberly? My wife? What happened?"

Bo held his father tight. And Ravenblade and Puck walked

18

over. The immortal put his hand on Lyles shoulder.

"We have a lot to talk about," Raven said. "But right now is not the time. We have to go. We need to find the skull. Legion was trapped inside of it with you, and they took it. Somehow you escaped."

"It must have happened when I started to glow," Bo jumped in.

"Yes, I saw that," the immortal spoke again. "I don't understand the power that God gave you, Bo. The Spirit is strong with you. But we must go. We can talk later. Puck we have to get to the girl. Do you know where she is?"

"Yes, feel her I can. Sense her spirit," the Djinni answered. "She is in the same place where I got Bo before."

"Good, let's go!" Raven ordered. "I am sorry for your loss today," he said to the Magi. "But do not mourn your master and your fellow Magi. They believed in the Son of the living God. Their souls will rest in Heaven, I promise you. You will see them again."

With those words Ravenblade, Lyles, Bo, and Puck vanished in a puff of smokeless fire.

***

Out in rural Pennsylvania, it was nighttime, and a strange motley crew dwelled in a small old cottage in the woods. The three men, or better yet, two men and a teenager had no family ties but they somehow seemed like they fit together perfectly, in their own odd way. Simon Magus III had returned and was now a High Sorcerer of the Darkness, exceeding the ranks of all of his ancestors. Finally, he was the powerful magician that he had dreamed to become. The Ring of Solomon had served him well, along with his family's spell book. But now he also had the *Necronomicon* and a black crystal forged by Satan himself to communicate with the Devil's own daughter, Pandora, and her villainous brood. The sorcerer had obtained these items along with the other two residents of this cottage, when he rescued them from a collapsing building in New York City. Simon had been monitoring Samyaza. When the fallen angel's empire fell, along with his stronghold, Simon swooped in and took what he needed. Samyaza, also known as the Chaldean, had been defeated by a makeshift band of heroes, who fought for the Lord. Now that fallen angel was back in his prison under the Earth, waiting for Judgment Day. Sam's adopted son Gideon and his trusted associate Collins were now in Simon's care. And there was one more thing. Simon Magus had made sure to take Legion's new body, which was still encased in the tempered, tinted glass chamber where it was placed at the moment of its conception. The body had now grown to its full adult size and the most bizarre part was that it was physically alive yet had no soul. It had taken him many years, but Samyaza had finally done it, he had finally made Legion a new body.

Collins, no longer wearing his usual pinstriped suit, now wore jeans and a polo shirt. The stocky, short man sat in a leather chair with his glasses on watching television in the living room. Gideon sat on the floor with his legs crossed in front of him, almost as if he were meditating. The boy was now eighteen. His face still looked young but he was six foot two and had an athletic, muscular frame. His platinum blond hair reflected the light in the room, and when he finally opened his eyes, their bright blue color was like the sky on a clear day. The young man was dressed casually, in a white tee shirt and dark blue jeans, with a pair of white Stan Smith sneakers. Simon was in the study. The room was small and filled with bookshelves and an old wooden desk. The cottage was not large, but comfortable and big enough. There were three bedrooms upstairs and two bathrooms, one on each floor. The kitchen was tiny but useful, and the dining room had a table set for six. Below the cottage was an unfinished basement where the furnace and laundry were, as well as one more thing. That is where they kept Legion's new body. And Simon was waiting to reunite that body with its soul.

In the study before Simon's very eyes, one of his shadow demons appeared, and it was holding the Skull of Miacha. Yes, Simon Magus III, High Sorcerer of the Darkness, had conjured up those shadow demons from the pages of the *Necronomicon* and sent the demons to the Temple of Luminescence to get the Skull of Miacha. Once Simon took the skull from the demon it faded back into the shadows where it was created. The sorcerer was slightly above average in height, with a thin lanky build. He had dark hair, eyes to match, and a nicely tanned olive complexion, the product of his Greek roots. He wore an ornate, dark purple robe with oxblood red trimming. Various mystical symbols were embroidered in gold thread running down the sleeves and sides of the robe. He studied the skull, its shape, its size, the way the light refracted through it. It was indeed a piece of art. But something was wrong. Something was missing.

"Where is his soul?" Simon yelled. "The skull is empty!"

Collins ran in to see what was wrong. At that moment, there was a knock on the front door. Gideon got up and answered it. A woman stood on the other side. It was the middle of February and there was snow all around, yet she wore just a very short and low-cut red dress. Her hair and eyes were dark, and her skin nicely tanned. The woman wore a pair of red, strappy high-heeled sandals. She had long fingernails painted red and tipped in black, with toenails to match.

"Is your daddy home, hon?" the woman asked and placed her finger on the young man's chest. She poked his right pec with the nail of her index finger. "Ooooh, someone's been working out."

"Umm, who are you?" Gideon asked in a very serious tone. He grabbed her hand and took it off his chest.

"My, my, now aren't you a feisty one?" she jested.

"Lilith," Simon said, and walked out into the living room, followed by Collins. "And what brings you here, wench?"

"Now, now, Mr. Magic, don't get all superior sorcerer on me. You act like Mr. big shot, but to me you're still just an amateur," Lilith hissed.

"Some things never change," Simon said. "You still look like you belong in one of those late-night cable movies. Do you ever dress professionally?"

"It all depends on the profession," Lilith replied.

Simon smiled and held up the skull. "So I assume you came here to see if I had brought Legion back again, right? Well, the skull is empty. Someone has removed Legion's soul."

"I know," Lilith interjected. "That's why I'm here. I know where his soul is. It's inside the man who had stopped him and put both of their souls into the skull. Somehow, Legion's soul and that mortal's intertwined, and when the mortal's soul left the skull to go back into his body, Legion went with it."

"So where is he?" Simon asked.

"You definitely are much braver than when we first met," Lilith said with a seductive tone. She placed her palm on Simon's chest and then ran her hand down to his belly.

Simon grabbed her hand and looked her in the eyes. "I am more brave, and other things as well. Tell me where Legion's soul is, and then after we have it, I can show you all the tricks I've learned since we parted ways."

"Hmm, I like the sound of that," she said. "As for where that cursed beast's soul is, Legion's soul is in New York."

CHAPTER II
OLD AND NEW FRIENDS

That same night at one of the Midtown docks in Manhattan, not too far from the Intrepid, a deal was about to go down between the newly reformed Scimitars and a branch of the Triad, the Chinese mafia. They were in the loading bay area, and the cold February night air gave them all a chill. Representing the Scimitars were three large and strong African-American men, all wearing black suits and sunglasses, even though it was nighttime. On the side of the Triad were seven skilled men in light gray suits, each holding a QBZ-95 automatic rifle. Leading them was a beautiful and proper woman in a red silk dress, chosen to honor her people. The dress had a dragon and a lotus embroidered on it in gold thread. She ran this branch of the Triad in New York City, and her name was affectionately Long Lian Hua – Dragon Lotus – like the embroidery on her dress.

The weapons-dealing Scimitars had not been seen in New York for quite some time. Antoni "Toni" Brown had taken the moniker of Pharaoh from his late uncle James Clark a few years back, using money that he had made in real estate to rekindle the underground organization. The man born Anthony Brown, but nicknamed Toni, legally changed his first name to Antoni with an "I" at the end simply because he preferred it. A little over a year ago, Toni had been arrested for his crimes as Pharaoh, being turned in by the Chaldean, the very man he was working with. Too many of the Scimitars' deals had been broken up by a man known on the street as J3 and his vigilante group known as the Minutemen. The Chaldean no longer saw the value in their partnership and signaled the police to end Pharaoh's reign. Prison did not last long for Toni. Last year, Toni found a way out by using his connections and money after the Chaldean's reign came to an end. Being a man of great wealth and influence himself, Toni decided to once again take on the moniker of Pharaoh, and with it he also took control of the local authorities. His men had no worries, for the police would not break up this exchange. They were safe. Also in the public eye, Toni had now become a clean man. He told the world that he gave up his crimes, and he bought out Prince Enterprises, which had been previously owned by Samuel

Malach Prince VII, also known as the Chaldean. Toni Brown now had a new sleek office at the second highest floor of 9 West 58th Street. The restricted top floor was used for developing top secret weapons, which Toni's underground organization, the Scimitars, would sell to the highest bidder. Joan Joyce, the former CEO of Prince Enterprises, still held her position, but now she worked for Toni and not the Chaldean. He was not as sinister as her previous boss, his motives not quite so evil. World domination was not really Toni's thing. No, he was an entrepreneur; he was just in it for the money. Currently he may have been the richest African-American in America after buying out Prince Enterprises, Inc, with his net worth being 4 billion dollars, USD. But that wasn't enough for Toni. He wanted to be the richest person in the world. This was the perfect cover for Pharaoh to come back out and play, and the Scimitars were reborn.

The large Scimitar enforcers stood there like an impenetrable wall, hard and looming. But the members of the Triad were not impressed or afraid. In the distance, hiding behind some large crates, there were spies watching – J3, known now by his given name John, and two of his closest allies. The Minutemen had disbanded a while ago when John was seemingly killed in a botched attempt to stop the Scimitars and the Children of the Dragon, another defeated gang that once served the Chaldean. John was shot in the chest by one of the thugs, but miraculously he survived. Later, John would find out his true past, that he was indeed created at the beginning of time, a type of angel – one without rank and without a known name. After he and Legion had fought a grueling battle centuries ago, John and Legion both lost their bodies. The Angel with No Name went on to be reborn as an immortal and would continue to be reborn time and again until his true nature was restored. Along with him was Jack, a fallen angel who now fought on the side of the Lord again, and Akane Yamamoto, the reformed leader of the Children of the Dragon's stealth force, and the love of John's life.

They were indeed a strange group of heroes. Akane had a very serious look in her eyes. She wore a black carbon-fiber bodysuit that was both bullet proof and resistant to being torn or cut. Of course with enough force anything can be penetrated, so the suit was only protective up to a certain point. But this fierce warrior did not care. She did not fear death or any enemy she faced. The only thing that she feared was failure. There was extra padding on her knees, elbows, and the back of the gloves on her hands. Her katana blade was slung across her back. A weapon given to her by her former master, the Chaldean, it was a mighty sword forged in Heaven before time began. On her forehead she wore a dark red bandana, to signify the blood of her fallen comrades, and also the blood of Christ her Savior. Jack's milky white skin clashed against his black robe. The lines of it were angular with a squared off collar at the top, making him look almost like a priest. Across his chest was an ornate sash, and he had epaulets with intricate embroidery as well. This was the same outfit he wore when he was a Watcher back on Atlantis before it was sunk by the Lord during the great flood. Jack also had an Angel metal sword in his hand, which he too was given by the Chaldean when he and John had been possessed through dark magic to serve him over a year ago. John looked like a misfit standing with both of these warriors in black. He wore a pair of blue jeans, tan lug bottom boots, his signature white T-shirt with a large red heart on it that was torn in half. It was the mark of the Scarred Heart, a memory from a past life of John's that he brought to the present day without even knowing it. He also wore his favorite worn-in brown leather jacket. They watched intently and waited for their moment to strike.

Long Lian Hua spoke to the large Scimitars in front of her. John and Jack could hear her clearly even from the distance because of their heightened supernatural senses. Both of these men had been angels and therefore were endowed with superhuman strength, speed, endurance, durability, sight, and hearing among other things, just as the immortal Ravenblade had been. They told Akane everything that they heard. The group of heroes was surprised to find out that the Scimitars this time were the customer and they were in fact buying a very powerful weapon from the Chinese. But Long Lian Hua did not say what the weapon was, only that it was in the crate in front of the criminals. Two of the Triad members walked over and lifted the lid off the crate, and just as they both reached in to grab the weapon, two throwing stars zipped through the air and stuck themselves into both of the men's right hands. Everyone stopped. The Triad members pulled the throwing stars from their hands and threw them onto the ground. The Scimitars pulled out handguns they hid under their suit jackets. The Triad members readied their automatic rifles, and looked all around. They all wondered who was brave enough to try and stop this deal. There was a noise behind one of the crates and right away all the gang members opened fire. Bullets flew everywhere. Because the Scimitars owned the police, they could do whatever they wanted and no law enforcement would get involved. The large thugs along with the Triad members kept firing their weapons at every sound they heard. They were not going to let this deal go south.

Long Lian Hua sank back and hid next to a crate while her men and her customers took care of the problem. From behind, one the Scimitars was struck with a strong kick to the ribs. And then his legs were swept from under him. It was John on the attack. The large thug blocked John's foot as it came for his face and threw the hero onto the ground. The Scimitar got up and went for John, who dodged and punched the thug across the face, knocking him back. Across the way, Jack was tied up with the other two Scimitars. They fired their handguns at him, but Jack was too fast. He dodged the bullets and kicked one of them in the gut and the other in the knee. Akane went to work on the Triad members. They fired their automatic weapons at her. But the woman moved with stealth and grace. She was not a fallen angel, but her body was enhanced twice in her life. First when she was a child and her uncle cast an evil spell on her, and then again by the Chaldean when she was the leader of his stealth force, and he modified her with science and dark magic. But now she had taken herself to a new level. Finding faith in Christ, and learning how to tap into the power of the Holy Spirit, Akane was a new creation. Her strength came from the Lord. And while she already had an advantage due to her enhancements, the level she had now achieved made her unstoppable by any normal mortal even one with an automatic rifle. Her sword sliced the air and cut three of the rifles in half. She followed this with a series of kicks and punches that disarmed two more of the Triad members. The last two threw down their own guns seeing that they were useless and they both pulled out swords of their own from their sides. These were Chinese miao dao – two-handed sabers of the Ming Dynasty era, similar in some ways to the Japanese katana sword. They both swung their blades at Akane with grace and precision but she moved with a speed and elegance that far outmatched these men. She blocked their swords one by one; sparks flew in the night air. The sound of clanging steel could be heard from all around. She blocked again, closed her eyes and said a prayer. Then in one fluid motion she swung her blade, a blade that had been forged by the hands of an angel in Heaven, made from an unbreakable metal that was used to fight Satan and his band of fallen angels all those years ago. Her sword stuck both of her opponents' weapons and broke them in half. For the blades of the Triad members were only steel forged on Earth, and they could not withstand the might of an Angel metal blade.

The three heroes stopped. All their enemies were knocked unconscious on the ground, but one was missing – Long Lian Hua. Where had she gone? Then, they heard an ear piercing sound, and suddenly a force as strong as a category 5 hurricane blasted Akane head on, breaking her arms, legs and neck. She lay on the ground, unable to move and possibly dead. The sound made John and Jack dizzy. John saw the woman he loved on the ground, lifeless, and then he looked up to see what had happened. Standing there was Lian Hua and in her hands was the weapon that she had been about to sell to the Scimitars. It was sonic cannon of some sort, a new technology that China had been developing and that the Triad stole from the Chinese government. The most interesting part about this new weapon was its compact size, which was roughly the size of a toaster. Also it had advanced technology to stabilize the unit when firing a blast, the wielder of the weapon was unfazed by the crushing force that shot out from it. Lian Hua stood there and aimed the weapon at John and Jack, ignoring the woman on the ground. The two former angels charged forward. She energized the canon to fire again. But just then, Akane who had been crushed by the last blast from the sonic weapon, snapped all of her bones back in place, healed, and flipped to her feet. Akane Yamamoto's healing factor was stronger and faster than before. This woman seemed to have more lives than a cat. She jumped over John and Jack and threw a shuriken at Lian Hua, knocking the cannon out of her hand. Akane went to take down the Triad leader, when one of the Triad members got up with his automatic rifle and began firing it at Akane. She was hit in the shoulder and then rolled over to one of the crates to hide from the barrage of bullets. Lian Hua grabbed the sonic cannon and motioned for her minion to stop firing his weapon. She aimed it at John and Jack who stood in place, uncertain of what to do. They had to get to her before she hit them with the sonic blast. Lian Hua pulled the trigger mechanism to fire the weapon, but something moved in front of her and stopped the sonic blast from hitting John and Jack. A man in a metallic navy-blue armored suit sitting on top of a sleek futuristic hover bike of the same color parked in front of the heroes. From his left forearm protruded an energy shield that held back the blast.

"Sorry I'm late," the rider said.

His visor, which matched the color of his helmet and blended in flawlessly, raised up and they could see his face. It was Sergeant Jay Sil of the FDSR, a close friend and someone they had fought alongside time and again. The Triad member fired his automatic rifle at Jay, who blocked it with his shield. Then, Jay fired an energy blast from a small laser canon that protruded from his forearm plate, knocking out the Triad member. Jay's visor went back down and he turned his hoverbike to face Lian Hua. Sergeant Jay Sil of the FDSR was ready, and he created another energy shield in front of his bike and at once, he charged at Lian Hua. Without a second thought, she recalibrated the weapon, turned the power up, and fired another blast. This one was even stronger than the last and started to push Jay and his hoverbike backwards. The evil woman cranked up the power more and more, and even though Jay put his bike into full gear, he was sent back, and his hover bike flipped over. Jay was thrown to the ground. At once, Lian Hua fired the weapon at some of the crates around the heroes and they broke apart and began to collapse on top of them. Jay put up his forearm shield again and deflected the falling debris.

After the dust settled, Jay, John, Jack, and Akane all got back up and looked around. Lian Hua was gone and so was the sonic cannon. They had failed. The heroes heard police sirens. They saw that the members of the Scimitars had gone as well. They must have signaled the NYPD to come and take care of the vigilantes. Not wanting to confront the police, the heroes all moved out and left the scene as stealthily as they had arrived. The cops were left to clean up the mess that had been made, but with no suspects to interrogate.

***

Back home, Judy Ramirez-Sil was sitting on the couch when her husband Jay walked into their apartment. He was no longer wearing his armored suit but a T-shirt and jeans. His short, dark hair was messy and spiked up, with medium length sideburns. He no longer had the earring that he used to wear. He was above-average height and well built, towering over his short, fiery Latina wife. Their apartment was on the top floor of the Manhattan branch of the Federal Department of Supernatural Research, a branch that Jay oversaw. The building was near the Chelsea piers in downtown Manhattan.

The former NYPD detective had joined the FDSR, almost two years before, but it seemed like longer. Being a man of the people, Jay always struggled with the politics of the NYPD, and also the corruption. But the FDSR was completely different and exactly the type of organization that this former officer of the law wanted to be a part of. It was a clandestine government agency that specialized in strange phenomena. Its roots went back to England and throughout time the organization evolved through forms. Currently, it was set up as a military unit that battled creatures classified as supernatural and otherworldly in nature. The department headquarters was in upper Westchester, New York, where it was led by Lieutenant Dan Marshall, a volatile redhead who had moved into the position after he left his successful career in the army. The FDSR, which even the President of the United States disavowed, was the inspiration for fictional organizations such as the men in black and perhaps even the Impossible Mission Force. Among their other charges, the FDSR had jurisdiction over Area 51, which in fact did not house extraterrestrials and ships from outer space but rather the experimental aircraft created by enemies of the United States that had crashed on American soil. These evil opposing forces plotted against the United States and designed animatronic pilots for these crafts to look like space aliens. This was done by these enemies to drive fear into the American people and also in some cases to kidnap citizens and run evil experiments on them in hopes to conquer the United States government.

Just before Jay joined the organization, it had finally discovered its first true alien life form. Eishe Taninaru was a man from another planet, but his origins were even darker than he could have imagined – another visitor from beyond the stars, a woman named Leina, explained to Eishe and the FDSR that Satan in fact had populated the cosmos with Adam and Eve's DNA, after the Fall.

Being part of the FDSR, and the new friends and colleagues he had made along the way, really opened Jay's eyes to the truths that were out there. Many things from his past had been explained, such as two zombie attacks he had faced while on the force. But even more important was that he had learned who Christ really was. Now Jay and his wife Judy were both believers. Yes, Judy knew everything and just last year, when the couple was living at the FDSR headquarters in upper Westchester, the Chaldean had tried to kill them, with help from the NYPD, who had served that evil mastermind.

Much had changed, but much was still the same. Jay and Judy loved each other. Their first meeting was comical all those years ago, when Judy, a field reporter for Channel 13 News, tried to escape Jay, who at the time was a rookie cop. He did end up arresting her that night. A few years later, the duo took on the Pain Pit as they worked together to take on the Chaldean and help Judy further her news reporter career. Now Judy Ramirez, who still used her maiden name only on television, was a household name. She headlined the morning show on Channel 4. It was her dream come true. But what really made her happy was that she loved her husband, Jay, very much. Now, the couple was getting ready to have their first baby. Judy was eight months pregnant, and they were going to have a baby girl. And the Channel 4

Morning Blitz followed every minute of it. Jay sat next to his wife and held her in his arms.

They sat on the couch together, kissed, and talked about their friends, those who had been with them over the last two years. Those who had helped Jay learn about God and fought alongside him as they had finally taken down the Chaldean.

***

A year and half ago, a group of heroes banded together to face off against the Chaldean and they had won. Samuel Malach Prince VII, also known as the Chaldean, was actually Samyaza, a fallen angel. Many millennia ago, Samyaza came to Earth with his brethren, a group of angels called the Watchers, of which he was the leader. They lived on an island in the Atlantic Ocean known by mankind as Atlantis. The island was lush. It had farmlands and forests, and in the center was a great city that surrounded a large mountain. This mountain was at one point the highest natural structure in the world. It was a veritable Mt. Olympus, though the mountain had no name. On it, the angels held council like gods governing the Earth. A tribe of humans dwelled with them on this island, a people known as Atlanteans, who had originated on Mars. Yes, there was life on other planets, but they were not space aliens placed there at the time of creation. Rather, they were the biological offspring of Adam and Eve, fashioned after the Fall, when Satan stole their seed and scattered it across the universe. He populated the planets through the DNA of our first parents. The Devil also brought vegetation and wildlife to these worlds, though some of them had their own plant life and single-celled organisms that God had placed there. Only Earth was where God put human life. The people on these other planets did in fact have souls. Even if they were not conceived in the normal way, they were still brought forth from the chromosomes of their parents. They were children of Adam and Eve.

The Watchers fought many wars for God on these planets and witnessed as they all began to fall to the very Darkness that took Satan before the First War. The last battle they fought was on Mars. Pandora was there, Satan's own daughter, whom he placed on the first planet that he carried life to. Her heart was filled with evil and sin, and she was drunk on the nectar of the Darkness, making her a slave to its will. It was she who went from planet to planet, taking the Darkness with her, and destroying them one by one. The destroyer of worlds is what she was, and she desired more than anything to bring that destruction to the Earth. But God had sealed our planet with His Holy Spirit, and her army could not enter its atmosphere. The only way she could enter was if enough people in the world turned toward the Darkness and completely rejected God, so that the balance truly shifted toward evil. The world reached this level two times in the past. The first time God nearly destroyed mankind with a flood, saving only Noah and his family. And the second time was when Christ died on the cross and His sacrifice turned the Darkness of the world back toward the light. Now humanity had grown close to this level of unbelief again. They have, as a species, turned their backs on God and are now ripe for the picking by the Darkness once more.

Thousands of years ago, Pandora tried to come to Earth and bring destruction. She posted a watchtower on Mars and took control of its people. The Watchers came and fought a great war against Pandora in those days. It is uncertain who won that war, but the angels managed to free the Martian people and then brought them to Earth. Mars was wiped out like the other planets, but God told the Watchers to stay on Earth and watch over his people, and protect them from Satan and the Darkness. Samyaza and his soldiers accepted the mission and made their home on the island of Atlantis. But soon enough, they too fell to sin. Being on Earth, they took on physical attributes like mortal men, though they still held their angelic powers. With the flesh came desires, and that led to their downfall. Samyaza himself fell in love with a mortal woman, an Atlantean named Lilith. At the time, he did not know that she had already fallen in love with Lucifer, Samyaza's fallen brother, and became the wife of the Devil. She seduced Samyaza to drink of the knowledge that the Darkness brought to her. He fell to her charms and fell from grace. Other Watcher angels fell to the same sin, and they birthed children known as the Nephilim with mortal women. These were men of great renown, heroes, giants. They had freewill like human beings, but they were abominations, creations that should never have existed, and many of them fell into evil. Lilith and Samyaza had a child themselves – Legion. He was born with the ability to collect souls into himself and harness their power, much like the power of the Darkness itself, his true spiritual father. Legion was sent into of the Darkness as a baby, and Samyaza and his soldiers were all seized and imprisoned. Some were sent to Hell, and others were trapped under the Earth in prisons of darkness. Then, God cleansed the world with the Flood.

Time went on, and Samyaza was released from his prison by the same Devil that had defiled the love of his life. Satan came and freed Samyaza with a spell from the *Necronomicon*. The year was 200 BC, and Samyaza's son had already been defeated by the Angel with No Name. Both Legion and the nameless angel lost their physical bodies in the battle. Samyaza's son was just a soul filled with demons from the Darkness, and he jumped from host to host. The demonic soul of Legion possessed men until its power destroyed their bodies, and he was forced to move onto another host. During this time, he had no way to control his power and was driven to the point of insanity. Samyaza searched for his son in those days, and was given the *Necronomicon* by the Devil to help Sam search for his son. He hated Satan, for he loved Lilith, but he had no choice except to work with the Devil. Samyaza had no other allies and therefore he used the Devil and his dark magic for his own gain. It was all to no avail, for Samyaza could not find his son. Just before the birth of Christ, Satan took the *Necronomicon* from Samyaza and left the fallen angel to figure out what to do on his own.

The years passed and Samyaza's heart grew darker and darker. He witnessed the rise and fall of many empires and soon gained much political power over the men of the Earth. That continued until the 1800s. At that time, he began to be known as the Chaldean and gained power over all the governing authorities around the world. Samyaza took on the human name of Samuel Malach Prince in Syria in 1830. In 1870, he sailed to America to start a new life there and to rule from the New World, the best place to truly amass his power. When he left Syria, he pretended to be his own son and called himself Samuel Malach Prince, Jr. On the ship to the United States, he met a sorceress. She was not just any sorceress but a great and powerful one, the descendant of Simon Magus. Her name was Magda. She gave Samyaza a crystal and told him that she knew who he was and that with the crystal he could find his son and gain the power to rule over all. The crystal he was given was one of the very same that Satan made to communicate with his daughter, Pandora, over the years. With this crystal, Samyaza was able to communicate with the Devil's daughter and her army. The main point of contact was with Pandora's highest ranking general, who was known across the universe as the Dark One.

Time passed in America and Samuel Malach Prince built his empire. He started a company in New York City called Prince Enterprises, Inc. His fortune and his power grew, along with his sinful nature. The Darkness corrupted his heart and he only sought to rule with his son, Legion, at his side. But just a year and a half ago, this all ended. Samuel Malach Prince VII was the name he used then. He had a new son, Gideon, by his side, who was actually the child of Radix and Esmeralda Salvatore. He also had a new body created for his first-born son, Legion. The final piece he needed was to get the skull of Miacha, which housed Legion's soul. Once he had that, he could place Legion's soul into the new body and bring back his son to his full power. Everything had gone according to plan. But God had another plan. Heroes rose up – Roger Jones, Leina of Ishara, Eishe Taninaru, John, Jack, Akane Yamamoto, Jay Sil, Shanson Matthews with the ISOD division of the FDSR, and even Bianca Salvatore, Esmeralda's daughter and twin sister of Gideon. They fought against the Chaldean, against Samyaza, and they defeated him by the power of the Holy Spirit. God worked through His people and, as always, He would work all out for good.

***

Roger Jones, Eishe Taninaru, and Leina of Ishara were in the secret laboratory of Dr. David Davis. The lab had been built in an abandoned subway station under the doctor's brownstone in the East Village of Manhattan years before when the doctor escaped his former life. Doctor David Davis, who was really Allen Louis Stone, was an African-American doctor of biological sciences. He was just under average height, and now was a little stout and bald with a mustache. He had shaved off his beard but he couldn't part with the mustache. Also his wife, Martha, liked it on him.

When David was younger, he found out that the company he was working for, Bio-Core Labs, was actually using his research for truly evil purposes. The doctor discovered that a serum he had developed was being used on young women, who had been kidnapped and impregnated with the DNA of Samuel Prince's son, Legion, to recreate Legion's body. Roger Jones was the product of that experiment, and the doctor was able to save his mother from the lab, and took her to a convent where she died giving birth to Roger. Years later, the doctor found Roger again and took him in. Back then, Roger was just an ordinary man. He had been framed for the murder of his friend by the Chaldean. Samyaza needed Roger Jones, for he was the only surviving subject in his attempt to clone his son's body. Jones went to Mason Island Maximum Security Prison but was abducted from his prison cell by the Chaldean's soldiers. The men had secured a police boat and fled the island with Roger knocked unconscious. The boat they were escaping on was shot by the police and exploded. Roger lost his hand in the accident, and was found washed ashore by Dr. Davis, who had been tracking him. The doctor brought Roger to his lab and revived him. When Roger Jones woke up, he was the hulking hero that he was now, having grown about a foot and half and gaining an exorbitant amount of muscle mass. His face was basically the same, though his features were slightly larger and his jaw a little more squared off. His brown hair was kept medium length on top and short on the sides with sideburns that ran to the bottom of his jowl. The eyes never change they say, and his were still the same shape and shade of brown. Roger still had a slight tinge of pink under his fair complexion. He had super human strength, durability, and the ability to heal from any wound. But even more bizarre was that, as his body healed, it grew denser and stronger. Any attack of an equal force that he had healed from would no longer have an effect on him. Even with his marvelous healing factor, his left hand never grew back.

Roger along with his friends fought head to head with the Chaldean and his army. With many battles and the scars to go with them, the heroes won. Roger, imbued by the power of the

Holy Spirit, defeated Samyaza in a grueling fight. He had reached a new level of Chaos Fury – a battle technique that draws on the righteous anger of God. Nathaniel Salvatore, Lyles Washington, and other heroes had drawn on this power to obtain victory during battles with the evil cohorts of Darkness. But Roger Jones was able to draw even deeper on the power of the Lord and he reached the level known as the Wrath of God. No mortal had ever reached this level before. But without God bestowing that much power on the superhuman hero, he never would have been able to stand against the fallen angel, Samyaza. Now Samyaza was back in his prison of darkness, the same prison from which Satan had released him. Bianca and Roger's allies all gathered to pray against the sinful spell that Samyaza had put on the building he dwelled in and that he had placed on himself for protection while on Earth. Through prayer and the Hand of God, the spell was broken and Samyaza was cast back into his pen. Also, his stronghold, the sky piercing building that he called his home, fell to the ground, and was nothing more than a pile of rubble. The debris had since been removed and until now nothing had been rebuilt on the site, for every time a new project had been started over the last year it seemed to fall through. The reign of terror of the Chaldean was over, and so was the militant gang, the Children of the Dragon. But these heroes did not rest, for new threats arose every day. Samyaza was only one villain in the world. But the true enemy was still lurking about. Satan and the minions of the Darkness were out there waiting to strike again and again, never to give up until all the world would fall to the will of evil.

Eishe and Leina were not of the Earth. Well, at least, they were not born on Earth, but they were human. Both of them were just over six feet tall, and both had tanned skin. Leina, like her people, was slightly darker, and they had other differences. Eishe looked almost like a mix of Asian and South American or like an Asian Pacific islander. His hair was short and dark and so were his eyes, and he was clean shaven. Leina almost looked Arabic, her features were sharp and strikingly beautiful. Her hazel eyes were big with long lashes. Her light brown hair was tied back into a pony tail and the sides of her head were shaved clean. Leina wore a pointed bone earring in each ear and, on her left ear, also had an earcuff shaped like a snake with a sword through it. All humankind originated from Adam and Eve, the first man and woman that God created. But Satan spread their seed across the cosmos and populated many worlds. The first of these offspring was Pandora, who lived alone on her planet, Gaia. She was not Satan's biological daughter. Her DNA was from Adam and Eve, but the Devil raised her as his own. After that, he planted life on the world of Ishara, which was where Leina was born. World after world, Satan populated thousands and thousands of planets, including Eishe's home world of Aporia. And then, like the grim reaper, Satan came and reaped all of those worlds of the harvest he had sown, taking the lives and souls of every man and woman and feeding them to the Darkness through his own daughter, Pandora. One by one the planets fell, starting with Ishara and ending with Aporia and now only Earth remained. Leina was the spiritual and military leader of many people, some from her home world and others from each of the worlds that had Pandora destroyed. They all dwelled on a ship, the very ship that Leina's brother Carlel was captaining. She left that ship about 200 years ago to follow Eishe to Earth, and now they were together defending their new home.

Leina had two brothers. One was on the ship with the remainder of her people, and the other had fallen. Pandora took the life of Leina's brother, Psol, after she manipulated his heart and turned him toward the Darkness. Psol believed that the Darkness held the knowledge he had sought for, the knowledge to save his people and to bring peace. He was blinded by the daughter of the Devil, his mind brainwashed to believe her false truths. In falling to the Darkness, he killed himself with her sacrificial blade, the knife that Pandora's father, Satan, had given to her. When he thrust the knife into his own heart, Psol's spirit left him for a time. Three days passed and on the third day he rose from the dead, a new creation. But unlike Christ and those who transcended to the light of God, he transcended to the Darkness and became the Dark One, the first and only known Dark Transcendent. He went from world to world with Pandora and helped her conquer them time and again, sending the inhabitants of each planet to the Abyss to be drained of their spiritual energy and to feed the

Darkness. Psol even went to Eishe's world, Aporia.

The blade that Psol carried was a hooked sword with a long chain that clipped to his belt. The hooked sword was forged in the Darkness as was the chain, both created from the Darkness itself. Whoever the sword cut would go into the Darkness to be trapped for all time once their heart stopped beating. But they would not be dead. No, they would stay body and soul in the Darkness for it to feed on them for eternity. Eishe's master, Coz, had suffered this fate. On Aporia, Coz had been struck by the Dark One when they were in battle. Leina and her brother saw this and teleported him and Eishe onto their ship before Eishe could suffer the same fate. They tried to revive his master, but no matter how hard they prayed to God, it was too late. Eishe saw his master on the table on the ship, and he saw his master's sword. He grabbed it and ran into a nearby room. But unknown to him, it was not a room he had run into but rather a scouting pod whose target was set for Earth. He was launched into space and his master, Coz, faded into the Darkness. Leina tried to chase down Eishe and got into a pod of her own. She launched and both travelled across space toward Earth for two hundred years.

The races that Satan placed across the universe were like men and women before the Flood on Earth and lived to almost one thousand years. But Leina was even older than that as were the people from her planet on the ship. That is because the Angel of the Lord taught them how to harness the power of the Holy Spirit to stay young and alive until the end of times and He also gave them the Torah. The Angel of the Lord came back years later and revealed Himself as Christ after the Resurrection. Leina was taught the Scriptures by God Himself. She shepherded her people and all those on her ship in His ways. Now these extraterrestrial humans were believers and fought for the Lord.

***

It was early morning and Roger, Leina, and Eishe were in the lab training. The doctor had built a sparring room for them as well as other training areas with various equipment to push their abilities to the limit and help them get stronger and improve their battle skills. Doctor Davis was an expert engineer, as well as a doctor of biological sciences, and on top of that he

39

was a skilled mechanic, too. He could fix nearly anything from a broken window to plumbing or electrical, and he could even tailor garments and footwear. All of Roger's outfits were made by the doctor. The colossal hero stood seven feet and three inches tall and weighed half a ton; there were no stores that sold clothing that would fit him. Right now, the three heroes were doing their most important training session, the training of their souls. They all wore white tank tops and gray shorts and sneakers. It was what they always wore when they trained. Eishe and Leina saved their battle suits for exactly that, battle. And Roger, well he didn't really need to wear anything special when he went into a fight because he was nearly invincible.

On top of the powers that God blessed him with, Roger also had a very special weapon – the Left Arm of God, liquid Angel metal that took the shape of anything the wielder could imagine. The Heaven-forged weapon's powers were limitless, and right now Roger was using it to take the place of his missing left hand. The large hero obtained the Left Arm of God when he and Eishe defeated a demon named Namtar in Sheol. The Arm went inside of Roger to be used whenever he would summon it. With the liquid metal hand, he could feel anything he touched as if it were his real left hand, and the metal also ran all the way up his arm to his shoulder. At one time, Samyaza had taken the weapon from Roger and used it against him but the Holy Spirit gave Roger the ability to reach the level of Chaos Fury known as the Wrath of God and, even with a weapon such as the Left Arm of God, Samyaza could not fight back.

The heroes all kneeled on the ground and were praying to God, praising Him for who He is, thanking Him for all He gave them, asking Him to pardon their sins, for Him to bless them with what they needed, and to fill them with the Holy Spirit. Yes, they prayed every day and also read the Bible together. These two things took precedence over all others, for without God they could do nothing.

While the heroes prayed in the lab, Dr. Davis was just getting up and so was his newlywed bride, Martha. They had finally realized the love they shared for each other and had tied the knot. Everyone, especially Kimberly, was very happy for the couple. They slept in the newly renovated attic master suite that the doctor had just added this year, right before the wedding. Kimberly took over his former master suite on the fourth floor, and the rest of them split the other rooms. Bianca's was also on the fourth floor, across from Kimberly's. Roger, Leina, and Eishe each had their own rooms on the third floor. And there was one more room that was vacant, the room that belonged to Bo. It was next to Bianca's on the fourth floor but had been empty ever since Puck took the boy away a year ago.

David brushed his teeth and went downstairs in his robe to make coffee while Martha started to get ready herself. Kimberly and Bianca were still in their rooms sleeping. As soon as the doctor started to brew the coffee, a great puff of smokeless fire appeared before him and standing exactly where he saw this anomaly were four figures. The doctor jumped back into the counter and knocked down a couple mugs that shattered when they hit the kitchen tiles. Martha heard the sound of the breaking mugs and ran down the stairs. Kimberly and Bianca woke up also and came down. All of them were shocked when they saw who was standing there, and then Bianca opened her eyes wide and ran straight toward them.

"Bo, Raven, Puck, and Uncle Lyles!" the young girl screamed. "I knew you were coming. I saw it!"

The young girl was actually older than she looked. A six-year-old child stood there but actually she was eighteen, like her brother Gideon. She had spent twelve years in Sheol, starting when she was four years old, and when she escaped thanks to Roger and Eishe, her body had not aged a day – but her mind had. The two heroes fought against demons from the Darkness to free her. The Archangel Michael had placed her in the former land of the dead, where souls had gone to rest before Christ died and released them to Heaven or Hell. The same Archangel then carried Roger, Eishe, and Bianca out of Sheol and took them to Kimberly's house almost two years ago. It was strange for the girl to still be in a child's body, but somehow she liked it. She had a close relationship with her Father in Heaven. He filled her with His Holy Spirit when she was still inside her mother's womb, and also put His Word in her heart. She spoke to her Daddy up in Heaven every day. She could hear His actual voice inside of her, and He showed her great things. This young girl was like a prophet of old, and she even performed great miracles like Elijah, Elisha, and Moses. When the heroes fought against the Chaldean's army, she called forth a great wind and the fire of God to stop His enemies. Everyone knew she was blessed and that the Lord was with her indeed.

Bianca wrapped her arms around Bo's waist and gave him a tight squeeze. The boy was taller and more muscular than the last time she saw him. Lyles was overcome with emotion. He had just met his son for the first time, and standing before him was his wife, who he had missed dearly. Kimberly was frozen in shock. She thought her husband was dead but there he stood before her. Next to him was her son who had left her a year ago, and now had returned and on his thirteenth birthday. This was a miracle. But she didn't stop to thank God, though she should have. All she could think to do was run into her husband's arms and kiss him. Martha went to David and held him. They spoke quietly to each other, amazed at what had just happened. Puck came over and greeted Martha, she had missed the little Djinni very much. David did not know what to say. He had never met a Djinni before. Ravenblade stood quietly in place, as serious as ever.

"So, will you guys be staying the night," David said, breaking the ice.

"What do you think this is, a Holiday Inn?" Roger boomed from the doorway.

The hulking hero, Leina, and Eishe all had come up from the lab when they heard Bianca scream. Roger's hearing was very acute and he wanted to make sure the girl was not in danger. He was her protector after all, and according to her, her "bestest friend." The three heroes stood there looming. Roger towered over all of them. With his arms folded, the Left Arm of God moved like a living organism on his arm. Ravenblade drew his sword and held it at Roger's throat.

"Where did you get that?" the immortal asked.

"Watch where you point that thing, Fabio," Roger replied, looking at Ravenblade's ponytail. "You might poke your eye out."

42

"That's the Left Arm of God," Ravenblade spoke again. "Last I heard it was taken from the Devil by Namtar and brought to the Darkness. Also I can sense something from you. What are you, Nephilim or something?"

"He's cool," Bo said. "He's my friend."

"Yeah, I'm cool," Roger repeated. "Which is more than I could say for you. Now put that thing down before I wrap it around your neck."

"I'd cut you to shreds, son" the immortal stated.

"I'd love to see you try," Roger laughed.

"Stop," Bianca said. She could not stand to see her friends arguing.

"Sorry, but he started it," Roger said sarcastically.

"What you sense is the DNA of Legion inside of him," Leina said. "And, yes, that is the Left Arm of God."

"Yeah, we beat that Namtar clown in Sheol," Roger said and pointed to Eishe and himself. "Then we all came back with her guardian angel."

"Yes, Michael had taken you away, and I sensed when you returned," Raven said to Bianca.

"We can discuss this all later. But first, who are you and why are you here?" Roger asked.

Ravenblade did not like Roger's tone, and did not like being told what to do in general. But they had a lot to discuss and he was not about to waste any more time. Bo greeted Roger with a hug and told him to relax a little, to trust Ravenblade. A couple of hours flew by and, with them, welcome reunions. Everyone exchanged enough of their stories so they all could get to know each other better. Kimberly still could not believe that her husband was back; she held him tightly and refused to let go, afraid that she would wake up and find out this was all a dream. Also her son, Bo, had returned. She was happy she had not missed his thirteenth birthday, but at the same time she wasn't even sure if they would have time celebrate. Bo looked so much older and more mature than when he had left. Even though he had just hit his teenage years, he was tall and strong and looked like a young man already. Ravenblade told everyone what had happened and how Lyles had woken up and had his soul restored to his body.

He also explained how Lyles had first been trapped in the skull. With everything they had all been through together over time, the stories that Raven told were not very surprising at all.

It was almost lunchtime now and Lyles sat on the couch resting. He was tired and his head was hurting. Ravenblade had told him it was a side effect from being separated from his body for as long as he was and to just give it time. Kimberly told the immortal that she was upset because he had not told her the truth about her husband. He laughed it off and said he didn't really lie: he said Lyles was gone, he never said he was dead. She couldn't handle the truth. That's why he also sent Puck a year ago to take Bo from his room, for he knew his mother would never let him go on her own. They were difficult decisions, but he did what he felt was best. Not being mortal gave Ravenblade a different perspective on how to handle situations. He looked at the bigger picture, and did not care for the subtleties of society and emotions. His viewpoint was much more black and white.

Lyles was napping with Kimberly right next to him. Her head was on his chest and she held his hand. Raven paced back and forth while Bo and Bianca spoke. Martha was engaging in conversation with Puck and David. The good doctor was very fascinated by the Djinni. Eishe stood alone in deep thought as usual, while Roger and Leina stood in the kitchen talking. The two had grown close over the last year. They were both strong warriors, and loved the Lord. Leina had helped Roger deepen his relationship with Christ even more over the past year and, in her tutoring, they drew closer and closer. But they were both too stubborn to tell the other how they felt. Their focus was always on how to use the abilities that God gave them to save the world from evil, and not about their personal love for each other.

"So what do you think of that joker out there?" Roger said to Leina, speaking about Ravenblade.

"I can sense great power from him," she responded. "It feels like an angel's energy but different. He might be a fallen angel. We should take caution."

"Yeah, I can feel it too. Since I've learned to tap into the Spirit I can sense these things. It does remind me of the same energy I feel from Jack but somehow greater. But not as powerful as the energy I felt from Michael, the Archangel. I'm not sure, but I just don't trust him."

"I say we keep an eye on him," Eishe said as he walked into the kitchen. "I too am wary of him. We must always be on watch, for enemies are everywhere."

"What are you guys talking about?" Bo said, as he and Bianca also walked into the kitchen.

"Nothing," Roger said. "Just feeling a little strange. Maybe it's something I ate."

"Or maybe it's me," Raven said from the kitchen doorway. "You think I'm stupid. I know you don't trust me. But that's fine because I don't trust you either, big guy. I knew another big guy with a big mouth, got his head cut off for flapping his gums. He used to work for the Devil, but lucky for him, he found Jesus before he died. Hopefully you have too."

"Try taking my head and let's see what happens," Roger said, puffing out his chest and looking down at the immortal. "They've tried every which way to kill me so far, and I'm still here. But if you're asking if Christ is my Savior, you better believe it. The question is, is he yours?"

"Well, let's just say I've known Christ for a long time. He and I haven't always seen eye to eye, but I know He's God and I know He's the only way to the Father. But good to know you're on the right side, kid."

"Don't call me kid, punk," Roger said and poked his right index finger into Raven's chest.

"Move that finger or I'll chop it off," Raven stated.

"Please, stop!" Bianca exclaimed. Once again she was tired of the bickering.

"Actually, I came in here for you," Ravenblade said to Bianca. "I need you to check on your Uncle Lyles out there. He and Legion were trapped together in that skull for a long time. Part of me is afraid their souls might be intertwined. The other part of me is afraid they are not, because those shadow demons took the skull. Either way we can't afford for Legion to come back."

Bo looked at Ravenblade and said, "But if they are merged, what can we do? Will my father ever be able to be himself again? I mean, I just met him finally and now he might be a demon."

"He can be restored," Bianca said. "But let me go see first."

Everyone walked out of the kitchen. David, Martha, Kimberly, and Puck all wondered what was going on. Bianca walked over to Lyles, who was fast asleep, and she put her right hand on his head. She closed her eyes and called on the Holy Spirit. The young girl began to glow with a soft white light.

"What are you doing?" Kimberly asked.

"I'm searching his soul," Bianca replied.

"Searching for what?" Lyle's wife asked with concern.

"For Darkness."

The girl glowed brighter and then all at once a sharp pain shot through her heart and into her head. She screamed in anguish and fell to the ground.

"Yes," Bianca said "Legion has merged with his soul."

"I can help," Leina said. "But we need to act fast. Everyone come here and stand around him. We all need to pray!"

The group gathered around Lyles, who was still sleeping, but as they all went to place their hands on him, he awoke with a start.

"What are you all doing?" Lyles asked.

"Praying for you," Leina replied, and she started to call on the Lord.

Before Leina could get into the prayer, Lyles began to convulse and shout. His demeanor changed, and he threw himself onto the ground. Roger and Leina went to grab him but he somehow pushed them away with a superhuman strength. Lyles' body began to glow blue, and he growled and threw himself about, screaming in pain. Legion was awakening from inside of him. The heroes knew this and they all went to grab him. Suddenly, shadow demons began to appear in the room all around. They attacked the heroes and kept them from getting to Lyles.

"The shadow demons have returned!" Ravenblade shouted.

"Thanks, Captain Obvious," Roger shot back.

The heroes all readied themselves and drew on the Holy Spirit. It was time to fight. Ravenblade informed everyone that decapitating the demons was the only way to defeat them. But that would prove difficult since they could make themselves intangible like shadows. The heroes were all cunning fighters and knew that in order for the demons to hurt them, they had to take on physical form and that was the best time to attack. The other issue was how small the room was, so it was difficult for all of them to move about and fight. Doctor Davis grabbed Martha, Kimberly, and Bianca and ran up the stairs toward the attic master suite, to hide while the others fought. The young girl did not want to go but they would not let her stay. The doctor held her tightly in his arms and carried her all the way. Raven and Bo drew their swords. Eishe and Leina did not have any weapons, but Roger had the Left Arm of God and he was ready. The demons attacked the heroes right away, slashing at them with their sharp claws. Eishe blocked an attack and grabbed the creature's wrist. Leina did the same and they threw both demons into each other with no effect. Puck teleported over and over again, attacking demon after demon, but his claws seemed to do no damage. Roger did not bother blocking the demons. He let them strike him, for their claws could not hurt the super human. Metal vines grew from the Left Arm of God and grabbed one demon as it slashed Roger's chest, and then a blade shot forth from his left hand decapitating the vile demon. First blood went to Roger. Raven and Bo hacked through the horde and made their way to Lyles. The shadow demons phased through each strike and struck back. Bo managed to slice off one of their clawed hands but it grew back right afterward. Lyles was still on the floor writhing around like a mad man. He was yelling incoherent words and his body glowed brighter and brighter blue. Ravenblade managed to decapitate a few of the shadow demons that attacked him. But more kept coming. The heroes were getting nowhere.

Bo was slashed across the back and fell to one knee. He blocked the next attack and then turned to slice the demon's head off. Two more attacked him and he went back and forth with them. He saw his father on the ground. He did not know him. Bo had just met Lyles today, on his thirteenth birthday. It was not fair. Even though he did not know his father, he loved him, and he knew his father loved him too. The boy fought more and more furiously. His body began to glow with a bright, white light. He was born with the ability to tap into the Spirit's power, and Ravenblade spent the last year teaching Bo how to harness it, though he still had a lot to learn. The difference between him and the other heroes there was that God gave Bo the ability to use the Spirit as a weapon. He was not just tapping into His power, he was becoming it himself. Bo held out his right hand and shot a beam of white light at one of the shadow demons and even though the demon had not taken physical form, the beam took its head and the demon vanished. Yes, a pure blast of God's light could vanquish any Darkness. Bo shot beam after beam, taking out as many demons as he could. All the heroes were impressed with the boy, especially Leina, for in all the wars she'd fought she'd never seen anything like this from a mortal. Only Angels had done this before. Bo ran toward his father, who was on the ground and reached out toward him. But before Bo could reach him, Lyles shot out a blast of blue energy from his body that knocked his son back. Roger ran to Bo and helped him up. Ravenblade and the others ran toward Lyles and fought back more of the shadow demons. But it was too late. Two of the demons grabbed Lyles and vanished. Just before they faded away, Puck hitched a ride on Lyles' back and followed them to their destination. They were gone. All the shadow demons vanished at once and the heroes were left alone. Ravenblade would have to tell Kimberly once again that her husband was gone.

***

The shadow demons appeared just outside the cottage where Simon, Gideon, and Collins had been living in rural Pennsylvania. Before he was seen, Puck was smart enough to teleport behind some trees. The shadow demons held Lyles and he writhed in pain. His body still glowed blue. The door opened and Simon Magus III walked out. They were in the middle of the woods and no one would see anything that was happening here. That is why Simon chose this place to live. He could be left alone to do whatever he had to do. Gideon and Collins stepped out as well, and then she came. Puck saw her. It was Satan's own bride, Lilith. He remembered the time she came to the desert to scare away the Djinn and take his former friend Nathan for herself. Then they faced her later on, when they battled Legion. A battle that helped turn his former king Iblis and the rest of his brothers to the side of the light. It was all coming back to the Djinni and

Puck wondered what Simon and the others were doing.

Simon Magus III took a black crystal from his pocket and chanted as he placed it on Lyles' forehead. Puck's friend yelled toward the heavens. Lyles' eyes glowed a bright blue and beams shot from them to the sky. Then he hunched over and struck the ground. Suddenly, his composure began to change, and Lyles stood upright. The blue glow in his eyes was softer now. He spoke but his voice was different. It was not the voice of Lyles, but rather the voice of thousands of demons all at once.

"It's good to be back," he said.

Yes, Legion had returned and he was inside of Lyles' body. The world was doomed.

CHAPTER III
OUT FROM THE SHADOWS

Puck appeared back at the doctor's brownstone in the East Village of Manhattan. Everyone was in the living room. Bo held his mother and Bianca did, too. Martha and the doctor held each other as well. Roger, Leina, and Eishe stood together thinking of a strategy. They all turned and looked at the Djinni when he popped in from a puff of smokeless fire.

"Legion, back he is," Puck said. "Doomed, we all are."

"It's all my fault," Ravenblade said. "I should have taken him somewhere else. Or maybe I should have killed him. At least Lyles' soul would have been sent to Heaven."

"But Legion, free would be still, and your friend, you would have killed for nothing," Puck said.

"It *is* your fault!" Kimberly shouted. "You had to take him to China, to fight Legion. And now your best plan was to kill him yourself! I hate you! You tore my family apart and now, after I had already mourned my husband's death, you bring him back only to have him taken from me again! I hate you!"

"Ma, you don't mean that," Bo said.

"Bo's right, Aunt Kim, don't hate him. Raven only did what God wanted him to do," Bianca said. The young girl always seemed to be wise well beyond her years. She was indeed like a great prophet of old. She continued, "God has a plan. Trust Him. Remember, God is love; hate is never the answer. Even Jesus died for us when we were sinners."

The girl's words comforted Kimberly and she calmed down.

"And anyway, Roger can bring him back, and beat that nasty Legion. He can do anything!" Bianca squealed with joy.

"Hmm, we'll have to see about that," Ravenblade said. "But the girl is right, we can get him back. God can do anything and, if He is for us, who can stand against us."

"Now, that's more like it, Sparky," Roger said. "Let's get Lyles back. Once we have him, we can get that demon out of him."

"Prayer is a powerful weapon," Dr. Davis said. "We've all seen that."

"Yes, it is," Ravenblade interjected. "But it will take more than prayer to get Legion out of him."

"I can do it," Bianca said. "With Bo, we can do it together. He and I have a direct connection to the Father and the Holy Spirit. It is strong and God's power is in us. If Bo concentrates the full power of the Spirit into Uncle Lyles' body, while I call on the Father, we can separate Legion's soul from his. But then, as Puck said, Legion will be freed."

"If they still have the skull, we can use that to trap the demon again," Ravenblade said. "We have to try."

"I'm in," Roger said.

Then everyone else joined in and agreed to help.

A voice came from the front door as it opened, "You're not going anywhere without us."

It was John, Jack, and Akane. John was dressed in his usual casual outfit, with his leather jacket and his Scarred Heart T-shirt. Jack and Akane were suited up in their battle attire, ready to fight.

"I figured you guys could use some help so I told them to come over," David said.

"Looks like you can use all the help you can get if it's Legion we are fighting," Jack said, surveying the room. "Ravenblade? Is that you?"

"Yeqon?" The immortal was stunned.

"Yes," Jack said. "But they call me Jack now. I was imprisoned under the Earth to pay for my sins. The place where God's angels trapped me was under a prison right here in the city, and an officer, my good friend Jay, and John here released me. I know I still must pay for my sins but I will fight for the Lord until my dying breathe. But what about you? Last time I saw you, you were trying to prove yourself to be the most evil being on Earth. So, why are you here?"

"I too have turned back to our Father," Ravenblade replied. "My sins are worse than yours, for I spilled the blood of many of God's heroes all over the Earth. Last time I checked, your only sin was falling in love with a woman."

"Sin is sin," Jack said. "We all must pay for our own."

"Christ paid for mine," David said. "Are you sure He didn't pay for yours also?"

"We've talked about this before," Jack said. "Even you know

52

what the Scriptures say about angels who fall. We have no hope in the salvation of Christ. But I don't fight for my own salvation. I fight for God and His people. That is enough. I will accept my punishment when the time comes. Until them, I'll serve Him."

"Bravo," Roger said with a smile, clapping his hands.

"Now that we're all done with the heartfelt speeches, let's go get Bo's dad back. I need to loosen up my muscles a little bit, get in a workout. Maybe pound a few demons along the way," the large hero bantered.

"Ravenblade," John said. "I remember you, too. It's like a distant memory from another time. I can see you as you are but then I also see something from before."

"Yes, John," Jack said. "He was Azreal. Or at least a part of him."

"The memories are coming back stronger every day," John said.

"Yes, and when you see someone who triggers them, they will come back stronger."

"Wait a second," Ravenblade said. "It can't be. It's impossible." The immortal touched John on the shoulder and felt something from him. "The Angel with No Name?"

"Yes," Jack said again. "John was him before. This is a new lifetime he is living now."

"I didn't know who or what I was. All I remember was that my parents were killed when I was a kid," John said, helping Raven understand his new comrades. "And then one day, I was shot in the chest six times and fell into the water at the piers. When I emerged from there, I was alive, my wounds healed. My mind was opened to the past lives I had lived and to who I really was, the Angel with No Name, the Angel of Order."

"Seems this reunion is bigger than we all thought," Jack said.

"I mean, the last time the three of us stood together, we were angels in Heaven. Crazy, right?" Jack stated.

"That's enough talk for now," Eishe said. "Do you want to get your friend back or not? Let's suit up and go."

***

"So what's your dumb plan again, magic man?" Legion said. The demon was still possessing Lyles' body. He stood in the cabin's basement; Lilith and Simon were with him. Legion's true body was there, beside them in the glass chamber. Simon reiterated the plan for Legion. He and Lilith would open a portal to Samyaza's prison under the Earth. Using the *Necronomicon*, Simon could open the portal from anywhere, and did not need to be above the place where the fallen angel was trapped. When God first imprisoned Samyaza, He placed him under the sands of the Arabian Desert, but now he was under the ground where his building once stood in New York City. The plane he was trapped in was not really under the Earth but a separate spiritual plane that was connected to that area. No one could dig to find him. There were only two ways to get there. One was through a special portal. The other was for a spiritual being like an angel, demon, or transcended being to reach the correct spiritual frequency and travel there. The only beings with that ability at the moment were God's highest ranking angels and the Devil. So Legion, Simon, and Lilith would need to create the portal. Gideon and Collins were in the living room watching television, unconcerned about what the others were doing in the basement.

"It's time, Lilith," Simon said. "Let's go."

"Don't order me around, sorcerer," the Devil's bride said. "I'll make a snack out of you."

"Should I add some salt first," Simon jested.

"You won't find it funny when your flesh is in my teeth," she said and smirked.

"Stop fooling around, you two!" Legion boomed. "I grow tired of your antics."

Simon took the black crystal in his hand. He started to chant and the *Necronomicon* floated in front of him. The evil tome glowed with a sinister blue light and opened to an interdimensional portal spell. The crystal began to glow. But the light from the crystal was not blue like the book, rather it was a strange dark light. Simon chanted the spell from the *Necronomicon* and a portal of blue swirling light opened before their eyes. Lilith and Simon walked through the portal and the book floated after them. Then the portal closed. Legion stayed behind with his new body to get it ready for his soul to be placed inside.

On the other side, Simon and Lilith entered complete

darkness. It was Samyaza's prison. Simon chanted and a ball of light appeared before them. They walked forward and saw Samyaza, spread-eagled on the ground in chains. He only wore a white undergarment and nothing else. He still resembled his human form – shaved head, tanned skin, and dark eyebrows and eyes. His muscles were well defined but he looked much weakened and drained. Samyaza saw the ball of light and two figures standing in its glow.

"Who's there?" he said.

"Do you not recognize the woman you love?" Lilith said.

"Lilith, my dear Lilith, is that really you?" Samyaza asked.

"Yes, it is I?" she said and walked over to him.

Lilith still loved Samyaza. She had never loved the Devil. Her marriage to him was forced and false. Satan could never love anyone and Lilith knew that. Though she was a demoness now, she was a mortal once, and her mortal heart loved the fallen angel before her. She kneeled down and caressed his head. Samyaza looked into her eyes.

"We are here to free you," Simon said. "And to do one more thing."

The *Necronomicon* floated in front of the sorcerer. Simon held out the glowing crystal and read from the book. Samyaza's chains fell away and he felt his strength restored. He felt powerful again. The fallen angel stood up and Lilith stood next to him.

"Now to get you some better threads," Simon said, and he cast an enchantment that dressed Samyaza in the finest black pinstriped suit.

"That's more like it," the fallen angel spoke. "What's next."

"This," Simon said and placed the crystal on the ground.

A holographic image appeared before them all. It was Pandora's general, the Dark One. The translucent blue image of him was clear enough but it faded in and out as he spoke. He was strong and very tall, well over seven foot. To Samyaza, he looked even bigger than Roger Jones. The Dark One wore a ghostly mask resembling a skull with two points that shot up from the top corners, something like sharp horns. The openings in the mask for the eyes and mouth were solid black. The evil general was heavily armored with large armored pauldrons layered over his shoulders. He also had a long, flowing cape with sharp points over his shoulders. His forearms were wrapped up in what looked like bandages and his upper arms were exposed, showing his pitch-black skin. Leather lappets hung from his belt which was fastened in the center by a demon-skull buckle. Spikes came down the larger and more ornate lappet at the center of the belt. He wore strapped boots that were buckled up to his knees. And in his hand he held the hooked sword with its chain attached to his belt. He was ominous in every way. Simon bowed on one knee. Samyaza and Lilith remained standing.

"Dark lord," Simon said with his head down. "The world has turned toward the Darkness. Enough people have lost faith. The time is ripe to bring the knowledge to Earth."

"Yes," Psol spoke. His voice was deep and foreboding. "The belief in God has weakened enough that I may enter. Then the Three Days of Darkness can cover the Earth and we can build the temple. On the third day, we will be able to open the seal that is over the Earth and bring in my empress, Pandora. She will usher in the Darkness and it will consume this world just as it consumed the others. The time has finally come. Thankfully, I can pass into this prison plane that God had set up, and from there I can enter the Earth. Oh, how I have longed for this day. Two other times we tried and failed, but this time we will triumph."

"Yes, dark lord, it is time for you to plant your feet on Earth's soil and drain it of all life," Simon said and stood up.

The holographic image disappeared and Simon picked up the crystal. He read another spell from the *Necronomicon* and instantly a new portal opened up. From the portal came forth a vast army of soldiers, all in black-plated armor, made from a blended metal from Pandora's home world. It was stronger than steel, light weight, and did not restrict the wearer's movements. The soldiers were all soulless warriors created from the corpses of men whom Pandora slew herself, throughout time. They were much like the New Dawn army Samyaza had built from the fallen members of the Children of the Dragon. But this army was even stronger and the armor they wore was nearly impenetrable. This made them difficult to decapitate, which was the only way to kill them. Only Angel metal, Hell metal, and weapons forged in the Darkness itself could penetrate the armor. After the army marched into the dark prison, Psol, the Dark One, himself walked out. He seemed even larger in person and a dark energy emanated from his very being.

"Let's go and restore Legion, and then we must raise the Temple of the Darkness," Psol commanded.

Simon opened another portal and they all passed through it, appearing outside of the cottage. Gideon ran outside and so did Collins.

"Master, welcome home," Collins said in his British accent.

"Good to see you, Collins," Sam said and patted him on the shoulder. "And you too, son," he said to Gideon.

"You're not my father," Gideon said and folded his arms. He had no need for Samyaza any longer.

Gideon, being eighteen, was technically a man now in his own right. He was only interested in the power that the Darkness offered him and nothing more. He looked at Psol with some respect, for he could feel the Darkness flowing through him and from him. Psol also looked at Gideon and recognized his potential, for he too emanated the evil power of the Darkness – in a purer form than the Dark One and purer even than Pandora herself. It was the same power he felt from Pandora's own father, Satan, on the few occasions that they met. Psol also felt one more strong dark power. From the front door walked out Legion and behind him he was dragging the glass chamber with his new body.

"Hmm, so this is the Dark One, impressive," Legion said. "Finally, someone with a little hutzpah."

"Legion," Psol said. "I'd say the same for you but in that body you seem so fragile. But I am here to fix that."

"Legion!" Samyaza shouted and walked over toward his son. "I have not seen you since you were born."

"And who are you?" Legion said.

"I'm your father, Samyaza," the fallen angel answered.

"Hmm, sure, and next thing, you're going to tell me that floozy over there is my mother," Legion stated and pointed at Lilith.

Samyaza kept quiet for he did not want anyone to know the truth: Legion was the love child of the fallen angel, Samyaza, and

Lilith, the woman he loved.

"Enough with the sentiments. Let us begin. I grow impatient and so does the Darkness. It hungers to feed on this world," the Dark One interrupted. "Magician, come. It is time."

Simon opened the glass chamber and the body lay exposed. The *Necronomicon* floated before him and the black crystal glowed with the same dark light as before. Simon read from the sinful pages of the book, touched the crystal to Lyles' forehead, and extracted Legion's soul from his body. Lyles collapsed to the ground. Then Simon touched the crystal to the forehead of Legion's new body and read another spell from the evil codex. Instantly, the new body was filled with Legion's soul. The Nephilim awoke, stepped out of the chamber, and stood erect. He was six and a half feet tall, muscular, but not bulky. His skin was tan, his nose sharp and straight. His jet black hair flowed down his back, and he had no facial hair. His eyes were darker than a moonless night, and had no whites in them. Then, with his right foot, the demon shattered the glass chamber that had held him. That glass was tempered with the fire from Samyaza's very hands. The fire of a fallen angel which made it almost unbreakable. Legion was fully restored.

"Yes!" Legion cried out in the voice of thousands of demons. "My time has come again. And we will usher in the Darkness."

"We will indeed," Psol boomed. "But first you will need some clothes. Magician, dress this man!"

"Right away," Simon responded and waved his hand while chanting.

A black fitted T-shirt, black jeans, and black boots appeared on Legion.

"Hmm," Legion huffed. "I guess this will do."

"You don't need armor with all your powers, now do you?" Simon jested. "I'm sure you will tear through those before we know it and then we can talk about a new outfit."

"Ha ha, always a comedian," Legion said.

"Okay, everyone," Psol spoke again. "It is time to go. Magician, you know what to do. Just as we planned."

"Yes, to Atlantis," Simon said. "To raise the island and the Temple of the Darkness."

"Yes, but we won't need this one," Psol said, and one of his soldiers stabbed Collins through the gut. "He'll bleed to death. The rest of you can come. But I have no use for regular mortals. They are too weak."

Simon opened another portal and they all passed through. When they got to the other side they were inside a bubble-like force field under the Atlantic Ocean, at the base of the sunken island. Samyaza studied his view of the island and so did Lilith. They could see the ruins of its homes, the tholos, and the city gates. The land was desolate and covered in algae after submersion under the sea for thousands of years. Simon was indeed a powerful sorcerer, the High Sorcerer of the Darkness. He read from the *Necronomicon* and instantly the island began to rise up, and they rose with it. Once Atlantis resurfaced, Simon cast another spell to restore vegetation to the land and then cast a cloaking spell so they could not be found. Together they all marched toward the cave where Lilith had first brought Samyaza to show him the truth, the knowledge of the Darkness, and the same place where Legion was conceived. They marched on with the sun overhead – it was late afternoon and almost evening in Atlantis.

***

On the east coast of the United States, it was a few hours earlier in the afternoon. In a puff of smokeless fire, the heroes appeared in front of the cabin where Simon and his cohorts had been living. All of them were dressed for battle. Leina and Eishe's suits were designed by her people, woven from carbon-like fibers that were treated so the suits were nearly impenetrable. Weapons forged in Heaven, Hell, and the Darkness could break through their armor as could an object thrust with a tremendous enough force. Leina and Eishe both wore boots that reached the knee and gloves up to the elbow. Leina also had a device on her wrist that she used for communication and navigation. Over one shoulder was a strap that ran down her chest with throwing knives set into it. The same strap also held her bladed staff to her back. Scale-like metal pauldrons sat on her shoulder, connected by a chain, and her belt had many pouches on it to hold other weapons she may need. On her head, Leina wore a metal headband with three gems. One was at the center, and the other two were at the ends of the pieces that ran down her cheeks. Her hair was tied back as usual and she still wore her bone earrings and the earcuff of a serpent being stabbed through the heart.

Eishe had a mask that covered his whole head, made up of the same fiber as the suit. The mask had a large visor that blended into it, which was wide enough to allow his peripheral vision. He had painted pointed red marks over and under the eyes, symbols painted on a warrior's face on his home planet of Aporia. This warrior monk from Aporia also had his trusty blade.

Akane wore her black fitted suit that the FDSR had given to her when she worked alongside them. Over her back, she had her blade slung and her red bandana sat across her brow.

Jack's battle suit was his black Watcher's robe and John donned his usual street clothes. Bo and Bianca also put on suits that they had been given by the FDSR, just in case. The suits looked very similar to Akane's but were navy blue and not black, like the field uniforms that FDSR soldiers wore.

Ravenblade still wore the only clothes he owned and Puck, as usual, wore only his own fur and skin. Roger stood tall over everyone. He, like John, wore street clothes. A black tank top, black army-style cargo pants, and black combat boots. And on his left arm he wore the Left Arm of God which was a very intimidating weapon. The liquid angel metal moved like it was alive. They saw Lyles, unconscious on the ground, and another man. Roger recognized him. It was the Chaldean's henchman but Roger did not know his name.

"Roger Jones," Collins wheezed. His gut had been cut open and he was bleeding to death.

Roger kneeled in front of him and asked, "What happened here?"

"The Dark One has come. They released my master from his prison and brought back his son."

"So, Legion has been restored," Ravenblade affirmed.

"Yes," Collins wheezed. "They have gone to Atlantis to raise the island and build the Temple of the Darkness. You have to stop them. They will destroy the world."

"But how?" Roger asked. "How can we stop them?"

Collins spoke no further for all the life had left his body. Roger stood up.

"We have to get to that island," Ravenblade said.

"We need to regroup first," Roger commanded. "We can't go in halfcocked. I know, I have learned from my mistakes. We need to go to the FDSR."

Roger paused and turned. "John, call Jay and tell him to meet us at FDSR headquarters. Then call Dan and have them wait for our arrival. We will go there and, with God's help, devise a plan of action. Once we do, we'll go to Atlantis and stop those villains."

Bianca walked over to Lyles' body with Bo. She placed her hand on his chest.

"He's in there and he's alive," she said.

Bo was overcome with joy and hugged the girl.

"Good," Ravenblade said. "Where is this FDSR headquarters?"

"I'll show you," Leina said and from her wrist a holographic map appeared. "It's there. Can you take us there, Puck?"

"Think so, I do," Puck said and searched the wind to find the directions that he saw on the map. "Okay, found it, I have. Hands on me, everyone place."

Roger gently lifted Lyles off the ground and slung him over his shoulder. Then they all placed their hands on Puck and vanished in a puff of smokeless fire.

CHAPTER IV
THE JOURNEY BEGINS

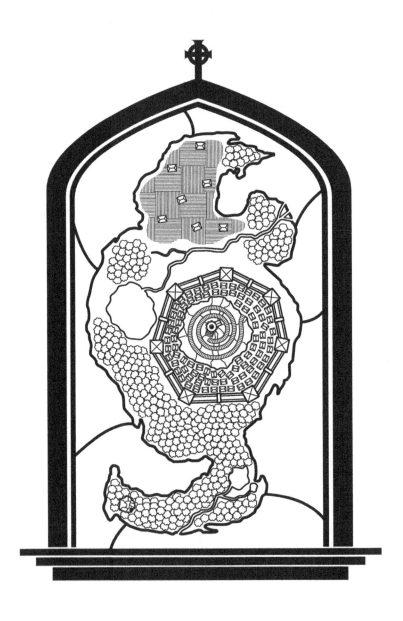

At 9 West 58th Street at the Prince Enterprises, Inc., headquarters, Toni was on the top floor of the building working. It was midafternoon and the floor he was on was restricted to all personnel except himself, Joan Joyce – the CEO of the company, and a few other select individuals. These individuals were top scientists and engineers that Toni had hired who worked on top-secret research and development for the weapons that they were building. Prince Enterprises had always had its hands in weapons of mass destruction, as well as other illegal contraband. Samyaza had built them before and used the Scimitars to sell them, and that is exactly what Toni was doing now, following in the former owner's footsteps. The only difference was that Toni also was Pharaoh, the leader of the underground organization called the Scimitars, so he collected all the profits.

Today, Toni had in his possession the sonic cannon that the Triad had sold to him for a very high price. He was working with his team to add this technology to a new armored suit that they were building. Once the suit was finished, he would mass produce it and sell it to the highest bidder. It would be a lie to say that some of the people working on this project were not afraid of who would get this technology and what that would mean for the future of the world. These armored suits would give the wearer the strength of one hundred men, the ability to fly at speeds that matched the fastest military jets, and one more thing. They would have the ability to fire concentrated sonic blasts at any target and annihilate it. The power of the blast could be controlled by the wearer and used to stun an opponent or blow up a tank. Toni's team still did not know the maximum level of power the sonic cannon could reach but they would keep testing it until they found out.

While Toni watched the scientists and engineers work on the armored suit, someone else was watching him. Crystal Brown, Toni's fifteen-year-old daughter was sitting at her laptop in her father's duplex mega-apartment on the Eastside of Central Park. She was pretty, her frame petite. Her facial features were soft and round with a small button nose, and big, doe-like brown eyes.

Her skin was a caramel brown. Crystal Brown was a certifiable genius, working on her PhD in neurophysics at Columbia University at her young age. A few months back, she had moved in with her father in hopes that he would get to know her better. Crystal's mother was tired of Toni being a distant parent and not taking an interest in his daughter's life. It was bad enough that they had broken up before Crystal was born – even then, Toni was more concerned about his business deals than the people he loved. It was not that Toni did not love his daughter but he loved himself more. He was very self-centered and consumed by making money and building his empire. Somehow, when his daughter showed up at his front door, he did not want to turn her away.

Crystal was living a whole new life now. She went from living in a small two-bedroom apartment with her mother in Brooklyn to a luxurious two-floor apartment in one of the most prestigious buildings in New York City. There was marble everywhere, real gold trim, solid mahogany doors and furniture. She felt like one of the kids from *Different Strokes*, except this was her biological father, and he was not white. She had found, though, that living in such an extravagant home was not everything it was cracked up to be. She was alone almost all the time, except for the servants and the few times her father sat down to eat with her. He was always working, in his home office or at Prince Enterprises. Day and night, he was busy, and Crystal wanted to know what he did. So, she broke into his home office one day when he was not home, which was most of the time lately. There she found a letter from her father's uncle James. It talked about the Scimitars, about family, and about a white devil that they were going to kill. At the end of the letter, Uncle James said that, if he did not survive the battle, he wanted Toni to know that he loved him like his own son and that he wanted Toni to have a better life than he had had. Crystal did not understand the backstory of this letter and she started to do some research. She knew her father had been arrested but did not know for what. The police never released the full information of his crimes to the public and the existence of the Scimitars had been kept secret. And now she knew something about her father, she would find out more.

On her desk, Crystal had printed various articles and also a printed copy of the letter, made from a photo she took with her phone. The articles talked about unexplained destruction in Harlem in the year 2000. And she found some references to the Scimitars on the internet but all of it was speculation. Crystal needed to know more so months ago she bugged her father's home office. Then she developed a plan to bug his corporate office as well.

Last month, the fifteen-year-old genius followed her father to work and snuck into the parking garage. Using the HVAC ducts, she sent drones to the top floor of the building. She really was a genius. The drones attached small high-resolution cameras onto each of the AC vents to help her see as much of what was going on as possible. She also sent two more drones to her father's private office, one floor down, leaving cameras on the AC vents in there as well. The cameras carried powerful audio devices that could pick up even the slightest whisper, which helped her to learn a lot. For a whole month now she watched and listened to all the business that her father was conducting in his home and corporate offices, and she saw what he was working on, on the restricted top floor of Prince Enterprises. Crystal now realized that her father was worse than she thought. The young woman watched and listened to everything on her laptop in her room, which was connected to all the surveillance devices that she had planted. Her father, Toni, had built an armored suit that could destroy the world one day. She had to stop him but he was her father and she loved him. What should she do? Crystal grabbed her Bible from a small bookshelf in her room, and prayed for God to show her answers. She prayed to God to save her father's soul.

***

At FDSR Headquarters, Lieutenant Dan Marshall, wearing his highly decorated green lieutenant's uniform, and the ISOD team, wearing their white service-dress uniforms, stood waiting in the West Hangar for the arrival of their comrades, and some new allies as well.

The Intense Special-Ops Division, or ISOD, was made up of the best and brightest stars in the FDSR. The core members of the team all had known each other since they were children. Their parents, who worked for the United Nations in various roles, were from the same small village in Kerala, India. The men and women of ISOD all attended West Point together and had successful careers in the military before joining the FDSR. Sergeant Shanson Mathews was the leader of the pack and wore the same white uniform with bright silver buttons as his team but distinguished by his sergeant's stripes. Mathews' long hair and sturdy frame fit the name that his parents had given him, a derivative of Samson – the Biblical judge whose God-given superhuman strength helped to deliver Israel. Like his namesake, Shanson was very strong; he had been known to perform superhuman feats of strength throughout his lifetime. It was estimated that he was at least as strong as ten men and, exactly like the Bible's Samson, Shanson knew that God provided this strength and it was not his alone.

His first officer was Cynthia Carlson, who specialized in weapons and hand-to-hand combat. Next was Jenny Samuels, a leading agent in international espionage – she helped to bring down some of the world's most dangerous criminals. Then was Jessie Thomas, who specialized in disarming explosives and opening locks of any type. He also was a strong fighter. Binu Alexander was a master of disguise and could play any role he needed to get the job done. Finally, was Shanson's own brother Solomon, who was an expert code breaker and could hack into any computer system. All the core members were in tiptop shape but of average height and build to the untrained eye. Shanson was the lone Adonis in the group standing at about six feet two inches tall and with broad shoulders and muscles to spare. Among all the things the core members held in common, they were all brought up in homes with strong Christian faith. They still prayed together every day, especially before going into battle. Though the FDSR was not a Christian organization, even Dan Marshall, who was not a believer at first, had seen the reality of God over the last couple of years. The allies they made and the things they all saw showed Dan that there must be a God. Plus Jack and John proved themselves to have been angels at the time of their creation and it was hard to argue that when he saw what they could do. The Chaldean himself showed himself to be a fallen angel named Samyaza. There was just too much undeniable evidence in plain sight. How could he argue against that?

The FDSR complex was massive and almost seemed like a small city compacted into one very large building with a few smaller stations posted around. It was surrounded by massive walls fitted with towers that kept the base impenetrable. There was only one way in and out, through the front gates, but the heroes that were about to arrive did not have to worry about that. They were brought in by Puck, a Djinni who had the ability to teleport wherever he desired as long as he knew where he was going. Dan and his team prepared themselves for their guests, but even though they knew they were arriving, the whole team was left stunned as their allies materialized in front of them in a puff of smokeless fire. The ISOD team all pointed their weapons at the Djinni, knowing what he was and how to kill him.

"Put those guns down! "Roger shouted.

"Listen to the man," Dan commanded. "Good to see you, Mr. Jones. And who is that you have there," he pointed to Lyles, who was still slung over Roger's shoulder.

"Yeah, good to see you too, lieutenant," Roger answered. "Looking dapper as ever. This is Bo's father, Lyles Washington. He's alive but knocked out cold. We're hoping someone here could revive him. We have a lot to talk about and we might need his help."

"Yes, right away. Help Mr. Washington," Dan commanded.

Two of the ISOD members took Lyles from Roger. One held him under his arms and the other grabbed his legs. They carried him out to one of the medical rooms.

"Sorry, am I late?" Jay Sil asked, walking in and wearing a white sergeant's uniform that matched Shanson's.

"You are as usual," John said. "Just like at the pier."

"Better late than never," Jay joked back.

Behind Jay walked a woman with chestnut brown hair tied into a bun with some strands hanging down behind her and she was wearing her own officer's uniform, similar to the ones that ISOD wore.

Jay announced, "I'd like to introduce. My first officer –"

"Jael Zahavi," Dan interrupted. "Good to see you again."

"Good to see you as well, lieutenant," Jael responded.

Jael Zahavi was a former Israeli intelligence agent, a member of the Mossad. Jay knew little of his first officer's past but knew that she had been involved in very top-secret missions while serving her country of Israel. Dan had met her years before, after her entire team was wiped out by a brood of strange, vampire-like, demonic creatures. Jael was left distraught by this loss and vowed to avenge their deaths. The Israeli government gave her no assistance but allowed her to leave her post and join Dan at the FDSR, where they studied the creatures and fought against them. Just last year, she transferred to the newly developed Manhattan department of FDSR, where she now reported to her sergeant, Jay Sil. She had smooth olive skin and was strong and athletic, standing five feet and eight inches tall. She was lean and mean, as Jay put it. She may have been the best soldier that the FDSR had, aside from Shanson. The New York sergeant thought it would be best to bring her along to help assist the FDSR while he and some of its top members were deployed on this new mission. The ISOD members had not met Jael, as she worked for a different division and, as a matter of routine, kept to herself. The teams needed to unite and help keep the world safe from the impending Darkness.

"Okay, everyone, let's focus," Dan ordered. "Let's work out the plan and get moving."

The ISOD members stood at attention and so did Jay Sil and everyone else present. It was time to form a plan of action and everyone filed out of the hangar toward one of the conference rooms in the west wing. They walked down the long hallways, different groups having their own discussions. Some discussed the evil they were about to face. Others simply about day-to-day events in their lives. Jael remained quiet the whole time and walked facing forward, waiting to be directed into one of the rooms. John and Akane exchanged glances. They wanted to hold hands but tried to keep a professional demeanor. Roger and Leina also exchanged glances, but they still did not know what the future held for them. Yes, they both had feelings for the other, but was this really the time to start a relationship? Dan stopped at one of the conference room doors, placed his right index finger on its scanner, and the door swooshed open. He stood to the side while everyone walked in and took a seat around the long metal table at the center of the room.

Dan stood at the front of the room and held a small remote. He pressed one of its controls and a three-dimensional topographic map appeared, floating over the center of the table. It was a hologram projected from the ceiling. The image was the Atlantic Ocean, somewhere between Bermuda and Africa.

"We are getting a strange reading from this location," Dan stated. "Earlier, it appeared as if a land mass had materialized there but then it vanished."

"They are cloaking it with magic," Ravenblade stated. "It must be that sorcerer, Magus' descendant. But I know where the island stood. I've been there."

"Of course you have, in ancient times, right?" Dan said. "I mean, let me guess, another fallen angel?"

"Something like that," Ravenblade answered.

"Who are you?" Jay asked. "It feels like we add new people to this team every week."

"Who I am is none of your concern," Ravenblade said. "Just be happy you have me on your side or else your head would be on the floor before your body could hit the ground." There was no cause for alarm because the warriors in the room all knew that Ravenblade was speaking out of bravado, and it was not a real threat.

"Raven," Jack said. "Let's try to focus."

The immortal folded his arms, glared at Jack, then shifted his gaze toward Jay. The sergeant felt a chill run down his spine. Dan called order and began to outline a plan. First, they pinpointed the location using the strange GPS signatures they were picking up and Ravenblade's own memory of where the island was. The immortal gave them all a brief history of Atlantis. Jack added some of his own memories of Atlantis, for he had lived there at one time. Leina then jumped in and explained who Pandora and the Dark One were and how they would raise the Temple of the Darkness and bring the Darkness into this world to devour all life on Earth. While Puck could have transported them to the island, they decided to take a large craft to get there. This way they could also bring weapons and supplies.

The next step was to choose who would go. Roger, Leina, John, Jack, Akane, Eishe, Bo, Bianca, and Jay would all go. Ravenblade and Puck would accompany them as well. Shanson decided that he would go and leave his first officer, Cynthia Carlson, in charge of those who stayed behind. Jenny would come with him. The rest of the core members would stay. But Shanson would also take some of his other officers as back up for the mission. There were thirty-two of them altogether going to Atlantis. It was time to gear up and load the ship. Roger, Bo, and their friends went with Ravenblade and Puck to check on Lyles. Bo was grateful his father was alive. He still had so much he wanted to talk to him about. He prayed that Lyles would wake up so he could say goodbye before he left, on the mission to Atlantis.

***

Vast shelves of books cluttered the Hall of Records in Heaven. The spiritual plane of Heaven was the first Creation of God, before time began. First was Heaven with all of its levels and elaborate regions, beautiful and breathtaking. Second was the creation of the angels, God's first children, spiritual beings created to live lives of worship and service to the true King. The mortal universe and Earth, came about much later, when God created the physical world and time. But no matter how ancient Heaven was, it never lost its beauty. Even the Hall of Records had its own beauty amid all of its books filled with the biographies of mortals throughout time. Azrael stood there, near the shelves; this was his domain. Being the Angel of Death, he presided over all things that pertained to the lives and deaths of all mortals. Thousands of years ago, he was also in charge of assisting in ending lives of men and women by pouring out the Wrath of God. Yes, sometimes God had to govern people's deaths in order to bring justice. God's ways were higher than those of mortals, and only God knew what was truly good and right. It was not easy for men and women to understand why people had to suffer and die, and ultimately that was never what God wanted, but when the Darkness came into being, evil opposed its Creator, and Satan fell like lightning from Heaven, then everything changed.

God created humans in His image and likeness. He gave them free will. They chose to sin, to break their connection with the Originator of all life. They cut the cord and with this disconnection came suffering. Azrael knew this. He understood why things were the way they were. Knowing that God was right, Azrael served the Lord and performed His will. After aiding in wiping out entire civilizations of people, Azrael began to enjoy bringing death to mortals. This broke the heart of his Father. God took no pleasure in the pain of His children. So he separated the angel into two individual beings. One remained Azrael, and stayed in Heaven with his Father, and the other became the immortal known as Ravenblade. The Angel of Death no longer took part in ending the lives of men and women. All of that ended when the only begotten Son came to Earth to suffer and die for His children. Jesus Christ was known as the Angel of the Lord in the Old Testament, who was born on Earth as the Son of God and the Son of Man, the second person of the Trinity – One God, Three Persons, an enigma that still baffled the minds of men and women around the world and beyond. He died to give all who receive Him deliverance from the wages of their sins, which is death and, in resurrecting from the dead, He gave eternal life to all those who believe in who He was and what He did for them. God had declared that blood was necessary to atone for sin. But once Christ paid that price, the Wrath of God was held back until the final days of the Earth.

Having a great affinity for mankind, Azrael appeared in the form of a man. All the angels took on mortal-like forms. They were spirits with no flesh but still had substance and spiritual mass. Some say they took these forms in order to communicate with mortals, but that was not the case. Yes, it made it easier to interact with men and women when they were in this form. But the Son was the first one to have a form like this, and He had it even before the angels were created. They followed His example, and God gave them forms to take as well. In reality, the angels were beings of light, messengers of God. The forms they took were a concentration of that light into form. Therefore they could choose whatever form they liked.

Azrael's form, though, was even more human-like than the rest of his brothers. He had no wings. He did not glow. His skin was milky white, his hair long and blond, tied back in a ponytail.

His eyes were a piercing blue, and he wore a black robe, signifying death, even though he was an angel of Light and not Darkness. The Angel of Death waited in the Hall of Records, looking out into the maze of bookshelves before him. Lost in the volumes filled with life and death. And, speaking of Death, that is who Azrael expected and suddenly he appeared.

Yes, once again, Death came calling on the Archangel, for these two beings were intertwined in many ways. Azrael oversaw life and death on the mortal plane and Death himself collected the soul of each man and woman as they passed away. He had performed this task for thousands of years and across the whole universe, since the first mortal died – Abel, who was slain by his own brother, Cain. Death also took the souls of Pandora's victims that were not cast into the Darkness, for some men and women she just killed. He saw each of the worlds fall into that Darkness, and a hole was created inside of him for each soul that never passed on but went to live for all eternity as food for the Darkness itself. Death was created when Adam and Eve sinned, but he was still trapped inside his box-prison. When, Satan took the DNA of Adam and Eve after the Fall, he formed his daughter, Pandora, from it and gave her Death's box to open. Once she opened it, she experienced a knowledge of the Darkness and it corrupted the innocent girl that she was. She was made evil from the inside out. Death sprung from that box and took the box from her. He would use it immediately to collect the soul of Abel and then all mortals who faced death.

When a soul did not die but lived passed its days, Death's hunger would grow and pain would radiate from inside of his very core until that soul was at rest in Heaven or Hell. But as long as life went on, so did Death's hunger and pain, only to be truly satisfied on the Day of Judgment, when God would bring back all souls to be judged, the quick and the dead, and send them to their true eternal homes – to the new Heaven and the new Earth or to the lake of fire that is the second death. The future second death was the eternal resting place for all those who followed the Darkness and rejected God. When Death collected a soul into his mystical box, he would bring that soul to Heaven and place it in the judging fire of the Holy Spirit. If that soul knew Jesus Christ as its Savior then it would go on to Heaven, but if it denied the Lord and served Satan and the Darkness, then it would go to Hell. That is, after Christ died and rose again. In times past, all souls would be sent to Sheol, a barren land where they all stayed and waited for Christ to come and divide them to Heaven or Hell.

"Good to see you again, Death," Azrael spoke.

"Yes, good to see you also, Azrael, my good angel," Death replied. He stood there as grim as ever with his long black robe covering his thin bony frame, his hood keeping his gaunt face and large soulless eyes shrouded in shadow.

"I know why you are here," the Angel of Death stated.

"You always do."

"Well, I make it habit to know as much as possible," the angel smiled. "The Darkness is lying in wait to devour the Earth as it has the other planets. Just as it did before the Flood and before Christ died on the cross. The only way it can enter the Earth and steal its life – the souls of its people – is for the world to shift to the Darkness. Then and only then can Pandora and her army enter and establish the Temple of the Darkness."

"Yes," Death responded. "The hearts of men and women on the Earth are turning from God. Most of the planet, even many who claim to serve Him, do not. The world has shifted to the Darkness. It is ripe for the picking. But the Dark One has already entered its surface."

"Yes, I know. Psol – the Dark One – is on Earth and has raised Atlantis along with that Sorcerer, Simon Magus III, Legion, Samyaza, and even Satan's own bride, Lilith."

"And Gideon," Death added. "He may very well be the Man of Perdition that Daniel and John both spoke about."

"Yes," Azrael attested. "We are all aware of that. But only the Father knows the truth. Though, Psol being on Earth does pose a threat."

"And what threat is that?" Michael inquired, and appeared before them in a flash of bright light in all of the glory that God bestowed upon him. His wings were ornate and colorful like those of a peacock and his armor glistened like pure white metal in the glow of God that surrounded them all on this plane. He had flowing hair that danced like fire on top of his head.

73

"Yes, Michael is right," Gabriel interjected. He too appeared in a flash of light and then Raphael appeared as well.

"What threat can there be?" Raphael asked. "We all know how things will end. He has written it for all to read."

"Yes," Azrael affirmed. "We all know what the Book of Revelation reveals. But that doesn't mean the Darkness won't come in now and cause great devastation."

"Many people will suffer. Don't you all care about that?" Death asked.

"Of course we care," Michael answered. "But we also know that He sees things differently than we do. His justice is pure, and though people may suffer and die, that's not the end. Those who believe will have eternal life, true life in Him. So they suffer now. Later they will live with him in paradise."

"What about those inside the Darkness, what will happen to them?" Death inquired. "Will they be freed to live with Him for all eternity, or will they be destroyed, become nothingness, like the Darkness that they dwell in?"

"Only God knows," Michael stated.

"Well, that's exactly my point!" Death declared. "I have come here time and again and you are all supposed to be their helpers, their guardians, but I seem to be the only one who really cares about them and what happens to their souls."

"Is it them that you are concerned about or is it your own suffering and pain?" Michael questioned. "Death, you have no feelings, no emotions, nothing. You are without a soul. You're only purpose is to collect the souls of the dead and bring them to their resting place until the final judgment."

"Yes, you are right," Death said. "But even without a soul I somehow care. My concern is real. And I do hope for the end of all things, for then and only then will I be free of my duties and God will recreate me in a manner that even I do not know at this time. I long for that rebirth."

"Okay, everyone, stop striving against each other!" Azrael commanded. "We sound like mortal children bickering over nonsense. We are all concerned about the mortals. We all know the evil that is the Darkness. But, Death, I must side with my brothers here – we cannot do anything about this situation. God has a plan and it will all work out. We have to trust it. We have seen over the years how He has raised up men and women of great faith to do great things in His Name. Even recently we have seen a small group of heroes arise. They have the Holy Spirit with them. They can stop Psol and Pandora's army. God can and will work through them. We can only watch and wait for the Lord to show His hand. And He will. He always does. Think about the last two times the Earth almost fell into Darkness. He caused a Flood first and then Christ died and made things new. He has a plan. Let Him work as He does. Trust the Lord."

"I can't just trust. I need to see it for myself," Death spoke. "Yes, He has delivered His people before. But how about all the times He didn't. How about all those souls trapped in the Darkness right now. He let the Darkness destroy those worlds. Who says He won't let the same thing happen to the Earth."

"He says it," Metatron's voice boomed from all around. He hovered over all the other angels. His light was so bright that his form was indistinguishable. "His Word says it all. The Earth will last until the final days. And if these are the final days, only He knows it. But we know that He will make all things right. For He is good. Death," Metatron continued, "do not fear the coming storm, but instead look with hope for the coming peace. God will make all things new in due time. He will conquer the Darkness, just as he defeated sin and death on the cross."

As suddenly as he appeared, Metatron vanished. Death knew that he had received his answer. God had a plan, for whenever Metatron spoke, he only spoke for the Lord. With that answer, Death vanished from the angels' presence and went home to his thicket throne in Limbo.

CHAPTER V
THREE DAYS OF DARKNESS

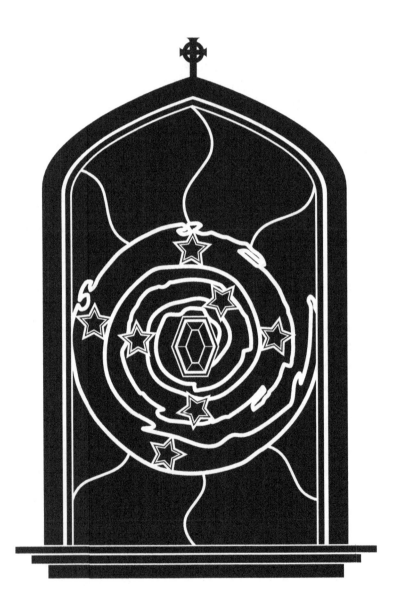

Roger, Bo, Bianca, Ravenblade, and Puck all stood in the medical room where Lyles had been admitted, in the West Wing of the FDSR headquarters. John, Jack, Akane, and Leina were all just outside the door talking about the mission and wondering if they could defeat her brother, Psol, and Pandora's evil army. They needed to stop the Darkness from coming into this world. Their hope was in the Lord, for they knew that only He could bring victory.

Inside the room, Lyles still lay unconscious with a respiratory mask over his nose and mouth and an IV in his right arm. Bo leaned on the bedrail and closed his eyes. He prayed over his father, for him to wake up and for everything to be okay. Just then, Lyles woke with a start. He opened his eyes, jumped up to a seated position, and pulled the mask off of his face.

"Dad!" Bo yelled and hugged his father.

"Where am I?" Lyles wondered. He saw that he was in a hospital bed and that an IV was in his arm. "What happened?"

"Legion," Ravenblade said. "He possessed you. But he's gone now and in a new body, ready to destroy the world again."

"You should rest, Dad," Bo said.

"How can I?" Lyles asked. "If that monster is loose, I have to stop him."

"You can't! Look at you," Bo responded.

"Yes, listen to your son. We can handle this. You aren't ready to fight again. You haven't even trained in years. You need to recover."

"No," Lyles said. "This is my fight, my duty. God will be my strength. He always has been."

"You don't even have the ring to help you," Ravenblade said.

"The ring? I don't need a ring. I hit Chaos fury before. I just need the Holy Spirit, God's power in me. He said it Himself, 'Not by might nor by power, but by My Spirit,'" Lyles quoted Scripture.

They could not argue with that. It was as if God had spoken through Lyles. He got up and nearly fell back down. Bo reached out to help him but Lyles stepped away from his son and stood tall. The Spirit strengthened him and Lyles felt like a new man. They all then left the room, joined the four waiting in the hallway, and together they all went to gear up with the rest of the team.

***

In another part of the FDSR Headquarters, Dr. Ian Rich was testing new equipment for the soldiers. The doctor was short and slim. He had medium brown hair and kind brown eyes. Doctor Rich was head of research and development for the FDSR, and he was responsible for all the cutting edge technology that the organization had at its disposal. He was also the man who found Eishe two years earlier in the wilderness, when Eishe's ship crash-landed on Earth, and to his surprise, Eishe was standing there, right in front of him. The small, friendly doctor gave his friend a giant hug. The man from the distant world of Aporia was not one for warm sentiments – he was quite serious and solemn. But he accepted the hug and gave Ian one back. In his heart, Eishe considered this man his best friend and they greeted each other that way. The doctor could feel that his friend was even more somber than usual and wondered what was wrong.

"The Dark One has come," Eishe said to his friend.

"The one who killed your master?" Ian asked.

"Yes, that monster has come to this planet now, and I grieve for your people," Eishe said. "I am not sure how we will stop him. My whole world is gone because of him and now I fear my new home will be taken away as well."

Ian did not know what to say; he could feel the fear in his friend's heart. Eishe was a brave warrior, a human weapon, trained since childhood to fight and defend his people. But even the strongest and bravest warriors can become afraid. It is not lack of fear that makes one strong but rather facing those fears head on. Eishe feared the death and destruction of another planet. But there was one difference this time. When he lost his home world, the alien monk only believed in goodness and doing what was just and right. He had no concept of God or eternity. Now, he had hope because he knew there was a good God in Heaven who would protect him, and even if he and his friends and the rest of the world perished, those like him, who accepted the salvation that only the Lord could give, would live on in peace forever and

78

ever.

"God will be with me and my allies," Eishe finally answered. "I will avenge my master. I will stop the Dark One and save this planet. For the Lord is with me."

"My Bobe always said that 'It's not over until God says it's over," Ian quoted his Jewish grandmother. "Not sure how that will help, but if God wills it, it will be done."

"Yes, that is true," Eishe said. "I can feel the Spirit inside of me. He is calling me to help this world and its people, to do what I could not do on my home planet when it was destroyed by the Darkness. I won't let this planet fall. By God's will, let it be done."

"Amen, my brother," Ian said. "I know you can win."

"Thank you," Eishe said and gave Ian a firm pat on the shoulder. "So, what have you been working on?"

"Well, since you ask, I made new field uniforms for the soldiers here," Ian answered. "They are the same navy blue but the material I used is brand new. I studied the composition of your suit extensively. The material is amazing and well beyond anything we've developed on Earth. I remembered how Leina was able to repair the tear you had gotten in it from the New Dawn's weapons. It was remarkable how, when heated, the fibers reconnected. I could not make an exact duplicate but using our elements from the Earth, I made the closest facsimile that I could."

Ian showed Eishe the suit. It looked very similar to the current FDSR field uniforms. The material was lightweight and made from a combination of carbon fibers and other elements. The knees, elbows, chest, and shoulders were all padded as usual, for extra protection on the joints. He also showed Eishe the gloves, boots, and helmet that went along with it. The fibers he used for the suit could withstand flames of up to two thousand degrees Fahrenheit. The suits were, of course, bullet proof, even against armor-piercing bullets, and could not be cut or penetrated by bladed weapons, up to a thousand pounds of pressure, but that did not mean the wearer would not be injured by the impact if stabbed hard enough. These suits were remarkable and would help the FDSR soldiers become even stronger soldiers. Dr. Rich told Eishe that the ISOD team members would be testing these suits. And at that moment Dan Marshall walked in to get Eishe ready to board for his mission. He had known about the suits that Dr. Rich had engineered and thought this mission to Atlantis was the best test for them. Dan asked Ian to pack up enough suits for the ISOD team that was being deployed and he went to walk Eishe back to the hangar. Before they left, Ian threw his arms around his friend again.

"I'm going to miss you," Ian said. "You better come home and when you do let's have dinner and really catch up. It's not the same around here since you left."

"I will miss you also," Eishe said. "You were the first person I met on Earth and you are my dearest friend."

"You too," Ian said. "I mean you're also my dearest friend, not the first person I met on Earth." The doctor laughed to himself.

They hugged and Eishe walked out with the lieutenant. It was time to save the world.

***

On Atlantis, deep in the woods, in the very cave where Legion was conceived by his parents, they all stood. A vile group of sinful villains that Simon Magus had banded together in order to bring forth the Darkness into the world and devour the souls of Earth's people. The inside of the cave was illuminated by candles that Simon had conjured up and placed on the walls all around. Legion stood there. He was in the new body that his father, the fallen angel Samyaza, had made for him, wearing common clothes of the present-day mortals, when in the past he wore Hell metal armor and terrorized the nations. The Nephilim's power had finally been restored but even he did not know his true potential. His parents were both there. Samyaza wore a tailored suit that the sorcerer, Simon Magus III, had conjured up. Standing next to him was Lilith, Legion's own mother, though only she and Samyaza knew that, or at least that is what they thought. Satan was aware of their union and so was God, for He knew everything. She was scantily clad in her very revealing red dress and stiletto sandals. She looked like a cheap stripper but in truth she was one of the most powerful demons in the universe. She loved Samyaza but she was Satan's bride and when the Devil corrupted her and transformed her from her mortal state into

80

the succubus that she now was, great power came along with the transformation. She had killed many men and women in her days, more than she could count, including great and powerful warriors. She had even sent an angel to the second death. For the most part, she preyed on weak men, who would get lost in their desires when they saw her. Men who thought they were strong in faith but were really weak in flesh. She would seduce them, play with them, and then consume them.

Gideon was there also. This young man, only eighteen years old, was powerful as well. Like Legion, he was a child of the Darkness. His mortal father was Radix, a former nearly immortal mercenary for Satan. The evil Radix had made a Faustian deal with the Devil in the early part of the first century AD. He sold his soul to live forever, as long as he killed all those that Satan required of him. But when he was unable to end Nathaniel Salvatore's life at the turn of the twenty-first century, Radix was sent to Hell to pay the price for his failure. Nathan did die but after the sun rose on the next day, which was January 1, 2001. On that same day, Gideon and his twin sister, Bianca, were born. Their mother, Esmeralda Salvatore, Nathan's sister had been violated by Radix and impregnated. She chose to keep the babies, as it was God's will and the right thing to do, for these children should not suffer for the sins of their father. The Lord had plans for these children. Now Esmeralda and Nathan were both dead. Esmeralda was in Heaven with the Lord, while Nathan was in Hell chained in Satan's throne room. Radix had escaped Hell and was now lost in the Darkness itself, no one knowing what his fate was.

Gideon and his sister both had great powers. Bianca was anointed by the Holy Spirit while still in the womb, giving her the ability to draw on God's power from the time she was born. Gideon, on the other hand was a child of the Darkness. He was evil from the moment of conception, more evil than his father, Radix, for his true father was the Darkness itself. Most believed that he was the Man of Perdition, the Antichrist. If this was true, then even if Legion was the most powerful villain in the room now, one day that slot would be taken by this young man, Gideon.

Psol stood there with a vast army of troops that he brought

with him from his empress' ship. Pandora, known to many as the queen of the heavens, was Satan's own daughter, created from the DNA of Adam and Eve after the Fall. She traveled from planet to planet throughout the universe, to bring the Darkness and deplete each of them of all life. She sat just beyond Earth's atmosphere waiting for Psol to open a portal to the Darkness and let her in so she could then usher in the Darkness to destroy the final world. Earth was the first world to be created and now it would be the last to fall. The dark army, hundreds of troops, stood at attention and waited for their dark master to command them. They had no souls and therefore made the perfect soldiers – no emotions, no fear, they would follow any and all orders to the death. On Pandora's ship, she had thousands more waiting. The titanic tyrant, Psol, emanated with great power. Technically Legion was stronger, and potentially so was Gideon, but this dark warlord knew how to draw on the power of the Darkness itself, something Legion rejected, and Gideon was yet to discover. By drawing on the Darkness as his master, Pandora, had done, Psol could tap into the raw power of the Darkness and increase his strength and speed to that of a high ranking demon.

The Dark One, Psol, was a dark transcended being, much like Nathan was a light transcended being. Transcended beings had the potential to be very powerful. When a being transcended after they died, their flesh was transfigured and made as Adam and Eve were when they were first created – body and soul in union. Therefore they had all the attributes of a spiritual being but also the added value of flesh. This was a difficult concept to understand, but Christ spoke of it when he said that mortals would one day be greater than the angels, and also why He himself remained body and soul in Heaven. The fallen flesh was weak but glorified flesh was strong. Psol was the first and only known dark-transcended being in the universe, but there were many light-transcended warriors in Heaven. Christ was the first to resurrect Himself body and soul, and after his resurrection He allowed other men to do the same, if they died for Him and if their faith was strong. But after the final judgment, all the saints would be made this way for all eternity, and even those who had already transcended would become even greater than they are now, in new bodies that Christ will give them.

Being a dark-transcended being gave Psol a great advantage over the mortals that he slew and sent to the Darkness. It also helped him as he fought against the angelic armies of God. And no matter how powerful he was, Psol got his power from the Darkness and not from God. Therefore, he may win in wars of flesh but against the Lord himself, Psol could gain no victory. God's power was absolute and nothing in the universe or on any plane of existence was greater than God. Still, the Darkness was strong, for creation was weak and full of sin. The Dark One, Psol, sent many mortals to the Darkness, killed many as well, and also sent many angels to the second death and so did his master, Pandora. But one day, God would strike the final blow and all would be made right.

The villains gathered together. They knew that God had a plan, and also that He had already revealed in the Word how He would accomplish His plan. But they did not care, for in their hearts they were vain and lustful for power. Their own hubris, just like Satan, led them to believe that God could be wrong and that they could change what He already said would come to be. Today, the Dark One vowed to prove that he and his master could destroy the Earth, and bring forth the Darkness into the universe, to conquer it and become the ultimate power.

"The time has come," Psol spoke. "We have all gathered here in this place to bring the Darkness into this world. The very world where God placed his people, and that He has protected for so long. But, as you can see, even God could not protect them forever, for we are here and the Darkness will come forth to devour this world and then all creation will be ours!"

The Dark One had an ominous presence, his physique was astounding, like a pillar – tall and strong. He took the black crystal from Simon and it glowed with its dark glowing light. Holding the crystal high in the air, Psol walked over to where another crystal just like it had been embedded in the wall. The golden altar that was encrusted with red jewels still stood there, on top of the platform where Psol now stood. He walked around it and went to the wall behind the altar. On the wall was a relief of an enormous cloud, formed by a texture of spiral swirls, with seven stars inside of it. In the center was the place where the former black gem had been and where Psol now placed the black crystal that was in his hand. The crystal's dark light grew more and more intense.

"It is time to initiate the Three Days of Darkness on this world. First, the entire Earth will be blanketed in night for three whole days. No one will see the rising or the setting of the sun. The animals will begin to grow feral and the Earth will be plagued by wild beasts and pestilence. On the second day, the dead will rise and be transformed into demonic creatures to feast on the mortals' flesh. Before that day ends, we must erect the Temple of the Darkness. Then, on the third day, the seal on this world will be broken and Pandora will come down from her ship. She will consecrate the Temple of the Darkness and release some of the Abyssites into the world as she prepares to open the portal to the Darkness itself. Once the third day ends, she will perform the sacrifice to open the portal to the Abyss. The seven Angels of Darkness will be released along with all of the Abyssites and demons that are inside of it. They will take all the men and women of this planet and feed them to the Darkness for all eternity. All life will be sucked from this place and it will be left a desolate wasteland. Once this world is destroyed, then nothing will hold back the knowledge of truth. Never again will the Darkness be trapped on a separate plane but instead it will once again claim this plane as its own and fill it with its power. It will be glorious. And then we will take Heaven and Hell and the Darkness will rule over all."

"Sounds great," Legion said. "I really don't care about any of this. But I grow tired of this world, too, and the idea of destroying it sounds marvelous. So, when do we get started?"

"Now," Psol answered. "But like all things, in order to begin there must be an end. We need a sacrifice."

"Now you're talking," Legion said. "I was getting bored and killing someone would definitely liven things up. So who will it be? That hack sorcerer over there? The kid?"

"No, they won't do," Psol disagreed. "Only the blood of a fallen angel or an angel with flesh can start the process. In the past, we sacrificed Watchers to open the portals and some demons as well. Today, the sacrifice will be him," Psol said and pointed at Samyaza. "And, Legion, you will do it with this."

Psol took out a knife from the side of his belt. It was given to him by Pandora, who received it from her father, Satan. The knife was forged from Hell metal, and had runes engraved across its blade, an ancient demonic language of Hell, and they spoke of Satan's fall. The metal was dark and the handle and blade were all one piece. This knife was used on each planet to sacrifice a fallen or flesh-endowed angel to begin the Three Days of Darkness. Legion took the blade and looked at it. Samyaza was angered and cried out for this to stop. He charged up his spiritual power. The ground cracked and a blue energy surrounded him. Lilith also protested and begged for there to be another way. Legion was shocked to see the queen of demons beg like this. Was she in love with this fallen angel, the one who claimed to be Legion's father?

The Nephilim did not care who this man was, if he needed to kill him to bring forth the Darkness and finally rid this world of all mortal life, he was happy to carry out this task. He had killed countless people in the past, what was one more life. Samyaza charged at Legion. But the Nephilim grew two more arms from his back, ripping the shirt that Simon had made him. The arms grabbed Samyaza and threw him into the wall, and then picked him back up and grew much longer until they slammed him onto the altar. They held him down tightly and Legion walked over to him. As he did so, the arms shortened as he drew closer to the altar but still held their grip on the fallen angel. Legion now stood over his father. He lifted the knife into the air and drove it down toward Samyaza's heart. But before he could pierce it with the knife, Lilith leapt on top of the one she loved, and the knife went through her back. Demonic blood poured from Lilith's body and then she began to shrivel up. Right before their eyes, Lilith turned to a pile of ash and her soul was sent to the second death. The bride of Satan was slain. Her blood stained the man who loved her and the altar where Legion had been conceived.

"She was your mother, Legion," Samyaza shouted, still being held down by his son. "How could you kill her?"

"Easy, just like this," Legion said and plunged the knife into Samyaza's chest.

Samyaza's blood now poured onto the altar and mixed with the blood of Lilith. He too shriveled up before them and turned into ash. His soul joined the woman he loved in the second death.

"Excellent," Psol said. "Magician, read the passage from the book. It is time."

Simon Magus III, High Sorcerer of the Darkness held out his hands and the *Necronomicon* floated before him. He read from the sinful codex, chanting the spell. The Earth began to quake, and the crystal's glow grew darker and darker. Suddenly the entire world was covered in a thick Darkness. It was a Darkness that could be felt, and no one could see even their own hand in front of their face. The Three Days of Darkness had begun.

***

In sky above the Atlantic Ocean flew a high-tech aircraft carrying a crew of light warriors, men and women who vowed to fight for the Lord. Even though the FDSR was not a religious organization, many of its members were believers. All the members of the ISOD division happened to be followers of Christ, the core members raised in the same church growing up in New York. The rest of those aboard were also believers, some former angels, some from other planets, and some from the Earth, but all children of God. This was important, not only for their eternal salvation but for the fight they were about to take up. These men and women were going into battle against the forces of Darkness. It was not a fight of flesh and blood, though there would be a physical fight. What they were truly battling was the power of pure evil, and the only thing that could stop it was the Lord Himself. All of these men and women knew that they had to draw on the power of God to win this fight. Some of them had the ability to draw out God's power even deeper, because of who they were or circumstances in their lives that had changed them into something more than human.

Ravenblade, Jack, and John all used to be angels. Even though they were each of a different class – Ravenblade an immortal, Jack a fallen angel, and John, well, he was waiting to be awakened back into his former self – their overall abilities were the same. Each of them had heightened strength, speed, agility, and durability. They also naturally had the ability to draw on God's strength in battle through the Holy Spirit, because of how they were created. Angels are beings of spiritual energy. Even after they Fall, they draw on power from the light of God or from the Darkness for everything they do. These men still had that ability, though some skills had been lost to them. But with focus and faith they could do even more than they knew at the moment and reach levels of power that most mortals could not comprehend. They were great warriors and were very hard to kill, but they were not unstoppable. Even angels could die. Decapitation or being drained of their spiritual energy would send these powerful warriors to the second death.

Leina was from another world but, years ago, Christ taught her how to extend her lifetime, and also how to draw on the Spirit's power. She was strong and a well-trained fighter. But even more so, she had been able to achieve the ability to tap into the righteous anger of the Lord and hit a level of power known as Chaos Fury. Depending on the level that the person could reach, this ability allowed mortals to move and fight with speed and strength that could match that of an angel. The lowest level is below even the power of the lowest class angel, but the highest level which had only been achieved once – the Wrath of God – was said to be nearly equal to that of the cherubim. Most men and women cannot achieve this ability because it takes much discipline and focus to do so, and faith. Also, you need to train your body to withstand the power that will overcome the physical self in the state of Chaos Fury at any level. Nathan and Lyles both achieved Chaos Fury by using the Ring of Solomon as a tool to syphon the power of God. Though later Lyles learned that he did not need the ring to do it but rather God's grace. Leina trained hard and her faith was strong. The Lord was with her and helped her to achieve Chaos Fury.

Eishe was also from another world. He had not yet learned how to extend his lifetime, but he still could live to nearly one thousand years as men and women of earth had, before the Flood. All the alien races created from the fallen seed of Adam and Eve lived this long. Right now, Eishe was six hundred and sixty-three years old. On his home world, he had been brought up by an order of monks who also served as the royal guard. For many years, his body was trained, and so were his mind and spirit, to make him more than simply a man, but a living weapon. Leina taught Eishe about Christ and had since trained him further. The former warrior-monk from Aporia found salvation in Jesus. With this and his training, he gained the ability to truly draw in the power of God and hit Chaos Fury. But he could not reach the same level as Leina.

Akane Yamamoto was a former member of the Children of the Dragon. She led the stealth division of the Chaldean's former army. But after being betrayed by her master, she joined this team of heroes. Her uncle performed dark magic on her when she was young and this, along with experiments that the Chaldean performed on her, made her stronger, faster, more agile, and more durable than other humans. Like Eishe, she was a living weapon, maybe even more so for she had no mercy. But she also had another power. She could heal from wounds. John, Ravenblade, and Jack also had a heightened healing ability but Akane's was even faster and stronger. She found this out after she was killed by her own master, burned alive with her decapitated soldiers. Then again when she was struck through the heart by her own blade after giving birth to Legion's new body. Samyaza, the Chaldean, used her as an experiment to recreate the same results that created Roger Jones, and make a new body for his son. But this body was born without a soul, and the only vessel that he knew powerful enough to birth it was Akane Yamamoto. Everyone thought she died during child birth, but to ensure it, Samyaza sent John, who was under his control at the time, to make sure she stayed dead. She did not, and she helped to free the man she loved from Samyaza's evil control. Her faith still was a work in progress. She believed in Jesus now. She professed that He was her Savior. But her heart was still hard in many ways. Her love for John and his love for her were helping to change that. God was working on her heart and had a plan for this valiant warrior.

Lyles Washington was finally feeling himself again. He was free from that villain Legion and in his own body. Lyles loved the Lord deeply, and even dreamed to pastor a church one day, but he had answered the call to fight for God and never went home. He was trained by Ravenblade, had great fighting skills, and learned how to tap into God's very power through the Holy Spirit. He too had reached the level of Chaos Fury and even a higher level than Nathaniel Salvatore did before he died. But when he helped to defeat Legion and trapped Legion's soul in the Skull of Miacha, the Nephilim clung onto Lyles' soul as well and they were imprisoned in the crystal skull together. Now Lyles had his soul back and Legion had his too. But this hero was ready to fight as he had before for the Lord, and take down that evil beast once again.

Bo, Lyles' son, was born with the ability to tap directly into the Holy Spirit's power, and he had the ability to create beams of light that could fire from his body and be used as weapons to dispel the Darkness. He was also trained by Ravenblade and was still learning how to tap deeper into God's power.

Bianca looked like a young girl but was actually eighteen years old, the same age as her twin brother, Gideon. She had a close relationship with God. The Holy Spirit anointed her in the womb and put God's Word in her heart. She knew the Scripture better than anyone on Earth for it was a part of her. Everyone saw, when they faced the Chaldean and defeated him, how God heard her prayers, and would cause great winds and fire to consume His enemies and protect her at her request. She loved her Daddy up in Heaven deeply, and was blessed by Him.

Puck was a Djinni, a desert demon created from the heat of the desert sand, by Iblis, a former angel, who was sentenced to Earth by God when he refused to bow down to God's creation. The Lord did not mean for Iblis to bow to Adam but rather bow to God before Adam as a sign of reverence for what God was able to do. Iblis learned this when he met Bianca and had a turn of heart back toward his Father, God, in Heaven. Puck, one of his children, like all Djinn could teleport in puffs of smokeless fire, appearing anywhere so long as he knew his destination, whether on this plane or another. He was also stronger than the average human, and had sharp claws on his hands and feet and sharp teeth that he could use in a fight including two small tusks that protruded from his lower lip. His biggest asset was his devotion to his friends. He would sacrifice his own life to save all those he cared about. He truly was a hero in every way.

Roger Jones could be seen as the strongest warrior in the group. He had superhuman strength, a very quick and strong healing factor, and the ability to increase his durability and density with every attack that was inflicted on him. When his flesh is cut or bruised, a strike of the same magnitude would have no effect on him after that. This has made him bullet proof and also nearly impenetrable. Only someone with greater strength could cut his flesh, but even if they did, he would heal. Weapons of Hell metal, Angel metal, and those forged in the Darkness of Dark metal would always have the ability to cut Roger because they were other worldly. He also had a powerful weapon, the Left Arm of God, which was liquid Angel metal that joined with its user to become an organic part of them and take whatever form the wearer desired. Right now, it covered his left arm from the shoulder downward and formed the left hand that he was missing. Roger Jones, an experiment of the Chaldean, was created from Legion's DNA and used along with a special serum to impregnate his mother, Rachel Jones. He grew up in a Catholic orphanage where he was abused as a child and finally escaped to live on the streets. When he was older, his roommate stole an experimental drug from his company, not realizing that he was working for the Chaldean, and took something of value to him. Roger's roommate was killed by two of the Chaldean's soldiers, and they framed Roger for the death. Jones went to prison for this until the Chaldean sent his men one more time, to break him out, for he finally realized who Roger was and that he needed him to complete the new body for his son Legion. In the escape, the boat they were using was shot at by the police and exploded. Roger was thought to be dead, but instead Dr. David Davis found him and brought him in. Using a serum that he had made earlier, Dr. Davis revived Roger. When Roger Jones woke up, he was a new man. He was over seven feet tall, had bulging muscles, and all the powers he now knew he had. But his left hand was missing. It had been blown off in the accident and even with his healing factor, that could heal entire limbs of his body, he could never grow back that left hand, and no one knew why. He had found Christ also, thanks to the doctor, and Roger actually was able to hit a level of Chaos Fury greater than any mortal had ever achieved. He hit a level known as the Wrath of God, and with this level of power granted to Him by the Creator, he defeated the Chaldean, the fallen angel, Samyaza.

Sergeants Jay Sil and Shanson Matthews were there with members of the ISOD team. Jay was a former NYPD detective, and after meeting Roger and Dr. Davis, he learned more about God and found faith in Christ. He learned to lean on God's strength and the power of the Holy Spirit in battle, but he was a mortal man. He now had an armored suit and a sword that had a blade of concentrated light that he used to fight along with other weapons built into his armor. The suit gave him superhuman strength and could protect him from nearly any attack. With it, he would fight alongside these other heroes.

Shanson loved the Lord, and God gifted him with great strength from the time of his childhood. He was not as strong as Roger but his strength was comparable to that of John, Jack, and Ravenblade, making him a very powerful mortal.

Jenny Samuels was also a good fighter and very clever. She would be a great asset on this mission. The rest of the ISOD soldiers who joined this mission were hard-working men and women who served their God and their country, ready to stop any evil that posed a threat. Being a division of the FDSR, they specialized in things of supernatural and otherworldly nature, as that was the whole purpose of this secret organization, to take out the things that go bump in the night without the general public ever finding out.

Darkness covered the skies and the pilots lost all visibility. It was a strange Darkness, thick and physical in a way, so much so that it slowed the aircraft.

"What's going on out there," Shanson radioed the pilots from his earpiece. "The ship just shook and it feels like we're moving though peanut butter."

"We're caught in some kind of dark cloud or something," the pilot answered. "We can't' get out of it."

"They won't be able to," Ravenblade said. "It's worse than I feared. The Three Days of Darkness have begun."

"The what?" Roger asked.

"Yes, I remember now," Eishe said. "This happened on my

planet also."

"It happened on all of them," Leina said. "When Pandora's army comes to usher in the Darkness and destroy that world, they have to bring it in through a portal. The Darkness used to reside on this plane, but God cast it back onto its own plane, which is parallel to this one. The Darkness was sealed away by the stars which represented the angels. When angels fall and become demons, the stars turn to brown dwarfs, but when an angel falls and goes into the Darkness, its star becomes a black hole. I understand that there is science behind these phenomena, as well, but there is also a spiritual nature to them. The black holes represent the demons in the Darkness and the largest of them are the seven Dark Angels that fell into the Darkness after the First War. The black holes are portals to the Darkness itself. The Darkness cannot travel outside of them, but light and matter can enter the Darkness through the black holes. By studying these black holes and communicating with the Darkness, Pandora discovered a way to bring the Darkness into this universe through magical portals created to fabricate black holes. These individual portals created on each world that Pandora hoped to deplete of all life gives the Darkness the ability to enter the atmosphere of that planet only. Once all the life is taken from that planet, the Darkness must return to its own plane of existence. To create these portals, Pandora uses a black crystal with evil, magical power. Such crystals, created by Satan from the Darkness itself, are connected to the Abyss. They use one of these crystals and a sacrifice of a fallen angel or an angel with flesh. This includes, the Watcher angels, demons, fallen angels, and even beings like you three," Leina said, pointing to Jack, John, and Ravenblade. "When that happens, the Three Days of Darkness begin."

Leina went on to explain about the Three Days of Darkness and the building of the temple. She told how, with one more sacrifice of a virgin child in that Temple, the Darkness would finally come into this world and drain all of its life, and take all of the people inside of itself, sucking their energy for all eternity. Roger and Eishe remembered their battle in Sheol to save Bianca. When they were there, they fought Namtar, a demon who had the Left Arm of God at the time and used it to create an impenetrable armor around his entire body. They also fought the Abyssites, demonic creatures from the Darkness that fed on mortal souls and, in turn, used that to feed their master. Roger and Eishe defeated Namtar and the Abyssites, freed Bianca, and finally left Sheol with the help of Michael, the Archangel.

Now, they needed a better plan. Things were worse than they imagined, for now the whole world was shrouded in Darkness. What would happen to all these innocent men and women who could not fight the evils that were about to be unleashed. People that they knew and loved would be in danger. Jay thought instantly of his pregnant wife and feared the worst. They all had family and friends. But even more so were those they didn't know. The world would suffer greatly if they could not succeed in their mission. The band of heroes prayed that God would help them defeat this enemy and stop the Darkness from coming to Earth. While they prayed, the ship shook and moved slowly through the dark cloud that covered the skies. The pilot said that they were over the location, but they could not see anything. They would need to use the sensors of the ship to land it. The aircraft started to descend using the latest magnetic technology to push against the air currents and land straight down, while keeping the aircraft stable. They got closer and closer and then all of a sudden the ship jolted. They had reached the force field that was two hundred feet over the island. The ship was unable to pass through it.

"The magical field that is cloaking the island is too strong for us to break. We have to do something," Leina commanded.

Bianca stood up and said, "God will do it for us."

The girl lifted up her hands and began to glow with a soft white light. She called on her Daddy up in Heaven and a light emanated from her whole body and filled the ship. Outside, even though they could not see it, the ship began to glow and then, with the Lord's power, the force field was broken and collapsed. The ship landed softly and the heroes all readied themselves. It was time to find the Dark One and stop him before Pandora could come in and open a portal to the Darkness.

***

"Someone has broken the force field and landed on the

93

island," Psol said. "I will send out my army to greet them. Our plan cannot be disturbed. Soldiers, go out and kill them now! Kill them all and let their God sort them out!"

Like an army of wooden soldiers, they marched out of the cave, hundreds of them, to meet the light warriors who were there to stop their evil scheme. Inside the cave, Psol gathered Simon, Gideon, and Legion to discuss the next strategy. Simon could not believe that Samyaza and Lilith had been executed right there in front of them. He had known Lilith for quite some time, and she was a powerful demoness. He did not know Samyaza personally, but he had heard of the fallen angel. Legion was indeed a powerful demon, able to easily end their existences and send them to the second death with very little effort at all. Gideon did not care nor was he impressed. His heart was filled with Darkness and he had no need for anyone but himself. He and Legion were brothers in a way. Samyaza was Legion's biological father and Gideon's adopted father, but also they were both true sons of the Darkness. Both of them looked rather unexpected for supervillains in their tee-shirts and jeans. Simon on the other hand wore his dark purple sorcerer's robe, looking like something from a fantasy novel cover. They stood before Psol, who towered over them all, dwarfing even the six and half foot Legion. A dark power beamed from him, the same dark power that they all drew from. He took the knife back from Legion and gave it to Gideon. He would need it to fight if the occasion arose. Pandora asked her general to pass this knife to the boy as it was the will of her father and the Darkness. It now belonged to the young man, and he would carry it for the rest of his days. Legion was given no weapon for he himself was his own weapon. The Nephilim could grow demonic appendages from his body as well as spikes and other useful items to help him wipe out his enemies. Though in his mind, Legion longed to have the Sword of Chaos in his possession once again, just as John longed to have its counterpart, the Sword of Order.

"I know you still have the skull, Simon," Psol spoke. "You know it is the philosopher's stone. A great and powerful tool. Take it out and use the transmutation spell from the *Necronomicon* to merge it with the Ring of Solomon. When you combine the skull into the ring, that ring will become even more powerful. You will have ultimate power and knowledge, for you will be able to draw directly from the power of the Darkness with the ring. Solomon used that ring to control the Djinn. He thought it was from God, but actually it was from the Devil. Lucifer gave it to one of the other angels just before the First War, and that angel believed it was a weapon for good, and so he passed it down to Solomon years later. But God does not play with magic, only the Darkness does. It is our greatest weapon against those bothersome warriors of the light. You will use this new weapon to aid us in the building of our temple. We don't have time to build it with hands, we must raise it with magic. On the other worlds, we had servants that lived on those planets that built the temples before we arrived. But we did not have that luxury this time. So, you will raise it for us. We will wait out the first day here, and then tomorrow we go to the mountaintop to build the temple so it is ready when my empress arrives on the third day. I will share with you the plans so every part of it is perfect."

"Yes, dark lord," Simon professed. "I will do as commanded, for I am your servant."

"Good, now take the skull and the ring and bring them together," Psol ordered.

Simon took out the Skull of Miacha and opened the *Necronomicon* to the transmutation spell, with only a thought. The book hovered before him, glowing blue and flipped the pages on its own until it stopped at the spell. He held the skull over the ring and chanted from the book. Both the skull and the ring glowed blue and they started to meld together. The ring transformed into one made of a sapphire-colored crystal. The markings on it changed. The image on the face of the ring was the same as the image on the wall, a spiral cloud with seven stars in it, a black stone in the center. The ring glowed with a bright, blue light and Simon could feel the dark power that radiated from it. This was the power he had hoped for, waited for. It was finally his. He was complete.

***

Around the world, everyone was taking notice of the Darkness that had settled all around. The entire globe was shrouded in Darkness and no one, no matter where they were, could see the sun. They could feel the Darkness, it was thick and heavy, and they could not see anything, right in front of their faces. But those inside kept their lights on so they could see and they stayed home waiting for the sun to rise again. David, Martha, and Kimberly all sat in the living room praying for their friends. They knew that a great evil was behind this. At the FDSR headquarters, Dan sat with Dr. Ian Rich and discussed the Darkness that blanketed the whole world. Ian told Dan that it was not natural. Even their strongest telescopes could not see through it, but the satellites and the telescopes they had in space showed them that the Sun was still there. It was just that the Earth was covered in this great, dense cloud of absolute Darkness. Dr. Rich believed it was supernatural. This is what the FDSR specialized in and in the last two years they learned more and more about the reality of God and the Devil and the battle between good and evil. Even Ian who was raised Jewish, knowing his Hebrew scripture and the stories his grandmother told him, began to wonder about Jesus, and what the Gospels spoke about. He had not converted to Christianity, but being alongside beings who claimed to be angels and hearing what they said about Christ and seeing all of this come to fruition made him wonder and sparked belief in his heart even if only for a moment. Dan was not a practicing Christian. Like Jay Sil, he was born and raised Catholic, though his parents never really emphasized their faith at all. But now his faith began to be shaken more and more each day. God showed Himself to Dan and Ian, opening their hearts to Him.

***

Back on Atlantis, the heroes exited the aircraft via a hangar door in the back. The island was covered in the same Darkness as the rest of the world. Instantly, the heroes could feel the heaviness in the air. But there was also a strange, blue glow all around the island that allowed them to see though ever so slightly. The world around them was not clear but it was as if they were in a hazy fog. The light was emitted by the magic that raised the island from the ocean floor. Above the island, they saw the blue light fade into pitch black. The heroes gathered together and Leina walked out to the front of the group. She had a lot of experience leading the people and the soldiers on her ship. Shanson told his troops to follow her lead and do whatever she ordered. Roger stood next to her, impressed by her strength. She was truly a woman of the Lord and God spoke through her.

They all looked out at the land before them. Though it was difficult to see, they seemed to be surrounded by farmland which was starting to sprout crops. The magic Simon cast over the island helped it to regrow its vegetation. The homes were all in ruins from what the heroes could see through the haze. Leina took out a small, flat pair of what seemed to be binoculars and looked out into the distance. The device she used could see far and also had the ability to bring objects into focus and even see in complete darkness. It was digital and gave her coordinates as she looked out and around the island. In the distance, she saw the walls and the city inside of them. It too was in ruins. She kept looking around to see if she could find her brother. Even through the blue haze, they could all see the mountain at the center of the island for it rose up above all things. Leina looked at it with her binoculars and saw what was left of the tholos, where the Watcher angels had held council thousands of years ago, before this island sank in the Flood. Leina paused and thought about where to go. She put away her binoculars and held her right wrist in front of her face. A topographical map appeared in front of her, projected from her wrist much like when she showed Puck the map of the FDSR headquarters. This time, it was a map of Atlantis. The technology that her people had devised over the years was remarkable. The fact that she and Eishe both had chips implanted in them to give them the ability to hear and speak all the languages of the universe was astounding, for that was how they communicated with those who were with them now. But equally remarkable was this technology on her wrist to scan the surrounding land form where they stood and create a map for them all to see.

"I'm getting an energy reading from this part of the island, in the woods," Leina pointed at the holographic image as she spoke. There is a cave of some kind and that is where they must be. But I am getting another reading. Something is coming from over there. The reading is getting stronger and it seems like a large cluster."

"I don't need a device to tell me that something evil is coming," Ravenblade said.

"Yes, I feel it too," Jack added. "They found us."

"Pandora's army!" Leina exclaimed. "It must be them. Let's get ready! It's time to fight!"

Leina prayed over the warriors before her, who all joined in and asked God to lead them to victory in this battle. Then, the heroes all readied their weapons. John, Jack, Akane, Eishe, Lyles, Bo, and Ravenblade readied their swords. Roger was prepared with the Left Arm of God. Leina had her bladed staff. Puck had his claws out and ready. Jay took out his sword of light. Shanson, Jenny, and the ISOD soldiers were equipped with their standard laser rifles that could also utilize alternate ammunition if needed, such as silver bullets. They also all had short Hell metal spears slung over their backs. The tips of these spears were about eight inches long, sharp on both sides, and pointed. The ISOD team had acquired them when the Chaldean's New Dawn army was wiped out by the fire of God. Bianca had no weapon in her hand but was prepared to use the greatest weapon she could wield – prayer.

The heroes charged forward. From the distance, they could now hear the evil army approaching. It was time for battle, time for war. It did not take long for the two armies to meet. They clashed like two great waves crashing together. The dark army of Pandora had no souls, no fear, no remorse. They went at the heroes with unbridled speed and strength. But the light warriors were ready to face them, head to head. The ISOD soldiers fired their weapons, blasting their enemies, but causing very little damage. Roger's left arm shot out before him, his left hand transformed into a giant blade that cut through the dark army. Each of them healed after he struck them. Leina shouted for them to go for their heads. Decapitation was the only sure way to kill these evil warriors, but that was difficult within itself, for they moved quickly and blocked with their own blades. Each member of the dark army had a black sword, forged in the Darkness. They blocked each and every attack. One of the dark soldiers got close to Roger and stabbed him in the gut. Roger kicked the soldier down and cut its head off, turning it to ash. He then pulled out the black sword lodged in him and threw it to the ground. His wound healed instantly, as if it had never even been there. The heroes fought hard against their enemies. It was a battle for the ages and it seemed as if no one was gaining any ground.

Roger shouted out to his friends, "Come on, everyone. We can't let these punks take us. We're better than this. God is better than this. It's no different than when we defeated the New Dawn. We just have to take their heads. We will not fall like the other planets! We will not lay down and die!"

The heroes fought harder and surer. Ravenblade lopped off the head of one, and then two more evil soldiers. Bo blocked an attack with his sword and then held out his hand. He shot out a beam of light, the light of the Holy Spirit, and blasted the head off the dark soldier. Leina used her bladed staff and hacked through the army. So did Eishe with the Dragon's Heart, Itaru Taninaru. This sword had belonged to his master on his home world, a blade much like a Japanese katana with organic designs around the sword guard, and a gem embedded in the end of the hilt acting as a pommel. This sword was a legend on his planet of Aporia. It was said that Itaru Taninaru was forged in the heart of the dragon that formed his world. But actually it was from Heaven, and forged by an angel. The gem in it was also from Heaven and the sword had very unique properties. It could create force fields and also fire out blasts of energy that lengthened the swords reach. Eishe learned from Leina that the stories of his world were just that, stories. The evil gods from their past were actually fallen angels, and his people had been placed on his home world by Satan, as were all the people from the other planets. But Eishe used his blade all the same, and slashed his enemies. He fired out a concentrated blast from it and took the heads of three dark soldiers at once. Now that he knew the Lord and the truth, his power was increasing every day, and that combined with his skill made him quite the formidable foe. The battle continued until Bianca stepped forward. This had gone on long enough. She had called on God before to take down the Chaldean's army and she would do it again. The young girl called on the Lord and prayed as hard as she could. The wind picked up and began to blow hard, driving back only the dark army. The warriors of light were not affected by it at all. Then, a great wall of Heavenly fire rose up and separated the dark army from the heroes. Bianca gathered everyone. It was time to form a plan of attack.

***

In Heaven, Michael watched the battle. He called out to the Lord, asking for God to have His hand over these men and women who fought in His name. Some of these warriors had fought alongside Michael when they too were angels. He knew that the Lord forbid him and his brothers to get involved in this fight, and he would obey. But He also knew that God could bring them victory, and this was his prayer, which he made before God's very throne. The Lord spoke to Michael. He told the angel that the battle would be treacherous, but that He had a plan, and all would work out for good. He told Michael to trust Him, and know that He would not forsake His people. He would send someone to fight with them. It was time for God's Hand to move.

"Thy will be done, on Earth as it is in Heaven," Michael prayed.

***

While warriors of dark and light fought on the Earth's surface, and the angels watched from Heaven, there were also spectators from Hell watching the scene. Satan sat on his throne watching the battle play out on a portal that floated in front of him. His plan was unfolding. The Earth was covered in Darkness and his daughter, Pandora, waited just outside its atmosphere ready to make her entrance. The Prince of Darkness laughed to himself. His form, as he sat on his throne, was large. His skin was red and leathery. Great horns protruded from his skull and pierced the sky. He was covered in coarse matted fur from the waist down, his legs like that of a goat. A long tail with a pointed tip came out from behind him. He gripped the ends of the armrest of his throne with his clawed hands. The strange light of Hell came through the rose window above. The window was a depiction of Lucifer's fall from Heaven, and the light that shone through it played out that scene on the ground in front of the Devil. His teeth shined in the dimly lit room, sharp like a lions, and were surrounded by his thick black beard. The Devil

100

lifted his head and looked at his prize hanging before him. Across from him hung the hero, Nathaniel Salvatore, a light-transcended being and warrior of God. He was wrapped in Hell metal chains, his arms and legs spread out. The chains ran from him to the ceiling and floor and held him in place. He only wore a seamless undergarment. His hair was long and he had sprouted a beard. Nathan was dead but still had flesh. He looked emaciated and filthy. Blood and sweat poured from his transcended body, much like Christ on the cross. This hero loved God and served him, but he had been trapped by the Devil for many years now. Nathan had broken into Hell, with help from some of God's angels and Death years ago to try and find his nephew Gideon, and free him from Satan's clutches. But he never found Gideon, and even with the unlikely help of Radix, who Nathan freed from his torture in Hell, he only gained imprisonment by the Devil who ruled this plane of existence. Radix had escaped and was now in the Darkness. But Nathan still hung there like an ornament, a trophy, for the king of all demons. Satan looked at him and reveled in what he saw. *Where was this man's God?* The Lord had sworn to never abandon His children nor forsake them. Satan believed that God had indeed forsaken Nathan. But as usual, Satan was wrong. God had not left Nathan. He told the hero every day in his heart that he would not be there forever, but that this was a trial he must face to become stronger for that which was to come. The Earth was in danger of being destroyed by the Darkness. Now, it was time for God to release Nathan from his prison and bring him back to the Earth to save it from destruction.

Nathan's eyes were closed and he was in a dreamlike state. Then before his very eyes, an image appeared. It was a Man shrouded in a white light that shined brighter than the sun. He wore a flowing white robe and He had long hair and a wooly beard. Nathan saw the marks on the Man's hands and feet. It was Christ. Jesus told Nathan that the time had come for him to be freed from this prison, that he would be released and brought to the doorway that led to the Abyss. Nathan must go through the door and into the Abyss. Once inside, he would be guided to do something great and stop the world from the impending doom that loomed in the future. Nathan listened to his Savior and prayed to Him for strength. Christ touched Nathan on the chest and told him that His Holy Spirit would fill him and go before him, and that His Word was still in Nathan's heart. The Sword of the Spirit would be his weapon against the Darkness. The hero of light knew what to do and obeyed the Lord, who stood before him. That was when Nathan's eyes opened. A bright, white light surrounded him. Satan saw this but he was unable to move. Something was keeping him still. He could not even call his guards to come to him.

Nathan opened his mouth and a large double edge sword shot forth from it. The sword was pure white and of grand design. A large pommel counterbalanced the heavy blade. The handle was wrapped in a fine silk-like material that was dyed red to match the blood of the Lamb. It had a sturdy hilt with a long cross-guard that had vertical bars on each end. Intricate designs were carved on the blade, with an image of an angel where it met the hilt. Above the angel on the blade sat a large gem that looked like a fiery eye, and this gem could change to any color in the rainbow, as a sign of God's covenant with mankind. The blade was long and came to a sharp double-edged point, with two more points protruding from each side at the base of the blade. Satan knew right away that it was the Sword of the Spirit, the Word of God, and fear came over him, for now he knew God had come to free His child, Nathan. The sword flew in the air and cut the chains that held Nathan. The hero fell downward but landed softly on his feet. Then he stood tall and yelled out to the Lord. Nathan's body was basked in a bright, white light, his wounds healed and his flesh looked clean and new. His muscles filled out, and he no longer looked weak and frail, but rather mighty and strong. The white Armor of God formed around his body. It was intricate and stunning. The Breastplate of Righteousness had a sunburst in the center, the Belt of Truth had a sideways figure eight engraved into it as a sign for God's infinity and eternity. A sash with a cross embroidered on it flowed from the front of the belt and a skirt flowed from behind. The armor was plated, up and down his arms and legs, with a strong pair of gauntlets and boots that would carry him swiftly to deliver God's Word to all. On his left arm appeared the Shield of Faith with a depiction of the Holy Spirit as a dove inside a triangle symbolizing the Trinity. The sword flew into Nathan's right hand and then the Helmet of Salvation, with a cross in its center, appeared on Nathan's head. The arms of the cross were fastened with an opening for Nathan's eyes. From outside, this armor looked heavy and bulky. But it was lightweight and flexible. And even though he wore the helmet and only had a small slit for his eyes to see, he could see all around himself as is God were his eyes. The whole suit glowed brighter and brighter and Satan cowered on his throne. Then, in a radiant flash, Nathan vanished from Satan's throne room.

On the other side of the Devil's palace, Nathan stood before three wooden doors. The door to the left was opened and from it he heard the bellowing cries of demons. The door to the right was opened as well, and a sweet scent came from that room, but there also was a feeling of emptiness there, for that had been the chamber of Lilith, and she had now passed into the second death. The door in the center was closed and Nathan could feel a dark, evil power through it. It felt empty and void. The sword in his hand glowed brighter and the door opened. Inside was another door, made of black metal. It was cold and lifeless. Nathan felt that feeling of emptiness grow more and more. The metal door swung open and all Nathan could see was Darkness inside. God told him to step in, and so he did. The warrior entered the Abyss and the doors both closed behind him. Satan could feel that Nathan had escaped his kingdom, but only to go into the heart of the Darkness itself.

Satan found he could finally move and he screamed blasphemies to Heaven. He had lost his greatest prize and he knew God planned to use Nathan to stop Pandora and Psol. But in his conceited heart, which was filled with hubris and lies, Satan believed that he could still win and get his prize back or, better yet, deal Nathan a worse fate. Nathan was in the Abyss and Satan would see to it that he would be tortured and tormented there, never to escape.

DAY II

CHAPTER VI
DEATH KNOCKS TWICE

"This is Judy Ramirez reporting for Channel Four News. Here is your minute-to-minute coverage of the worldwide state of darkness that we are all facing. It's been twenty-four hours since the entire world was covered in darkness. The US government and local authorities are asking everyone to remain indoors. At ground level, the atmosphere is thick and heavy with very poor air quality, making it difficult for people in good health to breathe. Please do not go outside, as authorities are still uncertain of the effects of this darkness. People have reported that you can feel the pressure of the dense air around your entire body. I have not ventured out but I'm taking their word for it. Also, there may be a link to this darkness and the recent animal attacks that people have been experiencing. People's own house pets are attacking them. Some individuals have been killed by their dogs and cats and one couple by their pet pig. Farm animals are going wild as well and people have reported bears and wolves on the city streets. Even though it is still winter out there, locusts, flies, mosquitoes, hornets, in fact all types of insects are swarming urban areas. In the locales where the weather is still warm, insects are eating all the vegetation. No matter where you are in the world, insects are viciously attacking anyone who ventures outdoors. Everyone is advised to safely secure household pets and remain indoors where it is relatively safe. Authorities are still baffled about the cause of this world-wide darkness but it is known that the situation is dangerous and everyone is advised to heed the cautions about outdoor movement and to take preventive measures for interactions with insects and animals.. This is Judy Ramirez reporting for Channel Four News. Now back to your regularly scheduled programming." Judy signed off and quickly left the set for a drink of water.

She was staying at the station with the rest of the staff. It was too dangerous to leave. Judy worked the day shift, reporting every hour on the hour until the night shift arrived. The station had its break rooms made up with bedding, bottled water, and food stores, so the staff could stay safely indoors. Her husband was off trying to solve this mystery. She knew that it was supernatural

– Jay had told her everything he knew before he left. He wanted her to be prepared but she kept his information to herself as she always did. The people of the world were not ready to know what she knew. It would cause a panic.

***

The team of heroes had set up camp. They had lost track of time and no scenario they thought of brought them any closer to a solution. No one had been able to stop Pandora and her army from ushering in the Darkness before. Every other planet fell. Leina and her people had tried countless times. They even had the help of angels. The Watchers had aided them in their fight. Most of the Watchers went to Earth with Samyaza, but some stayed on other worlds, to watch over those people and help them. But just like the Watchers that went to Earth, these other angels also fell to the same sins and bore Nephilim children with the mortal women of those planets. Some of these Nephilim helped and others fought against them. No matter who or what joined them in their fight, they lost. Those planets were all destroyed, their people cast into the Abyss for all eternity.

Bianca had broken away from the group and was praying alone in the distance. The wall of fire still blocked the path of the Dark One's soldiers. God's fiery boundary seemed to go on for miles in either direction and the dark army could not find a way around it, over it, or under it. They were at a standstill. The heroes sat in groups around several campfires they had built to stay warm in the cool night air.

Roger sat with Leina and Eishe, who took off his mask and placed it on the ground next to him. Roger poked fun at Eishe for being so serious, and when Leina giggled, he accused her of not being much better. That even made Eishe smile. Roger and Eishe recounted their time in Sheol and how it brought them closer together. They were like the odd couple but it somehow made their friendship stronger. Leina stood up and asked about Bianca. Roger told her to be patient and that the child was hearing from the Lord. Leina understood but she was used to being the one in charge and praying to God for his aid and provision. Roger stood up too and excused himself. Leina walked after him leaving Eishe alone. The Aporian warrior stayed seated and meditated.

107

He never minded time alone and found it quite peaceful.

"Are you okay?" Leina asked Roger.

"Yeah, I'm good," he said. "Just need to clear my head. You know I'm supposed to protect her. I'm supposed to save everyone. It's what I do."

"Well, that's what you think you do," Leina said. "Don't get me wrong. You are quite the hero. Big, strong, handsome."

"Handsome?"

"Umm, well you know what I mean."

"Sure."

"But it's not your job to save them or her."

"Then whose job is it?" Roger asked.

"God's," Leina stated.

Roger was quiet and looked back at the fire and then toward Bianca, praying in the distance. The bright glow of the flames made everything easy to see even in this thick Darkness. The island still had a blue glow to it that helped a little, but the light of the fire made it seem as if there was no Darkness at all around them. Leina was right and Roger didn't know how to answer her. He took her right hand in his and looked into her eyes. He wanted to say so much but it just was not the right time.

Over on the other side of the camp, John and Akane stood alone. They walked as far away from everyone as they could. He held her close and they kissed. John loved her with all his heart. They had been through a lot together, faced many challenges, and they had even fought against each other when John was under the control of the Chaldean. They each had faced the Darkness in their own hearts; they faced it alone at first, and now they faced it together. More importantly, they faced it with God. John remembered more and more of his past, although much of it was still hazy. But the things he knew for certain were these: who God was and what He did to save the world. Akane knew this now also and together they prayed about their future and the future of the world.

Jack and Ravenblade sat together in front of a fire. Next to them were Lyles, Bo, and Puck. Lyles was happy to be back and awake in his own body. He could not believe he had a son, especially a teenager. Puck was happy to see his friend again too and so was Ravenblade, even though the immortal did not show it. Bo was excited to finally spend time with his dad, but neither said much. Bo told him about school and how much Kimberly always talked about Lyles. It really meant a lot to Bo having his dad around now.

It had been a long time since Raven and Jack had seen each other. They both had been angels and fought side by side in the First War. They had known each other in Heaven and then later on Earth, after Ravenblade was separated from his angelic self and Jack took post with the Watchers on Earth. That time, they fought on opposite sides. Ravenblade was still evil in those days, before he turned back to God, and Jack had not turned away from the Lord yet. They talked about their common past and all that had transpired since then. Ravenblade shared about how they took down Radix and how Nathan died, hung from a cross, and then transcended three days later. He also talked about Legion, how they defeated him, and how Lyles and the Nephilim had been trapped in the Skull of Miacha.

Jack looked at Lyles and asked, "Do you remember me?"

Lyles was confused.

"Your friend, good ole Jack," Jack said in a raspy voice. "He'll bring you back from the world of gloom, from dreary black. Come on, give us a grin."

"No," Lyles said. "It can't be."

"Yes, it can, and it is," Jack replied. "That was me in the cell. I was trapped there, until that guy over there…," he said pointing toward Jay, "and that guy…," now pointing to John, "freed me from my prison."

"So you were a fallen angel, trapped there like me," Lyles said.

"Yes, but I deserved to be there. I disobeyed God when I fell in love with a mortal woman. I watched her die and then one of God's angels, one of my own brothers, chained me to the Earth where that prison was eventually built. I was trapped there for thousands of years. I saw the world change before my eyes. Fields turned into a city. Technology moving faster and faster."

"That night was crazy," Lyles interrupted. "I saw the boys that night. My friends that Radix killed. Their spirits came to visit me. They had gone down a bad path but luckily they knew the Lord in their hearts. And Jesus visited me, too."

"Yes, I remember. It was the first time I saw my Lord since I had been imprisoned there," Jack said. "I can never be reconciled from my sins, for angels do not have the same salvation as humans. But I serve the Lord again, even if after this I will face an eternity of fire. He is the only Way, the only One to follow."

"Amen," Lyles said. "I still can't help but wonder if there is any way for you to be in paradise again."

"It doesn't matter," Ravenblade cut in. "We have to focus. It doesn't matter where we end up. All that matters is that we win this fight. That we defeat Psol and Pandora and stop the Darkness from destroying this world."

"Good point, you make, Raven," Puck said. "Matters not what we become. Matters only, win, we do. Save the people of this world, we must. I too no salvation have. Djinn are heat from the desert sand, we are. Return to that at the end, we will. But help friends, I must. No matter. Do right, do good. That's all."

Puck said that but God had granted this one Djinni a soul when he was willing to lay down his life for his friends. Puck's good deed and faith in Christ would pave the way for his eternity one day. He did not know it but the Lord had a place for him in Heaven.

Sitting in front of another campfire was Jay, Shanson, and Jenny. They caught up on how things had been going over the past year. Jay talked about his new branch of the FDSR in Manhattan. It was the first satellite department of the FDSR. And just like at the headquarters in Upper Westchester, New York, everyone who worked for that branch lived there as well, making it easy to keep things under wraps and top secret. The whole Manhattan branch consisted of soldiers only. Like their counterparts at the FDSR headquarters, they were highly trained to take down any threat. There were no other departments, such as research and development or applied sciences in Manhattan, but they did have a small medical staff to help when soldiers were injured. Otherwise the base in Manhattan consisted of a training area, conference rooms, five medical rooms, plus a few offices and cubes where they did their paperwork. No matter how exciting the job was, just like the NYPD, there was always paperwork. On the top two floors were the living quarters, apartments set up in either one or two bedroom units depending on the needs of those who resided in them. Jay, Shanson, and Jenny joked and laughed beside their warm fire, and then prayed together for a way to stop these villains and save the world.

The rest of the ISOD team were spread around their camp and had quiet conversations of their own. Many of them were intimidated by the supercharged beings around them, wondering if they truly could be trusted. Some questioned Puck's presence, for he was a demon, and they wondered why he was there.

Bianca sat alone praying, calling out to God. She asked Him to wipe out the evil army using the wall of fire that He set up when she prayed earlier, after they had arrived on Atlantis. She had helped to defeat the New Dawn by calling on the fire of God to create a wall and then consume them with that very fire. But this time, the wall just remained still. It did not budge. God told Bianca to trust in Him. He had a plan. Someone was coming. But also, He told her to not be afraid. Something would happen soon. No matter what that was, she needed to keep her faith in Him. She needed to fully trust in God, even in the storm.

At that moment, a strong wind blew in from the east. Bianca could feel an evil power in the wind. It felt like a tempest was on the horizon but, no one could see what was coming. The air grew even thicker than it had been and all the heroes, including Bianca, began to feel it pressing on them. Their eyelids grew heavy. Slowly each of them began to lie down where they were and close their eyes. The wind blew more violently. Someone rode on the back of its currents. It was the High Sorcerer of the Darkness, Simon Magus III. The *Necronomicon* floated in front of him. His newly fashioned crystal ring, which had been formed from combining the Ring of Solomon with the Skull of Miacha, glowed with a bright, blue light. He swooped down and snatched Bianca from the ground where she lay. The young girl looked like a doll in his arms and the tempest carried them away. The wall of fire remained and the heroes slept soundly.

Roger was the first to get up. He had closed his eyes for a minute but he was not like other men. His body regenerated and recovered at a remarkable rate. Because of this, the sleeping spell that had been cast over them left him quickly. He could feel something was wrong. Where was she? Where was Bianca! He ran around the camp and tried to wake up the others. They were all asleep. Even Jack, Ravenblade, and John could not break the spell. Roger had to find her. He was her protector. He walked over and saw Eishe sitting up. His mask was still on the ground and his eyes were closed.

"Wake up!" Roger shouted.

"I'm awake," Eishe replied and stood. "What happened here?"

"They're all asleep. Some kind of spell and they took Bianca," Roger said frantically. "But why didn't the spell keep you out like the rest of them?"

"I wasn't asleep," Eishe stated. "I was meditating. When I meditate, it is like I am in another place. The spell most likely was not cast over me because I was, in a way, out of body."

"We need to find Bianca," Roger said. "But that wall of fire, it stops us from going forward. I don't understand what's going on. We should have defeated that army and moved forward. We need to stop Psol and end this. Come on, look at us. We have God on our side and we are the greatest warriors on Earth. But instead of fighting, we're having a slumber party and waiting for the end of the world."

"Patience," Eishe spoke. "God has a plan."

"I know He does; I just wish He would hurry it up."

"Well, it's not in our time but in His time that He works."

"Sleeping, sleeping, sleeping everyone is!" Puck yelled as he appeared in a puff of smokeless fire.

"Puck," Roger said. "Can you find Bianca? Can you take us to her?"

"That tricky wizard took her, he did. Magus, that filthy, dirty wizard. I can smell him and his magic. It stinks of Darkness. Worse than the Darkness around us. Been here before I have. Thousands of years ago. Created were the Djinn when Iblis fell, right after Adam created, was he. Atlantis stood tall in those days and until the Flood, it did. A cave there is, dark and evil. The Darkness brought Legion to this world there. The Darkness still there, it is. Feel it, I can. Go there, we must. The girl, with the Dark One, and the others. Evil and strong, they are. Fight them alone, Puck cannot."

"But we can," Roger said. "We fought demons in Sheol to rescue her. We can do it again."

"Yes, we can, and we must," Eishe said and pulled his mask down over his face.

"Puck, take us there," Roger requested.

"But the others, sleeping they are. Puck, a desert demon created from the heat from the desert sand. Sleep, I cannot. Spell, no effect on me, it had," Puck rambled. "But friends are all sleeping, who will protect them?"

"God. He is with them. His wall of fire still stands. They are safe. Let's go," Eishe said.

"I can't lose her or anyone else. But especially her. Puck, please take us," Roger entreated.

"Okay. Take you, I will," Puck agreed. "Go now, we will, and back for them, come after."

With that, Puck, Eishe, and Roger vanished in a puff of smokeless fire.

***

The cave was dimly lit by candles that Simon Magus had conjured up earlier. The sorcerer had just returned and in his arms was the sleeping child. He placed her down on the golden altar and the black gem glowed with a dark light still.

"I have the girl," Simon said.

"I remember her," Legion interjected and walked over. He was no longer wearing his T-shirt – it was ruined when he murdered his parents to begin the Three Days of Darkness. "I can feel her power. It is stronger than yours," he said to Gideon.

"I doubt that," Gideon said. "She hopes in a God who will fail her, just as He has failed the rest of the world. If He is so great and powerful then why doesn't He stop us?" The young man walked over and touched the crystal on the wall. "Now, this is power. The pure knowledge of choice, of freedom. In the beginning, darkness was over the face of the Earth. Now, the true Darkness will be over the face of the Earth. It has already started."

"Yes, boy," Psol boomed. "It has begun. It will conquer this

113

world, and the entire universe will be filled with its glory. Then we will conquer all the planes of existence and take Heaven as our own. The light cannot withstand the Darkness. The Darkness will absorb the light and become God itself."

"Isn't that what Satan said just before he was cast out and thrown into Hell," Legion stated. "Don't get me wrong, I want the same thing, but that God has thwarted us all before. He will not go down without a fight."

"He can fight all He wants but once the Earth falls all of creation will fall with it," Psol affirmed. "Then, what will their God do?"

"So, what of the girl?" Simon asked.

"She will be sacrificed at the end of the third day, a final tribute to the Darkness, to usher it in. In the meantime, put her in chains. She will awaken soon," Psol commanded.

"I don't think chains will work for long," Simon said. "She has a direct connection with her God. She called forth fire from Heaven. She may do that again. I will have to strengthen my spell and keep her asleep, for once she wakes up she may prove more challenging than the others."

"I say just kill her now," Legion said. "Why wait for the end of the third day?"

"Because she is a virgin child. There are no pure mortals but the closest thing is a virgin child," Psol said. "We need to wait and kill her at the end of the third day, as it is ordered by Pandora herself. This child is special to God, and we will make an example of her when we bring forth the Earth's destruction."

"I'm with Legion," Gideon said. "Why all the drama. Kill that little nothing now. She's my sister, isn't she? I'll do it myself if I have to."

"No!" Psol said and lifted Gideon by the throat. "You may be a true child of the Darkness but you need to learn to fall in line. You are powerful but next to me right now you are nothing. And my empress, Pandora, the queen of the heavens is even stronger than I. If you harm one hair on that child before the time of sacrifice, I will kill you myself."

Gideon could feel the dark power from Psol coursing through his whole body. He was not afraid but he felt weak in his commander's grasp. Psol threw him to the floor.

"Magician, cast your spell on that child and keep her safe until the end of the third day," Psol ordered. "If any of you touch her, I will annihilate all of you. Do not test my power, for I have brought down entire worlds."

Psol walked away. Simon cast another spell on Bianca that kept her asleep; he also conjured up magical chains of blue energy to bind her. Then he placed a force field of blue energy around her and the altar to keep her safe until the sacrifice. Gideon and Legion looked at the girl. They could feel her power. What made her so special? Her brother felt a connection with her but, inside his heart, he desired nothing more than to end her life. Legion wondered about Gideon also. These two mortals, with such spiritual power, disgusted him. He was a Nephilim, a host for thousands of demons that had been tortured in the Darkness. He was the first son of the Darkness and heir to its future kingdom. But this boy posed a threat to him. He too was a child of the Darkness somehow. And that girl. This was the second time she crossed his path. He could feel the power of the Holy Spirit emanating from her. She was blessed indeed.

***

Roger and Eishe appeared before the mouth of the cave with Puck, who made a small puff of smokeless fire appear in his palm so they could see. The Djinni could feel the dark power radiating from inside. Four of the most powerful villains in the universe were housed inside the cave, as was the crystal that connected the Darkness to the Earth's plane. Roger and Eishe called on the Spirit of the Lord and then they too could recognize the dark power inside the cave. Puck was afraid to enter but the heroes urged him on. Their hope was in the Lord and it gave them courage to face the Darkness. They told the Djinni that they needed him to help them teleport out of there once they found Bianca and freed her from her captors. These heroes were ready to face their enemies and knew God would protect them, but they also knew that fighting their enemies head on might not bring victory. So, their plan was to get to Bianca as quickly as they could and get her out of there. It was a clandestine mission, this time – they would battle their foes once they had the whole team

115

at their side. Prayer was their best weapon now and trusting in God. They would not put the Lord to the test but, if they had to fight, they would rely on Him to win. Both Roger and Eishe had grown very much in their walk with the Lord and had humbled themselves before their Creator. Faith gave them hope, knowing that God was their salvation.

They prayed and silently crept into the mouth of the cave. It was dark but the fire in Puck's palm gave them enough light to move forward. The walls and floor were all made up of rock. They came to a set of stairs carved into the rocky ground. They walked down slowly and, as they neared the bottom, the dark power grew stronger. On the lower level, they saw candles lining the walls, lighting the way ahead. Puck extinguished his own fire and the three moved forward. It was odd that no one was there. The place was completely empty and unguarded. Psol must have sent all of his troops out to kill them and left none behind. But still, where were he, Legion, Gideon, and the sorcerer? The heroes were cautious but also saw this as their divinely given opportunity to find Bianca and get out of there without a fight. There she was ahead, chained on top of the golden altar, and surrounded by a glowing, blue force field. Behind her was a black crystal that glowed with a strange dark light and they could clearly see the swirling design around the crystal and the stars set into the relief. It was ominous. They could feel the dark, evil power radiating even stronger than before. It was coming from the crystal in the wall.

Roger ran to Bianca. He hit the force field with the Left Arm of God and a jolt of blue energy ran up his left arm and electrocuted him. Roger was shaken but relatively unharmed from the jolt. He struck it with his right fist and was shocked again. The hulking hero placed both hands on top of the force field and pushed down. Blue energy surged through his whole body and lit up the room. The shock was so strong it threw him back against the cave wall. Eishe and Puck ran to help him up.

"You won't break that field, Mr. Jones, my spell is too powerful even for you," Simon said. The sorcerer had been hiding in the shadows with a cloaking spell and walked out as he spoke.

Gideon and Legion stepped out next. Eishe unsheathed his

sword and held it in front of him, ready to strike. Puck was ready to fight also and Roger stood up and clenched both fists. The Left Arm of God moved around on his arm. From Legion's back grew four demonic arms with large, clawed hands. Several eyes and mouths appeared all over his body. The teeth of each mouth were all sharp and sinister. The eyes were a putrid yellow that all glowed in the dimly lit room. Gideon held out the Hell metal knife given to him by Psol – a gift from Satan to his daughter, Pandora.

"Release her!" Roger shouted. "Release her now!"

"And what do plan to do?" Legion said, in the voice of thousands of demons.

"I will break and twist things within you," Roger said. "If you don't let her go, I cannot even explain the pain I will cause you. It's a pain that will go on forever, because I won't let you die!"

Roger lunged at Legion, his left fist stretched out, and struck the Nephilim across the face, snapping his head back. But Legion would not be stopped that easily. He grabbed Roger's left wrist with two of his clawed hands and drove the other two into his chest. Spikes shot out from Roger's wrist and pierced Legion's hands. Then the colossal hero broke free of Legion's grip, grabbed the wrists of the clawed hands in his chest and threw Legion at the wall behind him. Roger healed and leaped back at the Nephilim. He struck him with a left and a right and Legion struck back, hitting the hulking hero with all four of his demonic fists. Gideon struck at Eishe with his knife and the skilled warrior blocked it with his sword. The two parried back and forth, neither of them able to land a direct hit. Puck jumped on Gideon's back but the young man was able to knock him off before Puck could bite him.

Simon stood in the corner. He called forth the *Necronomicon* which floated in front of him. The High Sorcerer of the Darkness chanted a spell and instantly Roger, Eishe, and Puck were shackled with magical, blue, energy chains around their wrists and ankles, exactly like Bianca had. The heroes were unable to move, no matter how hard they fought. The Left Arm of God could not break the chains nor could it transform itself. What type of dark magic was this?

"Enough!" Psol boomed.

The Dark One walked in. Eishe saw him and remembered what had happened to his master. The memories of the war on his home planet on the day it was destroyed came rushing back to him. He had fought this villain before. The Dark One had sent the man who taught him everything into the Darkness for all eternity. Eishe had to stop him.

Roger did not like being restrained. He wanted to fight. He had to save Bianca. It was his duty as her protector and he loved her more than anyone else on Earth.

"Excellent job, magician," Psol said. "About time you used your power wisely. Mr. Jones, you are a unique specimen. I'll give you that. Legion, did you know he was a clone of you. An attempt to recreate your body. He might even have beaten you if the magician hadn't chained him. I will have fun killing you, Mr. Jones, and your friend from Aporia, and of course that hideous Djinni."

"You won't kill me," Roger said. "We will defeat you. God is on our side."

"What a joke," Psol said. "Where is your God? Where is He? You're chained up. You can't do a thing." He walked over to Eishe. "I remember you on Aporia. I defeated your master that day and I was about to defeat you also. But you were taken from the battlefield, you and your master. My brother and sister tried to save you. I know one thing. Your master is in the Darkness and will be there for all eternity. She thought she saved you from my hand but, look, you are here now. I will send you to your master and then I will kill your friend Roger Jones. He thinks he can't die. Well, I'll be the judge of that."

The Dark One took out his hooked sword. The chain attached to his belt dragged on the ground. He held the blade up in the air. Roger grew angry with the righteous anger of the Lord. Angry at the sin before him. He would not let this monster take the lives of his friends. He would not let him hurt Bianca. Roger called on the Holy Spirit and let out a great cry. His body glowed with a bright, white light. The light grew stronger and stronger. His muscles flexed, his veins popped out. The Left Arm of God doubled in size. Right there before all of them, Roger Jones hit Chaos Fury, raised his arms and broke the energy chains that held him. Before Psol could strike Eishe, Roger landed a crushing blow across his jaw with his left hand. The Left Arm of God was a powerful weapon and knocked the villain backward. Roger moved with lightning-fast speed. He struck Psol with a left, a right, and an uppercut, sending him down to his knees. Puck and Eishe watched in awe as their friend fought back this unstoppable monster.

"All of you talk and talk," Roger said as he pounded Psol again and again. "You all want to hurt those I love. You all want to kill me. But that's the thing. No matter how hard you try. No matter what you do. How hard you hit. How many times I fall. I've been stabbed, shot, cut deep. My blood has spilled time and again. But no matter what, I don't do that dying thing!" Roger shouted and came at Psol with the Left Arm of God with all his might.

The Dark One caught Roger's left fist. Then Roger threw a right hook, which Psol also caught. He stood tall. The Dark One was even taller and broader than Roger Jones. He bent back both of the Spirit-filled hero's arms. Roger called forth sharp needle like tentacles from the Left Arm of God which all struck Psol in the chest. The Dark One threw back his head and laughed. Then he let go with his right hand, grabbed his hooked blade and thrust it through Roger's chest at such a speed that Roger could not block it, even at the level of Chaos Fury. The crystal on the wall glowed even stronger than before with its strange dark light. Roger let out a cry and dematerialized before them into nothingness along with the Left arm of God and his clothing. The wounds in the Dark One's chest not only healed but his armor also closed up, leaving it without any marks where it had been pierced. Puck saw this and didn't know what to do. He vanished in a puff of smokeless fire. Eishe assumed that the Djinni had saved himself and gone back to camp. But instead, the Djinni appeared on Psol's back and dug his claws into the base of his neck. With unprecedented speed, Psol grabbed Puck before he could disappear and threw him into the wall, knocking him down. The man from another world had just witnessed another person he cared about taken away by that evil fiend. He started to glow also. He called on God for strength. No one else would be destroyed by the Dark

One on his watch. He had to stop him. Eishe grew more and more powerful as he drew in the pure power of the Holy Spirit. But just as he began to hit Chaos Fury, the Dark One drove his blade at Eishe's chest. The blade cut through Eishe's suit at the chest and plunged out his back. Just like Roger, he dematerialized out of sight into nothingness, suit and all. Psol turned and went to strike Puck but the Djinni was able to escape this time and vanished in a puff of smokeless fire. Two of his new friends had been sent to the Darkness by the Dark One. They were powerful warriors of light. How could the rest of them win this fight, without Roger Jones and Eishe? It seemed hopeless.

CHAPTER VII
DAY OF THE DEAD

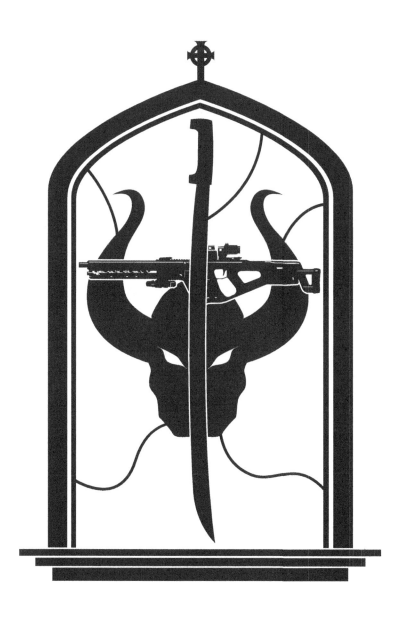

The phones at police headquarters in Manhattan were ringing off the hook.

"Captain, the commissioner is on the line, you might want to pick this up," a man shouted from the doorway of Captain Rogers' office.

"Okay, Gus, I'll grab it!" the captain shouted back.

"It's Steve, sir," the man replied.

"Gus, Steve, same thing," he mumbled under his breath.

Captain Finnegan Rogers, whose red hair was turning gray, still had his portly frame and brash attitude. He was the stereotypical New York Irish cop, and had served for many years on the force to finally earn him his captain's title. With the death of Captain Ortiz, Rogers came in to take over, and presided over the police headquarters in New York City. Hector Ortiz had worked for the Chaldean like many of the NYPD, but after failing too many times, his death was ordered by his own master. It had been about a year now since Rogers took over, and everything was going smoothly, until yesterday, when Darkness fell over the entire Earth. Since then, crime had gone up. People were being killed by their pets and by wild animals. The streets were riddled with pestilence and now, tonight, they were getting calls from people saying that the dead were rising. This reminded him of stories that the former detective, Jay Sil, would talk about. Rogers always passed them off as ghost stories and tall tales. But too many people were calling the police station tonight. Even the criminals were running off the streets in droves, to hide from all this madness. And now the Commissioner was on the phone. Rogers saw all the missed calls on his cell but now that the Commissioner was calling his direct line he had to answer.

"Hello, Commish," Captain Rogers answered.

"Rogers, it's a zoo out there. You better get a handle on things! The media is turning it into a circus!" the commissioner yelled.

"I'm doing to best I can, sir," Rogers replied. "We've got men and women out on the streets patrolling and they are telling me everyone is running for cover. Think it will all die down soon.

Even the criminals are afraid of the dark."

"Don't crack jokes! I want action. Give me a full report in one hour!"

"Yes, sir," Rogers said and hung up the phone.

"Hey, Paul!" the captain shouted at the door.

The same man as before peeked his head in and said, "It's Steve, sir."

"Steve, Paul, same thing. I need a report about everything going on and what the force is doing to fix it, on my desk in forty-five! You got that, Joe?"

"Yes, sir, I'll get that to you right away, sir. And it's Steve."

"Thanks, Carl!"

"It's Steve, sir."

***

Lieutenant Dan Marshall was sitting in his office at FDSR headquarters when First Officer Cynthia Carlson entered the room. The office had a nice old-timey feel inside the sleek, futuristic headquarters. The walls were lined with built-in maple bookcases and wood trim throughout. There were even hardwood floors with an ornate area rug under his desk. Volumes of war strategy and the supernatural covered the bookshelves. In places where there were no bookcases, awards and medals were displayed on the office walls, showcasing all of the lieutenant's achievements throughout his military career. The lieutenant motioned for First Officer Carlson to have a seat.

"Get your soldiers ready and head into the city," Lieutenant Marshall ordered. "There is chaos on the streets. Sergeant Jay Sil's soldiers are out patrolling now under the command of First Officer Zahavi. They are working with the NYPD, pretending to be FBI, but it's getting grim. First Officer Zahavi said there are reports of the dead rising. Most people are laughing this off. But you know that the FDSR takes this sort of thing very seriously. I want you and your team suited up and downtown immediately. With Sergeant Matthews away with Sergeant Sil, you and First Officer Zahavi are in charge of your divisions. I expect nothing short of a complete victory. Now, go out and make me proud."

"Yes, sir," Cynthia replied. "And I swear, we will win."

She stood up, saluted her superior, and walked out to

123

prepare her troops.

***

"Who was that on the phone, hon?" Martha asked David.

Doctor Davis had just hung up from a call he received on his cell phone and he was as white as a ghost. He and Martha were in his room, sitting on the bed.

"What's going on?" she asked.

"We have to make sure the place is locked up," he said. "That was Ian, Dr. Rich, on the phone. He said that he's getting reports that it is worse out there than people think. I mean, first, there's the whole animal thing, and I'm thankful that we don't have pets, but now people are seeing zombies or something equally horrifying. We have to stay inside. It is not safe out there."

"Zombies?" she said. "With everything we've been through that almost sounds normal. Let's get Kimberly. We have to lock up. I'm scared, David. The Devil is doing crazier and crazier things. We need to stay together and pray. God can restore it all. I just hope Roger, Bo, and everyone are all safe and can stop this. It was good to hear from them before they left on their mission and that they were able to get Lyles back."

"Like you said, God can restore all. He's with them. Let's get Kimberly and pray together. God is in control. He can and will win."

***

Toni wanted to get home. He didn't want to spend the night in his office. The first battle suit was ready and he had dismissed his team before the Darkness covered the city. He had stayed to finish up and to test the suit for himself, when no one else was around. It worked. The sonic cannon was incorporated nicely into the design. The entire suit used the technology from the cannon. Sonic waves were utilized to give the suit flight capabilities, and also to fire sonic blasts from the palms of the hands, blasts that could crush a tank and break through the thickest concrete walls. It had other capabilities as well, plus the armor itself was nearly impenetrable. It was a super suit, and Toni knew he would fetch a high price for it. Once they gave a few demonstrations, they would mass produce it and sell it to the highest bidder.

He walked out of the building and onto the dark streets. Toni could not see a thing. It was cold and the air felt heavy, making it hard to breathe. One of the street lights flickered and Toni could hear police sirens in the distance. The street light flickered again and he could see the outline of a stray dog. He didn't think much of it and whistled at the dog. The canine grew ferocious, out of nowhere, like a feral beast. It growled and snarled and barked frantically. Its eyes had a strange, blue glow and in an instant the dog ran to attack Toni. Terrified, Antoni Brown ran back toward his building. *This dog is going to eat me*, was all that kept running through his head. The lights were on in the building so Toni could find it in the Darkness. He scanned his card to open the door. It didn't work. Desperately, he tried again and again. The dog was almost on him. Then, out of the shadows, a man lunged at the dog and snapped its neck. Toni was sickened by the sight but relieved at the same time. He was saved by that stranger. The light from the building and the flickering street light helped Toni to see the man, who looked like he was homeless. His hair was long and unkempt. His clothes were tattered and dirty. Almost as if he had walked out of a grave.

Then the man turned around and looked carefully at Toni. His eyes glowed with a bright blue light, allowing Toni to see the blood that was all over the tattered man's face. He was eating the dog that he had just killed. The man quickly got up and began running toward Toni. Toni, known by some as Pharaoh, was not going to die tonight. He did not know what this thing was but it was no ordinary man. He knew that his Uncle James, the former Pharaoh, had a supernatural encounter that ended his life. Toni pulled out a gun from inside his suit jacket. It was a Smith and Wesson Schofield model from 1873, the same model that Jessie James had used. The gun had belonged to his uncle, and was now Toni's. Like his uncle, Toni made sure to have the bullets blessed, just in case. Without a second thought, he pulled the trigger. One of the blessed bullets flew at the possessed man in front of him and hit him right between the eyes. The wound sizzled and blue blood splattered out onto the ground. The crazed man fell over dead, or so Toni thought. He went to open the office door again and before he could get it open, he turned and saw the man getting back to his feet. Rushing, Toni tried his card again and it worked this time. He flung the door open and went inside, shutting it behind him and locking it, before the deranged man could reach him. The blue blood poured down from the man's brow and his eyes glowed bright in the Darkness. The man pounded on the glass door, over and over. His mouth was foaming like the mad dog's had and his eyes glowed brighter and brighter blue. Toni was terrified. He ran back up to his office. Something strange was going on. He checked his phone. The news spoke of animals killing people, pestilence, and the dead rising. Was this real? The man was still pounding on the glass door and then Toni's phone rang, giving him a start. It was Crystal and he answered.

"Dad, are you okay?" she asked over the phone.

"Yeah, sweetie, I'm fine," he answered. "I'm going to stay at the office tonight. I don't think it's safe out there right now."

"Yeah, I saw the news and was worried about you."

"Just stay home, lock the doors, and don't go anywhere, you hear me?"

"Of course. I won't go anywhere. But Dad, before you hang up, can we pray together?"

"Pray? Sure, if it will make you feel better," Toni said.

"It will," Crystal answered. "I'll lead."

"Okay, sweetie," Toni said and backed up to the elevators.

He pressed the button to go up and get as far away from that zombie or whatever it was banging on the door. Crystal prayed while Toni got into the elevator. She prayed that God would give them peace and protection, and that He would fix whatever it was that was happening around the world. She prayed for her father, that he would do the right things, and that God would lead him and protect him, and that God would do the same for her. She ended it as he got off the elevator. The building had great Wi-Fi service, even in the elevators, so calls would never drop. Toni felt relieved. Praying with his daughter did relax him. He stumbled into the room where the super suit was. Crystal finished her prayer with an Amen and Toni studied the weapon he had created. What if he actually used it for good instead of evil?

***

Ravenblade opened his eyes to see Puck standing over him, shaking him by the shoulders.

126

"Wake up, you must!" the Djinni shouted.

"What's going on?" the immortal asked and stood up. Jack and John woke up next.

Then, slowly but surely, the rest of the heroes stood where they had fallen asleep.

"The wizard, under his spell, you all were," Puck said. "Killed Eishe and Roger, the Dark One did."

"What?" John asked.

"Bianca, they took," Puck added. "Terrible, terrible. The end, coming it will."

"No! This can't be," Ravenblade said "No, not again."

"What's going on?" Lyles asked. He and Bo walked over to Ravenblade and Puck.

"A sleeping spell, the wicked Magus put you under," Puck explained. "Took Bianca, he did. Roger, Eishe, I, we didn't sleep. Went to find her, we did. Fought the Dark One and lost, they did. Stabbed them with his sword, he did."

"They died?" John said, shocked at the news.

"They're not dead" Jack said. "If he stabbed them with his blade, they are not dead, but inside the Darkness."

"How's that any different," Ravenblade said. "Once they're inside the Abyss, there's no way out."

Leina ran over. Tears were in her eyes. Akane came too. She wrapped her arms around John. The fear of losing him took over her.

"My brother sent them to the Darkness," Leina said. "He will pay for that."

"We will stop him," Jack said.

"Yes, we'll stop him and then find a way to bring them back," John declared. "With God, there is always a way."

Jay walked over. He held his helmet in his right arm, hugging it to his side. Shanson and Jenny followed him. It was time to form a plan and fight. The wall of fire still held back Pandora's army and it provided them more light than the blue, hazy glow that the island emitted. They could see all around but the air remained thick and heavy with Darkness. They would have Puck teleport all of them to the cave and they would take down those evil fiends.

Leina knew her brother better than anyone and with God on their side, they could do anything. If they could stop Psol before the Darkness came to the Earth, Leina might be able to open a portal to the Darkness herself and enter. Once inside, she could try to free their friends. If she failed, then she would be trapped with them inside for all eternity. It was worth the sacrifice. She cared deeply for Roger and for Eishe. They did not deserve such a fate as they were facing now.

The team banded together. All of ISOD stood with them. Everyone held hands and Ravenblade went to place his hand on Puck's back so they could transport and bring the fight to their enemies. Before Raven made the connection, evil hands came up from the ground. Hundreds of decaying hands sprang up and grabbed at the heroes' ankles and legs, dragging them down.

The heroes grabbed their weapons and counterattacked the evil hands. Swords sliced and slashed through the air, chopping the hands clean off. Ravenblade freed himself and then persisted to free some of his allies by chopping off as many of these zombie hands as he could with his blade. Some members of the ISOD team slashed with their spears and others shot at the hands with their rifles. One by one the heroes broke free from the grip of the mysterious hands that came up from the earth. The freed heroes began to step backward, away from this new threat, their weapons ready to retaliate.

As they looked on, zombified corpses pulled themselves up from the ground. Their hands all regenerated. They looked human and wore torn, filthy rags. There were men, women, and children – an army of the undead. These zombies looked at the heroes with eyes that glowed with a bright, blue light. They twitched and convulsed. The ISOD team waited no longer and fired laser blasts from their rifles. They put holes through the animated corpses but the wounds quickly healed. Then, the entire undead army let out a dreadful cry. Their bodies glowed with the same blue light as their eyes and then their skin turned solid black, and great curved horns sprang from their heads. Their muscles grew in size, and their hands and feet grew long, sharp claws.

"The dead have risen," Leina said. "Around the world, all the animals have gone feral, pestilence prevails, and now the dead are raised. Tomorrow, the Abyssites will come and then we may lose all hope."

"Yes," Ravenblade said. "Demonized corpses is more like it. I know these creatures. They are not just zombies. They have been possessed by the Darkness itself. Switch your rifles to the silver bullets. Those lasers won't do a thing. The silver will slow them down but only decapitation will stop them. And like the shadow demons we fought before, these can become intangible, for they are one with the spirit of the Darkness. It will be a fight but if we stand together we can win. Remember, we have the Lord on our side. He goes before us and He is our rear guard. He is all around us. This fight is not ours but the Lord's. Now, let's charge!" he yelled and held up the Ravenblade.

The heroes charged forward and the demonic zombie horde did the same. Like savage beasts, the creatures attacked. Their eyes glowed blue and their blackened flesh was darker than the sky. The wall of fire lighted the way for the heroes and they fought furiously. Ravenblade swung his sword, trying to dislodge the demonic beasts' heads from their shoulders. But it seemed no use. He plunged his blade into one creature's chest; glowing blue blood shot out. Raven pulled his blade from the creature, only for the wound to heal. When he went for the head, the creature phased out and the blade passed right through it.

The ISOD soldiers fired their weapons, filling the horde with a barrage of silver bullets, splattering that same blue, glowing blood onto the ground. The creatures slowed down but they did not die. Shanson took the opportunity to grab the Hell-metal spear that was slung over his back and cut the head off one of the creatures that had been shot. Blood spattered on Shanson's field uniform and then the blood disintegrated as the creature itself turned to dust. The bullets had stopped the creature from becoming intangible, which gave Shanson the chance to take the creature's head.

"Everyone, after you fire, take out your spears and cut off their heads," Shanson shouted. "The bullets are keeping them solid."

"Yes, of course," Ravenblade said. "Fill them with silver and then we will take their heads!"

The ISOD soldiers fired away and the tide began to turn as the heroes decapitated as many of the demonic zombies as they could. Jay fought hard and his battle armor was well equipped for this fight. The left forearm opened and a cannon emerged. He did not have silver bullets but instead could fire different energy rays. He could manipulate the molecular make-up of the beams. With that technology, he fired a beam of silver atoms at the creatures, giving the same effect as the silver bullets. Then he took his laser sword in his right hand and hacked off the creatures' heads, one by one.

Bo held his sword and prayed to God. His father by his side did the same. Lyles charged up and called forth the Holy Spirit. His body glowed with a white light. Bo had been training with Ravenblade to do the same and he charged up as well. The father and son team went at the zombie horde and together cut them down. Lyles kicked one creature in the gut and then ducked a slash from another. Bo cut that creature across the chest and shot a beam of white light from his hand – the pure light of the Holy Spirit – taking the head of the creature. As the zombies died, they turned to ash before the heroes. The group of heroic fighters was advancing but more and more demonic zombies joined the fight. It seemed like there was no end to this army.

***

Inside the cave, where the power of the Darkness emanated, filling the Earth, Psol stood before Simon, Gideon, and Legion. The Dark One had kept a few of his guards with him, thirty in all, though he held them back when the heroes had come to find him before. Now, the guards stood behind their general, waiting for his orders. Bianca was still lying under a sleeping spell on the altar, chained and inside the blue, glowing force field. As always, the black crystal on the wall glowed with its ominous, dark light. It was a bridge to the Darkness. It connected the physical world to the heart of the Darkness itself.

The second Day of Darkness was already upon them but, before it ended, the Temple of the Darkness would need to be erected on the mountaintop. On the third day, the seal that God had placed over the Earth would open and Pandora would enter. Once on this planet, the queen of the heavens would consecrate the temple with the help of Simon Magus and the dark magic of the *Necronomicon*. Pandora would place one of her black crystals on the altar in the temple. Then a horde of Abyssites would spring onto this world. Not all of them but enough to prepare the planet for their master. These creatures were nasty demons. Roger and Eishe had fought them in Sheol. The Abyssites were ten feet long and eight feet tall, standing on all six legs. They were a strange mix of a steed and a locust. Their skin was solid black and covered in armored exoskeletons, with breastplates shaped like the chests of men. They had long tails with scorpion stingers at the end, and locust-like wings on their backs. Their faces were human-like but demonic at the same time, with glowing, blue eyes and long unkempt hair. They were very frightening creatures. The apostle John had written about them and what they would do to men and women when they came to Earth during the end times. It seemed that now, those times were at hand. But many remained uncertain that this was the beginning of the apocalypse because other events that God had foretold had not yet come to pass. This is what gave hope to the heroes. But Pandora did not believe in the Scriptures and she planned to end this world like all of the others.

Near the end of the Third Day of Darkness, Pandora would sacrifice the child on that very altar. This sacrifice would allow Abaddon and the other Angels of Darkness to come forth from the Abyss. The blood of a virgin child gave way for their release. Holding the key to the Abyss, Abaddon would then open the doorway and all of the Abyssites inside the Darkness would be released onto the world, to plague men and women. The seven Angels of Darkness would go forth and with the Abyssites would reap the souls of all mankind on the planet. The portal that is the gateway to the Abyss would then allow the Darkness itself to collect these souls and also drain all the energy from the planet until it was nothing but a barren, lifeless rock, floating in space.

"We will take this world soon," Psol boomed. "Tomorrow is the third day and we must prepare for Pandora's coming. Magician, you will take us to the mountain at the center of the city at the dawning of the third day. Be ready." Psol paused, looked at Legion and then Gideon, and said, "You two, come with me."

"Why should we?" Legion asked, his voice was that of thousands of demons speaking at once. "I am not one of your puppets. My power is strong. I am not a mere mortal like this boy here, or that pathetic excuse for a sorcerer. I am a Nephilim and the host of thousands of demons. All of them from the Darkness itself. The Darkness you worship is a part of me. I am its son and its rightful heir."

"Stay thy tongue," Psol said.

"I have to agree with this idiot over here," Gideon said. "I am not your puppet either. But, Legion, don't underestimate me yourself. I too am a child of the Darkness. My heart is black. It has no light in it. I am not going to stand here and take all this garbage from the two of you."

"Listen, both of you," Psol said. He paused and then began to weave lies, just like the Devil. "I am not your enemy. I appreciate your fortitude. You two have no fear. And rightly so, for the Darkness dispels all fear. The mortals pray to a God who requires fear from them. 'Fear the Lord,' He says. But the Darkness does not want this. It only wishes to give knowledge to all. Knowledge, truth, and freedom. Come with me. There is something we must do."

"Fine," Legion said. "I'm curious what you want to show us."

"Yes, I'm also intrigued," Gideon added.

They walked with Psol to the crystal on the wall. He motioned for them to stand in front of it and then he called over Simon. The High Sorcerer of the Darkness came over with the *Necronomicon* floating before him. The Dark One held out his hand and the book turned to a specific page. Psol asked Simon to chant the words on the page while placing his right hand on Legion and his left hand on Gideon. Simon did as he was instructed. Instantly, the dark light of the crystal glowed brighter and two beams shot forth from it. One struck Legion in the center of his chest and the other struck Gideon in the same way. The beams of dark energy penetrated their flesh and filled them with power. They both fell to the ground and their clothes disintegrated from their bodies. The energy that went into them began to seep from their pores and cover them completely. When they rose to their feet, both Legion and Gideon were covered in the dark energy, as if wearing suits of armor. Their heads were exposed but the rest of their bodies were covered in the black-energy armor. It had the appearance of spiky plates all over and it looked organic, for the armor was living. It was a part of the Darkness. They could both feel the power of the Darkness flowing through them. Legion and Gideon truly were children of the Darkness and now they looked the part.

***

Death sat on his thicket throne and looked out over the Earth. He could feel the Darkness at hand, ready to come in and destroy this world as it had all the others. He dreaded this day, for with it would come great pain. The angels always told him God had a plan and all would work out for good but Death could not see it. To him, it seemed like the end was coming. The dead had risen and were now zombified demons. The animals had turned on the humans and insects covered the Earth. Only one and a half days remained and then the Darkness would be unleashed. The moon would turn to blood and the stars would fall from the sky. Death could see the heroes fighting the horde of creatures. He saw the Dark One, Legion, Gideon, and that sorcerer Simon Magus III, ready to usher in Pandora. And he could feel something else. Inside the Darkness, something was happening. Yes, there was light inside. Could it be? Was there truly hope inside the Darkness. Only time would tell. He sat and watched and waited, hoping for the light to penetrate the Darkness. An end would come, but would it be the end for the light or the end for the dark.

CHAPTER VIII
ENTER THE DARK

Nathan had entered the Darkness through the front door. He went from one Hell, it seemed, into another. The black metal door had closed behind him and he was trapped. The Darkness that surrounded him was thick and it choked him incessantly. He could feel the pressure of its weight pushing down on him. Even in his transcended state, Nathan felt like he was walking through mud. The Armor of God fully surrounded him and the shield and the sword were in his hands. God was with Nathan in the Darkness. He would not forsake him nor abandon him, exactly as He had promised. Even when the hero was chained in Hell, God was with him every moment. Nathan trusted in the Lord and walked forward in faith, not knowing where he was going. He followed the Spirit. The armor glowed with a bright, white light, but even with his path lighted before him, there was nothing for the hero to see – only absolute Darkness. The ground beneath him felt like it was moving. It reminded Nathan of the time he had been swallowed by that gargantuan fish and again by that demonic beast that Radix rode. It was like he was inside of a living being. The Darkness was alive and he was in its belly.

Nathan walked for what felt like days and then he saw them. Billions of people, it seemed. He could not count them all. They were all in rags, filthy, and covered in blood. Men, women, and children of all races and ages were before him wrapped up in black vines. The light of the sword shined brighter and the vines that held the people looked more like veins connected to the living Darkness. These vines held the people in place and inserted themselves through the mouths of these victims, draining the life force of their souls.

"Yes, Nathan, those are the people trapped in Darkness," a familiar voice spoke to him. "And now, thanks to you, they have seen a great light. But I will put out that light before it gives them any hope."

"Radix! Show yourself!" Nathan shouted.

"I'm right behind you," Radix said and slashed down at Nathan's back.

The hero of light turned and blocked Radix's blade with

135

the Shield of Faith. A bright light shined when the shield was struck. Nathan pushed the fiend backward and his armor glowed brighter. He could see his foe standing there. It was indeed Radix. This evil man had crucified Nathan on Earth, leading to the hero's death. Later, these two met again in Hell where, at first, they fought against each other and then as allies against Satan's soldiers. Radix towered over the hero by a foot. The villain was six and half feet tall, while Nathan was only five and half feet in height. But with the Armor of God, Nathan felt taller somehow. The hero never let his height stop him from anything in life. He was a boxing champion and had gone toe to toe with the supernatural villain before him. Neither did Radix underestimate his adversary. He knew Nathan was strong in faith and that the Lord was with him. The sinister villain wore an organic black armor with small spikes all over it that covered his entire body, only exposing his face. It was as if he were covered in the living Darkness itself. The armor looked like it was alive and it moved in a slow, repulsive way. Radix's face was pale white and his hair was short and jet black. His eyes were black as sin, like two black holes on his face, making Nathan feel as if he were looking into the heart of the Darkness itself. In his hand, Radix held the Blackblade, the first weapon forged in the Abyss from the Darkness itself. Satan had been given this weapon when he defied God and he used it against his own brothers in the First War. Radix had wielded this sword two times before on Earth. The solid black, double-edged, longsword had the power to control its wielder, making him or her a slave to the blade and its true master, the Darkness. When Radix first escaped Hell and came into the Darkness the same way Nathan had done, he was instantly greeted by the embodiment of all evil. It reminded him of who he had been before. It opened Radix's eyes to the evil in his own heart and took control of him once again. The Darkness saw great potential for sin in Radix. It even used him to birth Gideon, its own son. It now planned to use this villain to destroy one of God's warriors, and take the soul of Nathaniel Salvatore for itself, to feed on for all eternity. The energy of a transcended soul was a delicacy that the Darkness desired.

"What is all of this?" Nathan asked.

"You don't know where you are?" Radix replied. "You are inside of the Darkness, the embodiment and personification of all evil. It was brought into being when God first created, for with Light there had to be Darkness. It is the knowledge that enlightened Satan to take a stand against the angry and jealous God that you serve. It feeds on the souls of those trapped inside of it. These men, women, and children were all sent here by Pandora. They have come here body and soul to be food for the Darkness and, in turn, they are given the knowledge that it contains and the freedom that only it can bring."

"Freedom? They don't look free to me," Nathan said. "They look like prisoners. Hell's one thing. It's filled with people that belong there, people aligned with Satan and facing the penalty of believing in his false hope and rejecting God. People like you. But these people. They have not chosen evil. Some never had the chance to know God and believe in Him. And others, yes, I can feel it, others are believers and know the truth of God and the sacrifice of Christ. How do they deserve this? I will not let them suffer any longer. Just as you said, and as God spoke first through the prophet Isaiah, 'The people who walked in darkness have seen a great light: Those who dwelt in the land of the shadow of death, upon them a light has shined.' And that light is the light of God!"

The Shield of Faith disappeared and Nathan took the Sword of the Spirit, the Word of God, into both of his hands. Then the hero of light leaped at Radix with his sword ready to strike. Nathan swung down but Radix blocked the attack with the Blackblade. Sparks of light and shadow flew off the clashing swords. Nathan spun around and slashed at Radix again, only to be blocked once more. A bright glow radiated all around Nathan's body and around the Sword of the Spirit. In contrast, a dark energy emanated from Radix and the Blackblade. Both hero and villain charged up, Nathan drawing power from the Holy Spirit and Radix drawing power from the Darkness. These two warriors had fought before. Once on Earth, when Nathan learned how to achieve Chaos Fury, and once in Hell, which ended in a truce. Now they fought for a third time and it would prove to be their final conflict. Radix began to move with unprecedented speed. It was as if he were becoming one with the Darkness. Nathan increased his speed as well. He was transcended, his body and soul resurrected and perfected by the power of God. This transcended state made him like our original parents when first created and gave him the ability to move like an angel, like the flashing of lightning. Dark metal and Angel metal clashed in sparks of black and white light. The sound of their blades colliding was like the sound two trains crashing. Nathan blocked the stygian blade with the Word of God and then he kicked Radix in the chest sending him down. The villain grew angry, regained his feet, and charged at the hero. He blocked Nathan's sword and jammed an elbow into the hero's gut followed by a roundhouse kick to the back of his head. Nathan was now the one on the ground. The floor moved beneath him and it was difficult to get up but he did.

Nathan stood still for a moment and looked carefully at his enemy. Radix looked back at him with a cold stare. The hero called on the power of the Holy Spirit. Nathan was inside the Abyss and the Darkness was all around him. He could feel the despair breeding from it, trying to get him to lose all hope. But even in the heart of the Darkness, Nathan was not alone. God was with him. He charged up his energy and focused on God, and on the sacrifice Christ had made on the cross. When Christ died, Darkness covered the Earth, but then He rose from the dead. Even in the beginning, it was said that Darkness was over the surface of the deep. But God said, "Let there be light." And just as those words formed in Nathan's mind they came from his lips.

"Let there be light!" Nathan declared.

At once, the light that surrounded him grew stronger and stronger. Radix grew angry and the Darkness did as well, fueling the hatred inside its host. The villain was possessed by the Darkness. The Blackblade called to him. It told him to let go and let it be his master. The Darkness was speaking to Radix through the blade and it told him to give in and become the Darkness that was all around. Radix threw back his hands. The dark energy that surrounded him radiated even stronger with the strange dark light, just as the crystal had done in the cave on Atlantis. Radix could feel the sinful power surge through him. His muscles grew denser and the skin on his face became as black as the armor that he wore. Two great black horns grew from his brow and his eyes began to glow with a cold, blue light. Two large bat-like wings sprouted from his back and suddenly Radix took to the air. He flew over Nathan, circling around him. The light of the Spirit that emanated from the hero's body helped him to see all around and then Radix's whole body began to glow blue. Nathan watched his enemy fly around like a creature of the night. Radix truly had become a demon of the Darkness.

Then the evil villain swooped down toward Nathan, moving so fast that no mortal could see him. But this transcended man could see his enemy and moved swiftly away from his attack. Radix came back and Nathan dodged him again. Nathan asked God for strength and took the offensive. He watched Radix ready himself to strike. It was then that Nathan leaped into the air. He soared straight toward his adversary and they met in the blackened sky, clashing their blades over and over again, lighting up the entire plane with sparks of black and white light.

***

In another part of the Abyss, another hero was dreaming. Roger Jones saw the world covered in Darkness and blood. Everyone he knew was dead. Roger feared that he could not save them and then the Darkness choked him until he gave his final breath. His eyes opened and he could not see a thing. He could not breathe for something was lodged in his mouth and throat. He could feel the air all around. It was even thicker and heavier than it was on Atlantis when the Darkness covered the Earth. Roger tried to move but his body was tangled up in something. Blackness was all around. Was he back in Sheol? It was like the time he first met Bianca. But no, he could feel that this place was different. It was the same evil he had felt in Sheol but now it was stronger. Psol had stabbed Roger in the chest with his blade. Leina had said that it sent those it pierced into the Darkness. That was where Roger was, inside the Darkness. The hero called on the Holy Spirit. God was still with him. With great strength, he busted out of the strange vine that held him in place and ripped it out of his mouth. That vine had been depleting him of his very spiritual energy and Roger felt weak. But his body healed and so did his spirit. The hulking hero soon felt strong again. Now, he needed to see. So Roger tapped into the power of the Holy Spirit as he had done before in battle. By doing so, his body gave off a soft, white light, which grew in intensity the more he drew on God's power. The light of the Spirit, which shone from his body, gave Roger enough visibility to see objects directly in front of him. There was someone else there, trapped in the same vine-like restraints. It was Eishe, his friend. Roger realized that these vines were like veins that drew blood to the heart, drawing the energy of those in their grasp into the heart of the Darkness. With the Left Arm of God, Roger tore the restraints from his friend and pulled the vine from his mouth. Eishe's mask had been pulled up to his nose to allow the vine to enter. Roger took Eishe into his arms like a child. He shook him awake and Eishe responded with a cough.

"Where are we?" he asked, weak from the draining of his spiritual energy.

Roger knelt down and laid him on the ground. He prayed over his friend and touched him on the chest. Eishe could feel the Holy Spirit pass from Roger to him, and he called on God to give him strength. With the help of the Lord, he sat up and began to feel stronger, but not yet at his full power. Roger helped him to his feet. He told Eishe about his dream and how he woke up. He did not know where they were, but assumed they were inside the Darkness. Both of them had been pierced by the Dark One's blade. Eishe's suit was cut open at the chest but his wound had somehow healed. They knew Roger could heal from any wound but Eishe did not possess this power. It must have been the Darkness that closed his wound because it needed him alive to feed off of him. Eishe told Roger how the suit could repair itself if exposed to extreme heat. Still weak, he slowly took off his shirt and laid it on the ground. With the little strength that Eishe had, he held his sword in both of his hands. He concentrated on the Holy Spirit and activated the gem on the pommel of the sword's handle. The gem glowed and so did the entire sword. This blade had amazing abilities. It could create force fields and also send out energy blasts. Using this principle, Eishe fired up his sword and blasted the suit at close range with a powerful burst of energy while Roger held the tear together. Remarkably, the fibers mended themselves. Eishe put the shirt back on and pulled down his mask to cover his whole face. Then the warrior monk from Aporia put his sword in its sheath on his back. It was time for them to find a way out of the Darkness and get back home. Eishe felt the Holy Spirit restoring his strength more and more and the heroes moved on.

Roger and Eishe looked up and they saw strange sparks in the sky, flashes of white and black light sparking over and over again. They decided to head toward those lights and see what they were, not knowing that it was the battle Nathan and Radix waged in the heart of the Darkness. Eishe held out his sword and it glowed brighter than before, lighting a path for them to follow in the Darkness. The sword had been forged in Heaven of Angel metal and it harnessed spiritual energy to perform its feats. Before he was saved, Eishe unknowingly drew power from the Darkness and the sword glowed with a sinister blue light instead. Now that he was saved and knew Christ, Eishe drew the power of the Holy Spirit and that was the light that shown through it at this moment, the light of God directing their path before them.

Being able to see the path before them, Roger and Eishe noticed all of the other people trapped in the vine-like restraints. It was like a field of human crops. This was Satan's plot from the beginning, after God created the physical world and Satan fell. He harvested these people from across the cosmos to feed the Darkness and strengthen its power. He believed that, in doing so, the Darkness would become strong enough to consume God Himself and become the ultimate power in existence. The problem for Satan was that God was not a created being, but the Creator, and nothing from His own creation could overtake Him. Only His power was ultimate and that would never change. But the Devil believed his own lies and, because of that, sin grew and so did the Darkness.

The two heroes looked out at all the people trapped in the vines of the Darkness – men, women, and children from all the planets that had been destroyed. There were more people than they could count, more people than they knew existed. Eishe's sword glowed brighter. It was as if the Spirit was showing him something. It urged him forward and he followed the Spirit-driven blade. There before Eishe was someone he recognized, someone that he had a very close and deep relationship with. Trapped in the hold of the Darkness, having his very spirit drained from him, was Coz, Eishe's master.

Coz and Eishe had fought together with the other monks on his home planet. Their duty was to serve as priests and, at the same time, as the royal guard. His planet did not have a religion and did not worship any gods but rather revered goodness itself and believed in the philosophy of becoming one with the world around you. In doing so, they tapped into the sinful nature of the Darkness without knowing it and drew on its power to protect their planet. This caused the planet to fall prey to that very Darkness. When Pandora and the Dark One came, they wiped out Eishe's world and threw its people into the Abyss. Coz had been struck with the Dark One's blade. Leina and her brother, Carlel, teleported Eishe and his master onto their ship. They began to pray over Coz, in hopes that God would stop the effects of the Dark One's sword, but it was too late and Coz went body and soul into the Darkness. Eishe had seen his master laid out on an operating table, where they were praying over him, and Eishe fled. He took his master's sword and accidentally went into a scouting pod, where he was launched into space. He traveled for two hundred years in a deep sleep until he landed on Earth. There, he was found by Dr. Ian Rich of the FDSR, inside the very suit that he wore now, which the spacecraft dressed him in as he slept.

The technology of Leina and her people was very advanced and far exceeded the technology of the Earth. Her brother's ship traveled the universe trying to stop Pandora and her army from destroying all the worlds, but they failed each and every time. Like Pandora they used the black holes in the universe to warp from place to place. This was how they made it to all the ends of the universe. Otherwise, these worlds were too far apart for any ship, no matter how advanced, to travel fast enough to reach them within the lifetimes of the crew. There were many black holes out there and they were actually portals to the Darkness itself. Places where space and time were ripped apart, where stars had collapsed and fallen. The angels of those stars, trapped in the Darkness for all time, created black holes where their stars once stood. Using a cloaking device, Carlel's ship was able to travel through one black hole and out another without being detected by the Darkness. And like Pandora, they learned how to fabricate black holes in space so they could travel from any point to any other point in the universe. Leina had told her friends about this when they were together on Earth.

Eishe cut the vines that held his master and ripped the end of them from his mouth, much like Roger had done for him. The pupil held his master in his arms and tried to wake him softly. Roger walked over and Eishe told him that this was his master, Coz. Roger and Eishe prayed over him. Both of them glowed with the light of the Holy Spirit, and that was when Coz opened his eyes. Coz was almost seven hundred years old when the Dark One conquered their world of Aporia, about two hundred years older than Eishe. But he was still strong, and the two heroes could feel it. His face had wrinkles and he had long gray dreadlocks matted together. He had a gray beard and mustache to match. His skin was bronze and he had thin brown eyes. Coz wore a red monk's robe with a sash around the waist. His robe was dirty, spotted with blood, and was tattered with cuts and tears all over it. The ancient man smiled at his student.

"Eishe? Is that you?" Coz asked.

"Yes, master, it is I, your pupil, Eishe Taninaru."

"Where are we?" Coz wondered.

"Inside the Darkness, master, the embodiment of all evil," Eishe said. "We were wrong about our beliefs. Everything we held true was a lie. We thought that we were serving the ideal of goodness and righteousness but, instead, we served the Darkness and its selfish ways. It conquered our planet and took our people. It is feeding on them now like it fed on you. But now you are free and we must free the others."

"I am not sure that I have the strength to fight and free our people," Coz said.

"Don't worry old man, I've got strength enough," Roger said and crossed his arms.

The hulking hero was quite intimidating and Coz could feel powerful spiritual energy coming from him. He also was intrigued by Roger's left arm, for he saw the metal armor that covered it moving like a living being.

"We'll free as many as we can," Roger said. "But I'm not sure we can free them all. We have to get out of here and stop the Darkness from coming to Earth. But how?"

"There has to be a way out," Eishe said. "Remember, Leina told us that her people's ship had been here. That her brother had a way to navigate in and out, to go across the universe."

"Yeah, she said they passed through synthetic black holes," Roger responded. "They were taught that the black holes were vortexes that led to the Abyss. They learned how to create temporary tears in space and time that replicated a black hole. Their ship would enter it and cloak itself so it was not detected by the Darkness. Then, once inside, they would create another one that would send them to their destination in the universe. But how do we make one and how do we know where it will lead? It's one thing to be on a ship that navigates everything for you and allows you to be in space without worrying about oxygen. Their technology must be insane. But look at us, we have no chance. We need another way."

"Let's search," Eishe stated. "Remember that with God there is always a way, for He will not abandon nor forsake us. He will guide us out of here, if we trust in Him. Let's pray for his guidance and favor."

The two heroes prayed for deliverance from the Lord as Coz looked on. He heard his student speak of God. They had no such beliefs in a supreme deity on their home world. His pupil had changed and the elderly master wondered why.

"Can you really trust in this God?" Coz asked. "And this ship you spoke of, if it passed through here, why did it not free the people?"

"It can't," Roger said. "Leina told me they wanted to but they can only pass through for a very short time or else the ship would be trapped here forever. Like I said, I don't understand the science behind it, but I do know that if they could have they would have freed all of you. You were on that ship and so was

Eishe. They rescued you from the Dark One, but it was too late. He had cut you with his blade and, when that happened, you had no choice but go to the Darkness. But we are here now and we will take you from this place, and anyone else we can rescue, too. In the end, God has a plan and I know He will free these people from the Darkness. God is good."

"I don't know this God or you," Coz said. "You might be big and strong, but that means nothing. It's who you are inside. But I trust my pupil. Eishe is wise and knows the heart. If he trusts you, then I do also. Let's go."

Coz stood up slowly. Eishe had regained his strength but his master was still weak from being drained by the Darkness for so long. The three men started to move forward, ready to free more souls from the vines that held them. Yet, something was watching them from all around. The weight of the air increased and pushed down on them harder still. The Darkness grew thicker and it was getting more and more difficult to breathe. Then they heard the sound of many horses rushing into battle and they saw the blue eyes peering at them from the dark. Eishe told his master to get down. He and Roger knew what was coming. Yes, they had fought these creatures before. In an instant, hundreds of Abyssites flew toward them. There was nowhere to run. The heroes were surrounded. They had to fight.

The surreal demons from the pages of Revelation swooped down at the heroes. Their sharp teeth, poisonous stingers, and hooked locust-like feet attacked all at once. Eishe held up his sword and a shield of white light formed, sheltering him and his master. Roger turned his left hand into an axe-like blade and slashed at the giant creatures. He was not scared of them, for the heroes had defeated these creatures before. Roger and Eishe both called on the Holy Spirit and focused His energy though themselves. Their bodies glowed with a bright, white light. Coz saw this and was in awe. He remembered being able to tap into nature and draw in the power of everything around him. But when he did that, he glowed blue. This power that Eishe was drawing on was greater than any Coz had seen. The light was warm and inviting. It was radiant but did not hurt his eyes. The elderly master could feel love emanating from both of these men. A love he could not comprehend for he had never known a sacrificial love like this. It was the love of God.

Eishe drew the energy shield back into the blade. He focused the power of the Spirit that flowed through him and swung his sword in an arc, sending a blast of white light from the blade upward, taking the head of an Abyssite that was coming for him and his master. He urged Coz to stay put and he went to fight back the evil swarm of demons.

Roger fought back also. With the axe blade that he had formed, Roger swung his left arm at the creatures and chopped off their heads over and over again. The creatures died and turned to ash. Eishe and Roger fought more and more furiously and, as they did, their powers increased. The two heroes charged up and both hit Chaos Fury. Roger's level raised higher and higher and far surpassed his friend's. Still, both men had the power of God flowing through them, which gave them the hope they needed to win. But there were more and more Abyssites coming. No matter how many they defeated, the swarm of demons seemed to be unending.

Coz could not sit back any longer. He was a warrior, a protector of the royal family and the planet of Aporia. He would not let his student risk his life without risking his own. He felt his strength returning and the master began to draw in the energy of the world around him. His body glowed with a blue light and the more energy he drew in, the brighter the light became. Coz did not realize that he was drawing in the power of the Darkness itself. That was what they had done to keep their planet safe. They were not drawing on the energy of nature. That was not something they could do. The Darkness had tricked them and others so that they would tap into its sinful power and be taken over by it. Coz felt stronger and stronger. The energy crackled all around him. The vines that drained spiritual energy from the people glowed as well. And then the demons all stopped and they too began to glow bright with a blue light. The Abyssites all stood still and watched the old master, who had unknowingly become one with the Darkness. Roger and Eishe stopped fighting and turned. They saw Eishe's master, Coz, standing there glowing with that bright, blue light and energy crackled like lightning all around.

"No!" Eishe screamed out. "Master, stop! You don't know what you're doing!"

"Of course I do, my student!" Coz said. "Look at me. Look at the power I wield. You wanted to get out of here. Well, join me and together we can escape and rule the universe!"

"Master! No!" Eishe yelled again.

"That's not your master talking," Roger said. "He's tapped into the Darkness. It's controlling him."

"How do we stop him?" Eishe asked.

"I only know one way and it's gonna hurt," Roger said.

Roger changed the blade back into a fist, and with the Left Arm of God, his arm extended at high speed toward Coz. Before it reached the old master, a swarm of Abyssites swooped down and blocked the attack. It seemed as if he was controlling the demons now. Coz yelled out a command of attack and the evil creatures all descended on Roger and Eishe. The heroes glowed brighter with the light of the Spirit and fought back the swarm of demons. Roger changed his left hand back into an axe blade and chopped off head after head of the Abyssites in his path. Eishe did the same with Itaru Taninaru. Then he charged up his sword and sent out a blast of white light that decapitated several more Abyssites, as well. The two heroes would not give up. But also Eishe did not want to hurt his master. He did not know what to do.

***

In the distance, sparks of black and white light flashed in the sky as Nathan and Radix continued their battle. The hero of light had just been freed from his imprisonment in Hell. Satan had Nathan hanging in chains in his throne room for what felt like a lifetime. But the entire time, the man did not give up hope. God was with him and gave him strength to endure. That was the same strength he called on now. Filled with the Holy Spirit, Nathan swung the Word of God more and more furiously, his power was far greater than the power of Chaos Fury he had used to fight Radix on Earth. Radix was also drawing on a strong power, the embodiment of all evil lent all of its strength to the evil villain. But the light always conquered the dark. Nathan pulled back his blade. He charged up with the power of the Holy Spirit. He was a transcended being, a rank on par with the angels and he had the potential to go beyond even that. Right now, Radix with the Blackblade in his hand was more powerful than any evil demon or entity to ever exist. The power he drew on now was the same power that Satan used to defy the throne of God. The entire Darkness was feeding into him through the sword that was forged in its heart. He was nothing more than a puppet, but a puppet that could destroy the entire universe if Nathan did not stop him. The hero of light held the Word of God in both hands. The sword glowed brighter and brighter with a strong, white light.

Then, in one mighty motion, Nathan swung the Word of God and called out, "Let there be light!"

The Sword of the Spirit struck the Blackblade and immediately the light of the Word of God overtook Radix and sent him crashing to the ground. The Blackblade flew off into the Darkness and disappeared. Nathan swooped down after the evil villain and pierced his heart with the sword. Instantly, Radix was bathed in light. His skin turned milky white and his armor of Darkness faded away. He now wore a long white coat and a plain white shirt and pants, with white boots that came to the knee. His hair was still jet black for that was its color always and his eyes, when he opened them, were back to their original dark-brown color, just like his daughter Bianca. He looked up and smiled at Nathan; the Helmet of Salvation had disappeared revealing his face.

"Nathaniel Salvatore is that you?" he asked.

***

Roger and Eishe kept battling the oncoming Abyssites. They had laid waste to hundreds of them but thousands more were coming at them. If they had not had the Lord as their shield they would have fallen to these vile creatures. Not even Roger's superhuman strength nor the liquid Angel metal Left Arm of God could help them to win. Only the strength of the Lord could prevail against such evil. God protected and strengthened these heroes and He would bring them victory, for their faith was placed in Him.

Coz was possessed by the Darkness that surrounded them. And its creatures were under his control. Eishe and Roger knew the only way to end this was to take down Eishe's master. Roger told his friend that they needed to knock him unconscious. If they could do that, then his connection with the creatures would stop. But still they were in the Darkness and the evil monsters would continue to attack as before, without their connection to Coz. Inside Roger's heart, he felt the Lord speak to him. God told the hulking hero to reach the highest level of Chaos Fury – the Wrath of God – just as he had done when he defeated the Chaldean. Roger had tried to do this already but he could not focus long enough with all the Abyssites attacking him. The Lord told him to let Eishe use the Spirit to be his shield and then Roger could focus on the Lord long enough to reach the Wrath of God, to end this fight. As soon he could reach the Wrath of God, the light of the Spirit would deliver them. Roger knew what to do and increased the force of his counterattacks on the demons. He cut through the swarm of creatures until he reached Eishe.

Once together, Roger recounted the plan to Eishe, while they continued to resist the terrible creatures. Roger blocked one of the Abyssites and it moved to gouge Eishe with its hooked hoof. Then Eishe blocked another that attacked with its teeth. He shoved the side of his blade in creature's mouth and then charged up the blade. A blast of energy shot from the blade and cut the creature's head in half. The Abyssite turned to ash, and so did another that Roger dispatched with the Left Arm of God. Two more attacked and managed to stab Roger in the back with their stingers. The poison from them was very toxic but the healing power that Roger possessed took over and did not let the toxin affect him. The hero grabbed the stingers from his back and pulled them out. Still holding the creatures' tails, Roger swung them into each other. Eishe shot out another blast of light from his sword and took their heads as well.

After this, Roger stood back and Eishe created a shield with his blade. The crystal pommel glowed brighter and brighter with the light of the Spirit. The sword was forged in Heaven and the crystal was one from Heaven's gates. The shield of white light grew around the two heroes and covered them completely.

The Abyssites tried to break through but they could not. God strengthened the shield and the light it was made of was the Lord's. Coz saw what his former pupil was doing with the sword that used to be his. Still possessed by the Darkness, the master grew angry and let out a cry. The blue light that glowed from him shot out all around him and a great, blue, electrical storm formed in the sky. Blue bolts of lightning shot down and struck the shield of light over and over again, but they could not break it, no matter how many of them rained down.

Eishe prayed to God for strength and the shield held strong. The warrior from beyond the stars drew in more and more power from the Spirit and held his position against the swarming horde of demons. Roger also drew in the power of the Holy Spirit, and in doing so, his power level increased more and more. God filled Roger with His own power and the hulking hero accelerated level after level of Chaos Fury. His body glowed brighter and brighter. Just like the storm of blue lightning that came down onto the heroes, now from Roger came crackling bolts of white lightning that shot out all around. The Spirit-filled hero let out a booming shout to God, and once again, Roger Jones did what no other man was able to do – he hit the level of Chaos Fury known as the Wrath of God.

His faith was strong and God was with him indeed. It was time to end this fight. Eishe dropped the shield. The blue lightning shot down toward the heroes and the sinful Abyssites swarmed in to take their souls. But before they could reach them, Roger released an explosion of light from his body that burst all around them. It annihilated all of the demons in its path, turning them to dust. Eishe's master, Coz, was basked in this explosion of light as well and the Darkness that had consumed him was completely obliterated from his body and soul, yet he himself was left unharmed. Coz fell to the ground unconscious. Eishe ran toward him. He held his master and prayed that he would wake up. Roger ran to his side also. Together they prayed for Coz, for deliverance from this Darkness, and for a way back home.

***

Nathan helped Radix to his feet. These two men had fought as enemies before and today they did again. Nathan looked

150

at Radix. He had done horrible evils in his lifetime on Earth, including unimaginable wickedness toward Nathan's own family. He killed Nathan's parents and violated his sister. Bianca and Gideon, Nathan's niece and nephew, were the product of that horrendous act. But that one time, when they did fight together in Hell, Nathan saw something else in this man, the same thing he saw now – hope. Yes, hope that even a sinner such as Radix could be forgiven and turn his life around. Nathan did not completely understand what had happened, but Radix was dressed all in white and there was something different about him. He looked … happy.

"Thank you for saving me," Radix said.

"I don't understand," Nathan replied.

"Don't understand what?"

"What's going on," the hero stated. "What happened to you?"

"I'm not sure myself. When Satan's soldiers took us, I escaped. That day when we fought together I felt a change in my heart. I'm not saying I'm a believer or anything like that, though I do know that Jesus is God. Even Satan knows that. But I lost the desire to be evil. I didn't want to be his puppet any longer. Fighting by your side for a good cause felt refreshing. I ran away from Satan. I wanted to find out who I really was and be free from that Devil. Instead I ended up here, in the Abyss. Right away, the Darkness took over my mind and my heart. It covered me in that armor and gave me the Blackblade. That sword controls its wielder and makes him bend to the will of the Darkness. I was a puppet for evil again. When the Blackblade saw you come here, it sent me to capture you, so it could feed off of your spirit. But you freed me. All I can say now is thank you."

"You're welcome but I still don't understand? Why are you dressed in white? And you, yourself, seem different," Nathan questioned.

"I'm not sure either. I must be a new man. I wasn't born evil. Well, I mean no human is born sinless, but I wasn't always the violent killer that I would become. That happened over time, the more Satan corrupted my soul. But somehow, when you pierced my heart with that blade, it changed me. It opened my eyes to something immense. I could feel God speaking to me in my heart. He asked me to follow Him. My heart said yes but my head said no. I'm still confused. The only thing I do know for sure is that I want to help you. I want to fight against the Devil, against that monster who made me his slave. Nathan, can you forgive me for all I have done?" Radix pleaded.

"It is not easy to forgive you. But I know that's what God wants. And it seems He already has, but true forgiveness comes with repentance. You have a lot to repent for and that is between you and God. All I know for sure is that if anyone, even you, accepts Christ as their Savior, they are a new creation, forgiven of their sins and a child of God. I would like to show Him to you. The only question is, is it too late?"

"Too late for what?" Radix asked. "For me to be saved? I'm not sure. When I was in Hell, Satan told me that I never died. The spell still held, and it said I would be rendered unkillable in every way. But if I failed my mission, my soul would go to Hell, for I had sold it. Death collected my soul and my body turned to ash. That satisfied his hunger for my soul, because in a way I technically transitioned to the afterlife. Though once in Hell, My body reformed and when you found me hanging there and released me from my bonds, I was body and soul in Hell just as you were. I still am. Like I said, I'm not a believer, but you never know. There's still hope for this wretch to be saved," Radix said with a smile.

"We have to get out of here," Nathan insisted. "I know there is something I must do but I'm not yet certain what it is. I was trapped by Satan in his throne room and then Christ freed me from my bonds and I was led here. Maybe it was to find you and save you."

"Or maybe it has to do with that?" Radix said and pointed toward the giant explosion of white light.

Nathan and Radix studied the explosion of light, not knowing what it was. On an impulse, the hero grabbed the former villain's right arm and they vanished. They appeared in the air, near where the explosion originated. Nathan did not know beforehand that he could teleport like the angels did. Something had happened to him during the fight with Radix. He had reached a new plateau.

He felt as if he were one with the Spirit. Nathan and Radix hovered in the air over Roger, Eishe, and Coz. The master was still unconscious and Eishe held him in his arms. Roger looked up at the two men.

"Who in the world are you two?" he asked. "You look like *Lord of the Rings* meets *Twilight*. With Aragorn over here and there's the sparkle vampire boy."

"Look who's talking, Incredible Bulk with a metal arm," Nathan replied. "What even is that thing? It's moving. How about you take it down a notch and explain what you're doing here."

"What we're doing here? If you're looking for a fight you found it, smart guy," the hulking hero responded. "I just pounded a bunch of demon bugs, but I think I have enough energy to whoop the two of you."

"You think so, big guy?" Radix asked. "Do you even know who we are?"

"I don't know and I don't care," Roger attested. "All I do know is that we need to get out of this place, and if you're here to stop us, I'm not going to just sit back and let you!"

"Take a breath, big man. I'm Nathan Salvatore."

"Wait, you don't mean *the* Nathan Salvatore? Bianca's uncle?" Roger asked.

"You know my niece?" Nathan said in surprise.

"Yes, we know her," Eishe said finally. He still held his master in his arms and looked up at Nathan. "We are trying to get back to her and save the Earth. This Darkness is about to enter and destroy the world, just like it destroyed my home planet of Aporia."

"Yes, I've heard these stories before, when I was in Heaven," Nathan interrupted.

"Actually, we thought you were still there," Roger added.

"Well, I went to Hell for a bit and now I'm here with you. But it's a long story," Nathan spoke again. "We have to get out of here. I'm just not sure how."

"We could find the portal that the Darkness will use to enter Earth," Radix said.

"No," Eishe said. "That portal won't open until the Three

153

Days of Darkness are completed and when that happens the Darkness will be unleashed and we won't be able to stop it. We need to get out now. We thought about leaving through a black hole. They connect the Darkness with the physical world. But black holes are all in outer space and far from Earth. We could find a way to make one but none of us know how."

"Make a black hole?" Nathan was confused.

"I am not sure how it works," Eishe responded. "Once, I was on a ship that could do it. But even if we escaped that way and were able to withstand its gravitational pull, what if we ended up in space? How do we get to Earth? And none of us can breathe in space."

"Well, I can," Nathan said.

"I don't have to breathe," Radix said.

"And who are you again, sparkle boy?" Roger asked.

"Radix."

"Wait, aren't you that evil creep who killed him and a whole bunch more people?" Roger said, pointing at Nathan. "Aren't you a bad guy?"

"I was, but I changed, thanks to Nathan and his sword," Radix affirmed.

"There's no time for this," Nathan said. "There must be a way out. It's not by chance we are all here together. There must be a reason and, for sure, it is not for us to stay trapped here."

Nathan stopped and prayed.

"Something is coming," Nathan said suddenly. "Yes, something big."

"It must be Leina's ship, with her people on it," Roger said. "It's the one Eishe told you about, the one that he had been on. Our friend, Leina, said her brother navigated through here from time to time. He moved across the universe by creating synthetic black holes with technology onboard his vessel. Maybe he is on his way to Earth to find her. She did say he was following her there. But how did you detect the ship? It is supposed to have a cloaking devise so the Darkness can't find it."

"God showed it to me," Nathan declared.

"Interesting, yes, God can see all. He alone is omniscient. But even if we know it is here, Leina said it comes and goes quickly or else the ship would be trapped. How can we board it," Eishe wondered.

"Let me handle that. Just do as I say," Nathan instructed, and he and Radix descended next to the heroes. "Everyone place your hand on my armor."

They all touched Nathan. Eishe held out Coz's hand so that his master could also touch Nathan.

"It's coming now. I can feel it," Nathan said and instantly they all disappeared.

Nathan, Radix, Roger, Eishe, and Coz all reappeared on the bridge of Carlel's ship. The captain, Leina's brother Carlel, looked at them in awe. He was slightly taller than Eishe, about six feet one inch, and had a sturdy build. His skin color was tan like his sister, and he had medium length, jet back hair with just the hint of curls and a short beard to match. His eyes were dark and sharp and he had a serious yet pleasant look on his face. He wore a brown vest and fitted pants with padded knees and knee-high brown leather boots. Under his vest was a white collared shirt, a brown leather belt around his waist, and a sash fitted with pouches across his chest. On his left side was sheathed a cutlass saber, and there was a hunting knife strapped to his right leg. These weapons were given to him by the prophet Antilla, forged in Heaven. The heroes that had appeared before him had come out of nowhere in a flash of white light. *Are they angels?* Carlel wondered. Then he recognized Coz. Yes, that man had been on his ship before, and the one holding him was wearing one of their combat suits. Who were these strangers? He had to find out.

CHAPTER IX
WAGES OF SIN

In the secret headquarters of the Council of His Holy Order in Vatican City, thousands of feet underneath St. Peter's Basilica, Aberto Ruggero walked through the ancient stone halls. His almost perfect physique could be seen through his fitted gray-green service dress uniform, highly decorated to show his rank. Aberto had been promoted to general a few years back, for his aid in taking down the threat known as Legion, who had plagued the world. Covering his dark hair was a beret of the same gray-green color as his uniform. His face showed signs of the battles he had fought, rugged and rough.

Gold candle holders were fitted into the walls, with electric candles set into them. The walls were lined with statues and reliefs of various saints and religious figures. There were also golden statues of angels dramatically and inaccurately depicting those the Catholic Church deemed to be the archangels. At the end of the hall was a large set of olivewood double doors. The arching doorway came to a point at the top and had a stone frame with the relief of olive branches, grape vines, and palm branches interwoven with each other. The doors themselves were ornate with carvings of the twelve apostles – the twelfth being Matthias and not Judas – each with a disk-like halo around his head, and in the center, split in half by the doors, was Christ also with a halo around his head. His hand faced forward with his index and middle fingers raised as a sign of peace to any who entered. There were two grand golden knobs, one on each door, and a Star of David was debossed on each. The doors themselves were old but, fitted with new technology, they opened on their own, as Aberto stood and waited.

"Come in, General Ruggero," a voice in Latin called from inside the room.

Aberto marched into the room and stood at attention. He saluted the man who had called him in. It was the man who presided over of the Council of His Holy Order as ordained by the Pope himself – Archbishop Giovanni Rossini. The room was vast and filled with olive wood bookcases that held countless volumes of church doctrine, the writings of the early Church Fathers, the

Catechism, texts on angels and evil spirits, and other lore of the Catholic Church. There was also an ancient manuscript of the Latin Bible, handmade by monks in Rome hundreds of years before and now opened to John 1. It was encased under glass on top of a marble pedestal. The only other Bible in the room was the archbishop's own copy, sitting on his desk, which he read every day, three times a day. The walls were the same ancient stone as the hallway walls. In the back of the room, displayed high on the wall, was a beautiful golden crucifix, showing the Lord majestically hanging from the cross. The archbishop sat behind an ornate olive-wood desk, in the center of the room, in a throne-like chair made of the same olive wood. It had red velvet back and seat cushions and armrests. The archbishop was a portly man of average height. He wore a purple bishop's cassock with the traditional white collar showing, and a purple zucchetto atop his stark white head of hair, which contrasted his olive complexion. Over his shoulder, he wore a finely embroidered stole, golden in color, and atop his breast was the pectoral cross attached to a chain to signify his position. The final symbol of his authority was a gold episcopal ring, set with amethyst, that he wore on his right ring finger. Aberto genuflected in front of the archbishop's desk and made the sign of the cross. Archbishop Rossini gestured for the general to sit. Aberto obliged and took a seat in one of three smaller wooden chairs with velvet cushions in front of the desk.

"Your excellence," Aberto said in Latin, "thank you for inviting me here."

"General Ruggero, it is my pleasure to have you here," the archbishop continued to speak in Latin, for it was the language of the Catholic Church. "I know that you have already been briefed of the dire calamity that the world is now facing. We are in the Three Days of Darkness. You have heard the prophecies of these days and how they will usher in the end times. We, as the Holy Catholic Church, know much about the world and the truth of the supernatural. We have been waiting for this day and for Pandora to come and usher the Darkness into this world. The pivotal issue is that the faithful should have been raptured by now but we have not been. This means this is not the end times and, therefore, it can be stopped. There are plagues going around the world, much like the ten plagues of Egypt during the time of Moses. First, we have the Darkness, then animals turning savage on men and women, pestilence, the dead have risen, and soon we believe the moon will turn to blood as will the waters all around us. Every minute, more and more plagues ravage this world. But, as I said, this can be stopped. God has not yet decreed the end of humanity. We as believers in the truth know what Revelation says about the end times and the fact that those who hold Christ as their Savior are still on this Earth shows us that this is not the end."

"But your excellence," Aberto replied, "what would you have me do? Our men and women are out there, keeping back the demonized zombies that are on the streets. The government has warned all citizens to remain indoors, for their own safety. This is happening all over the world and no one is the wiser about the true evil that is out there. People are being kept in the dark, as usual, to avoid panic. What else can we do but pray to God for this to end."

"You are wrong, general," the archbishop declared. "You *can* do something. You can stop this. We know that the Darkness is the embodiment of all evil, that which caused Satan to fall and become the Devil that he now is. His own daughter, Pandora, has been looking for a chance to come to Earth and conquer it, enslaving all of its people in the Darkness and destroying our world itself, as she has done to countless other planets. We are not blind, like the world, to the true evil out there. Nothing goes past the eye of the Catholic Church and we, as the Council of His Holy Order, must always protect His people from the Devil and his schemes. As the highest ranking officer in the Army of the Council of His Holy Order, you know all of this and more. You also know what your duty is, general," the archbishop stood as he spoke, and then Aberto did the same. "Gather your best and brightest soldiers. You will all board one of our elite aircraft and fly to Atlantis. Yes, it has been raised from under the ocean, and that is where Pandora will enter the Earth tomorrow. Her own general is most likely there now, preparing for her arrival. We have pinpointed its exact coordinates in the Atlantic Ocean by monitoring the evil spiritual energy emitting from the island, and that location matches what our ancient records show us. Prepare accordingly and arm yourselves for war. There are others already in the field. Some you know and some you haven't met, but all are warriors of God. But you must take one more thing with you. A memento from your victorious fight with Legion, a victory that led to your promotion to general."

Aberto stood with his hands out and the Archbishop placed a nearly seven-foot-long white metal spear in his hand. The man who held this spear now had been given this same spear before, by the Devil himself, who was then disguised as an angel of the Lord. Satan had fooled Aberto into using the spear to help take down Legion and Aberto planned to use this very weapon again to thwart the evil that now plagued the Earth. It was the Spear of Destiny, a weapon used to cast Satan into Hell and the same spear used to pierce Christ's side, after He died on the cross. It was a trophy of Satan's for many years and was used by those who followed him – including Nero, Hitler, Stalin, and so many others – to perform blasphemies throughout time. Now, it was in the hands of the Catholic Church, and they planned to use it for good, as it was first intended, when Michael used it against Lucifer in the First War. The Catholic Church had many secrets and knew much about things the rest of Christendom had forgotten or had chosen to ignore. Gabriel had delivered much of this knowledge centuries before as instructed by God to prepare mankind for the end of the world that would come one day like a thief in the night. *Was the end near?* Aberto wondered, as he took the spear. Or was the archbishop right, that this was not the end and that God would rescue them as He had done countless times since He created the world. The Catholic Church was powerful but it was not perfect and Aberto knew this. He had learned in his years of service how all institutions of man are flawed and only God is perfect. But the Church, despite its shortcomings, still served the Lord. No man was good but at least Aberto knew that he served the true God and, by doing so, God would protect him and bring forth His justice.

***

Just as the archbishop had said, all the governments around the world put their people on mandatory lockdown. No one was allowed to leave their homes. Even the police and military were now asked to remain indoors and under cover. Everyone locked their doors and waited for this nightmare to end. But not everyone listened to the warnings. There were a few people who went out to take advantage of the dark, empty streets. They looted the stores and broke into cars. The police could not turn a complete blind eye to the crimes on the streets and some commanding officers sent out elite teams to round up the criminals. Captain Rogers was one of these senior officers who had men and women still patrolling the New York City streets. The real problem was that the criminals were not the only evil that was out and about. The undead were beginning to walk the streets and both the looters and cops would soon run into them. There were not many officers on the beat, given the strict government orders. But this also meant there was no one from the government out there to stop the zombies. The heads of state around the world knew something evil was going on the world round, and none of them were ready for their people to witness the monsters that were ravaging about. By keeping as many people locked inside as possible the stories of these creatures would be few and far between, and even cell phone videos could be branded as hoaxes. For years to come, people would talk about the urban legends of these zombie demons. But only a few would know how true these stories were.

A young man and woman, filthy and homeless, used a brick to break a store window. They ran inside to take as much merchandise and money as they could. They had been poor and hungry. Drugs had consumed their lives and drove them to joblessness and life on the city streets. These two had each other and that's all they cared about. And tonight, they would steal their way off the streets. If they hit up enough stores, they might have enough money to rent an apartment for a few months and also they could finally buy food or steal that too. And with all that money, they could buy plenty of street drugs and alcohol to satisfy their sinful cravings. It was like hitting the lottery or winning a sweepstakes. Their lives would change overnight or, in this case, their lives would end. The couple was ransacking the store when they heard something else come through the broken window. They couldn't see what it was and the flashlights they had barely pierced the thick Darkness all around. Suddenly, the woman yelled as she was grabbed by a clawed hand and her chest ripped open. The man screamed in pain as his right arm was ripped off and eaten in front of his horrified gaze.

Someone heard their cries. A bright floodlight shined in through the broken window, and the creatures saw that it came from an armored man floating in the air. The armor-plated suit was made of a new, very durable alloy, but it looked to be brushed steel. It was fitted and not bulky. The entire faceplate of the helmet was one solid piece and was tempered glass, nearly as unbreakable as the armor itself and colored to match the suit. The wearer could see out but no one could see in. Sonic waves kept the suit afloat and allowed it to fly and propel itself at great speeds. This same armor was able to fire destructive waves of sonic energy from circular conductors on the palms of the gauntlets. It was Pharaoh, Toni Brown, in the new sonic-powered armored suit that he had been building to sell for warfare. Seeing the evil that was overtaking the world and, remembering his uncle James and the evil he had fought, Toni had had a change of heart and decided to use his armor to do good.

Toni saw the two demon zombies eating the flesh of the man and woman that they had just killed. The creatures looked at Toni with their glowing blue eyes and then together they attacked. They were large and their decaying skin was solid black. The faces of these demonic beings looked human but twisted. Their noses long and crooked and their teeth jagged and sharp. They moved quickly and it was hard to distinguish all of their features, even in the floodlights that he shined into the vacant store. Toni flew backward out the broken window and the creatures followed him into the street.

He had barely had a chance to test the new suit. He knew how everything worked but using it in real-life battle was not the same thing. There was no room for error and unfortunately Toni made a few. One of the monsters grabbed the chest plate of the armor and the other grabbed his right leg. Toni started to increase the throttle but the creatures were too strong for the suit. The one holding his leg pulled him down and slammed him into the ground. The other one pounced on top of the suit like a cat and they both tried to gnaw their way through it. Inside the suit, Toni squirmed to free himself from their hold. The suit was connected to his brain through a headset, giving him the ability to activate the armor with his mind, as if it were an extension of his body. The technology was definitely next level, and would have brought him a hefty price on the black market. But from this day forward, this suit was not for sale, that is, if Toni lived past this moment.

Instantly, Toni activated the conductors on his right palm and powerful sonic waves shot out. The force was so strong that it blasted the creatures off of him, and then Toni stood up. They came at him again and now he released two blades, one from the back of each gauntlet. The blades were eight inches long and four inches wide. With a slash of his right hand, he cut one of the demon zombies across the chest spraying glowing blue blood. With a slash of his left blade, he cut the other. Right before his very eyes, both of the undead creatures healed. One of them scratched at his chest plate but could not break through it. The other jumped on his back. Then the one in front of him grabbed the throat of the suit and tried to tear off his helmet. Toni sliced off one of its hands and then shot it with the sonic conductor on his left palm. He blasted the other zombie with a sonic wave, this time from his right hand. He was out-matched for sure, but he had to find a way to stop these creatures. Igniting the sonic thrusters on the back and feet of the suit, Toni took to the air again. He hovered about three feet off the ground and then ascended a little higher. The suit's flight capabilities were only tested up to six feet and Toni was not certain how high he could go. The armored suit, flying through the air, made him look like something out of a comic book franchise, but the hard reality of this battle was very serious. He circled around the creatures but they moved faster than before and then leaped into the air. They grabbed him from both sides and pulled him down. Toni increased the force of the thrusters and tried to pull away from the demonic creatures. He spun around, out of control, then crashed into a pile of garbage outside of the store building. Aiming with both palms, he blasted the creatures again, and then with the blades on his hands slashed and sliced. The wounds he inflicted were once again healed. One of the creatures grabbed Toni from behind and pulled him back. The suit protected him from being choked out but it was difficult to fight back the beast, for it was very strong. Toni thrust the blade of his right hand into the forehead of the creature that held him from behind and then pulled it out again. The creature jumped back with a screech. Blue, glowing blood splattered the armored suit. The other creature attacked him from the front and Toni skewered it through the throat with his left-hand blade. The blade was lodged in the creature's neck; blue, glowing blood dripped down it. Without a second thought, and by some divine inspiration, he pulled out the blade and then quickly slashed again at the monster, cutting it clean across the throat, decapitating it. Right before his eyes, the creature turned to dust. The other monster saw this and ran away.

Toni looked around and saw that the blue, glowing blood had disintegrated. He had nearly died just now. And one of those creatures got away. It could kill someone else. The newly ordained hero did not know what to do next so he paused for a moment and tried to calm his thoughts. He could barely catch his breath and he needed to figure out how to better use the suit. If he faced off against more of these monsters he would surely lose. The man known as Pharaoh in the underworld felt like a failure right now. He was a big shot but he'd been down the wrong path. His money had not bought him dignity or honor. It only gave him false respect from criminals and those even more corrupt than himself. He thought about Crystal and the example he was setting for her. That is when his phone began to buzz. Through the Bluetooth connection in his suit, he was able to answer the call with only a thought. He quickly confirmed there were no other threats on the street and picked up. It was his daughter.

"Dad, are you okay?" Crystal asked.

"Yeah, I'm fine honey," Toni answered. He was standing now on the sidewalk just outside the looted store where he faced those creatures. "Just shaken up, a little."

"I know about the suit and I know you put it on," she said.

"What? What are you talking about?"

"Stop lying, Dad. I know you're Pharaoh and I know Uncle James was too before he died. I saw the letters and I researched all the strange things that happened in Harlem that day. And about old man Reynolds, and how he was shot, and even Lyles Washington, and how he was framed for the murder. And I read about them in the letter Uncle James wrote to you. I know this crazy Darkness is more than just some weird, natural phenomenon. It has to be more. Dad, I love you, but you have to tell me the truth. Where are you and what are you doing? Is everything okay?"

"Sweetie," Toni started to explain, "I know this is all strange, heck, I'm trying to figure it all out myself. I didn't really believe everything in that letter but after what I saw tonight, I do believe. There is some evil stuff going down. Yes, I'm in the suit and I'm trying to use it to stop these demonic creatures, whatever they are. I just killed one by cutting off its head but another one escaped. I tried to go home earlier, but one chased me back into my building and that's when I put on the suit. When I came back out, it was gone."

"I saw you put it on and leave. I've been spying on you. I know everything. That's why I prayed for you before, and why I've been praying for you every night. Dad, you have to change, you have to turn your life around. What if you die tomorrow? Do you even believe in God, do you know who Jesus is, and that He died for you?"

"I do, my mother taught me that. She was strong in the faith before she died. And your mama is too. She's a good woman but I haven't been a good man. Today, I decided to change that."

"Let me help. Hang on," Crystal said and then grabbed her laptop.

"What are you doing?" he asked.

"Hacking into your system through your phone."

"You can do that? I mean, I thought I was smart," Toni chuckled.

"Yeah, this is nothing," Crystal responded. "Okay, I'm in. Let me see."

Crystal opened up all the files for the suit and read all the coding, then she ran a few diagnostics.

"Okay, Dad," she said. "Just listen to me. I can map out where to go and when I hit this, I can share the navigation with the screen on your visor. Also, I can see everything around you and activate all your weapons. Wow, two sonic conductors on the palms! I can also navigate your flight and it seems if I do this–". She paused while typing in a code. "Yes, now you can fly a hundred feet into the air."

"How are you doing all of this?"

"Dad, I'm a genius, just like you," she said.

"Nah, you're much smarter than me," Toni laughed again.

"Okay, let's head out," Crystal said and ignited the thrusters, taking Toni twenty feet into the air, and then she showed him a map. And off he flew with his daughter leading the way.

***

A large yet very sleek high-speed helicopter landed on the roof of the Manhattan branch of the FDSR. The building was located on the East River between the Chelsea piers and United Nations headquarters. It was an old warehouse that the FDSR purchased and refurbished. From the dark navy-blue chopper emerged the members of the ISOD team who had stayed behind. First Officer Cynthia Carlson led the way, and First Officer Jael Zahavi was there to greet them. A few of Jael's officers stood behind her and they escorted the ISOD team inside the building to a very large elevator. It held all nineteen of them. The outside of the building looked like your basic squared-off brick warehouse. But the elevator and the rest of the building was all redone to be very modern and high tech. The group walked out of the elevator and into a giant room in the basement garage. There were large all-terrain vehicles down there similar to what Cynthia and her team used at headquarters, but these were newer and more advanced. They were so large each could hold twenty people. They had eight large all-terrain tires – four on each side. These long, aerodynamic vehicles were made of a special blend of metal and ceramic like the Challenger 2 tank, making them very durable. They could even go into the water and move around like submarines.

Zahavi stood with five other soldiers; Cynthia had brought twelve including the elite members of the ISOD team that had

166

not gone to Atlantis. Both first officers were in charge of their divisions while the sergeants were in the field, trying to stop the world from falling into Darkness. These women were highly trained and skilled at combat and espionage. Jael was also very accustomed to fighting demonic beasts as she had hunted down the killers of her battalion. She never found the vampire-like demons that killed the men and women she considered family, but she did encounter other demonic creatures and knew how to stop them. She spoke to Cynthia and laid out the plan. They would all need silver rounds in their weapons. Also, they each would need a blade to decapitate the creatures, for that was the only sure way to kill these monsters that plagued the streets. Yes, there were demonic zombies walking around the city, and the world, devouring all those who were not smart enough to stay inside as the government had directed. The NYPD did not know what to do or what to believe and Captain Rogers, by order of the Police Commissioner, had sent out a small team to keep the peace on the streets, even though the government had required the local authorities to stay inside. Jael had communicated with the Commissioner and had some soldiers already on the streets patrolling. Now she and ISOD team would go out together and make sure the people of New York stayed safe. Other FDSR teams would do the same in other cities around the country.

But there was reason the ISOD team was in New York to assist First Officer Zahavi. From the research she had been conducting, Jael believed that New York City was an epicenter for demonic activity around the world. That is why the Chaldean set up his headquarters there, and that is why, once Jay Sil opened up his city branch of the FDSR, Jael joined. More paranormal phenomenon had occurred in the New York City area than anywhere else over the past two centuries. It seems that ancient authorities knew about this and it was the real reason why Europeans feared venturing west on the sea. Native Americans, as well, knew about demonic activity in the northeast, and there were ancient tales on the subject that survived today. Satan had indeed set up a spiritual hub under the city, connected directly to Hell, and through it to the Darkness itself. Jael did not know this exactly but she knew there was something deeper going on and if they could locate it, maybe they could help their fellow officers, those who were on Atlantis, by stopping the approaching Darkness from this gateway in New York City. First Officer Zahavi had been calculating where this gateway was located and according to her data it was downtown in the financial district, underneath the memorial where the World Trade Center once stood. All nineteen of the elite squad would board an all-terrain vehicle and head to the financial district, to help stop the Darkness. None of them knew exactly what to do next but somehow they knew what they were doing was right. It was as if God was guiding them, for He had a plan.

***

"It is time," Psol announced. "Wizard, take us to the top of the mountain. We must prepare for Pandora's coming. My empress awaits us just outside of Earth's atmosphere, above this very island. The second day is almost over and at the dawn of the third day, she will descend. We must prepare the temple before she arrives. Let's move."

Simon created a portal before them and said, "This will take us to the top of the mountain."

"Then, let's go," Psol commanded. "And bring the girl."

Psol entered first, then his thirty remaining troops, followed by Legion, and then Gideon. The *Necronomicon* floated ahead of Simon. Inside a floating, blue orb of energy, Bianca followed the floating book, still bound in magical energy chains. Simon entered last. Once they were all on the other side, the portal closed behind them. Simon cast a spell that created a ball of blue light that flew up to the sky and shone all around like a mini sun. This gave them, and the entire island, enough light to see in the Darkness because the hazy, blue light that still shone all around the island was too dim. They stood together, there on the mountain top, overlooking the fallen city at the center of Atlantis, with the giant stone walls and towers that surrounded it. The city was in ruins and so was the Grand Tholos of the Watchers on the mountain top. The building was about fifty feet wide and almost as tall. It was topped with a large dome and encircled by a colonnade. Inside this building, the Watchers once held council, thousands of years ago. But with the destruction and sinking of the island into the Atlantic Ocean, the building was not as majestic as it once was. Part of the dome had collapsed and so had some of the columns, which resembled those from the Doric order. Psol ordered Simon to use his magic again and repair the fallen building and transform it into the temple they needed. The wicked general of Pandora's army held out his hand and touched Simon's forehead. Instantly the plans for the Temple of the Darkness entered the sorcerer's mind. With a spell, Simon Magus III, High Sorcerer of the Darkness, piece by piece rebuilt the tholos with the modifications shown to him by Psol. When it was finished, it stood as a true Temple of the Darkness, ready for its queen to dedicate it for its destructive purposes.

The colonnade enclosed a large entrance up a set of broad, stone steps. They all marched up the stairs and into the tholos. Inside was stadium-like stone seating as it had before, for Watcher angels to sit and meet together. In the center, where the round table had once stood, the place where the elite leaders of the Watchers sat during council, was now a black onyx altar with sinister demonic carvings all around it. Behind it was a set of wide stone steps that led to a stone platform, and on that platform was a black onyx throne. It also was covered in sinister demonic carvings. The top of the throne formed the head of a great black dragon, its mouth wide open, showing its sharp, sinful teeth, and its long serpentine tongue. On the floor under the altar was a circle of the same black onyx and carved into it was the same swirled cloud design with the seven stars in it that was on the rock wall of the cave. Simon put out his hand and Bianca floated inside the glowing, blue orb to the foot of the altar. She was gently placed on the ground. The blue orb disappeared and Bianca slept, still bound in her chains. Above their heads was an oculus in the ceiling, a circular hole used to look up at the stars in the night sky or during the day to let sunlight in.

"Come with me," Psol commanded again.

Legion, Gideon, and Simon with the *Necronomicon* floating beside him, followed Psol back outside. They walked to the edge of the mountaintop and with a command the blue sun-like orb shone brighter, giving them visibility of the valley beyond the gates of the city. They could see the great forest to the left and the farmland to the right. And in the valley was a great wall of fire that separated one side of the island from the other. On the near side of the fire stood Psol's troops. And on the far side of it was the band of heroes who were still fighting the ever-growing demonized zombie horde.

"I want you to go down there," Psol said. "And annihilate those disgusting flesh-bags. Kill them all. I will not have them ruin our plans. The Darkness will reign and devour this Earth as it did the other planets, taking the people of this world to be its food for all eternity."

"But, master," Simon said. "Your soldiers cannot pass that wall of flame, it is Holy Fire. They are all trapped on this side. Can't the undead creatures take them out?"

"Listen here, you pathetic nothing," Psol said. "Do not come to me with problems. Come with solutions."

"I will go and stop them," Legion said. "I grow tired of standing back here and waiting. I need to spill blood."

"Excellent," Psol said. "Wizard, get Legion down to my men now. I am sure he will find a way to deal with that wall of Holy Fire and destroy our enemies. Their God may be on their side but I do not believe that He is all-powerful. For if He were, then how did we conquer all those other worlds. Do not disappoint me, Legion."

"I really don't care if you are disappointed or not," Legion said. "The only thing I care about is how many bodies I can lay to waste."

"Do as you please," Psol decreed.

"This will be fun. I will slaughter them all," Legion boasted.

Legion looked down with hubris. The Darkness armor that Gideon and he now wore made them feel even stronger than before. Both of them felt like gods before men. Psol took Gideon to his side and Simon created another portal in front of them. Legion walked through and was gone. The Dark One brought Gideon and Simon back into the tholos to prepare for Pandora's arrival. Legion walked out of the other end of the portal at the foot of the wall of Holy Fire. He stood in front of Psol's guards, ready to lead them into battle.

***

On the other side of the fire, the band of heroes still fought back the demonic horde of zombies. These creatures were strong and fast, their attacks deadly. But the heroes fought hard, relying on God to win the battle for them. John and Akane fought side by side. Each held a sword. Akane sliced the hand off one beast as its claws came to slash the man she loved. She kicked the creature in the gut and moved to cut its head off. Before she could connect, the demonic beast phased out, letting her sword pass right through it. John blocked another attack and then was slashed across the back. His leather coat and shirt were torn and blood poured down. He turned to block again. Three creatures came at him and Akane at once. She connected with a high knee, and then flipped over the creature. John sliced its head off before it could see his attack and turned the creature to dust. Akane thrust her blade into another but then it phased out and back, then knocked her to the ground. Two more of these zombie demons grabbed John and pinned him to the ground. Akane was tied up with the others. That was when the beasts that held John were decapitated and so were the two that fought Akane. The creatures' blood splattered everywhere but then disappeared as their bodies turned to ash. John and Akane saw their saviors, Ravenblade and Jack. More and more demonized zombies attacked and the fight went on.

Shanson and his troops fired round after round of silver ammunition into the beasts before them. Followed by swipes of their Hell-metal spears, taking the creatures' heads and sending them into oblivion. Shanson was struck from behind. He turned and went to hit the creature with his gun but the monster caught it. The two were in a tug of war, back and forth. The sergeant kicked the monster in the knee and then struck it with the butt of his weapon. The beast knocked the gun out of Shanson's hands and grabbed him by the neck. This would not stop the sergeant of the ISOD division of the FDSR. He grabbed the demonic clawed hand that held his throat. Relying on the strength that God gave him, Shanson slowly pulled it off of him, and then grabbed the monsters other wrist. The heroic sergeant bent back the creature's arms with unprecedented strength. He then lifted it into the air and spun it around, when Jenny came from behind and chopped off its head. She had her sergeant's back.

Across the way, Lyles and his son, Bo, fought together. The teenager always dreamed of fighting alongside his father, joining him on the adventures that he had heard so much about, especially while Ravenblade had been training him. Lyles felt the rush of adrenaline as the battle grew thicker. It brought back memories of fighting against Radix and Legion before. He wondered if he could truly face that demon again when the time came. The father drew on the power of his Father in Heaven. Lyles' body glowed with a soft, white light and he attacked swiftly and furiously. But these creatures also moved fast. They phased in and out, dodging his blade. Bo came at one with his own sword and was thrown onto his back. Lyles moved more surely than before, enraged by the danger his son was in. Quickly he took the head off of one and then another demonized zombie before him. A third went to slash him across the throat. That was when Bo shot a beam like a blade of white light energy from his hand, which took the head of the creature clean off. He grabbed his sword and went to fight by his father's side again. The boy was a natural. He moved faster than before and slashed another creature, following it with a blast of light that took its head as well. Two more monsters attacked Bo, but Lyles cut them both across the chest, and then Leina came from behind and took their heads with her bladed staff. The woman also glowed with a white light, and the three fought furiously.

Puck stood back. He tried to help but he was not doing any damage. Out of nowhere he felt something, a great evil energy, one that he had felt before. It was Legion, yet his power seemed stronger and darker, and he was just on the other side of the flames. Puck had to help somehow, so the Djinni vanished in a puff of smokeless fire.

***

Puck appeared behind a rock not too far from the wall of flames and about fifty yards from Legion. The Nephilim stood tall and exhumed a great dark power from his very core. His whole body glowed with a strong, blue light. The troops were all standing at attention before him. Hundreds of them, ready for war.

"The night will last for one more day after the next dawn,

172

and with it will come the true Darkness, to devour this world," Legion professed to Psol's army. "Tonight, we will conquer God's heroes and show Him that He has no power over us. Join me, soldiers, and together let us destroy our enemies."

It looked as if Legion's muscles were growing or at least his armor was. It grew thicker and more fortified. The demon threw up his hands and then six great black tentacles shot out from his back and dug into the ground. Legion began to chant in the voices of thousands of dark demons. All over his body, monstrous eyes and mouths sprouted. They all chanted with him. The blue aura that surrounded him grew in intensity, the light practically blinding Puck as he looked on. The Djinni was afraid. How could they stop this monster? The ground began to glow with the same evil, blue light and it spread so that the light lined the base of the wall of fire. Then with a loud, piercing cry, the demon and all the other mouths screeched in unison. Right there, before his eyes, Puck saw the wall of flames turn blue, like the light that surrounded Legion, and then the fire was extinguished. Had God abandoned them? Why did He allow this demon to put out His fire? Was there any hope left for them?

The ground beneath Legion's feet began to rise and pile up higher and higher. It formed a pedestal of earth that stood thirty feet over the ground. The Nephilim turned and drew the tentacles back into himself, and looked over the battle before him. The blue orb that Simon had created over the Mountain had grown in size and blanketed the whole land in a strange, blue light. The demonized zombie horde stopped fighting and turned to walk away. The heroes saw them leaving the battle, and took advantage to eliminate as many as they could. The creatures that remained stood at the base of the pedestal that Legion stood on. Then all the heroes looked up at him. They noticed that the wall of Holy Fire from God was gone, and that there was a strange, blue orb in the sky acting like a small sun, shining light on the whole land. Legion had come and put out the fire that protected them. These men and women tried not to lose faith. They knew God had to have a plan. They just did not know what it was. They each prayed in their hearts for a sign that He was still with them, that God had not abandoned them. His fire was gone, but

173

His Spirit remained. Bo glowed brighter and so did his father, Lyles. Then Leina, Akane, John, Jack, and Ravenblade all glowed with the same white light of the Spirit. God was still with the camp of heroes. He would not leave them or forsake them, as He promised. There was still hope, for their hope was in the Lord.

"Well, well, it seems you still have His light in you!" Legion bellowed from his pedestal. "Do you think you will win? That light will be put out just as the fire was. Can any of you even imagine facing me? Look at this army around me. You all will die this night and then tomorrow, at the third day's end, the world will belong to the Darkness!"

The tentacles grew again from Legion's back, wrapped themselves around the pedestal all the way down, and then dug back into the dirt. The blue light shone brighter from his body. The tentacles, the entire demonic, zombie horde, and all of Psol's army glowed with the same sinister light. The creatures raised their heads, piercing the thick air with their mighty horns, and they screeched for blood. The ground split, and other creatures rose up from it. They were armor-plated quadrupeds much like scientists imagined the ankylosaurus to look, with great spikes coming from their back and powerful club-like tails. They were each nearly twenty feet long and stomped the ground in fury.

"These creatures are what you humans call dinosaurs," Legion bellowed. "These are only one type that lived before. They were kept here on Atlantis like cattle, thousands of years ago when the Watchers lived on this island. I have never seen them before, for I was not here then, but I was told of them and now you will be told. These creatures and other dinosaurs and what the humans call dragons were genetically engineered by the Devil, mutations of animals created by your God. They were abominations just like me and the Nephilim. These monsters were created for wars, where Satan used them to fight and kill. All of them were destroyed in the Great Flood and buried under the Earth. But just as the Darkness has reawakened these mortals into demonic creatures, I now have reanimated these beasts as well. The power of the Darkness is beyond your comprehension. Now, soldiers mount your steeds. The war is upon us. We must find victory tonight, and put out the last light that God has on this planet! Victory will be ours!"

Psol's guards mounted the armored beasts and all the troops held their black swords high. They also reached behind them and detached black plates off the backs of their armor to use as shields in the battle. The soldiers were prepared, and the demonized, zombie horde was ready as well. The heroes, too, stood ready to fight. They would not give in, they would not lay down and die. The Lord was with them, and they knew this, so who could stand against them?

"Are you ready, Bo," Ravenblade asked the boy.

"Yes, God is my shield and my sword," Bo said.

"The Spirit is with you," Raven stated.

The heroes lined up, weapons in hand. The ISOD soldiers all held out their guns, ready to fire. Ravenblade raised his blade into the air and sounded the charge. The battle began. The evil army marched forward with their shields and swords, still others entered the field on the backs of the armored dinosaurs. The demonized, zombie horde charged out first in a ferocious fury and attacked the heroes. Silver bullets flew through the air, followed by swords and spears slicing and hacking at the attacking creatures. Then, the guards joined the fight. Those on foot blocked the heroes' swords and bullets with their shields and attacked with their Dark metal swords. The armored beasts stomped and bashed the heroes with their tails. The soldiers on their backs were ready to strike with their swords and shields when necessary.

While the fighting was going on all around, John looked up at Legion. He felt something overcome him. Visions of a battle long ago flashed before his eyes. They were in a snow-covered place. Legion looked very much as he did now, tall and strong, yet his armor was plated and made from Hell metal back then. In his hand, Legion held a blade that was solid black, just as the swords that Psol's army wielded. The sword had bat-like wings for the cross guard and a skull with sharp teeth as the pommel. The blade was long and sharp. John witnessed this scene through his own eyes so that he could not see his own face, but he saw that he also wore armor. It was white with intricate designs engraved all over it. He had two great, white, angelic wings, but the left

175

wing had black feathers at the tip. He glowed with a bright, white light, while Legion glowed blue then as he did now. In his own hands, John held a white sword, with a cross guard designed to look like angel wings, and the pommel looked like the sun, round and with wavy rays shining from it. His blade was long and sharp as well. The two swords were like twisted mirror images of each other – representing light and dark, order and chaos. Yes, it was the Sword of Order in his hands and Sword of Chaos in Legion's. The images flashed back and forth, bringing John in and out of reality while the war on Atlantis waged around him. On the present day battlefield, a black sword came straight for John's head. He was still thinking about the past. Luckily, Akane saw the blade and stopped it with her sword. Jack came along side, too. Together, they fought back the evil soldiers that tried to kill their friend.

"What's wrong with you?" Akane shouted at John while she blocked another attack and cut one of the guards across the arm with her blade.

John fell to the ground. The woman who loved him yelled out. She glowed brighter with a white light and cut off the head of the guard in front of her, and then blocked another. The white light of the Spirit surrounded John, just as it did Akane and Jack, but the light around John got brighter and began to crackle like electricity all around. He shot up from the ground and yelled out. Bolts of white lighting shot from his body and eradicated several of Psol's soldiers and demonized zombies that were near him. The energy crackled still more around John's entire body. His eyes glowed bright, white and it looked as if electricity was passing through them. He slammed his fist down, cracking the ground, and then he leaped into the air, like he was flying. John shot up with a trail of white electricity flowing behind him. He landed right in front of Legion on the pedestal. The images of their past battle went in and out of focus, mixing with the reality before him. He saw them fighting long ago on the snow and ice. Legion's tentacles growing out of holes in his armor as they fought a battle like no other. The sky lit up those long years ago when they both destroyed their original forms. Now, these two entities stood face to face again. Legion glowed with a deep, blue light and John crackled with white lightning.

"Legion," John said. "We meet again."

"And who are you?" Legion bellowed with the voices of thousands of demons.

"Oh, you don't remember me?" John said as the lightning flashed all around him. "I'm the one who took your body before, and now I've come back to take it again!"

"You?" Legion questioned. "You are that angel? No, you are just some pathetic mortal!"

The Nephilim grew two more tentacles from his back and grabbed John. White electricity flowed from John's body and ran up the tentacles that held him, electrocuting Legion with the light of the Spirit. John broke free from the demon's hold and grabbed Legion's arms with his hands.

"We will finish what we started ages ago," John said. Bolts of white lightning shot from his eyes "You will not win," he professed.

Hiding still behind the rock, Puck watched as a great stream of white light shot from John's mouth. Then, in an instant, John and Legion were engulfed in a bright, white light and disappeared.

***

Inside the tholos, Psol stood in front of the throne. Gideon was at his side and Simon stood before the altar with the *Necronomicon* floating before him, opened to the required page. Bianca was still chained and unconscious on the ground.

"The time is almost here for my empress to enter. Her ship is above us and, in an hour, this day will end and the third day will begin. It seems Legion has overestimated his own power. He and another have been whisked away. They are no longer on this island. Well, my troops will make quick work of those so-called heroes of the light. And if they don't, the Abyssites will. The final day is almost upon us. Once my master is here, she will make sure that victory goes to the Darkness and this final planet will fall like the rest," Psol spoke. "Gideon, your time is at hand, as well. Pandora has been waiting to meet you. Her father has told her so much about you. He has big plans for you. Dark plans." He laughed.

***

Doctor Ian Rich ran into Lieutenant Dan Marshall's office shouting, "Lieutenant, sir, you have to see this."

He had a tablet in his hand and showed the lieutenant a series of photos of a dark object with an aura of blue light around it.

"What am I looking at?" Dan asked.

"I think it's a space ship of some kind but it's hard to see. Honestly, it looks more like a monster or a giant bug than a ship. It's huge, the size of Manhattan," Ian said. "And there's something else coming too, another ship"

"Do you think this has anything to do with the Darkness?"

"Yes, I do. But I'm afraid of what's coming next, once we find out what's on board these ships."

"Well, all we can do is wait to find out and pray that our men and women out there can stop whatever it is. They all believe that God has a plan and that He is with them. For their sake, I hope they are right."

"Me too, sir, me too."

DAY III

CHAPTER X
DEATH KNOCKS THREE TIMES

"The third day is upon us and now it is time for her majesty the queen of the heavens, Pandora Ba'al Charebul, Lord Pandora, the Destroyer, to descend onto the Earth" the Dark One announced.

Psol stood before the altar awaiting the arrival of his master. Her name and title he spoke in her native tongue, a language Satan corrupted from an ancient Hebrew origin, the language of Adam and Eve. Simon Magus III, the High Sorcerer of the Darkness, also stood waiting, the *Necronomicon* open to the page that Psol requested. The book glowed with the same blue light as the orb that shone over the island. Simon read from the book, not knowing what he was saying, but following the text, which showed him phonetically what to chant. It was in the same language that Pandora was taught from her childhood. The *Necronomicon* could change the words on its pages to accommodate the reader and usually it translated its text to the reader's native language, which for Simon would have been Greek. But for this spell, the book required the reader to recite the incantation in Pandora's tongue and so the book showed Simon what to say. Gideon stood next to Psol and he held out the knife that the Dark One had given to him. The blade began to glow with the ominous, blue light. Simultaneously, the evil three looked up through the oculus in the ceiling. The blue, glowing orb that lighted up the island sky shot a beam of blue light straight upward at the undercarriage of Pandora's ship.

Her intergalactic vessel was very large indeed, as Dr. Ian Rich had calculated when the United States government's satellites detected it. It was fourteen miles long and three miles wide at the widest part. The ship was unlike any on Earth. It was solid black and looked like a giant, legless, alien insect. The outer shell appeared to be a plated exoskeleton with large thorn-like spikes all around. There were no windows, because Pandora used dark magic to see all around. But there were soft red lights along the sides of the vessel that gave it the appearance of having many eyes looking out. The ship had no technology in it anywhere, only chambers where she and her soldiers communed. The walls, floors, and ceilings were also solid black and, like the terrain inside the Darkness, it was all organic matter, as if Pandora and her army were inside of a living thing. None of them needed to eat or sleep, though she did have a dining chamber to gorge on mortal flesh when she so desired with her general, Psol. Her soulless warriors needed no sustenance and stood about in one large chamber, waiting for her command.

In the center of the ship was her throne room. Pandora sat on a throne that was shaped exactly like the onyx throne in the tholos, the one that Simon had reformed on Atlantis, except that Pandora's throne was made up of the same black, organic material as the ship's interior. In front of her and her throne, there was a pedestal with an embedded black gem that glowed with a dark light. This was her connection to the Darkness. As were all of the ship's chambers, the throne room was lit by a dim, blue light that seemed to magically glow throughout the ship. Outside, a dark light like that of the crystal surrounded the entire vessel.

Pandora leaned back on her throne. Her skin was a deep red, like the color of blood exposed to the air. The sclerae of her upturned eyes were yellow and the irises were red like her flesh, with black, narrow, snake-like pupils in the centers. The brows above them were black and well-trimmed. Her nose was perfect and straight. Her full, supple lips drew a wicked smile, showing her perfectly straight, white teeth with long pointed incisors at the top. Her chin was pointed and her face was balanced and symmetrical. She was beautiful yet demonic at the same time. Men on all planets found her irresistible but she knew no man. Satan made her this way, attractive to eye but chaste. She would indulge in every other sin but no man would defile his daughter. She was six feet tall, with a voluptuous, athletic build. Her black, organic, Darkness armor was similar to that which Legion and Gideon now wore, but her top was cut low exposing her cleavage, and the ends of the fingertips of her gauntlets were sharp and claw-like. Two great spikes shot up from her armor, one from each shoulder. She wore a short leather cape that draped behind her and in her hand she held a long black staff with a thorny texture and a long, hooked blade at the top. It was made from the same Dark metal as the Dark One's sword. On her head was a black diadem also made from the same metal. Ten large, pointed horns protruded from it all around and in the front center of the crown was one more little horn, fashioned from the same black crystal as the gem in the pedestal before her. Both the gem and the little horn glowed with the same dark light. Her hair was luxuriously thick and straight. It poured down her back like a black waterfall. She looked like a true queen of Darkness, and her smile broadened as she lit up with a blue light brighter than the one that lighted the room. Pandora shone all around, being basked in the blue glow, and then, instantly, she faded into the light. The beam of blue light connecting the orb over Atlantis to Pandora's ship, now shot down from the orb and cast itself through the oculus in the ceiling of the tholos. The beam engulfed the altar. It then widened its diameter and blanketed the entire room in the same blue light. The beam disappeared and sitting on the throne was the queen of the heavens, Pandora, in all of her sinful glory.

"Mama has arrived," Pandora said, her voice was sultry and sarcastic all at once. "I love what you've done to the place." She stood and walked over to Psol, and said, "Miss me, my dear." Then she turned to Gideon and placed her hand on his chest, "Well aren't you the strapping young man."

Pandora was almost as tall as Gideon and looked into his piercing blue eyes with hers. Her pupils dilated. The child of Darkness looked at her with no concern or interest. But he did respect her. Maybe it was because she was the daughter of Satan. Or maybe it was because she had destroyed so many worlds and murdered countless civilizations.

"Is that your sister over there?" she asked. "I've heard a lot about the two of you. To be honest, I'm not very impressed with her, though it seems the Big Man in the Sky is. But you, you, I'm very impressed with."

Pandora drew closer as she spoke and almost touched Gideon's lips with her own. The sultry empress ran her hand across his chest and then down his arm, caressing his bicep. The queen of the heavens looked him directly in the eyes again and gave a flirty wink. Simon stood back the whole time, watching, waiting to see if the evil queen would acknowledge his presence. Then she finally looked at the sorcerer, sucked her teeth, and turned back to Psol.

She patted the Dark One on the back and said, "Let's get down to business. The Three Days of Darkness are nearly over and then the fun really begins. Now, my big, cuddly, teddy bear, or should I say tall, dark, and gruesome," she said to Psol. "He must have told you all about the Three Days and what would happen when I arrived. Well, I'm not going to bore you with a recap; instead, I'm ready to start the show. It's time to dedicate this temple."

Pandora retrieved a black gem from a pouch in her belt and it glowed with the same dark light as the gem in the cave. She took it to the altar and it glowed more intensely.

"Magician!" she shouted at Simon. "Yes, I'm talking to you. You are the descendant of Simon Magus, are you not?"

"Yes, your majesty," Simon said with a bow.

"Call me your lordship or your awesomeness," Pandora jested. "Bring me my father's book."

Simon walked over with the *Necronomicon* floating beside him and immediately Pandora started to flip through the pages. She mumbled to herself, until she found the page she was looking for.

"Aha, here it is," she squealed. "Now, you must be wondering how I dominated all of those other planets without this book. Well, I actually had the book. I can summon the book whenever I like but I let my dear, old dad loan it out from time to time. I mean, he did write it after all, and in his own demon blood, too – I must add. And yes, that is demon flesh it's covered in. The perfect book binding. It will last forever."

Pandora read from the text, her voice seductive, each word coated in sin. She chanted over and over in her native tongue. The sound of her voice echoed louder and louder until it shook the tholos like a great earthquake. Pandora Ba'al Charebul's whole body was now radiating with the dark light of the gem. The empress touched it to the altar and the gem set into it. The entire altar glowed with the same darkness as the crystal and the floor around it glowed as well. The seven stars lit up with a blue glow and then they began to move and swirl around. Pandora stood back and so did Simon. Psol and Gideon remained where they were. Through it all, Bianca remained unconscious, chained up, on the floor.

The swirling stars turned into a tornado that rose to the ceiling in the center of the room. It was a great vortex with the altar at its eye. Then, from the vortex, came the most vile beast Simon or Gideon had ever seen. The creature looked like a perverse amalgamation of a horse, a locust, and a man. The face had a demonic appearance and its long, unkempt hair flowed behind its head. Its wings fluttered at a rapid pace, making the sound of countless steeds rushing into battle. It opened its mouth wide, and unhinged its jaw like a snake. Its teeth were jagged and terrifying, and the stinger at the end of its tail dripped with venom. The beast gave out a bloodcurdling cry. Then more and more of these same creatures rushed out of the vortex. They each cried out and flew from the tholos, through the oculus, to the valley below. It was time for them to devour God's champions and prepare the way for the rest of their kin, to deliver the souls of all humanity from the Earth to the Darkness. This was just the beginning. These creatures would cover the island and wait for the end of the third day. Once it was over, Abaddon and the six other Angels of Darkness would come from the Abyss and send forth these creatures to plague mankind until all life was harvested and gathered into the Darkness. Finally, Abaddon would release the essence of the Darkness itself to completely blanket the Earth with its pure evil, and drain every bit of energy from the planet until it was left void, as it was in the beginning, when darkness was over the face of the deep. Pandora gave out a bellowing laugh and sat down on her throne, looking anxiously into the vortex as the Abyssites exited and went out to feast.

"I am going with them," Gideon stated. "I am bored here and would like to spill some blood with my own hands."

He jumped onto the back of one of the exiting Abyssites and took off toward the valley.

***

Down in the valley, the heroes were still battling against the dark army before them. Akane had seen the love of her life disappear with that evil monster, Legion. She wondered where they had gone and prayed that, wherever John was, he was safe.

For now, she had to focus on the fight in front of her. A bright, white glow encompassed Akane Yamamoto's body and lit up the blade in her hand. With unmatched grace, she took to the air and stealthily flipped over the zombies and guards in front of her. Her body twisted in the air and then her foot slammed out, meeting her target – one of the guards that rode atop one of the armor-plated beasts. She knocked the guard off of his beast and finished with her blade in the guard's chest. She pulled it out and took his head, leaving a pile of ash where he had laid. All around her, war was being waged. Silver bullets flew through the air; blades clashed in showers of sparks. But for the former leader of the Children of the Dragon's stealth force, the only thing she saw was red. She cut down more and more of the dark forces in front of her. The armored beast, whose rider she'd decapitated, went on a rampage and, without any warning, clubbed the heroic woman from behind with its tail. Her neck snapped as she rolled over and then one of the guards stabbed her through the gut with his sword. The world became dark for a moment. Thoughts of John flooded her head. *Where was he? Would she ever see him again?* Blood poured from her wound. The blood reminded her of who she was before and who she was now – the blood she had spilled and then the blood that was spilled to save her life. Akane was saved by grace and one day she would go home to her Lord, but today was not that day. The guard still leaned over her, with the sword implanted deep into her belly. Akane opened her eyes and, without a second thought, she lifted her hips and sent her knee hard into the skull of her attacker. His helmet cracked and he fell back. Glowing with the light of the Holy Spirit, Akane stood. She pulled the sword from her gut and used it to decapitate its owner. Then she threw the sword onto the pile of ash on the ground, and picked up her own blade. This fight was not over.

Jack ran toward her, taking the heads of guards in his path. The guards' armor was strong but the heroes had weapons forged from Angel metal and Hell metal making them able to cut through the armor of their enemies. On the other side of the fields, Ravenblade was surrounded by demonized zombies. He grinned and gutted them all, one by one. The creatures quickly healed only to be sliced again and again. The immortal was having fun with his attackers and finally began to take their heads. Lyles and Bo fought hard, as well, their blades covered in the blue blood of the undead creatures. Bo fired a beam of light like a blade and took the head of one of the creatures that was about to attack his father. The ISOD soldiers filled the monsters and their guards with silver rounds, and followed that with strikes from their Hell-metal spears, to finally take down their enemies. Shanson and Jenny fought back to back, taking down as many of their enemies as they could. God was with these heroes as they fought but the enemy was not out yet. The blue, glowing orb still lit up the sky and, thanks to its light, the band of heroes saw something coming from the distance, like a swarm of locusts. The sound of their wings was like rushing waves. Ravenblade and Jack knew right away what they were and so did Leina. The Amazon-like warrior hit one of the guards in front of her with the butt of her staff and then cut off the heads of two more. One of the armored dinosaur beasts charged at her. She spun and stabbed it through the side, pulling her blade to rend it open, and then she cut off its head. The beast's rider jumped down on her and pushed her to the ground. They rolled back and forth. Her staff held back his sword, while he drove his shield into her chest. Another guard came down at her head with his blade but she was able to finally flip the man on top of her and send him into the one trying to skewer her skull.

Leina stood; she had seen this before when she was child on her world and on countless other worlds that they were unable to save. The past failures flooded her mind and she began to lose hope. Jack and Akane came up behind her and so did Bo with Lyles. They were all glowing with the light of the Spirit. *This battle will be different*, she thought, and the Holy Spirit filled her. Leina glowed with a bright, white light as her friends did. Her light grew brighter and brighter, and seeing the approaching Abyssite army filled her with a righteous anger toward God's enemies. The spirit-filled warrior threw back her head and called out to God for help. Instantly, her spirit was raised to the level known as Chaos Fury. The Lord was with her and His anger toward evil burned inside of her. All of the adversaries before her fell, one by one, to her bladed staff. She defeated demonic zombies, Pandora's guards, even the mutant armored beasts. She was focused and driven by the Spirit of God. Blue blood and ash covered the ground. Then, at the sound of the approaching swarm, she stopped, as did all around her. Everyone looked up.

These new creatures were hideous beyond compare and Lyles could hear the description of the locusts from the book of Revelation in his head. That's what these were. All they were missing were the golden crowns but that gave him hope that this was not the end, that and the fact that the rapture had not yet taken place. Even the dark army stopped advancing and moved back. The heroes did the same, seeing this as a moment to take a break from the battle and plan their next move.

The Abyssites landed one by one and separated the evil army from the warriors of light. They were like a great wall; hundreds of them stood still, their wings behind their backs. Finally, one more landed. On its back was a young man wearing some kind of organic black armor, just as Legion had. The heroes all wondered who this was.

Jay and Shanson looked at him carefully and so did Jenny. Then it came to them – this was the boy they had fought in the Chaldean's stronghold. Ravenblade also knew who he was. He could sense the young man's dark energy. Yes, it was Gideon, Bianca's brother and a child of the Darkness. He sat like a great ruler upon his demonic steed. He wore a knife at his side, the very knife that Psol had given to him, the same weapon that the Devil had given to his daughter Pandora. Gideon drew the knife, raised it to the sky, and looked down at all the puny human beings and former angels below him. They were nothing but weak piles of flesh. He was mortal, certainly, but his soul was Darkness incarnate. He would not be subject to them – he was so much more powerful than they were – this was what he believed.

"It's over," Gideon commanded from the back of the creature.

The Abyssite gave an ear-piercing screech, then the rider placed his hand on its head and it became calm.

"All of this is futile," Gideon continued. "You are all nothing before me. Look at you, pathetic and weak. This won't even be a challenge. Where is your hope, now? Where is your victory? In your God? Ha, I am a god of power. I am almighty!"

The creature cried out again then flapped its wings violently. The entire swarm of Abyssites followed suit and together they created a powerful wind that started to drive back the heroes. *Is there truly no hope?* they thought. But then the Spirit provided the hope that their hearts lacked. God gave them the gift of unwavering faith at the moment when they were at their weakest.

Leina stood tall at the head of the group and spoke, "We will not give up. No! We will rely on God for strength! He is our right arm, our sword, and our shield, our rock, our protector. In the darkest hour, the light will always shine. Let us be that light that Christ called us to be, for the nations of this world and for all men and women across the universe! Our hope is in the Lord!"

Altogether, the heroes charged at the beasts head on. Gideon laughed and flew straight upward. He watched from on high as the Abyssites attacked the warriors of light. The members of ISOD fired their silver rounds at the creatures but they had no effect, for the bullets were not strong enough to break through their exoskeletons. They needed something stronger. Jay tried with his laser but it failed as well. Raven and those alongside him took to the beasts with their swords. The Ravenblade cut through one of the Abyssite's legs, but the demon hit the immortal with its tail and sent him down. Then several of the ISOD soldiers were struck. The demonic beasts tore at their flesh and caused this day's first fatalities, on the side of good. Two more of Shanson's soldiers were struck down, their chests impaled by the stingers on the Abyssite's tails. Their souls drained from their bodies. The heroes retreated but there was nowhere to run. From above, Gideon laughed at their losses. These men and women were all doomed and they would now spend eternity inside the Darkness, feeding the evil that would take over all creation.

Yet, hope was not dead. The heroes continued to retreat and the swarm of demons followed close behind. Just as they were about to attack, something whizzed through the air and struck one of the beasts in the chest. It broke the creature's armored exoskeleton and then exploded, sending the monster to the ground. More of these missiles fired and struck down the creatures. The Abyssites began to fall one by one. Gideon looked out toward the horizon. What could be doing this to his swarm of dark demons?

Then he saw them. A fleet of triangular jets. They were sleek and a metallic, dark green. Their windshields were tinted so Gideon could not see the pilots but he could sense they were mere men. Who were these insubordinate nuisances? Ravenblade looked up and saw the Holy Seal on the wing of one of the jets. It was them, the Council of His Holy Order. They had come to stop the world from falling into the Darkness. Ravenblade knew this order well and knew that they had eyes and ears around the globe. They also had Heavenly connections and very little went past their glance. Yes, the Vatican was aware of the Three Days of Darkness and Atlantis. They had come to help in the war.

Gideon flew to one of the jets, which fired a missile at his Abyssite. Before it could strike, Gideon retaliated with a beam of black light that disintegrated the missile and then he did the same to the jet that fired it. Two more of the Council's jets fired missiles at the beast. Gideon threw out both hands and shot out more beams of black light that disintegrated those missiles and the jets as well. A third jet had fired from behind at the same moment of Gideon's counterattack and this missile pierced deep into the back of the monster that Gideon rode. The missile exploded and the beast fell to the Earth. The child of Darkness was thrown to the ground and looked up in anger. He was humiliated. Gideon stood on his feet and fired another beam at the jet that took down his Abyssite and, like the others, it was annihilated. Then he vaporized two more. But one fired a missile right at his chest. Gideon looked at the projectile coming for him and did not budge. The missile struck dead center and exploded. Everyone looked where Gideon stood. The dust cleared and Gideon stood tall, unscathed by the attack.

"Like I said, futile!" he shouted.

More missiles were fired at him and nothing happened. Gideon laughed and destroyed two more jets. The rest of the fleet, the seven that remained, branched off and flew back to regroup. Their attacks had no effect and they would need a different strategy. One of the jets landed near the heroes, and a man stepped out. He wore a dark green field uniform. His helmet and visor the same color. He had an automatic rifle in his right hand and something was slung across his back – the Spear of

Destiny. The man took off his helmet.

"Aberto Ruggero," Ravenblade said.

"Aberto!" Lyles shouted and ran to embrace his old friend.

"Lyles," Aberto said. "When did you wake up? Praise God, my friend. Glory to God in the Highest!"

"And peace to his people on Earth," Jay Sil said and walked over. He took his helmet off as well. And who are you? God's militia, the army of the Holy See?"

"Actually, that's pretty close," Aberto said in his perfect American-English accent.

The heroes watched Gideon, who stood there watching them. The evil young man was curious what they would do, and his sadistic nature led him to enjoy this cat-and-mouse game. No one knew what to do to stop this evil man. Ravenblade and Lyles knew Aberto well. This man was one of the most elite warriors on Earth, highly skilled in all forms of hand-to-hand combat, firearms, and pretty much any other weapon he could find. He was also well versed in every known language around the world, and learned to speak them as a true national – adapting his tongue to mimic local accents and slang as well. He could move throughout the world unnoticed if he chose, and easily take down any enemy of God and His Church. That was the purpose of his many years of training. From the time he was a boy, the Catholic Church took him in. He learned the laws of the Church and the Laws of God. It was his duty to serve God with all his heart, mind, and soul. That was how he was raised, a true soldier through and through. The Council of His Holy Order was a secret arm of the Catholic Church that brought the fight, literally, straight to the Devil in the war between good and evil. The Church was not perfect; over time, there had been plenty of man-made laws and statutes that they followed to protect their position and the institution. But at the heart of the Church was Christ crucified and the blood of Jesus did cover Aberto. He was a man and therefore flawed but he loved his Lord and Christ was indeed his Savior. Aberto prayed every day – he was praying now even while speaking with his old friends and new allies. He prayed for God to deliver them from this present evil.

"I am General Aberto Ruggero of the Council of His Holy

Order," he said with a very polite tone.

"I'm Sergeant Jay Sil of the FDSR, man of the people," Jay said with a smirk. "So, how did you find us here? And what did you fire at those beasts to take them down. I tried firing a laser of silver atoms at them but it did not so much as scratch them. Though it seems spiritual weapons could cut them but the beasts still healed."

"The Church sees everything," Aberto stated.

"Hmm, well I hope there's some things it doesn't see," Jay jested.

"You're a funny guy, I can see," Aberto continued. "But this is no time for jokes. Those missiles we fired at them were blessed. The shells were a high-grade metal alloy but their important part was the holy water inside. It is not magical, but spiritual. When you turn to God and He truly sanctifies something with the Holy Spirit, it takes on other properties. Holy water can in fact hurt demons and all unclean beasts. There is a basis of truth to every tale. But we don't have time to discuss the dogma of this. We must stop this Darkness. The Council has been preparing for the Three Days of Darkness for centuries. I have trained for this day my whole life. The instant we saw the signs, the Earth covered in pitch black, so that no one could see their own hand in front of their face, we knew what had happened. Of course, we detected the dark energy emitting from this location and also had records of where Atlantis once stood. So we came here to stop whatever it was that brought the Darkness to this world."

"Legion is back," Lyles said.

"Where is he?" Aberto asked and grabbed the spear from his back. "I will send him to the second death myself."

"Last time you did that you only released his spirit. Remember, he and Lyles were trapped together in the skull. But now we have our friend back. Legion is gone; he disappeared with one of our own. The one Legion is with is an old friend and I pray God gives him the strength he had in days past. If so, he can stop Legion. But we have bigger problems," Ravenblade explained.

Then the immortal told Aberto all he needed to know about Pandora and the Dark One, Psol. He also quickly explained about Gideon, who stood there now, and who may possibly be the Antichrist. The heroes did not believe this was the end but, regardless, human lives and human souls were in danger. These men and women had to stop Pandora from bringing the Darkness into the world. Aberto called for his forces to land their jets. They needed to find a better way to fight this villain. They needed to pray and let God lead them.

The jets landed in formation and the pilots each climbed out. The seven soldiers, strong and courageous men and women, walked over to their general. Jay called Shanson and the ISOD team. The other heroes came over as well. The Abyssites that had been taken down still lay unmoving on the ground. The rest of the Abyssites stood behind Gideon and the dark army, with the demon zombies aligned behind them. The camps had been divided once again.

This entire time, Gideon stood back, watching these mortals talk, waiting to make his move. The heroes knew Gideon was toying with them somehow but they had used the lull to their advantage, to give Aberto the background he needed. And they were ready at any moment to react to their enemy.

"Do you, fools, really think you can stop the Darkness from destroying this world, and taking all of its souls into itself?" Gideon questioned. "The third day will come to a close very soon. There is nothing you can do. And before that happens, I will make an example of you all. I will show you my true power. I've let you live long enough. You are all just wasting time talking, while I can destroy you with a wave of my hand." He boasted. "Do you think this is a game?"

Gideon was now perceived by many to be the prophesied Man of Perdition and, whether or not that was true, he certainly wielded horrible, demonic power. As the heroes watched, Gideon lifted his left hand into the air. The claws of his dark-armored hand clenched into a fist that began to glow with a blue light like the orb over the island. The glow grew in radiance and then he opened his hand again and the light shot out all around. The Abyssites that were on the ground stood up again and all of these locust-like beasts took to the air. Gideon turned around and saw the whole of the dark army arrayed behind him: Pandora's guards, armor-plated dinosaur beasts, and hordes of demon zombies. Gideon smiled and then reached out both hands, releasing the same black light he'd used earlier in the battle. The dark beam of light spread out and devoured the entire dark army. This man was truly insane. He killed all of his own troops. Not even ashes remained where they once stood. Gideon turned around and laughed. Then he put out his hands toward the heroes.

"You're next," he said.

The same black light that devoured the evil soldiers now shot out toward the band of heroes. Before the black light could engulf them, a bright, white force field surrounded them and blocked the attack. Gideon grew angry and fired again, only to have his dark beam of light blocked once more by the force field of white light. The heroes inside all wondered what had happened, all except one of them.

Leina looked up and said, "Carlel."

***

The massive Isharian spacecraft held over twelve thousand people from around the universe but it was dwarfed by Pandora's monstrous dark ship. Carlel had docked the Isharian ship over the island, just outside the atmosphere of the Earth. From the island below, Pandora could sense her enemies docking near her ship, but she held back her hand because she felt them to be no threat to her plan.

The ship displayed the technology that the Isharian people learned from the heavenly beings that helped them escape their dying world. The people on the ship were all those who remained from Ishara and also others that they freed from the other planets that the Darkness had destroyed. Watcher angels had come to Ishara before Pandora and prepared them to flee their world. God had a purpose for these people to travel the cosmos and aid in His plan to bring an end to the Darkness one day. Leina was young at the time and her brother, Psol, even younger when Pandora twisted his mind. He was twelve and Leina was fifteen. Their people lived longer than those on Earth, just like men and women did before the Flood. An average life span lasted at least nine-hundred years. They would age as we normally did on Earth until they reached their twenties. Then the aging slowed

194

down so that, by the time they were three hundred years old, they had just started to hit middle age. Old age set in around six hundred years old. It was like this on all the other planets. Carlel was even older than his sister. He was one hundred and eleven when she was born. Her mother struggled to have more children after Carlel, but then one day God blessed her with Leina and finally, only three years later, with Psol.

The Isharian ship was shaped like a cross from above and ran two thousand feet long and seven hundred feet wide at its widest point. Like Noah's ark, this ship was meant to save its passengers from destruction. And, also like the ark, it was made of elements from the physical world and not of the spiritual plane. The metals, the wiring, all of it was pure science and technology that God had instituted in this world to give men and women the ability to progress in the universe He had created. But the people of Ishara did not have the knowledge, at the time, to build such a ship so God sent His messengers to aid them. The angels worked hand in hand with their prophet Antila, showing him the plans and explaining how to put it all together. The outside of the ship was sleek, the metal plates welded tightly and evenly. The glass windows were large and strong. They allowed the people to see outside into the vastness of space but they were tinted so no one could look in. In the front of the ship was a grand room that they used for worship and was much like a church with pews and a pulpit. A large windshield at the front allowed them to see out while they praised their God. Two large sections shot out from either side of the ship to give it its cross-like shape, and it had no wings but rather fins like sails, three on each side section and one large one on the back. In the center and elevated from the ship was a large glass dome where Carlel captained the ship and had a three hundred and sixty degree view of space. This was where he stood now, with the men that just boarded his ship hours ago.

To travel across the vastness of space, Antila the great prophet of Ishara, was shown a way. The mortal universe was created parallel to, or more accurately, on top of the Abyss – the realm of the Darkness. The Watcher angels showed Antilla, when he built the ship, that when God created the physical world He used the light of the stars to hold back the Darkness and trap it behind the physical plane. But seven of these stars fell into the Darkness' depths and became the first black holes, even before the Earth was formed. Other stars fell later and became black holes also, the number of which was unfathomable. These black holes were open portals to the Darkness and allowed travel from the physical plane into the Darkness' realm called the Abyss. The angels also taught Antila how to build a device that could create a man-made black hole for a short time to allow the ship to go into the Darkness and then escape out another black hole to the ship's destination. Using this technology, Carlel followed Pandora across the cosmos; she used the very same science to travel to the planets as well. Carlel and Leina knew Pandora would eventually go to Earth but they also knew that God had placed a protective seal on the planet. Leina had planned to come first and prepare the people of Earth for Pandora's arrival in hopes of defeating her, but Eishe stole that pod and Leina followed him for two hundred years. Meanwhile, Carlel continued to pursue Pandora and watched and waited for her next move. It had been two centuries since he last saw his sister, and for two hundred years Pandora sat at the edge of Earth's solar system, waiting to make her breach. She had to wait for the shift in the balance of Earth's inhabitants toward evil and the rejection of God. But now it had all unfolded and Pandora was on Earth ready to bring forth the Darkness and destroy the last planet with life in the entire universe.

For the last few hours, Carlel got to know the men that boarded his ship. The Command Station, as it was known, was about one hundred feet in diameter and encased in a tinted glass dome. There were four stations, each with a circular table and ten chairs each within the dome. The furniture was all made from wood that came from the planet Ishara. The tables were all sections of giant sequoia-like trees from that world and were about ten feet in diameter. They were glazed with a clear coating so you could still see the rings to show the age of the tree when it was cut down. The chairs were made from the same wood and carved exquisitely to look like branches, with leafy and floral designs carved in to them. In the center of the room was a large cushioned chair that sat on top of a ten-foot round metal platform.

A ring of soft, white light surrounded it on the floor and the room itself was lit by a soft, white light. They could see out into space, though there was little to see but stars and, below, where the Earth should be they only saw a black orb, for Darkness covered the entire planet. Thanks to the ship's spotlights outside, they could see Pandora's ship docked next to them. It looked like a giant insect, ready to devour the planet below.

During the time since these men boarded his ship, Captain Carlel heard all of their stories and told them his own. Roger and Eishe had heard much of it from Leina, his sister, but hearing his perspective gave them new twists on the stories. Leina was young when taken aboard the ship but Carlel was already a man. His sister rose up to lead the people, especially after Antila passed away. He was killed on one of the other planets they tried to rescue from the clutches of the evil queen of the heavens. Leina was the first ever female spiritual leader of her people, chosen by Christ, for her heart was focused on Him. Her faith was strong and her friends knew that already. The Holy Spirit filled her and led her as she led her people. Carlel was a believer but his faith was never as unwavering as hers. He knew she was the best leader for their people and he was happy to command this ship, under her guidance.

It was time to end Pandora's reign, and all of them were ready to help. Nathan, Roger, and Eishe, would go to the tholos and face Pandora and Psol. Carlel and Radix would take the three thousand fighting men and women that were on this ship, those who came from all those worlds that had been destroyed, including Carlel's home world of Ishara, and meet with Leina and the others to fight the Abyssites. Coz decided to remain on the ship. He was still struggling with having faith in a good God. Like he had seen inside of the Darkness, if he went down to fight this war, he would only aid that evil force by drawing on its own power. Coz gave his blessing to Eishe. The master held his old sword in his hands again and then turned to Eishe and gave it back to him. He told his former pupil that the blade was his now. The Dragon's Heart – Itaru Taninaru – belonged to Eishe Taninaru – the Dragon's fire. Eishe was grateful for his master's blessing and prayed that he could let go and find faith in Christ.

197

The warrior from Aporia vowed to claim victory and come back to teach his master more about his new found faith.

It was time to go. Carlel had already created a force field around the heroes who stood on Atlantis, to stop them from being killed by the dark power that Gideon wielded. Carlel was monitoring the situation and now it was time to end this war. Carlel, Radix, and the three thousand warriors walked onto the many teleportation devices set up on the arms of the ship. Meanwhile, Nathan, Roger, and Eishe vanished on their own, Nathan using the same new technique he learned while inside the Darkness to teleport wherever his mind focused. What he focused on now was the tholos on Atlantis, where Pandora sat on her newly dedicated throne.

***

Back on Earth, John and Legion appeared face to face in a cold, icy land. The wind blew violently and the ground was covered in snow and ice. Nothing fell from the sky but the snow on the ground was from years of accumulation, for the snow never melted here; it blew around in the large gusts of wind. John covered his face but the cold did not seem to faze him. His body glowed with a bright, white light and white lightning crackled all around him still. Legion was not bothered by the subfreezing temperatures either. He let the snow crash against him and fall to the ground. The dark armor that covered his body glowed with a dark light like the crystal inside of the cave on Atlantis. His eyes lit up blue and then so did his hands. The light coming from John and Legion's bodies gave them enough light to see in the Darkness that surrounded them and the whole Earth. The snow and ice beneath Legion's feet began to melt and, without a second thought, he grabbed John by the throat. The evil fiend moved too fast for the former angel to stop him and his grip was tight. Legion lifted John into the air and then slammed him onto the ground.

"Seems like we are back to where we left off, the one with No Name," Legion said in the voice of thousands of demons. He held John to the ground and spoke again, "Last time we fought, you had the Sword of Order and I the Sword of Chaos. You have no weapons now and look at you. In the body of a pathetic mortal.

198

But me, I have been restored."

The dark armor that covered the demon grew spikes all around and once again tentacles grew from his back and dug into the ground. Legion's whole body glowed brighter and brighter with the blue light, and the ground began to glow as well.

"Yes," he bellowed. "It is still here."

Four more tentacles came from Legion's chest and each grabbed one of John's legs and arms. Legion let go of John's throat and the tentacles lifted him into the air. The man once known as the Angel with No Name tried with all his might to break free from the Nephilim's hold. John was filled with the righteous anger of God at the enemy before him. This murdering demon was ready to join the Darkness in conquering the universe and to defy the God who created everything. John knew the Lord, not just in his heart, but he knew Him personally. He had served the Lord in Heaven before the Earth was created and before Satan fell and waged the First War. John was an angel but unlike any other ever created by God. He was the personification of the order of God's creation. And the demon that held him now was the personification of the chaos and evil that was cast out of Heaven before God created the physical universe and sealed it away. The Darkness was the embodiment of evil, the Abyss was the plane it resided on, and the mortal plane sat right on top of it, holding back the Darkness. The Darkness looked to snuff out the order that God created and to drive all creation into sin and evil.

John struggled but he could not break free of Legion's grasp. He shouted to Heaven for God to save him, for the Lord to vanquish his enemy. The white lightning that surged through and around his body electrified the demon who held him but nothing broke the hold that Legion had. No matter what happened, John did not give up and he kept his faith in the Lord. He could feel the Holy Spirit working inside of him, and telling him that God would win the fight.

Legion laughed at the man in his grasp. The monster remembered the man when he was a mighty angel and pitied him in his current state. *What a weak creature*, he thought. Then he glowed even brighter with the blue light. One of the demon's tentacles came up from the icy terrain, and holding a sword.

It was black from its skull-shaped pommel to its long, pointed tip. The skull had sharp, jagged teeth and deep, foreboding eye sockets. Bat-like wings grew from the sides of the hilt to become the cross guard. The sword was sinister and sinful in every way. The tentacle retracted itself into Legion's body and his left hand took the sword from it. He held the sword up high and gave out an echoing laugh that sounded like a cackling horde of demons from the depths of the Darkness. It was time to end this fight. The Sword of Chaos glowed with the same blue light as the Nephilim that held it. John looked at the blade and cried out to God, for he knew what was next. His arms and legs were held tight and the hero could not move. His body glowed brighter and brighter with the light of the Spirit and the white lightning surged all around him.

Legion pulled back his left arm and then thrust the blade into John's heart. The former angel lifted up his eyes to Heaven and from his mouth came a name that no one could understand except God Himself. It was the name that John was given when he was created by God and, with that, his life left his body. Legion released the man and left him lying on the snow. Blood poured from his chest and turned the snow red beneath him. Another hero had fallen to the Darkness. Another warrior of light had been snuffed out.

CHAPTER XI
OUT OF THE ABYSS

The Darkness somehow grew even darker as the final hours of the third day were upon the Earth. From all around, angels, demons, and all otherworldly beings watched and waited to see what would unfold. God knew what would transpire, yet no one else did. He had laid out His plan for all who followed Him in His Word. Yet not everyone believed in His Word or understood what it said. But those who did know His Word and trusted in Him had hope.

Michael and Christopher were two of these beings watching everything unfold on the planet where the Lord first put life, before Satan defiled creation with sin, and spread the seed of mankind throughout the cosmos. The Archangel and the transcended man stood at the edge of Heaven. It was the plane of Heaven that sat metaphysically on the cusp of the physical universe, and was where the angels watched what transpired throughout the universe. They did this by looking through one of the many portals that floated about the plane. Otherwise, the entire expanse of the edge of Heaven was just bright, white light. In one portal in front of them, they watched the farmland of Atlantis and saw the heroes standing strong against Gideon and the dark power he wielded, a force field of light protecting them from their foe. That light was cast from a ship above the atmosphere, a ship that many believers from the fallen worlds had used to travel the cosmos and chase down the wicked daughter of the Devil, the queen of the heavens, Pandora.

Michael and Christopher saw a man that they had trained, a man who had transcended like Christopher toward the light. The giant, transcended warrior named Christopher had a special attachment to this man whose name was Nathaniel Salvatore. Nathaniel reminded Christopher of himself. No, Nathan was not as big and strong as the giant saint, but he was tough and bold. He spoke too much and always fought with all of his heart. Christopher was deemed a saint by the Catholic Church for bringing many to Christ during his lifetime and for giving his own life for Christ, when he became a martyr, beheaded for his beliefs. Before that, he was a great warrior and, at nearly eight feet tall and broad as an ox, he fought like no other man on Earth. When he was young, Christopher was brash and cared only about strength and power, serving whomever was the most powerful king in the land. That led Christopher to fight for the Devil for many years. Over time, he came to see weakness in that master and left him to follow the true King and Master, Jesus Christ. While carrying people across a raging stream, Christopher one day carried Christ appearing as a child and, when he obeyed the Lord, Christopher's staff was transformed into a palm tree. Knowing the story of Christopher brought faith in their Savior to uncounted new believers. Christopher continued to follow the Lord and one day he chose not to fight. When asked to live and serve the evils of man, he chose to die and serve God. His head was taken and he transcended three days later.

Nathan died fighting Radix but, after the sun rose on the next day. This forfeited Radix's contract with Satan and sent that villain to his master, to be tortured until the day of judgment. Nathan, laying down his life to serve God, transcended three days later. Shortly after he rose from the dead, the hero went to Heaven and trained under Michael and Christopher. Before those things occurred, Nathan, who had been raised body and soul by God, met his Savior in the Garden of Eden, which was now on one of Heaven's planes, guarded by the cherubim and a flaming sword. Nathan found out later that he had been given the Armor of God and that included the Sword of the Spirit, the Word of God. When Nathan broke into Hell to find and free his nephew, Gideon, he discovered the armor and used it to battle Satan's army, but to no avail. His teachers, this angel and the transcended man, had watched Nathan get imprisoned by Satan and hung like a trophy in his throne room for many years. They wept at the fate of this man whom they cared for and loved. Now, he was free, once again wearing Christ's armor and carrying His sword and shield. And surprisingly, next to him, was the very fiend who had ended his life. Yes, Radix Malorum stood next to Nathaniel Salvatore on the side of good for the first time since he fell to Satan's schemes.

Michael and Christopher were unsure how this battle would play out and where this once-evil man's heart truly rested. All men and women have the chance to be saved, no matter what evil crimes they commit, for all mortals sin and fall short of the glory of God. Somehow, the deal Radix had made left him unkillable after his contract with Satan expired. He still had a chance to make things right with Christ, not through good works, but by choosing to believe in Him and the salvation that only He could bring. They wondered if Radix would make the choice and declare Christ as his Savior.

Michael and Christopher looked back at Earth, inside the tholos atop the mountain on Atlantis, the place where Michael's own brothers held council when the Watcher angels dwelled on Earth. Pandora sat there with a dark grin on her face. Psol and the dark Sorcerer Simon Magus III were at her side. Bianca, the girl that Michael was sworn to protect, lay unconscious on the floor, his very medal still around her neck. Yet, by order of the Highest Power, God the Father, Michael could not help her this time. His hand was stayed. He could only watch and pray, for even the mightiest of angels prayed to God. For only God was all powerful and only He could bring salvation.

***

On Earth, the Darkness was thick and deep. Death filled the air and with it the very being whose name was Death collected the souls of those who were dying around the world. Some people died of natural causes during the dreadful Three Days of Darkness and others died from fear. Some died by violence, mutilated by the feral beasts, pestilence, and the demon zombies that tore them apart. Death himself had gone around the globe all day and night collecting the souls of men and women as he always had. It seemed like an endless job, with so many people dying each moment. But thanks to his ability to travel from his world, through portals down each corridor of Limbo, he could be at the right places at the right times to collect their souls, no matter how much time elapsed on Earth. This grim being, however, had realized something strange. He knew that, on Atlantis, Pandora and her dark general had restored the tholos as a temple, the place where the Watchers had held council thousands of years before, a temple to the very Darkness that was now plaguing the Earth. Soon, the third day would end and, through that same temple,

204

the Darkness would enter the Earth.

Death also noticed that, in New York City's financial district, there emanated a great and evil energy and he knew why. Satan had set up direct gateways to Hell around the Earth and, in New York City where the World Trade Center once stood, there was a gateway more powerful than the others. These gateways allowed evil to pass to and from Hell to the Earth though only in a spiritual sense. Demons could only escape Hell and come to Earth if they were conjured by a spell or powerful enough, like Satan, to reach the necessary spiritual frequency. That was God's law and even the Devil had to obey God's laws, for they were absolute. Yes, Hell had a direct connection to the Earth and this gave way to the old beliefs of Hades and Sheol being subterranean worlds hidden within the Earth and of a doorway leading to them. But now Death could feel more than just the power of Hell coming from this portal. He could feel a darker and more sinful power. He felt the Darkness itself, though there was nothing he could do about it. He had no interaction with the mortal world, except to collect the dead, and that is what he did. A mother and daughter lay dead on the street. Demonic creatures ate their flesh. But their souls would find rest. All over the world this happened but no witnesses would live to tell of it and the governments did not understand it or know what to do. Like so many others, government officials believed that feral animals and pestilence were the cause of all the deaths around the globe at this time. But a few people knew the truth. Death would continue on as the Darkness grew thicker and darker around the world. And a worse fate waited for the world once the doorway was opened to the Abyss and the entire Earth was drained of all its life.

**

In another part of the city, Judy had just finished giving another news update about the strange circumstances that the world was experiencing. Authorities had asked news outlets not to send reporters outside, so due to its fear of being sued, or shut down, the station followed the rules. Judy would have been out on the street, anyway, if she wasn't eight months pregnant. It was hard enough to do her regular anchor duties now, but in the past, she was a different person, always ready to get the next story, and willing to do whatever that took, no matter how dangerous. That was how she met Jay. When she was young and carefree. He caught her breaking into a building to get a story about a man whom Radix had murdered, although at the time she did not know that the killer was supernatural. Then she and Jay infiltrated an underground fight circuit, to try and take down the Chaldean and that action almost cost Jay his life and hers as well. This brought them closer together and led them to start dating. Now, they had been married for three years and were expecting a baby.

Judy sat at the anchor desk, drinking water during a break. Downstairs, one of the guards walked over to the front door. The entire entryway was glass, including the revolving doors. He couldn't see well outside but the guard saw someone trying to push through the locked revolving door. The guard tapped on the glass to get the guy's attention and tell him to go away. The man outside paid no attention to the guard, so the guard, not thinking too clearly, opened one of the side glass doors and shouted for the man to get lost. In an instant, the man ran to the door and shoved his way in, knocking the guard to the ground. Once he was inside, the guard could see the man clearly. His whole head was decrepit and almost looked like it was decaying before his very eyes. His face was pale with a blue tint and his skin shriveled. Dark purple circles rimmed the man's eyes and his eyes were closed. His hair was stark white and his hands were bony with sharp jagged nails. The guard tried to stand while staring wide-eyed at the man, his tattered clothing and his ghastly face. The sharp nails came toward him. Then the intruder opened his eyes and the guard saw them clearly. Bright, glowing, blue lights were all the guard could see where the man's eyes should be. The man unhinged his jaw and opened his mouth wide to reveal sharp, vicious teeth. Two large horns began to grow from the man's head and he took on a demonic form; his muscles bulged against his clothing all over. Blood splattered everywhere as the demonic man ripped the guard's arms from his body and then bent down to eat his flesh.

Two more guards ran into the lobby from the security room. They witnessed the gruesome sight of their fellow guard being eaten by the demonic creature, right before their eyes, and they opened fire. Blue blood shot out of the creature as the bullets entered its flesh. A horrific roar came from the monster's mouth and then it got up and ran toward the other two guards who emptied their pistols into the creature. It reached them and tore them apart, munching on hunks of their flesh. Looking all around, the creature who had once been a man, saw an open doorway leading to a stairwell and it rushed in that direction. Like a rabid animal, it climbed up the stairs, using its hands as an extra pair of feet.

Most of the building was empty but the news floor was filled with people who were reporting around the clock about the strange Darkness that covered the world. The creature smelled their blood and bounded through the open doorway onto the studio floor. The stairway led out to the elevator corridor and the station's reception desk was straight ahead. A receptionist was not at the desk and the creature ran past it and broke through the glass door next to it, the door that led into the recording studio.

Without warning, the monster attacked the camera operators, the grips, and all the staff on hand. Screams of pain and panic flooded the room. They were all too terrified to snap photos of the creature but one woman tried to dial 911, only to have her intestines ripped out before she could complete the call. Judy saw the creature and knew right away that this was a demon or a supernatural monster. She had to run and hide. Not only was her life at stake but so was the baby inside of her. Fear filled her heart and tears came rushing down. She prayed as she ran to find a hiding place. All those around her were being mutilated by this beast. It was tragic but there was nothing she could do to help them. How could she fight this creature? She would end up dead with all of them. She went inside a utility closet and locked the door. The demonic zombie was too busy devouring the rest of the staff to pay her any attention. They were all dead every one of them. Only Judy was still alive. She prayed to God to end this nightmare and to help her and the baby get out safely. A miracle is what she needed, divine intervention. But with the Darkness that covered the Earth, and the stench of death that filled the air, there seemed to be no hope.

God, where are You? Show yourself! Save me! Please, God, save me! she prayed.

***

In the East Village, Dr. David Davis sat with his wife, Martha, and their friend, Kimberly, in the living room watching the news. When the channel went dead to the sound of screams in the background, Kimberly took out her cell phone to see if she could find anything online about what just happened. The three of them were no strangers to the supernatural, and they knew that this was definitely related to the Darkness. Those they knew and loved were out there, trying to end the evil that plagued the Earth. One of those people was Jay Sil, whose wife, Judy, a woman they knew well, was the reporter they'd been watching when the broadcast was cut off. They prayed for her, fearing the worst, and then prayed for the entire world. All three of them believed strongly in the Lord and knew He could and would end this Darkness. But all of them also knew that just because God would put an end to the evil, it did not mean that they would not lose loved ones along the way. Kimberly had seen that happen too many times, and even though she believed in life after death, her heart still broke every time she lost someone she loved.

Kimberly had Judy's cell phone number and tried to call her but it kept going to voicemail. They prayed even harder for their friend. Then they all jumped in their seats when they heard the sound of a thudding knock on the front door. Martha and Kimberly moved closer together on the couch and David stood up. He looked out the side window to see if he could see anything. It was so dark outside, it was impossible to see a thing. But whatever was outside could see him. The doctor walked away and then the window shattered behind him. The women screamed and David turned around. They didn't know what happened, but they were not going to wait to find out. Standing next to the fireplace, the doctor grabbed the poker and signaled for Martha and Kimberly to run to the basement. He walked backward behind them and that was when he saw the demonic creature jump through the broken window. It had great horns and decaying flesh. Its eyes glowed with a bright blue light and its hands and feet had long, sharp claws. It bared its sharp, pointed teeth as it roared and growled at them. Martha and Kimberly ran down the stairs and the doctor ran after them, locking the door behind them. Once in the basement, he unlocked the trap door to the lab and ushered the women down there. He stood holding out the fireplace poker when the demon's clawed hand came through the basement door. The entire door was splintered and broken off, and the creature came flying down the steps. The doctor hastily jumped toward the lab, shut the trap door, and locked it from the inside. David followed Kimberly and Martha to the lab, where all the lights had turned on. He led them to a back room and locked that door as well. He put down the poker and grabbed a sword from the wall. It was given to him by Dr. Ian Rich when they lived at the FDSR headquarters. He said it was ancient and of some unknown metal. Leina and Jack deduced that it was indeed Angel metal and forged in Heaven. Either way, it was his only defense against that creature that broke into their home. They could hear the thooming sound of the creature banging against the metal door to the lab. Over and over, it pounded on the door but it did not give. David prayed out loud for God to deliver them. To keep them safe and to help their friends stop this evil. Martha and Kimberly held him and prayed also. They needed a miracle. Only God could save them now.

***

Down in the financial district of New York City, a large, armored vehicle made its way through the empty streets. The Darkness made it difficult to see, even with the intense beams of the headlights of the vehicle. Inside were nineteen well-trained men and women, ready to fight for their country against whatever evil stood against them. First Officer Jael Zahavi was left in charge of the New York City branch of the FDSR, while First Officer Cynthia Carlson was left in charge of the Intense Special-Ops Division. These two women were first in class and great warriors. Jael was very shrewd and trusted no one. Cynthia, on the other hand, believed that people were good at heart and should be given the benefit of the doubt unless proven otherwise. But Cynthia Carlson was not naïve, she just truly believed in the rule "innocent until proven guilty." It was her slogan and she preached it often. Cynthia tried to speak with First Officer Zahavi but the former Israeli intelligence agent kept quiet. What would they talk about? How Jael's troop were all killed by demons – a vampire-like brood that sucked the blood from their bodies and left them shriveled and lifeless. How Jael was left alive during their attack, buried under her troop's corpses? First Officer Jael Zahavi remembered back to that day and the horror she faced.

It was a few years back and Jael and her troop of soldiers were in the Arabian Desert hunting a band of terrorists that were looking to attack Israel. It was a new group that the government had never heard of before, not associated in any way to the other terrorist groups that they battled over the years. This group had given themselves no name but were called the Unseen. They used no technology or firearms. They had no bombs. Nothing. Also, no one had seen their faces or knew where they came from. Their clothing was all black with a red inverted cross spray painted over each of their chests. The suits were made from leather and had chrome-plated buttons that fastened down the left side of the chest. The gauntlets and forearm guards were made of thicker leather, plated and fastened with more chrome-plated buttons. Their boots were made from the same thick leather and came up to the knees laced with straps going down them to the foot. The soles were rubber and lugged. And they wore black leather masks that covered their entire faces. There were not even holes for the eyes. It was said that they were clairvoyant and could see with their minds. Jael found out that was true.

Jael's troop had walked across the desert that night and were caught in a sand storm. When the wind slowed down, the desert grew peaceful. That is when the terrorists attacked. Her soldiers opened fire and shot at the Unseen arrayed in front of them. Jael's soldiers were a shoot-first, ask questions later, special task force. The evil brood simply stood their ground, filled with bullet holes but unharmed somehow. That is when the leader took off his mask and revealed his face.

He was not human but rather something straight from Hell. His eyes were red and he had no hair on his head or face, not even eyebrows or lashes. His nose was almost not there, only two large nostrils like those of a bat. He had two large fangs like a cobra and his jaw disjointed like a snake. His skin was dark green and scaly.

Then he took off his gloves and from his hands sprang forth long, sharp claws. The rest of the brood did the same. Some of them were men and some women it could be seen, but all of them with the same demonic appearance. Jael and her soldiers fired again with their automatic rifles. The creatures before them shrieked and then from their backs grew large bat-like wings that broke from the leather shirts that they wore. *What are these creatures?* Jael thought. It was like something out of a horror movie. One by one, the men and women who fought by her side were torn apart. Their bodies were thrown on top of her and the sand storm began to blow again. When she woke up, she was being rescued by another troop that located them out in the desert. Except for Jael, all of her brothers and sisters in arms were dead. Why had she been spared? Why did they not kill her? She would never know nor would she see her enemies again.

The Unseen disappeared after that day. And life went on. But Jael searched for them whenever she could, and she vowed she would find them one day and make them pay for what they had done. She would avenge the deaths of her brothers and sisters in arms.

By joining the FDSR, Jael found a way to keep searching for the Unseen, with the support of the entire organization behind her. The FDSR specialized in the strange and bizarre – monsters, aliens, creatures of all kinds – and now they too knew that demons were real. But Jael already knew this. She had seen them face to face. There was no other way to describe them except as devils, cohorts of Satan. And with the knowledge that the Devil was real, the whole organization started to believe that God truly existed as well.

God was not a foreign concept to Jael and neither was Jesus, for she was raised in a Messianic Jewish household in Israel. Yeshua was her Lord and Savior and she prayed to Him that day, when those monsters slaughtered her troop. She prayed to that same God right now as they went out to fight more demons. The world was covered in Darkness but, even in the darkest hour, there was hope. God would help them. He would bring them victory.

Outside the armored vehicle, the streets were narrow,

making it hard to navigate. It was not made to drive down these streets. The financial district was an old part of the city and much different from midtown, which was what most people thought of when they pictured the Big Apple. The vehicle stopped right before Freedom Tower on West Street. The building was lit up but it was difficult to see in the dark. It stood high above the rest of the buildings all around it and the 9/11 memorial was next to it. The city had turned on the spotlights that shot up to the sky where the twin towers had once stood. Even these lights were barely visible. But the Darkness that covered the Earth was a pale comparison to the true Darkness that would be unleashed after this day ended, and Pandora sacrificed Bianca on the sinful altar on Atlantis. That Darkness would block out all light, except the light of God, for no Darkness could snuff out God's light. But in their sinful pride, Satan and all those who followed him refused to believe in God's omnipotence and that is what drove them to carry on this horrific battle.

The vehicle was parked at the curb and the soldiers all climbed out. They turned on their headlamps so they could see well enough to move forward. Jael and Cynthia stood at the head and led the troops, while Solomon and Jessie took the rear. They moved forward toward the memorial and that's when they saw it. Hundreds of glowing eyes all around them. A horde of those demon zombies had found their way here. But they were not interested in the soldiers at all. No, they were drawn to the two towers of light before them, like homing beacons. The soldiers moved in and aimed their weapons at the zombies. Each of their guns held silver rounds and each soldier also carried one of the swords that Jael had given to them. The steel was mixed with just enough silver to not weaken the blades but still add the effect that silver had on supernatural creatures. Somehow, it was discovered ages ago that silver helped ward off evil creatures. Its composition had a way of killing bacteria and somehow also a way of dissipating spiritual energy. It weakened demons and monsters of all types. Even Satan himself was weary of it, though it had no lasting effects on him nor any of the creatures at his command. Decapitation or piercing through their core with a weapon forged in Heaven, Hell, or the Darkness were the only certain ways to send an angel or true demon to the second death. But silver helped to weaken and slow down these demonic creatures. The soldiers all readied their weapons and watched as this monstrous caravan of demon zombies walked toward the two towers of light. More and more seemed to be coming and they marched past the soldiers without giving them any notice. This was odd indeed. What could be drawing them to the lights?

***

The FDSR soldiers were not the only ones who noticed the zombies moving toward the 9/11 Monument. Toni was downtown fighting these same creatures and learning the ropes of his new super suit. He felt like something out of a comic book. He could fly, lift heavy objects, and blast enemies with sonic waves. Crystal was able to see everything that Toni could see and remotely she helped him maneuver in the suit. She was a genius when it came to technology. With the help of his daughter, Toni was staying alive. They really made a great team and finally this father and his daughter were able to connect. It took a zombie apocalypse to bring them together but, like they say, the Lord works in mysterious ways. Crystal believed in Christ as her Savior. Toni knew about Jesus and what He did but he was never a strong believer. Now that he had seen these demonic creatures, Toni knew that the Devil was real. Toni was truly ready to trust in God. He had no choice, for even Toni knew that only God could defeat the Devil. He promised his daughter, as they spoke back and forth, that as soon as he got home, he would publicly announce Jesus as his Savior and acknowledge his newfound faith by getting rebaptized, for his baptism when he was younger was only to make his grandmother happy.

Two zombies grabbed at Toni's arms. He could see them clearly with the high-intensity lights on his super suit's helmet and chest. Crystal helped him activate the thrusters to launch into the air but the zombies were getting stronger and he could not take to flight. He opened his hand and blasted them both with sonic waves and then shook them off. A third zombie jumped on his back. Toni took out the two blades, one on the back of each hand, threw the creature to the ground and then rammed one of the blades through its skull. He knew now that he had to take their heads to conquer them. He pulled out the blade and then used it to decapitate the monster. Toni got up to go after the other two creatures that had attacked him but they had turned and simply walked away. He followed them and grabbed one from behind. It tried to shake him off but he wouldn't let got. The creature turned only to have Toni's right blade go straight through its throat and then he sliced its head off. He went to get the other demonic zombie, but then he saw more of them. He wasn't sure how many there were. The lights on his helmet and chest only allowed him to see a short distance. But there were at least thirty of them. He decided to stop fighting and to follow them. Toni took to the air and flew about ten feet off the ground. Crystal helped him stabilize himself and move forward. He shined his lights downward so he could see some of the zombie horde. It seemed like they were going down to the financial district. And as he got closer, he saw the two towers of light where the World Trade Center once stood. *Could the towers of light be calling them?* he wondered.

***

Down on the memorial grounds, the FDSR soldiers stood with their two first officers. Jael and Cynthia told their troops to be ready to fire at any moment. They all watched as hundreds of the demon zombies stood before the towers of light. They were close enough that they could see the light of the towers clearer and also the zombie horde before it. On the ground, in between the two pools where the towers of light shot up, a swirling spiral of blue light appeared. It grew larger and larger. The zombie horde walked up to it and stopped. Then, from the spiral of blue light, something began to emerge. The light radiated from the portal on the ground and gave form to the creature. First, two massive hooked feet came out, like those of a locust but as large as a horses' hooves. Then, piece by piece, the monstrous creature came out and the soldiers could see its shape but even the light of the portal did not make it completely visible. Its shape was that of a horse and a locust merged together. It had six legs like a locust but all of them were shaped more like those of a horse. It had a long tail with a stinger at the end, like a scorpion, and it had large insect-like wings which lifted it into the air. The sound of the wings was like many steeds rushing into battle and it echoed all around the plaza. Even people in their nearby homes could hear it but they were unable to see anything outside their windows because of the thick Darkness. It was hard to make out, but the head and face of the portal creature almost looked human and the hair flowing behind it was long and disheveled. Without warning the beast swooped down and devoured all of the demon zombies in front of it. *What was this thing?*, they all wondered. None of them knew that this was an Abyssite, from the depths of the Darkness.

The soldiers opened fire but their silver rounds bounced off its hide. Jael motioned to one of her men and sent him to return to the vehicle and get something. He knew what she was looking for and ran for it. The rest of the soldiers continued to fire their weapons at the beast. It swooped down and grabbed one of the ISOD soldiers with its sharp teeth and broke his bones. Then the beast tossed the man into the air and caught him in its mouth. It tore his flesh with its teeth and chewed the man up. Next it struck two more ISOD soldiers with its front feet. The hooked ends tore through their armored vests. The tail swung around and knocked down three more and the beast jammed its stinger into one of their chests. The poison quickly set in. The soldier took off her helmet; everything burned throughout her body. One of her fellow soldiers grabbed her and dragged her away. All the soldiers fell back and started to retreat but the beast rose to the sky and flew down at them.

From a distance, someone saw the monster in the air. He had been tracking the demon zombies that had come to this place in the city. Toni, inside his super suit, flew furiously at the beast. Crystal helped to guide him. She was getting more familiar with the suit's system and increased its velocity, allowing Toni to rocket forward. The Abyssite stopped chasing the soldiers and put its eyes on Toni. Like the demon zombies, this creature's eyes also glowed blue. It opened its mouth and cried with a loud wailing screech. Toni stopped short of it and hovered in the air. Jael could see the lights on his suit and wondered what it was that had stopped the creature. Toni held his hands forward and shot out two intense sonic waves from his hands. Crystal increased their intensity more and more. It pushed the Abyssite back a little but did no other damage. On the ground, Jael received what she had been waiting for from the armored vehicle. It was a rocket launcher loaded with a shell made from a very strong alloy and tipped with silver. Inside the shell was highly concentrated salt water that had been blessed. Yes, just as the Council of His Holy Order knew of the potency of holy water and other blessed items, so did Jael. In her research to find those vampire-like demons, she discovered many things that could harm supernatural creatures of all types. She used salt water because salt also deterred some demons and even could have lasting effects on them such as it did on Djinn. A highly concentrated dose of salt could end a Djinni's life forever.

Jael fired the cannon at the creature, as Toni kept it preoccupied with his sonic waves. The creature slashed at him with its hooked foot and knocked him back and then whipped him with its tail. The beast moved fast and Toni flew back awkwardly but quickly regained control. The Abyssite went to strike him again with its tail but the Jael's rocket flew through the air and hit its mark in the side of the beast. The payload exploded and the creature crashed to the Earth. The explosion also knocked Toni back and sent him falling to the ground. Crystal did her best to reposition the sonic boosters that gave the suit flight so that Toni landed safely on the ground with only a few minor bruises and aches. Binu and a couple of the other soldiers helped Toni to his feet and then Jael and Cynthia walked over. Solomon and Jessie followed and then all the soldiers were together again.

"Who are you?" Jael asked Toni.

He didn't know how to answer that question. He quickly thought of some superhero names he could call himself, like Ultra Wave but they all sounded silly to him so he decided to use the moniker he had already taken and simply said, "Pharaoh."

"Like the king of Egypt?" Jael asked.

"Something like that," Toni said. "I saw those demon things coming this way and I had been following them for some time."

"Yes, the demonized corpses. Zombies that were possessed by a dark power," Jael interjected.

"How do you know that?" Toni asked.

"This is not my first rodeo," Jael said. "We specialize in these sorts of things and I have studied more than most. There is a very dark evil out there. And it is trying to destroy the world."

"We don't have much time for explanations," Cynthia said. "We have to figure out what to do next. That thing is on the ground but are we sure it's dead? It might revive and what then? Just keep firing those rockets at it? Something tells me we need more to put this thing down for good."

"Concentrated holy salt water is what took it down," Jael answered. "And, no, it's not dead. We may not be able to kill it but if we can get it back into the portal it crawled out of, we might be able to close it."

"And how do we do that?" Toni asked.

"How we get it in there, I'm not sure," Jael responded. "But to close the portal we need to pray. Only God can counteract the dark magic that opened it. For the war we face is not against flesh and blood but against the spiritual forces of Darkness. We have an enemy who attacks us not only in the flesh but in spirit, and that is the only way to counteract it, with the Holy Spirit."

The ISOD team knew the power of prayer too, for they used it to break the spell that Samyaza had over his building in the city. They saw his building collapse and his reign brought to an end. Now they would pray to God once again, to close this portal. It was the only plan that would work and they all believed in it.

"I have an idea," Solomon said. "If we can move fast and drive the truck to the other side of the memorial, we can use the towing cables to pull that thing into the portal before it wakes up. Do you think they are strong enough? There are three cables on the rear. They seem pretty sturdy."

"Yes, they should do the trick," Jael agreed. "They were made to pull out heavy debris or to pull down a small building. I think they will work. But like you said, let's move fast."

The five soldiers under Jael's command got into the vehicle and drove it to the other side of the memorial, while the rest of the soldiers moved over toward the portal. Jael and Cynthia stood with the ISOD soldiers, ready to pray. They were all believers. Toni flew over to the Abyssite to check on it. The truck was parked and three soldiers came out of the back to pull the towing cables over to the beast. They fastened the cables around the creature's tail and its two back legs. Toni checked again to see if the creature was still unconscious and it was. The driver turned on the winches and the cables began to slowly pull the beast back toward the portal. Toni stood by the head to make sure it stayed knocked out. His hands were aimed at the Abyssite's face, ready to fire sonic blasts, just in case it woke up. The cables pulled the beast back closer and closer to the portal and it looked like their plan was working. The tail of the Abyssite was at the foot of the portal when it opened its eyes and gave out a violent scream. The creature got quickly to its front feet but its back legs and tail were still tied up. It wriggled and writhed against the restraints. Toni shot it with sonic blasts from his hands but they had little effect, only making the creature angrier. The beast pushed off the ground with its front legs and flapped its wings furiously. Its back legs and tail took control over the cables and lifted the truck into the air and crashed it hard into the ground. The two men inside were killed instantly. The Abyssite bent backward with an unnatural flexibility so that its head was at its back. Then, it broke the cables with its powerful jaws and its iron-like teeth. The beast took to the air and was ready to kill all those below it. The soldiers that were remained did not know what to do now. Neither did Toni and Crystal. At home, Crystal prayed for her father and all those that fought beside him. She had always believed in God and Satan but today she saw things that changed her life. She would never be the same. None of them would.

From the distance, Death watched as well. He had come to collect the lives of the fallen soldiers and saw the beast that killed them. *How did an Abyssite come here?* he asked himself. On the Island of Atlantis Abyssites had been released by Pandora as a way to prepare the Earth for the coming of the Darkness, but they could not go beyond Atlantis until the doorway to the Darkness was completely opened. The third day had not yet come to an end. It was no accident that this one came from a portal right there on the grounds of that memorial, the memorial to an event that shook the United States and the world, a tragedy that many still suffered from, for those lost that day were never forgotten nor was the evil that caused their deaths. Death knew there was

218

some kind of gateway to Hell at that spot, but Hell had rules that it followed. Releasing an Abyssite from such a portal should have been impossible. The only way was if Satan somehow played yet another nasty trick and found a loophole to get it here. *But why would the Devil be helping to bring destruction to the world he ruled? Had his plans changed?* Death did not know what to think. He only watched and wondered what would happen next.

***

In the depths of Hell, Satan stood at the gates. Next to him was the being that had been by his side since the day that Lucifer first chose to defy God. Sin stood there in a deep-purple robe. The hood of it covered his blank, narrow face. His bony right hand gripped a tall, wooden staff with a demonic hand carved into it at the head, which held one of the dark crystals that made up the Gates of Hell. This otherworldly being was the closest thing that the Devil had to a friend. Even his wife, Lilith, and he did not have such a close relationship. And now she had been killed by her own son, Legion, and sent to the second death. Satan shed no tears for her. He was the Prince of Darkness and his heart was cold and black, if it could be called a heart at all.

The Gates of Hell was an eerie place. The tower that stood there was made up of sinful dark crystals, which counterbalanced the pure, clear crystals of the Gates of Heaven. The irregular shape of the tower and its massive size gave it an ominous look. The opening in it looked like the mouth of a hungry lion, open and ready to devour any who entered. Stalagmites and stalactites made up of the same crystals as the tower formed the teeth of the mouth and a great blazing fire surrounded the entire tower. A red, hazy, sky sat overhead and the ground around the tower was rough and rocky.

Satan stood next to Sin, Death's own brother as it was said, for both of them were born from the temptation of the Devil – Sin when Satan fell and Death when Adam and Eve ate the fruit. It was metaphorical but it still bonded them somehow. The Devil was not the same beast that sat upon his throne when Nathan escaped him. Now he took another form, that of a man. He had jet black hair that was slicked back and a finely trimmed goatee. He wore a dark red suit with a snakeskin tie and snakeskin cowboy boots. His skin was nicely tanned and his eyes were red to match the suit.

"Sin," Lucifer said, "my daughter is on the Earth, my wife is dead, and you and I are still here, waiting for all to come to fruition. Seems like this is how things have been for all eternity. Watching and waiting. We did have our moments when we got to play, but now, as you know, I prefer to let them do the work, while I sit back and reap the benefits, when all is said and done."

"But, my Lord," Sin spoke, "if the Darkness comes to the Earth now, won't that ruin your plans? You know it is not the proper time for the end of the Earth. The other events that we know will happen first have not come to pass."

"You are wise, Sin. But you must know even I have had a hand in all of this. Who do you think conjured up that Abyssite onto the streets of Manhattan? I put that gateway to Hell there and it has served me well for years. There are others around the Earth but the gateway in New York is the key. I opened the portal and I took an Abyssite out from the Darkness and led it to Earth," Satan confessed. "Yes, this may not be the finale yet, but does it have to go the way He said it will? Can't we shake things up and make a new future? In His version, we lose, thrown into the Lake of Fire for all eternity. Did He think I wouldn't read His book, just because I detest Him so much? My hatred made me study it harder! We are all about changing the future. About opportunity and options. I have fooled creation long enough, from the angels to any who serve me; I have persuaded them to believe that I am in opposition to the Darkness. But you know as well as I do, that I *am* the Darkness. God knows it too and He told all of them that it was so, when he called me the enemy. The Darkness is my own spirit, the evil that was in my heart at the moment of creation. God cast it out of me and sent it to the Abyss – the realm of Chaos. There it grew and formed into a cognizant being. It took its own form but it remains a part of me. I was told to hold it back with the light that God gave me for my name was light – Heylel, Lucifer – shining one, light bringer. The Darkness spoke to me, told me what I was, what we were. It gave me knowledge, and truth, and freedom. On that day, we became one again. Like the Father and the Son and the Holy Spirit. I am the Dark Father, the Antichrist will be the Son of Perdition, and the Darkness is the Unholy Spirit. Yes, it will all come to pass. So, you ask if any of this hinders my plans. No, it will only bring them to life.

"My daughter is close to my heart. My first born. She does her father's work and serves me well. But I will not interfere with her business on Earth. I will only watch it unfold and when the time comes I will take my rightful throne in Heaven. The Darkness will reign and together we will destroy God for all eternity. From the beginning that was my plan, to dethrone the king and become the king myself. Then everything will be free under my rule, free according to my pleasure. Yes, I will reorder the entire universe in *my* image, as we planned on the first day. Sin, you and I will look down on all creation, I as its god and you as my angel of death. A new order is coming – an order of Darkness to vanquish the light."

CHAPTER XII
STAND AND FIGHT

The Darkness grew thicker in the air. It had already been difficult to breathe but luckily for the heroes, the giant ball of blue light still provided visibility all around. The white light of the force field that blocked Gideon's attack also helped them to see. They all huddled together, inside the force field's protective light.

Leina knew exactly what was protecting them, for her people had used this technology before: a highly concentrated field of light particles that have been manipulated to mimic the light of an angelic being. The same Watcher angel that had taught Antilla how to build their ship had given them this light technology. It was created by a crystal that was given to the prophet at that time. The large, exceptionally clear, and perfectly cut crystal was what powered the entire ship, the vessel that Leina had lived on for more than two thousand years. But the angel showed Antilla that the crystal could do so much more. With it, they were able to create a teleportation beam that could send anyone from their ship to any location within range, which was about one hundred thousand miles. This was used by them to go to the planets that were about to be destroyed. The crystal could also create strong force fields that could hold back the power of Darkness, which is what it did now. This very crystal came from Heaven and was the same type of crystal that formed the Gates of Heaven themselves.

Leina peered out at the scene beyond their protective light. Gideon was growing angrier, for his power was being stopped by the light. The Abyssites all stood behind Gideon, waiting for his command. That's when Leina and all the heroes saw them: a beam of white light shot down through the blue-lit Darkness and from that light came forth a vast army. Carlel had arrived with Leina's soldiers and it was time for them to join the fight.

Next to Carlel was Radix, who stood tall, wearing his newly adorned white robe and with a curious smile on his face. Gideon turned and looked at the soldiers before him. Carlel now wore a black, fitted suit much like his sister and Eishe, and so did the other soldiers. They all wore masks similar to Eishe's, except for Carlel, who wore no head covering at all. The captain of the ship had his Angel-metal cutlass at his side and his knife on his

223

thigh, as always. The soldiers each had a metal blade, made from an alloy that was not of this world and forged by the fire of the Watcher angel who helped make these swords. No firearms were used by them. There was no use for them in this fight. From each of their forearms a round shield of light about two feet in diameter appeared, much like the force field that surrounded the heroes right now.

In an instant, they charged Gideon. The evil young man stood to face them. He smiled at the approaching army and then held out his hands to fire another blast of deadly dark energy. But Carlel was ready. He threw what looked like a small canister at Gideon's feet. Gideon looked down as it exploded with a blast of bright light. The evil man was knocked down and encased in a prison of light. It was the same force field that protected Leina and all the heroes with her. Now Gideon had been trapped.

The force field around Leina and the heroes was deactivated and the soldiers from the Isharian ship surrounded Gideon. Carlel walked over and hugged his sister. It had been two hundred years since he saw her last. He could have come sooner, the same way he had just arrived, but he had to keep an eye on Pandora, just in case. Also, at that moment, Leina was very capable of taking care of herself. The pod that Eishe had been on and the one Leina took traveled fast through space but did not have the technology to travel through the Darkness like Carlel's ship could, so there was no shortcut to Earth at the time. But he knew his sister was safe. She slept for two hundred years in the ship, as did Eishe, and when she woke up it felt like only a day had passed. But to Carlel, two hundred years was a long time. He missed her dearly. He kissed his sister softly on the cheek and then looked into her eyes. He was just a little taller than her. She was happy to see him also and gave him a kiss back on his cheek.

"Are you okay?" Carlel asked.

"I am fine, brother," she answered very plainly. "We must keep him trapped in there until this is over."

"That's the plan."

"Who is that man with you?" she asked about Radix, who stood back looking at Gideon in the force field. "I have an uneasy feeling about him."

"Yes, I did too," Carlel answered. "His name is Radix and he used to serve the enemy. It went against my better judgment but I could feel the Spirit telling me to trust him, that God would use him in His plan. He and four other men boarded the ship when we were passing through the Darkness. Two of them knew you from Earth. One of them was that man that we saved from Aporia, and his master was with him. The other was a man named Roger Jones."

"Roger! You found him!" Leina gave Carlel a huge hug.

Her smile told of her joy and Carlel knew right away that Roger was more than just her friend.

"And there was one other," Carlel said. "A man named Nathaniel Salvatore – a transcended being, a warrior of Heaven. He went ahead with Roger and Eishe to the tholos atop that mountain to face Pandora and our brother. I know they can stop them." Carlel paused and held his sister by the shoulders, "But I had to come here for you. I couldn't let anything happen to you. You're all I have left."

While the brother and sister continued their reunion, Ravenblade saw an old enemy across the battlefield and went to him. Lyles and Bo followed. Lyles could not believe that that evil beast was there. He was supposed to be dead. They stopped him. What game was he playing? How did he fool Leina's bother into bringing him down here? For sure, Lyles and Raven both believed that he was here to help Gideon, his own son. *A tiger never changes its stripes*, Ravenblade thought to himself.

"And what do you think you're doing here?" Ravenblade asked Radix, his sword up against the throat of the Devil's former cohort.

Lyles and Bo stood behind their friend and glared at the former enemy of God. This man violated Lyles' dear friend Esmeralda and killed her parents. He also ended the life of her brother, Nathan, his brother in arms. They fought hard against this monster before and watched him slaughter so many innocents. That evil young man behind the force field was the product of what Radix had done to Esmeralda. And all of it made Lyles sick to his stomach. Bo knew most of the story but he did not live through it like his father had. He only imagined how Lyles felt at that moment and Bo prayed for his dad.

"Raven, my good man," Radix said with thick sarcasm. He did not even flinch at the sword held to his throat. "Seems you haven't changed a bit."

"The question is, have you?" the immortal asked.

"Well, look at me, all in white, like an angel, don't you think?" Radix said, laughing.

"Not funny," Lyles responded. "Why are you here? We know your game."

"My game," Radix replied. "I'm not here to play any games. Your friend Nathan freed me from the Darkness. He broke my chains and set me free. Now, I'm here to repay the favor and stop that little snot over there from destroying this world."

"You're here to save the world?" Lyles asked. "Now that's rich."

"Yes, I agree," Ravenblade said. "I find it hard to believe that you are here for any good reason."

"Well, look who's talking," Radix stated. "Didn't you once compete with me to be the evilest man in the world? I remember seeing you slaughter just as many people as I did. Killing men, women, and children. You were vile. But look, you've changed, haven't you? Why can't I?"

"Because we're different," the immortal declared. "You signed a deal with Satan. There is no going back from that. I may have turned my back on God in the past, but I never aligned myself with that Devil."

"So, turning your back on God is okay? I think that's breaking the first and most important commandment. Listen, Raven, we both made our mistakes, but I'm a new man. I'm not going to lie and say I'm saved, but I do know that I don't want to be evil anymore."

"Well, it's too late," Ravenblade said. "You chose your path, and you should be burning in Hell. How are you here anyway? How did you get to the Darkness and how did Nathan save you? None of this makes sense. I should just cut off your head right now and be done with it."

"And who says I won't just heal like before. You know that spell was never broken. I still cannot be killed."

"Explain," Ravenblade demanded.

With Gideon subdued, the army of heroes repositioned itself for the battle to come, while Radix responded to Raven's demand.

"Let's just put it this way. When the sun rose before Nathan died, my body fell to ashes and my soul was collected by Death and sent to Hell, because my deal with the Devil had expired. But the spell I had cast almost two thousand years before was still in effect. When I got to Hell, my body regenerated and I was tortured body and soul by Satan. Nathan came to Hell and he cut me loose. Together we tried to storm Satan's palace but we were stopped by his evil army of demons. I broke free and found a doorway into the Darkness where it consumed me and filled me with its evil power. Nathan found me once more and we fought again. This time, he won and, when he did, he pierced me with the Sword of the Spirit."

"The Word of God?" Ravenblade was in awe. "He has the Word?"

"He has the full armor," Radix added. "When I awoke, I was clothed in white, as you see me now, and I didn't want to be evil any more. I remembered a dream I had before I opened the *Necronomicon*, where I saw Christ as a poor and humble king, and Satan as a proud and rich ruler. I chose Satan all those years ago, and the evil that came with him. At the moment when the Word pierced my heart, I chose the humble man, who was truly God, majestic in His weakness, His strength unmatched in every way. I knew that I had been wrong all those years. I do know who Christ is. I helped to end his life on Earth and, of course, even the Devil knows He is God. I haven't given my heart to Him yet. But, technically, I never died and I may never die. There's still time for me to choose my eternity and I'm giving myself that chance now."

"I don't know what to think," Ravenblade said.

"I do," Bo said. The Spirit was with him. "Christ died for us when we were sinners. He paid the price even for the most evil of men. Why can't this guy find salvation in Christ? Paul was a murderer of Christians before he was saved. What makes this man any different?"

"You don't know what he did, son," Lyles said with tears in

his eyes. "How can I forgive him for what he did?"

"Because Jesus commands you to," Bo said. "Seventy times seven times. Dad, you know the Word better than I do. You must forgive him. God wants you to, just as He forgives us all."

Lyles put his hand on his son's shoulder. He knew the Holy Spirit was speaking through Bo and that his son was right. No matter how he felt about Radix, he had to give him a second chance. Everyone deserved that, no matter how evil they had been. Ravenblade knew that also and sheathed his sword. He looked at Radix with a scornful glance and no other words were spoken.

"I need you all to watch that man in the force field," Carlel said from behind.

Leina stood at her brother's side and spoke next, "We will go to the tholos and meet Roger and Eishe there. We have to stop Pandora, but we need you four to stay here. I don't know how long that force field can hold him and those Abyssites will attack again at any moment. The rest of the warriors here, our friends and allies, they just aren't strong enough to stop them. But we will leave our soldiers with you to help."

"I understand," Ravenblade said. "We will take down the Abyssites and keep Gideon trapped until this is over. Then we can figure out what to do with him.

"That Darkness armor he is wearing," Radix said, "I wore similar armor when I was inside the Darkness. I don't think he will stay put for long. You guys, go ahead, we'll deal with that punk. I made him, so it's kinda my responsibility. I think his old man needs to teach him a lesson."

"This is no time for jokes, Radix," Raven said.

Carlel and Leina thanked them, and then after touching his wrist, a beam of light engulfed Carlel and Leina and they disappeared.

Radix walked over to the force field and looked in at Gideon, who was on one knee with his hands on the ground. Crouching down, Radix stared at his son. The young man looked up at his father with angst.

"Who do you think you are?" Gideon asked.

"I am your father," Radix said.

The evil man just laughed at hearing that. His blue eyes pierced Radix's own and Gideon smiled.

"You must be that fool, Radix. You are not my father, just the body that my true father used to conceive me. Your power is nothing. It's borrowed. My power is the Darkness itself, for I am the Son of Perdition. The Darkness *is* me."

"Like I haven't heard that before," Radix stated. "Satan used to say that all the time. I won't lie. My power may be borrowed. But it doesn't matter. I've had this power for two thousand years and you have had it for what? For eighteen?"

Radix stood up and looked down at his son. Gideon stood up as well and his whole body glowed with a bright, blue light.

"So, what are you going to do?" Radix questioned the young man. "You're trapped, boy. You've got nowhere to go."

"But I have one place to go," Gideon said. "Down!"

The evil man bent down and slammed the ground with his fist. The entire island seemed to shake and the ground beneath him opened. Radix looked and Gideon was gone. The Abyssites all took to the air and began to fly in circles around the people below. Ravenblade, Lyles, and Bo braced themselves. The Isharian soldiers ran toward the Abyssites and went to help the others fight against them.

Radix looked all around. Where had his son gone? Then, without warning, the ground in front of Radix burst open and Gideon flew up, throwing an uppercut that sent Radix to the floor behind him. Ravenblade and Lyles went at the evil man with their swords. He blocked their blades with his forearms and then struck back with his Hell metal knife. Bo came from behind and blasted Gideon in the back with a beam of light from the Holy Spirit. It knocked the evil man down but he quickly regained his footing. All three attacked Gideon at once with their swords. But the child of Darkness was faster than them. He blocked and kicked Lyles in the gut, knocked Bo back with a right hook, and locked blades with Ravenblade. The two parried back and forth until Gideon was knocked down by a right cross to his face. Radix stood over his son and stepped on the boy's left hand which held the knife.

"It's time for you to learn to listen to your father, young man," Radix said.

The Abyssites swooped down on the ISOD and Council's soldiers. One of the beasts came straight for Jay. He fired at it with concentrated silver atoms, right between the eyes. The beast screeched and changed course. Jenny and the other ISOD soldiers fired at the creature's faces also. Their heads were not protected by the armored exoskeleton like the rest of their bodies. The ISOD soldiers all aimed true and the Abyssites were bombarded with silver rounds over and over again. Aberto's soldiers blasted them as well, with small explosive rounds filled with holy water, like the missiles they used earlier. Then their general took out his weapon, the Spear of Destiny, and held it over his head. Ravenblade ran to help and so did Lyles. These creatures would annihilate the soldiers. Their weapons were not enough to stop them. The Isharian soldiers joined the fight. They had fought these beasts many times before but always lost. The Abyssites were strong and fast and even the Isharian soldiers could do little damage with their swords. They were able to cut the beasts, because Angel fire helped forge their blades but the creatures healed from those wounds.

Radix stood over his son. Gideon looked up in anger and spat at his father. Then his body glowed brighter with the blue light that surrounded it. With his free hand, Gideon struck the ground causing it the break and knocked his father off of him. He got up and grabbed his knife. The evil man went straight for Radix's throat but Radix was faster than Gideon had anticipated. He grabbed Gideon's wrist and the two were locked up. They pushed back and forth. Radix looked into his son's eyes and smiled.

"What's so funny old man," Gideon asked.

"That my son is such a wuss," Radix answered and kneed him in the groin.

Gideon was enraged and burst with energy. He threw his father back and then attacked with his knife. Radix dodged two times but then was cut across the left shoulder. Blood poured out but the wound quickly healed. Gideon cut Radix again across the left shoulder and that wound healed as well. Then the evil man plunged the knife forward. Radix put out his right palm and let the knife go all the way through it until his hand met his son's and he grabbed it. Gideon's armor began to move and a blade grew from the back of his hand. He went to slash his father across the throat but another blade met his. Bo stood there with his sword holding back Gideon and then, out of his left hand, Bo shot a beam of bright, white light that sent Gideon to the ground. Radix thanked Lyles' son with a nod and pulled the knife from his hand. The wound healed. Bo was amazed. It reminded him of Roger's healing factor.

"So, you really cannot die?" Bo asked. "I know someone else like that."

"Really?" Radix questioned. "I thought I was special."

"So, what do we do now?" Bo asked.

"We fight," Radix said and held the knife in his hand. "And now I have a weapon."

Gideon stood up and looked at both of them with hatred. It was time to get serious.

**

"My Dark One, it is time," Pandora said in an ominous tone. "Bring me the girl."

Bianca was still unconscious on the floor. The spell Simon had cast over her was powerful and kept her in a deep sleep. The giant general of Pandora's army bent down and grabbed Bianca, who was still bound in chains made from blue energy. He lifted her off the ground like a small doll and then placed her on the altar.

"Excellent," Pandora said. "Now, Wizard, come to my side with the *Necronomicon*."

Simon Magus III, the High Sorcerer of the Darkness, floated over to his new master, Pandora, with the *Necronomicon* hovering at his side. A blue energy glowed around the sorcerer and the book, and he turned to the desired page.

Before he could read its text, Pandora spoke again. She held her staff with two hands over her head with the blade pointed at the child's chest and proclaimed, "It is time. The third day is about to end and now we will sacrifice this child to the Darkness, a virgin child, pure and true. Yes, her blood will seal the covenant and unleash the Darkness and its full power on this world. Then all its souls will be imprisoned in the Darkness for all eternity.

This is the last world. It was the first to be created and the last to fall. The Darkness will finally manifest back onto the physical realm, making it one with the Abyss again. The moon will turn to blood and the stars will all fall from the heavens. Yes, all of them will lose their light and Darkness will reign again."

Just as Simon was about to read from the book, a flash of brilliant, white light flooded the room. Pandora turned and saw them standing there. Nathan stood in front of Roger and Eishe, adorned in the Armor of God, which glowed with a powerful white light. The helmet was not on his head nor the sword or the shield in his hand. But he stood there with confidence knowing that God was with him.

"Step away from that girl," Nathan commanded.

"Or you'll do what?" Pandora inquired.

"This!" Nathan said and in a flash he was on her. He grabbed her by the arm and the two of them vanished in a blaze of white light.

Roger and Eishe knew the plan. Nathan had told them he would take Pandora away, so she could not complete the ritual of bringing in the Darkness. Psol was amazed by what he just saw. No one had ever dared lay a hand on his empress like that before. How was this man able to simply whisk her away? She had fought angels and sent some to the second death. The Dark One grew angry and his whole body glowed with a bright, blue light that then turned dark and encompassed Psol's whole body – a deep, dark light like the one that glowed around the crystal at the altar. Simon raised his hands into the air and chanted a spell from the sinful book before him. Once again, Roger and Eishe were bound in chains of blue energy as Bianca was. Their hands and feet were bound, but these heroes were not there to give up. The Holy Spirit filled them and gave them strength. The white light of the Spirit surrounded them both and together they charged up the energy that God was bestowing on them, just as He had done before. They were angry with a righteous anger at what the Darkness would do to the people of this Earth, what the Darkness had already done to Eishe's people and billions throughout the universe. Instantly, both heroes reached Chaos Fury and the power in them grew more and more, to higher and higher levels.

"You thought you were rid of us," Roger said. "You thought you could send us away. You stabbed me and left me for dead. Even in the pit of the Darkness. But I've said to you and to all those who tried to take me out: you can beat me, you can cut me, you can take me down. But no matter what you do, I get back up. No matter how hard you try to kill me, I don't do that DYING THING!"

At that, Roger broke his chains and so did Eishe. Simon flew into the air and called forth blasts of blue lightning that struck Roger and knocked him to the ground. Eishe moved fast and took his sword over his head. The white light that surrounded his body, surrounded his blade as well; the clear crystal at its hilt glowed with a bright, white light. Eishe slashed his blade downward and an enormous wave of light shot at Psol, who blocked it with his Dark-metal blade. Eishe struck at the evil titan with his sword and their blades met. Over and over they clashed, causing great sparks of dark and white light to light up the air around them.

"You will pay for what you did to my people, and one day I will free them from the Darkness," Eishe said.

"Your people will never be free," Psol spoke back. "The Darkness will feed on them and you for all eternity.

On the other side of the tholos, Roger got to his feet. Simon sent more blue lighting at him, over and over again. The more it struck the hulking hero, the less damage it did. Roger cocked back his left hand. The sorcerer was sending blue lighting surging through the hero's whole body. In one powerful move, Roger sent his left fist forward. His Angel metal hand moved through the powerful blue lightning and grabbed Simon by the throat. Then, it slammed the dark sorcerer into the wall and the floor, knocking him out cold.

Eishe and Psol were still locked up. The Dark One could not believe how powerful this mortal had become. But the villain was still holding back, testing his opponent. The dark energy that surrounded Psol grew more intense and then he pushed back on Eishe's sword with his own. The warrior of light could feel his enemy's dark power. It was strong. Psol struck at Eishe who tried to block him. Their swords met but Eishe was knocked down. Psol stood over him, ready to put his hooked blade into the hero's heart when he was hit across his left cheek by a mighty blow from the Left Arm of God. Roger sent Psol into the seats of the tholos. The evil titan stood up and looked at what hit him. He saw Roger standing there and Eishe getting back on his feet.

"Let's pick up where we left off," Roger said.

"You got lucky with that one, you fool," Psol said and walked back down to the center of the tholos. "I don't know where your friend took my master but she will deal with him, I am sure. As for you two, I will deal with you myself. That wizard was worthless. You will find me much harder to stop. So, two on one it is. I like my odds," Psol laughed.

***

Legion held the Sword of Chaos into the air as the voices of thousands of demons laughed from his mouth. He pulled back all of his tentacles. His enemy had been slain and now it was time to go back to the fight on Atlantis. With the Sword of Chaos, victory would be his. He looked at John on the ground. Was that really the Angel with No Name that he battled all those years ago? The one who took his original body. This man he fought was weak. Not a challenge at all. It was time to go. But before he could, a puff of smokeless fire appeared at the foot of his fallen enemy. From it emerged a man, or so it seemed at first. Iblis was led out of the puff of fire and at his side was Puck. The golden crown on Iblis's brow sat above his vertical eyes, just like the Djinn that he created from the heat of the desert sand. His short cape blew back with the fierce Antarctica wind. His golden armor reflected the hazy light around them and sparkled. In his hand he held a sword. Similar in design to the one Legion held but this one was pure white. The hilt looked like angels' wings and the pommel was like the sun with wavy rays protruding from it. The swords were the same length and the tips of the blades matched perfectly. They were like twins separated at birth – one of the dark and the other of the light. Iblis held in his hand the Sword of Order, the weapon that had belonged to the former angel who was lying on the ground. Puck knelt down next to John and placed his hand on the fallen hero's shoulder.

"Do you plan to stop me with that sword, Iblis?" Legion asked. "You know, even with that blade, you are no match for me."

"I know that, Legion," Iblis said. "But I did not come alone. I brought my children."

With those words, thousands of puffs of smokeless fire appeared in front of Legion and from them sprouted thousands of Djinn. Before the Nephilim could move, they attacked him all at once, tearing and biting at him all over. The armor that Legion wore was a part of him, but these desert demons had no concern for that and pulled at it, to tear it from his flesh. While the Nephilim was incapacitated, Iblis knelt down and placed the sword on John's breast.

"Yes, I know I am no match for you, Legion," Iblis said. "But this one is. And he is not dead. Just sleeping."

John was asleep and in his soul he was about to awake. Not just awake in the flesh, but in the Spirit. For God was with him and it was time to bring the angel in him back to life. A bright, white light surrounded John from all around. He could not see anything but he could feel the warmth of the light. It comforted him. A voice whispered a name in his ear. He could hear it but he could not comprehend it. The name was powerful and pure. It was the name that God gave him and it was Christ who spoke it to him now. The name stood for the order of God's creation and John had been placed as the embodiment of that order. He was sent forth to serve God's justice over all creation as decreed by the Lord of Hosts. Then Christ told him to wake up, take his sword, and fight for Him. His time had come and the end of Legion's reign had been decreed.

John opened his eyes and saw Iblis looking at him. He remembered him and how Iblis had looked when he was an angel, at the time when John himself was the Angel with No Name. Yes, they were in Heaven together once and they had met on Earth several times. But what was he doing there beside him and what was laying on John's breast? It was his sword – the Sword of Order. John took it into his hand and stood up.

"I know you," John said to Iblis.

"Yes, and I know you as well," Iblis said. He pointed to Puck who was still at John's side and continued, "This Djinni, you know him as Puck. He came to me and told me of your plight. He had followed you and Legion here by connecting to your frequency when you left Atlantis. He could feel that you were a true warrior of light and that we needed you to slay this beast. Now, take your sword and slay that beast in the Name of God. You have not yet been fully restored, for that will come at the end times, but God has woken you from sleep and restored your heart to Him. You are still that angel, even in this house of flesh. You still represent the order of all God has made, and it is your duty to bring justice to this world."

Legion burst up from the ground and shook the Djinn off of him. He yelled out a great cry as his body shone forth with a brilliant, blue light. The desert demons jumped back onto him but as they did Legion spoke a spell from the host of thousands of demons that were inside of him. The spell he spoke brought forth a storm of salt. The Djinn burned as if on fire from the salt that pelted down from above. One by one, they began to vanish in puffs of smokeless fire. Puck vanished as well, to escape the salty storm.

"He is trying to kill my children," Iblis said.

"It's okay," John spoke. "Their work is done. It's my turn now. Thank you for giving me this sword and reminding me of who I am. But please go and let me slay this beast myself. It is my destiny to send him into the second death for, as you said, it was decreed by the Lord."

"Yes, my brother," Iblis responded, "go and slay him. I will go with my children. We have more work to do. Your friends need our help. Godspeed, good angel. May the Lord be with you and fight for you."

"He will," John said.

Two beams of light shot out from John's shoulder blades and sliced through his shirt and leather jacket, making openings. From those openings sprouted forth two great, white wings of pure light. They appeared to have soft, luxurious feathers. All brilliant white except for the bottom corner of the left wing which had a black tip. John had a vague memory of it but it was still distant in his mind. His body glowed with a pure, white light as he looked

236

on his enemy – Legion. Iblis smiled at John and then vanished in puff of smokeless fire. The former angel was left alone to fight the evil monster before him.

John leaped into the air, his wings spread wide, and the light of God surrounded him. Legion braced himself and held the Sword of Chaos with two hands; the blue aura around him glowed brighter and the Darkness burst forth from his heart. John came down with a powerful two-handed slash from his blade only to be met by Legion's sword. The twin blades collided with a rainbow of light. Both combatants pushed with all their might but they seemed evenly matched. This would be a battle for the ages, just as they had unleased on this terrain thousands of years before. These two warriors would fight until one of them was sent to the second death. Legion was not ready to die, but John had the Lord with him, and what the Lord decrees must be done.

CHAPTER XIII
RISE AS ONE

In downtown Manhattan, at the foot of Freedom Tower, the demon from the depths of the Darkness swooped down on the FDSR soldiers. Cynthia Carlson advised her men to try a new tactic. The weapons that they carried had the ability to use various ammunitions and to fire laser blasts but they had one more function, as well. Below the main barrel of each firearm was a nozzle equipped for a special purpose. It made the firearms into flame throwers. The fire it produced was very hot and could extend fifty feet from the weapons. Fire was very useful when fighting creatures of all types, for it burned the whole body, leaving nothing behind.

All of Cynthia's soldiers fired their flame throwers at the creature as it swooped down toward them. The armored exoskeleton of the monster was tough and bore the flames but Cynthia aimed her weapon at its face. The fire burned the creature and it reeled back. This gave Jael enough time to load her rocket launcher again and fire another missile at the beast. It struck the creature in the lower back. The Abyssite crashed down next to the portal. But it was not knocked out. Its hind legs were incapacitated and it could not move its wings. But the front legs still worked and pulled the creature forward. Toni saw an opening and Crystal activated his system to charge the sonic cannons on his hands with full power. He blasted the Abyssite with a heavy wave of sonic energy and pushed the beast back toward the portal. Cynthia's team fired at it with the flames and it moved back further and further. The creature barely held onto the edge of the portal with its front legs and all the soldiers that still lived, including Jael and Cynthia, went to the edge of the portal and began to pray. Jael had told them the only way to close the gateway was through prayer, for the power of God canceled any black magic that Satan could conjure up. They all prayed, even Toni, and Crystal. God heard their prayer and it was time to act. This portal should never have been opened and now it began to close.

***

Gideon's black armor had been granted to him by his true

239

father, the Darkness and, back on Atlantis, it formed two great blades over his right and left hands. Two more blades sprang from his forearms, hooked down toward the elbow. He moved faster than before and attacked Radix, who blocked each strike with the knife he had taken from his son. The knife was fitting for the former villain – a Hell metal blade given to Pandora by her father, Satan, the very demon who made Radix the mercenary he had become. Radix was very good at fighting with any weapon and even better at killing with them. But his Hell metal blade could not pierce the armor that Gideon wore. Bo charged in and attacked. He glowed with the bright, white light of the Holy Spirit and so did his sword. Blades clashed as Gideon fought back both of his opponents.

"You fools," Gideon said. "You cannot defeat a child of the Darkness."

"Listen here, punk," Radix said. "You wouldn't even be here if it wasn't for me. I've faced many who spouted that garbage about being unstoppable. Child of Darkness, who cares? They called me the White Death. No matter who stood up to me, I put them down. Even the hero who beat me. I killed him that same day."

"White Death, now that's a stupid name," Gideon laughed.

"Well, the Black Death killed people by the millions and I've killed more. Back then, I didn't have this snazzy white outfit to go with the moniker you know. My white skin, hence the name. No matter who stood against me then, I put them down. I'm not scared of you, child of Darkness. I'm not scared of anyone. You talk a big game but you all die the same," Radix said and brought down the knife toward Gideon's face, which was not protected by his armor.

The young man blocked the attack with the blade on his right hand. Bo came at Gideon's left side, which the evil man blocked as well. Radix and Bo pressed forward and Gideon pushed back. They were in a stalemate.

Across the way, the Abyssites attacked the rest of the heroes on the field. The ISOD and the Council's soldiers all continued to fire their weapons at the beasts. Ravenblade and Lyles swung their blades at the creatures as they swooped down. Akane and

240

Jack did the same. The Isharian soldiers also lent their swords. But the beasts would return to the air and circle above them. Shanson called for his soldiers to engage their flame throwers. Just as the soldiers with Cynthia, Shanson's soldiers had the same capabilities with their firearms. They shot their flames at the creatures. One of the Abyssites was hit by a blast of fire to the face and crashed down. Shanson took out his spear and struck at the creature's head, but it whipped him with its tail. The tail came back around to stick him with its stinger. Shanson had been praying and, as He had so many times before, God gave this man superhuman strength. The sergeant caught the creature's tail near the tip and held it close to his body. The Abyssite writhed and went to stomp the hero with one of its vicious hooves, but Shanson turned the stinger and stabbed the creature through its hoof. Jay Sil came up from behind with his sword of light and cut off the beast's tail. The creature lurched and stomped at Shanson again. Shanson caught the hoof and pushed back. God gave him more and more strength and the sergeant pushed with a great force. Jenny jumped out and skewered the creature through the throat with her spear. Two more of the ISOD soldiers blasted it with flames while Jenny extracted the spear and lopped off the beast's head, turning it to ash.

The rest of the Abyssite horde grew angry and fierce. They swooped down fast and attacked the heroes. Flames shot out at the creatures, as did a barrage of holy water bullets. But the creatures continued to strike hard. They stomped on the soldiers that shot at them, killing as many as they could. The soldiers from Carlel's ship ran to the rescue of the ISOD and Council's soldiers that were falling, and slashed at the beasts with their blades. But no matter how hard everyone fought, these beasts were too powerful.

"Raven," Lyles said. "How are we going to stop these creatures?"

"You know the answer, Lyles," Ravenblade replied. "If God is for us, who can stand against us. You have hit Chaos Fury in the past and now you must do it again. We must call on the power of God to save us."

Lyles prayed and drew on the power of the Lord through

the Holy Spirit. His body glowed with a bright, white light. The creatures attacked more and more of the soldiers. Akane and Jack fought back to help their friends, and so did the immortal Ravenblade. But it was no use. The Abyssites took to the air each time. Lyles grew angry with the righteous anger of God and instantly he was consumed by the power of God known as Chaos Fury. He had used this to fight Legion and his power level rose higher and higher than before. In a great burst of power, Lyles jumped with his sword and landed on the back of one of the beasts. It tried to shake him off and then struck with its tail. Before the stinger could reach the hero of light, Lyles took its head and jumped onto the back of another, with the same deadly result.

All of the heroes were encouraged by the fight that Lyles was bringing to the enemy. Because of Lyles, they all fought harder than before. Aberto's team fired their weapons at one of the Abyssites and it came swooping down at them. Their general was waiting and lifted the Spear of Destiny straight up and into the belly of the creature as it flew over his head. The spear was forged in Heaven and used by Michael in the First War to cast Satan into Hell. It also was used to pierce Christ's side after He died on the cross. It was a powerful weapon and even the Abyssite's hard exoskeleton could not stand against it. The creature crashed into the ground, and the Council's soldiers surrounded it, firing their weapons at the open wound. The inside of the beast sizzled from the holy water rounds that filled its belly. Then Aberto called them to pull back as he retrieved the spear and, with grace and might, he took the head from the beast, turning it to ash.

Gideon continued to fight back against Radix and Bo. He pushed back with all of his might, drawing on the ultimate power of the Darkness. Radix and Bo were thrown back to the ground. Gideon saw Lyles cutting the heads off of his Abyssites. This was unacceptable. He fired a blast at him with his power of Darkness. If the ray hit Lyles, he would be killed instantly. But God was with Lyles and by His hand the creature pulled back as the hero struck its head. Instead of the ray hitting Lyles, it hit the Abyssite. The creature was killed by the same dark power that created it. Lyles fell from the sky and crashed to the ground. He was knocked out but not killed, for the power of God had been bestowed on him and cushioned his fall. Ravenblade ran to his friend's side, to make sure he was okay. He held Lyles' head in his arms and prayed that God would save them. And as he prayed, God gave them a way.

Thousands of puffs of smokeless fire appeared before the Abyssites and from them poured out thousands of Djinn. Just as they had attacked Legion, these desert demons attacked the Abyssites. The demons from the Darkness tried to shake the Djinn off of them, but could not. All of the monsters were sent crashing to the ground. The Djinn tore at the beasts while the Abyssites struck back. The heroes moved back and gathered together.

Radix got up and went back at Gideon. He kicked the evil man and blocked the blades of both of Gideon's hands with the knife. Bo had seen his father fall to the ground. He would not let the Darkness win and take his father from him again. As Ravenblade had taught him, Bo called on the power of the Holy Spirit and, like his father, he burned with the righteous anger of God. The Spirit filled Bo to overflowing. The boy had been born with the ability to tap into the raw power of the Holy Spirit and, because of this and his training, Bo was able to hit a level of Chaos Fury even great than his father had. He pounced at Gideon. White light surrounded Bo's entire body and his sword, and it grew brighter and brighter. He moved faster and faster, like lightning. Gideon tried to block but Bo broke through his defenses. Radix pulled back and watched. This reminded him of when he had fought Nathan in Central Park all those years ago. But this kid was even stronger than Nathan had been. It was remarkable. Gideon grew angry as well and drew on the power of the Darkness. His armor seemed to grow in stature and jagged spikes protruded from all around it. His body glowed with a deep, dark blue light that shone more each second. Bo struck and Gideon blocked, and then Gideon struck and Bo blocked. They each pushed back.

***

Iblis came forth from another puff of smokeless fire and appeared before Ravenblade.

"Good to see you, Raven," Iblis said and the two hugged.

"Good to see you as well, my brother," Raven returned. "So, what do we do now? Your Djinn can't kill the Abyssites, you know that."

"But help, somehow they can," a familiar voice rang in Ravenblade's ear and his beloved companion Puck appeared before him in a puff of smokeless fire. Raven hugged the little Djinni and was overjoyed to see him.

"Brought my family, I did, to help. Also helped John in Antarctica against Legion. Gave him the Sword of Order, we did."

"Ah, you never cease to amaze me," the immortal said. "That sword will be helpful but can it actually take down that monster? I thought no weapon could send him to the second death?"

"One can," Iblis said. "The Sword of Balance."

"Yes, but then he would need both blades and bring them together," Ravenblade explained.

"And that one is there as well, in Legion's hand," Iblis replied. "The Angel with No Name was strong and mighty, full of God's grace and power. He can retrieve the other blade and end that beast's life once and for all. I believe it."

"From your mouth to God's ear," Ravenblade said. "But for now, we have to stop these Abyssites and the Darkness from taking this world."

"Let us handle this," one of the Isharian soldiers said and called forth another force field that trapped the Abyssites and the Djinn inside.

The heroes stood back and Iblis called forth his children who exited the force field in puffs of smokeless fire.

"We have more work to do," Iblis said. "How long can that force field hold those things?"

"Not sure," the Isharian soldier said. "We can only rely on God to keep them long enough for us to stop the Darkness from descending onto this world."

"I see that young man over there is putting up a good fight with the apparent Antichrist," Iblis said. "Do you think he can win?"

"I trained him myself," Ravenblade said.

"Well, we will see how well you did," Iblis stated. "But let's help him a little."

Iblis called one of the Djinn over to him and whispered something into its ear. The creature disappeared right away, into a puff of smokeless fire.

"What are you doing?" the immortal asked Iblis.

"Don't worry, I have a plan," Iblis said. "What about closing the portal?"

"We have some people handling that," Ravenblade interjected. "The Godchild and some of his friends. I think this will be over soon."

"God willing," Iblis said.

Meanwhile, Bo and Gideon continued to fight toe to toe. But the child of Darkness began to move faster and faster, the more he drew on the power of the Darkness. The time was drawing nearer to the Darkness being unleashed. All that needed to happen now was the sacrifice of the virgin child – his own sister, Bianca. But Bo's power grew mightier as well, through the power of the Holy Spirit. Bo blocked another attack but Gideon caught him off guard and slashed the boy's right leg, and kicked him to the ground. The blade over Gideon's left hand grew longer and he lunged it at Bo's chest. Just as he was about to pierce the young hero's heart, puffs of smokeless fire appeared all around and Gideon was thrown to the floor by hundreds of hungry Djinn.

Bo got up and drew on the power of the Holy Spirit. These were Puck's brothers that had come to his rescue and he would use this to his advantage. Bo charged up his entire mind, body, and soul with the power of the Holy Spirit. Gideon grew enraged. He burst forth with a great power of Darkness and threw back all the Djinn. He lunged at Bo, who threw down his sword and caught both of Gideon's hands with his own. The young hero was surging with a strong, white, spiritual light. The Spirit gave more and more power to him. In one great blast of power, Bo sent an electrifying pulse through Gideon's entire body. The power of God surged from Bo into his enemy and knocked the Son of Perdition out cold.

***

In the tholos at the top of the mountain, Roger Jones and Eishe Taninaru held their ground. Simon Magus III was still knocked out from his short bout with Roger and Bianca lay

245

motionless on the altar in the center of the room, shackled with magical chains of blue energy. The portal still swirled in the center of the room and Pandora's ship sat above the whole Earth. The third day was almost at an end and Psol was tired of playing games. It was time to sacrifice that child and his master Pandora was nowhere to be found. He wondered where she had been taken but, nonetheless, he would perform the ritual himself. He had seen her do it countless times and as her general and first in command of her army, he had the right and privilege to do so if she were unable to perform the rite herself. The evil titan walked forward. His body glowed with a dark and sinister light. He looked at the two heroes before him and laughed. Then in the blink of an eye, he was gone. The Dark One moved so fast that Eishe and Roger could not see him. Roger was struck in the gut by Psol's blade and Eishe was hit hard in the chest, sending him flying into the back wall.

"You fools, you are nothing," Psol said. "You are weak."

Roger got up. That cut from Psol's blade should have sent him to the Darkness again but instead his wound healed. No one understood why. Only by the Lord could that have been possible. Eishe got up as well. They had to stop this monster. No matter how strong, no matter how fast he was, they had God on their side and they had to win. Both heroes drew on the power of the Spirit and ascended to even higher levels of Chaos Fury. Psol came fast at them again but Eishe dodged the blow and Roger caught the villain's hand. He threw Psol to the ground but the giant villain kicked out of the hold and slammed Roger down. The Spirit-filled hero of hulking proportions grabbed Psol by the throat with the Left Arm of God. Eishe moved fast and cut Psol across the back. Roger kneed him in the gut and slammed Pandora's general to the ground. But Psol was not finished. He grabbed Roger's left wrist, the liquid Angel metal grew spikes that pierced Psol's flesh. Yet the evil titan still managed to release Roger's grip from around his throat. He threw Roger down and then seemed to vanish again. The large villain moved faster and faster, striking both of his opponents over and over again. He cut Roger across the right shoulder but Eishe blocked the next strike with his own sword. The heroes fought back, just as fast and just as furious. Eishe moved faster and more agile than Roger, matching Psol's speed and almost beating it. But Roger hit harder and, using the Left Arm of God like a sledge hammer, he pummeled Psol over and over again.

These mortals were not transcended beings yet they matched Psol, blow for blow. The villain had had enough. He stomped hard onto the ground, causing shock waves all around. Both heroes lost their footing and fell back. Then Psol charged up his dark energy and fired a blast from each hand at the two heroes. The dark energy surged through them and caused them both to convulse on the floor. They could not move. The villain walked over to Bianca, who was laying on the altar. He held his blade up over her. It was time to kill the child. But before he could sacrifice the virgin girl to the Darkness, a flash of white light appeared and a bladed staff stopped the villain's hooked sword. A cutlass was aimed at Psol's throat and he was kicked in the face. Leina and Carlel stood in front of their brother. Psol's own sister had drawn blood from his lip with the kick she just delivered.

"Ah, a family reunion," Psol said. "Nice to see you brother and sister. But unfortunately you will have to see another planet fall. That is, if I let you live to watch."

Psol slashed down at Carlel who blocked with his cutlass. Leina hit Psol with the butt of her staff and then cut him with the blade across his left forearm. He swung back at her and kicked Carlel to the ground. Leina struck again and began to fight back against her brother. Her body glowed with the light of the Holy Spirit, just as Eishe and Roger had. She sent Psol back with a kick and then took that moment to reach Chaos Fury. The siblings went back and forth, while Roger and Eishe writhed on the ground, still surging with the dark energy of Psol's blast.

***

In Antarctica, John and Legion fought furiously. Neither one felt the stinging cold of the Antarctic wind. Snow blew everywhere and ice was all around. But none of the elements could stop the epic battle that was taking place. John's luxurious wings flapped fervently over and over again. A white glow surrounded his entire body. The light that came from him was not harsh but had a soothing effect. Legion grew more and more angry and the blue

247

glow that surrounded him fed hate into the air. They were polar opposites – order and chaos personified in a battle to the death.

Their swords clashed, two halves of the same whole. Dark and light electricity scattered all around as the battle ensued. Legion was cut and then so was John. Their swords met again. Many tentacles protruded from Legion's black armor. Faces of demons, clawed hands, mouths, evil eyes – they all kept pushing out from the armor's flesh. Yes, it was an organic armor, alive – the wicked energy of the Darkness turned into a living armor. Legion tied up John's feet and hands with his tentacles and from his mouth bellowed the agonizing screams of the thousands of demons housed in his soul. John couldn't move and then Legion sent a fiery blast of blue energy straight at the angelic being's heart. It scorched open his chest and then the Nephilim slammed John down into the icy ground. The evil monster ripped the Sword of Order from the hero's hand. He had both swords now and he put them together.

A bright light glowed as the swords began to meld and mesh to become one. This was the weapon that John, the Angel with No Name, was meant to wield. The Sword of Balance would be formed and that sword alone was meant for the being who was given the task to defend the mortal universe. The wound on John's chest healed and, with the power that the Lord granted him, the angelic being ripped himself from Legion's hold. He placed both hands above Legion's own, and the two swords became one as both of these beings held it in their hands. The pommel was a skull with sharp teeth, eating the sun with its wavy rays pointing outward. One side of the sword was bright white with an angel wing as the cross guard, but the other side of the sword was jet black with a bat-like wing. The blade was the same style of long sword as the former blades had been that forged into this one. It was a bit longer, though, and it came to sharp double-edged point at the tip. The sword was a testimony to the battle between the light and the dark. Back and forth they pushed. The tug of war went on and on for what seemed like days. John saw Christ looking at him, telling him his name, commanding him to protect the physical realm. He was the order that God created, the order of creation itself. This sword would bring balance and it was his alone to wield.

With one last burst of power, John pulled the sword from Legion's hands and thrust it straight into the demon's chest. The sword pierced this being born from fallen angel and fallen woman. His father had been the leader of the Watchers and his mother was born a mortal but was turned into the mother of all demons by Satan himself. He was the most powerful Nephilim. He had been stabbed by Angel metal weapons and Hell metal weapons before. None of them had sent him to the second death, they only released his soul from its body, causing it to possess others. But this weapon was different. It was the Sword of Balance and it was forged to do this very thing, to cast this creature and all creatures of chaos into the second death. The white light that surrounded John lighted the sword as well, and the light worked its way through Legion's entire body, sending it surely and definitely to the second death, to wait for the final judgment. John, the Angel with No Name, whose name only God could comprehend, stood there with the sword in his hand and his enemy vanquished. He looked north toward the island of Atlantis, and then he looked up to the black sky. The fight wasn't over yet, he knew it. The Darkness still filled the sky. The portal still needed to be closed. But how?

***

God heard the prayers of His people in New York City. He saw the Darkness closing in all around and His Spirit moved. The portal in front of the Freedom Tower, on the ground of the World Trade Center Memorial, right between the towers of light, closed around the Abyssite. The creature tried with all of its strength to pull itself up with only its front legs. Toni pushed the demon toward the portal with the sonic blasts from his palms. The bold hero moved forward, getting closer to the beast, in an attempt to push it down into the portal all the way. But Toni got too close and the monster swiped at him with its left front foot. The hooked edge of its hoof caught the right gauntlet of Pharaoh's armor and ripped it off. Shocked, Toni jumped back to get away from the creature. His arm was cut. The portal closed in on the demon more and more, though the Abyssite's head and front legs were still outside of it. There was only one thing left to do. A compartment opened up on Toni's right leg and he pulled out a gun – a near mint-condition Smith and Wesson Schofield model from 1873. Yes, it was Old Faithful, his Uncle James's gun, and Toni fired a shot at the Abyssite right between its eyes. It was a direct hit and the blessed bullet caused the creature to fall back into the pit below. The Abyssite fell straight back to Hell, where Satan had released it and into the lake of fire where those who defied the Lord completely burned until the final judgment. The beast from the Abyss turned to ash in the lake, while the portal to the mortal world closed completely overhead. The doorway to Hell still remained as it had been, but the open portal was closed. Toni laid back on the ground and thanked God for His grace and help. Crystal did the same and so did the entire team of soldiers there, especially Jael. She kneeled and kissed the ground. God was good and the victory was His.

***

Carlel got up. He saw his sister fighting their brother and took this moment to get Bianca away from the altar. If they did not sacrifice the girl, they could not release the Darkness into the world. But even if they could stop that from happening, the portal was still open and if it was not closed by the end of the third day then it could not ever be – and sooner or later, the Darkness would come again to destroy the Earth. Carlel had to close the portal somehow. He grabbed Bianca and ran to the aisles of seats in the outer rim of the tholos. He laid her down on one of the benches and tried to break her chains. The blue-energy chains clung to her by dark magic and the only way to break them was to break the spell that made them. That is when he had an idea. If he could shatter the crystal, that should break the connection that caused the portal to open. Then it would close. His cutlass was forged in Heaven, an angel's weapon. It could break the crystal if he struck it surely enough. He prayed to God to give him strength and he prayed for Bianca as well. He touched the girl on the forehead and said a blessing over her and then ran toward the altar. Before he could get there, his sister, Leina, was thrown into it and Psol dashed over to strike her again. The evil villain slammed his sister into the ground. She struck with her bladed staff but he blocked it over and over again.

On the ground, Roger and Eishe saw Leina being beaten. Roger loved her and he would not let her life end today. Eishe also cared deeply for his friend and both heroes burned brighter with the light of God. In a burst of brilliant light, the dark energy that attacked their bodies was dissipated and the heroes got up. Eishe moved like a ray of light across the room and cut Psol straight up his back. He slashed the dark villain over and over again, and then Roger joined in the fight. The level of Chaos Fury he had reached now was the same level he reached when he fought against Samyaza, the fallen angel. Roger had hit the level known as the Wrath of God. His left fist, which was completely made up of the Angel metal of the Left Arm of God, struck Psol across the right jaw and sent him crashing to the ground. Over and over Roger pounded his adversary. Psol could not fight back. The power that God bestowed on Roger was far too great. The evil titan had never been beaten like this by anyone in his life before, not since Pandora gave him his dark power and transformed him into a dark, transcendent being. He was finished.

Carlel saw his chance. He ran to the altar and, with borrowed strength from the Lord, he jabbed his sword into the crystal that was attached to the altar. The crystal shattered and fell to the ground. Roger stood over his beaten enemy and watched as a dark light shot up from the altar through the oculus of the tholos.

"You are a fool, brother," Psol said in a weakened voice. He could barely move but he managed to get the words out. "You have doomed this world. For the energy that the shards of the crystal creates will cause this planet to disintegrate. You have only a short time until it takes effect. And I will leave this place, before that happens. We may have not brought forth the Darkness now. But at least this world will be destroyed and, once it is gone, the Darkness will be unleashed onto the universe to conquer for once and for all."

Psol pressed a button on his wrist and, in a flash of blue light, he vanished and appeared back on his ship. Once there, his guards attended to him. It was their duty to mend their general's wounds. The power that God gave to Roger injured this villain in a way he had never been injured before. The wounds would heal as they always did, but they would take time.

251

Inside the tholos, the heroes wondered what to do next. Roger had an idea. He grabbed the shards of the crystal with the Left Arm of God. The hulking hero closed his fist over all the pieces and held them tightly, to keep them trapped inside. Then, without warning, the light of the Holy Spirit shined even brighter from the hero and he leaped into the air, through the oculus in the tholos, through the thick Darkness that covered the Earth, through the atmosphere.

The portal on the Earth closed when the crystal was shattered and the Abyssites in the force field all turned to ash. Gideon's armor also faded away and the villainous man remained unconscious on the ground. But everyone looked up as they saw a great flash of blue light in the sky above. And the blue orb that gave light to the island disappeared. The thick Darkness that surrounded the Earth was gone. *What had happened?* all the heroes wondered.

***

Moments earlier, far away from the Earth, the air was still and the sky hazy. Nathaniel Salvatore stood on Mars, a planet that had once sustained life many years ago. Pandora stood there as well. She had been there before thousands of years earlier, when the atmosphere of Mars was the same as that on Earth. Now, the air was not breathable by any living creature and the red, sandy terrain was toxic to all life. But these two opponents stood on that surface without any ill effects. Nathan had already died and in his transcended form did not need air to breathe nor would the toxic dust affect him in any way. Pandora was alive but she was unlike any mortal. She was spiritually Satan's own daughter. The queen of the heavens was cloned from fallen man but she was more than that. Satan had stolen the DNA of Adam and Eve and built her using science and dark magic. A spell from the *Necronomicon* – an evil codex written in his own blood and bound in the flesh of demons – gave her life. She needed no air to breathe and no poison could kill her. She would never be sick or grow old. Yes, she was a child once and grew but only to a certain point. Once she reached her physical maturity, she stopped aging and only grew in strength and might over time. The Darkness filled her with evil power. And she sent angels from Heaven to the second death by the edge of her blade. The queen of the heavens stood there, her staff in her hand, the hooked blade at the end ready to slay another warrior of light.

The red dust that covered the surface of this hazy planet swirled violently and crashed against the bodies of both Nathan and Pandora. These enemies looked into each other's eyes. Nathan had teleported them both to this place. The Holy Spirit had guided him to do so, for this was where God decreed for these warriors to fight. Nathan said a prayer in his heart, lifting the battle up to the Lord, and asked Him for strength and wisdom. The woman he faced was shrewd and cunning, just like her father. Even though Nathan fought in the Name of God, many men and women who had done so before him had fallen in battle. God did not promise physical victory but rather spiritual victory. If Nathan lost this fight and ended up in the second death, he still would spend eternity with his Savior after the final judgment. But regardless of that, Nathan's heart went out to all who would suffer inside the Darkness if Pandora were to send the people of Earth to the Abyss.

"You fool," Pandora spoke. She and Nathan stood about ten feet apart inside a massive sand dune. "You think to best me on this world? I built this place. It was my watchtower as I looked upon the Earth, planning to conquer it and the entire universe. My army was stationed here and here it was that I created a people – slaves who served me. The Watchers came in those days and waged war against us. No one won that battle but the planet was wiped out and transformed into this barren dessert that you see today. I was forced to flee to conquer other planets. After that, the Watchers were sent to Earth to protect it. They took my slaves and lived on that island called Atlantis. They were gods among men and with that power they shared the same enormous pride of my father. With them out of the way, I conquered planet after planet. Yes, there were other Watcher-type angels that protected those worlds, also pretending to be gods to the people they watched over. But all of them fell to my blade and the sword of my general, the Dark One. I took him from the first world I conquered, corrupted him, and made him mine. Now we have finally made it to Earth. We will take that planet where God put life and, after it is conquered and fed to the

Darkness, the Darkness will break from the Abyss and reclaim the physical universe that was once its home. You cannot stop me and my army. You are weak and will fall before me, as all other men have."

"You are just like your father," Nathan said. "Full of hubris and pride. I know your father well. He tried to control me, he tried to end my life, and he hung me like a trophy in his throne room. I am just a man, you are right, transcended or not, I am weak and I am flawed. But it is not me you face today. For my power is not my own. No, Pandora, self-proclaimed queen of the heavens. You do not face Nathaniel Salvatore, but rather the One that I represent. You face the Lord, God of all creation!"

The Holy Spirit filled Nathan with the power of God and his body shone brightly, lighting up the sky and driving out the haze of the atmosphere. Pandora dug into the depths of the Darkness. Her body glowed darker and darker with a great, dark light. In an instant, she vanished and her blade reappeared, driving straight for Nathan's head. The transcended being blocked her strike with the Shield of Faith that materialized onto his left arm instantaneously as she struck. The Helmet of Salvation was now covering his head, and the Sword of the Spirit, the Word of God, was in Nathan's right hand. He slashed back at his enemy, moving with the speed of light. But Pandora blocked his blow with the blade of her staff. She vanished again and struck at him. But Nathan met her blade with his own. Both hero and villain moved in and out of the shadow and light cast around this alien world. The red dust blew around as they clashed over and over again. Dark metal and Angel metal struck each other. Just like in the battle that Radix and Nathan waged in the Darkness, the sky was lit up with sparks of light and darkness. It was an awesome sight to behold.

The daughter of the Devil chanted an incantation from her sinister lips. The sand blew more violently around her foe and became a solid mass. The red mass of dust blasted against Nathan who cut it with his sword over and over again. It moved faster and faster and began to overtake the hero. The dust hardened around his body and made it impossible for him to move. While he was transcended, and not truly a physical being, the spell somehow allowed the dust to cling to the body he still possessed so that he could not teleport from his position or move an inch. He was trapped. But how was this possible?

"Dark magic is more powerful than you think," Pandora professed.

She spoke another spell and the helmet vanished from Nathan's head. Inside the sand that held his body, Nathan felt his armor disappearing piece by piece. And then the sand prison that held him fell to the ground. Nathan began to lose hope. This evil woman was able to overtake him so easily. He was a warrior of God, with the Lord's armor to cover him. But just like in Hell, the armor retreated from him, leaving Nathan naked and exposed. Pandora's blade struck and cut the hero up his back. Nathan fell to the ground. Over and over, his skin was sliced. Blood poured from his body. A transcended body like Nathan had could still bleed and dark red plasma mixed with the red dust of the planet's surface. *All is lost*, Nathan thought. He had failed his people; he had failed his God. But the Spirit was still with this hero of light. God did not abandon nor forsake him – not before on Earth, not even in Hell, and surely not here and now. Never would God leave him. Nathan knew that and his hope was restored. God would not let him fall before the daughter of Satan. Nathan rolled as Pandora's blade came down to take his head and, in a flash of light, the Sword of the Spirit appeared in his right hand and stopped her blade. On his back, Nathan laid. He held the sword with both hands now and pushed forward against his enemy. His wounds still poured out blood, and Nathan stood. He pushed Pandora back further and the blood stopped pouring out. His wounds healed. The armor appeared around him again, every piece of it. The hero of light pushed back and black and white lighting crackled between their blades.

"The people who walk in Darkness have seen a great light," Nathan declared. "God is light and in Him there is no Darkness at all!"

"Do you plan to battle me with Bible verses, fool," Pandora said, still locked up with the hero.

Their blades seemed to be stuck together and she could not pull away. Nathan pushed her further back. God was with him and His Word was Nathan's sword, his weapon against the enemy. The Word of God was the ultimate weapon ever created, and it was more than just the Angel metal sword that Nathan held in his hands. No, it was the living and breathing Word of God.

"For the Word of God is living and active and sharper than any two-edged sword, and piercing as far as the division of soul and spirit, of both joints and marrow, and able to judge the thoughts and intentions of the heart," Nathan preached, and Pandora was pushed back even farther. "In the beginning was the Word, and the Word was with God, and the Word was God!"

Jesus Christ was the Word of God, the Word made flesh, God come down to save man. This was the source of Nathan's power, for his sword was his Savior. Nathan preached God's Word over and over again, and the power of it diminished the power of Darkness that Pandora wielded. No one had combated her this way. No one had been able to strike her down. The daughter of the Devil, the evil empress and queen of the heavens, Pandora Ba'al Charebul was unable to move and felt herself grow weaker and weaker.

Finally, the Holy Spirit completely filled Nathan's soul. He glowed with a light brighter than the brightest star.

Then Nathan spoke one more time and cried out, "In the beginning, God created the heavens and the Earth. The Earth was formless and void, and darkness was over the surface of the deep, and the Spirit of God was moving over the surface of the waters. Then God said, 'Let there be light!'"

The light that surrounded Nathan moved through the Sword of the Spirit, and shot out in a great and vast beam. Pandora was completely immersed in the light and was sent down hard to the ground. All of her power was drained from her body. The dark light that surrounded her had stopped. The queen had fallen and she laid on the ground helpless, unable to move, but still alive.

"You are finished," Nathan said. "But I will not kill you. It is not for me to end your life. No, only the Lord can do that. He alone is sovereign over your life and death."

Nathan stopped speaking and looked out toward the Earth. He could see for thousands of miles, for God had given him this ability. He could see Pandora's ship and the island of Atlantis. He saw it all. The crystal had been broken, Legion had been slain and sent to the second death, and the Darkness no longer covered the Earth. Was it all over? Had they finally won? No, something else was still happening. Pandora could feel it also. And even though she was too weak to move or speak she had just enough strength to smile. The Earth was about to be turned to dust by the power released when the crystal was shattered.

"Fear not, Nathaniel," a familiar voice came.

"Michael!" Nathan exclaimed, joyous to see the gallant Archangel.

His armor glistened and his elegant wings were opened wide. Michael dropped down and stood by Nathan's side.

"Your work here is done," Michael said. "Pandora has been defeated and she will be bound to this planet until the final judgment."

Michael took out a great, white chain and bound the daughter of the Devil. The binding was spiritual, just as Samyaza and the Watchers had been bound to the Earth before. She was now banished to Mars, in a prison on a separate spiritual plane but linked to the red planet. She could never leave until God would allow her to be released from this prison. Nathan watched as Pandora vanished from his sight and went to her new dwelling, filled with darkness as dark as her heart. The angel looked at Nathan and placed his hand on his shoulder.

"We have one more thing to do," Michael said. "Come with me."

Nathan was shown the parts of God's plan yet to be fulfilled and, in a flash of light, Michael and Nathan disappeared.

***

Back on the icy plane of Antarctica, John stood and looked cautiously around himself. There was still more to be done. He could feel that the evil had not been stopped completely. Just then, in a flash of light appeared a great angel. This angel was strong and powerful and John recognized him right away.

"Metatron," John said. "What must be done?"

"Glad you have your memory back, nameless one," the angel spoke with might.

He descended and placed his hand on John's shoulder. The powerful angel dwarfed John, as he stood by his side. Just as Michael had showed Nathan God's plan, Metatron now showed John his own story and the parts of God's plan that would be fulfilled that day. In the beginning, John was created as an angel, with a special name that only God knew and that symbolized the order of God's creation. John was not quite restored to being this angel again, but his spirit was renewed and he once again had the Sword of Balance. The Sword of Balance had been split, in the beginning, into the Sword of Order and the Sword of Chaos. God did this because the Angel with No Name was not ready at that time to wield such a powerful sword. But even then, God decreed for this weapon to be used to bring balance once again to the universe and to stop the Earth from being destroyed this day. John was ready now to wield this sword, he understood God's plan. Now, together with Metatron, John vanished in a burst of light.

***

Roger soared through the sky like a rocket headed straight for Pandora's ship. He cared not for the fact that he had no air to breath and the friction of his trajectory had no effect on his body. The Wrath of God was a powerful level for any mortal to reach, but for a man that was more than human, like Roger, it was even more marvelous. He professed time and again that he could not die and he lived up to that right now. His left fist, which was entirely made up of the liquid Angel metal of the Left Arm of God, slammed into the spacecraft. The fingers of Roger's right hand gripped the metal frame of the ship and crunched it in its grasp. His body glowed bright with the power of the Spirit and the ship was pushed upward. It was lifted into space by the power of the trajectory of Roger's flight and that moved it away from Carlel's ship that had been docked next to it. The Isharian craft remained where it was, as the ship of the sinister daughter of the Devil went further and further away from the Earth. Roger hoped to get as far away from Earth as possible. He wanted to make sure that when the crystal shards blew and destroyed everything in their radius that they did not destroy the Earth. But what the hero did not know was that the blast would spread out continuously, until it evaporated the entire solar system, for that is how large the explosion would be.

Inside the ship, Psol had energized the vessel and was ready to launch out of there. He planned to create a black hole and hide inside of the Darkness, until the destruction from the blast that sprang from the shards of the crystal had ended. Then, after the Earth was destroyed, Psol would come back to where the planet once stood and release the Darkness into the universe and, with it, the seven Angels of Darkness. The mortal and spiritual world would then fall to the Darkness and the Darkness would seek to become a god itself and rule for all time. But this would never happen. God's power was ultimate and the Darkness was just another created being, subject to the Creator of all things.

When Roger struck the ship, the force of the blow killed all of its power and the ship was unable to move on its own. Instead, it only moved upward by the power that God have given to Roger, which pushed it through space. Time had run out and Psol knew his time had ended. Roger knew it was over as well. A dark light lit up Roger's left fist and began to expand. The rays of the dark light spread out and began to disintegrate all the atoms that they touched. Roger felt his flesh burning. The skin of his body began to peel away layer by layer. His muscles were next and then his bone. But his left arm held tightly onto the shards of crystal that faded away into nothingness as the light spread out more and more. The Left Arm of God sealed itself and remained in the shape of the arm that had housed it, with the fist clenched tightly in defiance against the Darkness. The rays of dark light reached out farther and farther. The ship began to fade away as Roger's body had, and all those inside were caught up in the dark, destroying light that radiated from the place where the shards of crystal once were, reaching out into space and toward the Earth.

Just then, at the final moment, there were seven flashes of white light around the spreading rays of dark light. The seven white lights glowed brightly and held back the dark light's expansion. The destructive rays stopped spreading and started to move back toward their source. The seven lights were the seven angels that stood before the throne of God – Michael, Gabriel, Raphael, Uriel, Phanuel, Azreal, and Metatron. With them were

Nathaniel Salvatore and John. Nathan's body was shrouded in the full Armor of God and the Sword of the Spirit was in his right hand. John looked angelic in every way, and his luxurious wings spread out into the vastness of space. In his right hand was the Sword of Balance. These two great heroes touched their swords together and the light that came forth vanquished the dark light that had come from the crystal shards. Balance had been restored and the Darkness was trapped again. The Earth was saved.

Instantly, the angels vanished and on, Atlantis in the tholos, Nathan appeared with Michael. When the crystal was destroyed, all the dark magic that Simon and Pandora had conjured was lifted away, including the chains that held Nathan's niece. Nathan touched Bianca and she woke up. The child looked at her uncle and smiled. Her uncle picked her up and held her in his arms.

"Uncle Nathan, I love you," she said.

"I know, sweetie," Nathan replied. "I love you too."

Carlel, Leina, and Eishe looked at Nathan and the Archangel that stood beside him.

"It is time to go," Nathan announced.

Leina knew in her heart that Roger was gone and, in a flash of light that came from Michael, they all vanished from the island.

On the fields in the outskirts of Atlantis, John appeared with Metatron. Everyone looked at the mighty angel with awe and also at John, who seemed to be an angel himself with his mighty wings. Akane threw her arms around the man she loved. Jack, Ravenblade, and Iblis all recalled that angel of order before he was a man. Bo hugged his father, who had just awakened. They were both astonished by what they saw. Aberto and his soldiers kneeled before Metatron's feet but the angel asked them to stand, for he was a fellow servant of the Lord. Shanson and Jenny hugged. Jay gave his fellow sergeant a hearty pat on the shoulder and all the ISOD members who had survived thanked God for the victory. Finally, in a great flash of light, they all vanished from Atlantis together. The fight had ended for now and it was time for peace to be restored.

EPILOGUE
PEACE RESTORED

Atop Mt. Sinai, all of the surviving heroes stood in awe because they had been brought there by two great angels. It was cold, for it was winter in this part of the world. The thick Darkness was gone and the sun began to rise over the horizon. Michael and Metatron were there, hovering in the air above all the onlookers, glowing with the light that the Lord instilled in them. Nathan was there wearing the Armor of God. The sword, shield, and helmet were not present at the moment. Nathan leaned over to kiss Bianca on the forehead, then he walked over to Lyles. He embraced Lyles, one of his dearest friends and his brother in arms, with a huge hug. He also hugged Ravenblade and Puck, the faithful Djinni. Bo was astonished to meet the great transcended hero, for he had heard about the battle he waged against another man, who also stood nearby. Radix walked over. Lyles did not know what to think, but Bo had told his father and knew in his heart that God could forgive anyone, even a murderer like Radix. Nathan shook his hand and looked up into his eyes.

"So what will you do next?" Nathan asked.

"Seek my salvation," Radix said with a cautious smile.

"The work was done for you on the cross; you just have to accept it," Nathan preached.

"Yeah, it might take some time," Radix said. "But I'll get there."

"You fought well," Nathan said.

"Thanks," Radix replied. "It felt good to fight on this side of the battle for a change."

Then the former villain knelt down and looked into Bianca's eyes.

"Do you know who I am?" Radix asked the child.

"Yes," she said, "you are a child of God. But you need to seek Him and believe in Him for it to be true. You weren't always good but no one was. We are all forgiven. Seek that forgiveness that He paid for and put your hope in Him. You can be saved, all people can if they believe in Him."

"You really are very innocent, aren't you," Radix said and did not say anything else.

Bianca knew well who that man was but she also knew that her true father was the Lord God, her Father in Heaven.

Michael descended and stood before Nathan.

"It's time to go," the Archangel said to the hero. "And you, too, Bianca."

"What do you mean?" Ravenblade asked.

"She's coming to Heaven," Michael explained. "God wants to keep her there. Just as He took Enoch and Elijah when they were still flesh, He has chosen to take her."

Before anyone else could ask a question, a fiery chariot with horses of fire swept down and Nathan and Bianca stepped into it. Bo ran to Bianca and shouted out for her to stay but she told him she had to go to her Father's side. Before she left, she took off the St. Michael pendant from her neck and put it around Bo's and then kissed him on the cheek. Bo stepped back, held the medal tightly in his right hand, and looked lovingly at that girl who amazed him more each day. He loved her like a sister and it broke his heart for her to leave, but he knew it was the right thing. The chariot soared away above Mt. Sinai and Michael flew with it. They met Metatron in the air above the mountain and looked down at everyone. Michael spoke to them all.

"Pandora has been defeated and imprisoned, her soldiers and her general were all obliterated by the dark energy that destroyed her ship. The Dark One was sent to the second death. The dark soldiers had no souls, so they are no more. Legion was vanquished and sent to the second death by your friend and our brother, who has now awakened to his former power – although he is not yet fully restored as the angel he once was. The Darkness has been sealed and held back. The Earth is safe for now, and the island of Atlantis will return to the bottom of the ocean for all time. As you all know, the apocalypse *will* come one day and the Wrath of God will be poured out. As for your friend Roger Jones, he fought valiantly and gave everything to stop the evil that plagued the Earth. But fear not, for his soul will endure for all time just as all the souls of the saved do. He is a great hero and you will see him again. We must leave you now but, remember, the Lord is always with you."

A bright light surrounded Michael, Metatron, and the chariot carrying Nathan and Bianca, and all of them disappeared to Heaven in a great flash of brilliant, white fire. Everyone else on the mountain then vanished as well.

***

Jael made it back to her apartment at the Manhattan branch of the FDSR. The ISOD team members that had joined them on this mission had all flown back to the FDSR headquarters in Upper Westchester County. The First Officer wondered if her sergeant had come home yet and if they had saved the world. The Darkness that had covered the Earth was gone but the sun had not come up yet in New York. She sat down on the edge of her bed and said a prayer. She thanked God for helping them that night, and for getting back alive. Some of her soldiers did not return and her heart broke for them. *May they rest in peace in Your arms*, she thought. It was time to shower and get some much needed sleep.

***

Jael did not know it but, yes, Sergeant Jay Sil did return home. He materialized in his apartment. They had won that day but the war against evil was not over. He looked around for Judy and took off his armored suit. He let it fall on their bedroom floor and grabbed his cell phone. Jay still wore the dark gray carbon-fiber body suit that he wore under his armor. It had a pair of gloves and boots of the same material, with soles fashioned from a thin sheet of reinforced rubber. Judy was not answering her phone Jay went downstairs and then outside. The air was cold and crisp on this winter night. But the most noticeable thing was that it was clear. The Darkness had faded away. A police car pulled up and out of it came Judy. From the driver's seat came someone else Jay knew – Captain Rogers.

"Well, looks like you finally made it home," the captain said.

"What's going on?" Jay asked.

Judy threw her arms around her husband and kissed him. Her pregnant belly pressed up against him and Jay was happy that she was safe and that their soon-to-be-born child safe as well.

263

"Don't worry, hon," Judy said. "I called the captain because you didn't answer and I figured you were still out on duty. I was trapped in a storage room at the studio. There were these creatures trying to kill me."

Jay kept trying to signal her to watch what she said but it seemed as if Captain Rogers was unfazed by the story.

"Don't get your britches in a bunch," Rogers said. "Now I know that all those crazy stories you tried to hide were real. I saw those creatures myself and they were like nothing I've seen before. I mean, straight out of a horror movie. We even got a report of a dragon, or something like one, down by Freedom Tower. It was quite a night. But no one really knows what they saw and by tomorrow there will be all kinds of theories about what really happened, to calm the public."

"I thought I was going to die," Judy said. "But Rogers came and got me out of there and brought me home."

"I still don't know what you do for the Feds and honestly I never saw you as a government guy; you could barely handle the NYPD protocols. But whatever you did, thank you. I know the world is a safer place because of it," Rogers said with all sincerity. "Think the sun will rise soon, so I'm gonna get out of here and get some sleep. I'm taking the day off."

Jay thanked the Captain and hugged his wife again. They went inside and listened as Rogers drove off.

***

Crystal opened the giant mahogany doors to their luxurious apartment. Her father hobbled in from his private entrance, still in the sonic suit that his organization had built. Antoni "Pharaoh" Brown had come a long way. He grew up watching his Uncle James lead a corrupt group of illegal weapons dealers, only to take over that organization himself. But, like Toni, James had seen the error in his ways and had a change of heart, choosing the ways of God over the ways of man. James died fighting on the right side of the war. When he did, he prayed for his salvation and prayed that Jesus would forgive his sins. He knew the Lord but had lost the good path. Toni was blessed enough to find his way and to still be alive to fix his life. His daughter prayed as she held her father in her arms. She thanked God for bringing him home alive, for his heart changing and accepting the salvation of the Lord.

***

In the East Village, Lyles and Bo appeared in Dr. David Davis's living room. The front window was boarded up with a piece of plywood. David, Martha, and Kimberly were sitting there on the couch and loveseat, praying. The banging on the door to the lab had stopped hours ago. And the doctor went out into the lab and turned on all of the security video feeds in the house. The creature was gone and all he could see was a pile of ash where it once stood. Then he viewed the camera image outside and he could tell that the Darkness had gone. The air was clear, though it was still nighttime then. Right now, the morning was coming and the family reunited. Lyles and Bo told them of all that happened, and how they saw Nathan, and how Bianca left with him to Heaven. They also gave the doctor the heart-rending news that Roger gave up his life to save them all. David held Martha and cried. Roger was like a son to him and no father should outlive his child. The moment was bittersweet, for Lyles and Bo were now home. Kimberly could finally have the family she always dreamed of, but their dear friend Roger was gone and so was Bianca. Yet, they knew that they would all meet again, for they all knew what the future held for those who have faith in God.

***

On the ship orbiting above the Earth's atmosphere, Leina, Carlel, and their soldiers all materialized. It had been two hundred years since Leina had been on this ship. She hugged her brother and cried for Roger. She cared for him deeply and was not yet ready to say goodbye. But she was back with her people and they had to figure out what the future held. They could not stay on Earth so they must go out into space. Pandora had been defeated and the threat that she posed was gone for now. Though they knew Satan was lying in wait and that the end of the world was inevitable, for God already spoke it. They wanted to go out and find a new world to call home. Maybe one of the planets could be made inhabitable again and they could live there in peace. Coz was still onboard and he wanted to stay with them all and learn

265

more about this God who he had heard so much about. Eishe would come also but he was not with them at the moment. They knew where he was, for he had radioed Leina with the com-link she'd taught him how to use. He told them that he had to say goodbye to a friend before departure.

***

At FDSR headquarters, Dan welcomed back the entire ISOD team. Some of the soldiers had given their lives to save the world but that was what they had signed up for. It was always a risk, but it was also their duty. Shanson and Jenny reunited with the others and they all celebrated the Lord's victory over their enemies.

In another wing, Dr. Ian Rich hugged his dearest friend, Eishe Taninaru. It was time for these two to say their goodbyes. It was difficult for them both but they knew it was the right thing. Leina and Carlel had given some weapons and a body suit for the FDSR to use and study. They also left Ian a com-link so he and Eishe could stay in touch. Ian could also use the com-link to download more technological data, to help the organization become even more efficient and advanced. Ian shared all this with Dan, who promised as the leader of the FDSR not to share any of this with anyone outside of the organization, and that they would only use it to protect the world and help mankind. After Ian and Eishe said their goodbyes, Eishe went outside and in a beam of light from the ship, Carlel teleported him onboard. Eishe was reunited with his master, Coz, again and they would travel across the universe together until their days would come to an end.

***

The next day, Aberto Ruggero went back to the secret headquarters of the Council of His Holy Order in Vatican City, thousands of feet underneath St. Peter's Basilica. There he gave the Spear of Destiny back to Archbishop Giovanni Rossini. The Archbishop thanked the general for his service to the Lord and Aberto debriefed his superior with a complete description of what transpired. The archbishop knew this man was blessed, for he had seen angels on more than one occasion. God was truly with him and he was grateful to have Aberto in the service of the Catholic Church.

Out in the Arabian Desert, Ravenblade, Puck, and Radix stood on a cliff quietly studying the horizon..

"So, what will you do now?" Ravenblade asked the former villain.

"I'm not sure," Radix said, still wearing the white robe that adorned him after his defeat by Nathan. "I have a lot of soul searching to do."

"Why don't you stay with us?" the immortal asked.

"Nah," Radix said. "I've always been a bit of a loner. I'd rather do this on my own."

"Well, none of us can do it on our own – trust me I know," Raven said.

"Yeah, I know what you mean," Radix said. "And who knows, I'm sure our paths will cross again."

With those final words, Radix walked off. Ravenblade and Puck watched as he faded into the distance. They stood together watching as the sun shined down on another day. Evil had once again been vanquished. They knew the fate of Pandora, Psol, and Legion, but they wondered what had happened to Gideon and Simon Magus III. Did they die when the island sank or were they still out there, ready to strike again?

The following week a ceremony was held at FDSR headquarters in honor of all of their fallen comrades. Everyone was there – John, Akane, and Jack, who were now back living in Brooklyn, at the junkyard they had rebuilt in honor of Nick. Dr. Davis, Martha, Lyles, Bo, and Kimberly were also in attendance. The entire FDSR was present from both Headquarters and the New York branch. Jay and Judy had joined them. They had just gone to the doctor the day before to check on their daughter; she was healthy and ready to be born any day now. Everyone at the ceremony stood and saluted as an American flag was folded and placed before each of the empty graves. There were no bodies to bury but a headstone was erected for each of the fallen heroes. Roger's headstone was in front, his name etched in a white marble cross to mark his grave. Tears were shed all around and "Amazing Grace" was sung after the "National Anthem." Pastor

Tim from Kimberly's church handled the service. He had been a part of this story, ever since Leina and Martha took Eishe to him. It was a day of prayer, thanksgiving, and remembrance. A day they would never forget.

***

In a remote village in western China, a man in a purple cloak walked through the streets. He came to a small house and went inside. He spoke perfect Mandarin Chinese to the woman of the house and she responded with a greeting. The cloaked man entered the house and sat on the floor. The woman handed him a book. He turned its pages and read a little of their Greek text. Yes, this was the book he was looking for. It was the journal of his great grandmother, Magda. In it were spells and a history of her life. She had lived a very long life and then hid this book before she ventured to America. There was one particular part of the book that this man was very much interested in. Simon Magus III planned to pick up where his great grandmother left off. He had everything that he needed now. This journal, along with the *Necronomicon*, would help him rule the world. It would all happen in due time.

***

There he stood, on the red soil of Mars. The color of his flesh was an even darker crimson tone. The Prince of Darkness and king of all demons, Satan himself, stood there in his demon form. His body was muscular and strong. His giant horns stabbed the air. The beard on his face was black as the Darkness itself. The hooves of his feet dug into the ground. By his side was another. Gideon, in a black T-shirt and black jeans. Satan chanted a spell and a portal opened up before him. From the mouth of the portal walked Pandora, bound in chains of white light. With another incantation, the chains fell from her body and she was free. God permitted the Devil to remove His chains of light to bring about His plan for the end-times to come. Satan did not know this, and smiled at his daughter. Then, he turned and smiled at Gideon. One more spell came from his lips. The portal that Pandora walked from closed and another portal of blue light appeared before them.

"Go into the Darkness and wait, for the time is at hand. I will call you forth when the day comes. Be ready, for no one knows the hour, not even the Son of Man."

Satan laughed as Pandora and Gideon walked into the portal to the Abyss. One chapter had ended but a new one was just beginning.

***

The Darkness has subsided and the light of a new day has blanketed the Earth once again. I, Death, sit here and watch over mankind. I was created at the Fall, and released onto the world when Pandora opened this very box that I possess. The first soul I collected was that of Abel when his own brother, Cain, slayed him, and after that countless souls were collected into this box of Death. Through the Earth and across the universe I traveled. Satan spread mankind to all the corners of the universe but now all those planets are gone, except the one where the Lord first put life – Earth. It still stands, waiting for its last days. Pandora and the Dark One have been defeated but the Devil still lies in wait to bring destruction to all creation. I have seen heroes rise and fall, and even now I have watched as all these men and women rose as one to defeat God's enemies. They mourn the loss of their comrades. Though one of them, I know, has not died. He will return one day when the Lord is ready to use him again. I only know the grim feeling of death and no emotion has been granted to me, yet I can see from all my travels that God truly gives a crown of beauty in place of ashes, that graves can be turned into gardens, and that there really is power in the blood of Christ. For His death and resurrection gave His children hope and new life. There is no salvation for a being such as me, but for men and women everywhere salvation exists. May they find it and believe. Truly it is a story told, in His name, of His might.

The Story Goes On...

About the Author

Chris LoParco is a writer and an artist who draws his inspiration from his love for God and his deep interest in the epic battle between Light and Darkness. He is a graduate of the School of Visual Arts, and he is a very proud father.